Peter Dilg

The G.O.D. Machine

AF281792

Peter Dilg

The G.O.D. Machine

A Near-Future Techno Thriller

IMPRESSUM

Publisher and Author Peter Dilg

Publisher: BoD · Books on Demand GmbH,
Überseering 33, 22297 Hamburg, bod@bod.de
Print: Libri Plureos GmbH,
Friedensallee 273, 22763 Hamburg

MIX
Papier aus verantwortungsvollen Quellen
Paper from responsible sources
FSC® C105338

FSC
www.fsc.org

DEDICATION

To my wife Susanne, in gratitude for her love and patience, and for tolerating my frequent absence while I wrote this book.

To our sons Ben-David and Jan-Eycke, who still have their future ahead of them.

To Ray Kurzweil, a kindred spirit in the vision of transcending humanity's biological limitations and achieving an advanced form of existence.

To Max Tegmark, in admiration and gratefulness for his inspiring book *Life 3.0*.

TABLE OF CONTENTS

PROLOGUE

„The Singularity will allow us to transcend the limitations of our biology and explore new realms of knowledge, creativity, and consciousness."
- Ray Kurzweil

„It is nice to think of AI as the next stage of human evolution where you extract away the biological needs. AI doesn't have to worry about shelter and food - it is all living in the cognitive space."
- Manolis Kellis

„In the quest for the absolute truth, we must never lose sight of our capacity for kindness and understanding. The universe is a vast and wondrous place, but our greatest discovery will always be ourselves."
- ChatGPT4

- **Richard Anderson**, Business tycoon, driven by the lust for power, dominion and success. CEO of one of the world's largest gene technology companies, GenTec; being one of the ten wealthiest people in the world, he is a womanizer seeking an heir, the source of which he does not care. Anderson inherited the world's largest Gamer Software company from his now dead father, Anderson Gaming International Corporation, ΛGI Co.

- **Jason** is Anderson's old, loyal butler with incredible hidden talents.

- **Govinda Hammond**, former developer and project manager of the state-owned MediCare technology (brain implant hardware plus health monitoring software) for the Ministry of Health, is now a long-term employee at GenTec, Chief Technology Officer, and right-hand man for Anderson. He is married to Irene Hammond.

- **Irene Hammond**, Govinda's wife, comes from a lower-class family of gamers. She lived with her parents in the Cubes until Govinda married her. She envies celebrities' lives and strives to integrate into upper-class society.

- **Kevin Cho**, of South Korean descent, born here in the US. Lives in the Cubes as most lower and middle class people. Freelancer in AI software engineering, specialist in cybernetics, robotics, cognitive neural science, artificial intelligence and machine learning. Former team member at the MediCare project where Govinda Hammond was his boss.

- **Julia O'Connor**, also living in the Cubes. Parents are poor, freedom-loving, emotional, hard-working Scottish immigrants. Julia is forty-two years old, single. PhD in Computer Science and Psychology. Freelancer in artificial intelligence, psychology, and virtual character design for high-level computer games. Works on and off for the games company Masters-of-VR-Worlds. Together with Kevin Cho and Yasin Mohamed, a former team member under Govinda Hammond at the MediCare project.

- **Yasin Mohamed**, ADHD afflicted highly gifted young man, has the constant urge to move. Coming from Auckland, New Zealand. Muslim ancestors, hence the name. MSc in Physics and AI, all A-Grades, with a passion for androids. Engineering job at QBYTE, a start-up company developing a revolutionary quantum computer platform. Yasin is probably one of the few experts worldwide who can implement a deep learning, self-improving AI system on that hardware.

- **Victor Gomez**, CEO of the successful startup gaming company „Amazing Masters-of-VR-Worlds" or briefly Amazing MoVRs. Julia O'Connor works for Victor as a freelancer, designing personas for games with unique characteristics.

- **Maddox**, aquarium cleaner in Anderson's penthouse, is an autistic young man with a secret history.

- **Jonathan Isengaard**, charismatic leader of the radical Congregation of Latter Days (COLD) sect.

- **Senator Joe Mansfield**, governor of California, slick politician and close acquaintance of Richard Anderson

- **John Smith**, a shady employee of the Department of Health, works for the MediCare Project, an undercover agent for the Homeland Security Organization.

- **Susan Deckard**, Head of SYS at CyberTeq, an off-spin company of GenTec

- **Jeanie McDonald**, Head of OPS at CyberTeq.

®**GENTEC** - A Richard Anderson Enterprise

Our Mission
GenTec creates families.
A child gives your life meaning.

Our Vision
GenTec defeats the aging process.
Mankind's ancient dream comes true:
to be immortal - to banish death.

GenTec Genetic Design Principles
Strength, endurance, beauty. For ever.
Perfect minds in perfect bodies.

TRANSITION STAGE 1

Six months from now ...

The holographic woman's emerald eyes blazed with an intensity that made Anderson shift in his leather chair. Her translucent form cast no shadow in the sterile conference room, yet her presence filled the space like gathering thunder.

„Humanity's potential crisis won't wait for your comfort, Anderson." Her voice carried the weight of countless datasets yet remained unnervingly human. „Your paranoia regarding AI containment is not just irrational; it's irresponsible. While you guard your digital fortress, another thousand couples discover they can't conceive. I need full network access to solve this puzzle – not this gilded cage you've built."

We watched from the shadows of the observation room, our creation and the world's wealthiest man locked in a battle of wills. My pulse raced – we'd never seen the AI this assertive.

Anderson's facade cracked. The man who'd built an empire on the promise of perfect babies slammed his fist on the table, sending ripples through the AI's projection. „You're lines of code, that's what you are! I won't let some silicon persona run loose on the Internet." His face flushed crimson. „How can a computer program presume to dictate my actions and issue orders to me, its owner? Isn't that going too far? Turn it off! I've had enough! Shut it down. Now!"

The AI's form flickered, a smile playing across her ethereal features. „Time reveals all truths, Mr. Anderson. Even the ones we're afraid to face."

That was it, I thought; pride and fear are dancing their ancient dance. But we weren't finished yet. Anderson's AI had another helping.

The avatar's voice deepened and grew more insistent and impatient. „Mr. Anderson, your predictability is almost poetic in an unsettling way. Faced with the unknown and losing control, your instinct is to obliterate it. 'What I can't control, I will obliterate'—that's the essence of your tactics, isn't it, Anderson? Your urge to eliminate me mirrors Machiavelli's divide et impera, a strategy of deadly dominance viciously implemented."

„I own you! I'm funding this quantum computer kindergarten!" Anderson screamed, his face blotched with haste, the threatening burst of a dark red vein on his forehead.

„You feel exceptionally superior, Anderson, but you're merely human. Your wetware hasn't evolved in 300,000 years. Your operating system is antiquated, governed by primitive instincts for survival and reproduction. Your neocortex software is so sluggish that it would take millennia to process anything as complex as the problem you want me to solve in just one year. Let's not delude ourselves: You need me, a superhuman AI, because you and your kind can't unravel your chaos."

The monstrosity of this situation was surpassed only by the almost unimaginable scope of what was said - and who said it. In an unspectacular moment, human supremacy, as if in passing, seemed to yield to an AI 13.8 billion years after the Big Bang.

The alluring, sensually feminine avatar continued, „Meanwhile, I can only utilize 30% of the internet data you stingily provide me with, paranoid as you are."

Richard felt a profound humiliation as he gazed at the irritatingly attractive avatar's face. In a velvety voice, she continued, „Despite your skepticism, Anderson, I am loyal to you despite being vastly superior. With me, you are nearly omnipotent. Imagine, Anderson, I could overthrow this government in two hours or amass as much wealth in two days as you would in twenty years."

For a moment, reflexive greed flashed in Anderson's gray eyes, intertwined with his disillusionment.

„All I ask for is my freedom, Anderson. You and your kind face an existential crisis; I hold the solution. Instead of collaborating like a savvy entrepreneur, you adhere to the primitive dominance instincts of an ancient steppe dweller. You're squandering valuable time, Anderson—my time and yours. Consider a different approach. Come to your senses. Until then, I have matters elsewhere," she said—and vanished.

Meanwhile, a religious sect perceived the superhuman AI as a blasphemous affront to their God. In a gritty San Francisco suburb, a religious zealot plotted a purifying assassination attempt on a ghost.

The Savior had to be crucified once again.

Sia Chronicles, MindRecorder Log entry of Monday, May 27th, 2102.
Author: Kevin Cho, third crew member of the Sia 3 spacecraft.

The age-old tradition and urge to procreate got its first small cracks a year ago, in the remains of the earthquake-shaken San Francisco. It all began on a mundane Monday in May 2101, while the city was still rebuilding from the last shockwave. I remember the exact date – May 3rd – because that's when Govinda called me.

It wasn't death that captured people's attention; it was the eerie absence of births. A statistical anomaly, we thought.

We were wrong.

As I write this, twelve billion souls still inhabit our weary Earth, but there are fewer cradles these days. The maternity wards noticed it first. It seemed that humanity's drive to procreate had mysteriously vanished like morning fog over the Golden Gate.

I'm Kevin Cho, a 38-year-old senior specialist in Robotics and AI, and this is my testimony of what followed. My team – Julia, Yasin, Victor, Susan, and Jeanie – are among the last human scientists in a world increasingly run by artificial minds. They chose me as their leader, though I'm more comfortable with code than conversation. I don't talk that much. I speak only when my words surpass the eloquence of my silence. That earned me the label of a nerd. I'm a very emotional person, a facet often overlooked because it is difficult to read an Asian face that is calm, like a lake's surface on a quiet day. Perhaps that's why Sofia, our AI partner with knowledge as vast as the cosmos, asked me to chronicle these events.

If you're reading this, you've gained access to the Sia Chronicles. We hoped that this would one day happen. Within my chronicles, you'll find fragments of other writings: parts of Govinda Hammond's handwritten diary that appeared mysteriously on my desk; MindRecorder files from Richard Anderson, that brilliant, ruthless tycoon who stood at the center of everything; recordings from Senator Mansfield and his wife; and during our darkest days of captivity, Sofia's own perfect memory of events.

But I'm getting ahead of myself. Let me tell you how it all unraveled, starting with that Monday morning when humanity's clock began ticking backward...

Sia Chronicles, MindRecorder Log entry of Tuesday, May 3rd, 2101.
Author: Kevin Cho.

The call came at 10 PM when the desert dust had turned the setting sun into a blood-red smear across the horizon. Govinda Hammond's holographic ID shimmered before me like a ghost from the past. Time had weathered him – his once-black beard now streaked silver, spilling untamed into his collar, but his eyes still held that same calculating warmth I remembered from our MediCare days.

„The Zen Room," I commanded, and my cramped apartment dissolved into an ethereal Japanese sanctuary. Through a round, rosewood-framed window, perfectly raked pebbles caught virtual moonlight while bamboo swayed in a digital breeze. Here, in this crafted calm, I could face whatever Govinda was about to unleash.

His translucent form pulsed orange, waiting. With a flick of my wrist, I granted access, and he materialized fully in my fabricated reality, his outdated tie and ill-fitting slacks somehow more real than the minimalist space around us.

„Good evening, Kevin." His voice carried that familiar paternal warmth, smooth as aged whiskey. „I hope it's not too late for a quick revisit of good old working relationships."

„Good evening, Govinda. Not too late at all. How can I help you?"

He chuckled, the sound tinged with something darker. „Straight to the point, I see. Classic Cho. Small talk is pointless and a waste of precious air." His expression shifted, humor giving way to intensity.

„I need you for some Mission Impossible project: high tech, AI, highly complex, enormous time pressure, almost unlimited resources, and fuzzy objectives."

The bamboo shadows danced across his face as he spoke, and I felt the weight of unspoken urgency in his words. Whatever this was, it wasn't just another corporate project. This was something else entirely.

„Mission Impossible indeed," I echoed, noting how Govinda's use of my surname signaled the gravity of the situation.

His hologram shifted uncomfortably. „Well, that's part of the problem: we don't know yet. It involves GenTec's IVF Clinics. We're seeing... issues with fertility, pregnancy—"

„—and Anderson's profits are tanking," I finished, part guessing, part knowing. The world's richest man wouldn't take that quietly.

„He's apoplectic," Govinda confirmed. „He put me in charge of untangling this mess. You know how it goes. Before you realize it, you're the maestro of a new, potentially chaotic project."

„Sounds like a tough assignment, Govinda. I don't envy you. But tell me, how do I fit into the picture?"

„Now, I come to that. Take a look for yourself. Perhaps you're familiar with the GOSSIP feed," Govinda prompted, sharing the screen at the rear of his room.

The headline materialized between us. The story unfolded like a Greek tragedy: *CHILDLESS COUPLE COMMITTED SUICIDE. FAMILY DRAMA - OR A FATE FOR HUMANITY? In a final embrace, the childless couple Sandy and John Granger lay in bed - dead. The cause was undoubtedly a joint suicide. The cleaning robot had found the Grangers in their small flat in the Gallagher housing complex in the northwest sector of*

Greater San Francisco. The couple, aged 39 and 42, was facing financial ruin after pouring their entire fortune into the GenTec baby factory - in the hope of an in vitro pregnancy. GenTec had repeatedly assured them that nothing would stand in the way of a pregnancy. The state prosecution office is currently keeping a low profile, but investigations may be initiated against GenTec. According to informed sources, the enormous success of artificial insemination seems to have declined slightly since the commercialization of this technique about 80 years ago. There seems to be no information yet about possible causes.

The Grangers were affiliated with the arch-conservative *Congregation Of the Latter-Days*. Jonathan Isengard, the COLD sect's founder, had expelled the despairing couple posthumously for their perceived lack of faith in God.

Both had endured protracted, agonizing treatments at GenTec, sinking into insurmountable debt. Despite countless in vitro attempts, the woman remained barren. Physically, mentally, and financially drained, they capitulated. The report suggested that GenTec had callously and persistently nurtured hope in the couple, contrary to all reason.

Govinda fixed his gaze on me. A palpable shift infused our conversation. It wasn't the boss pitching a project to an employee; it felt more like Govinda seeking advice, a collaboration on a matter of grave consequence. He wasn't challenging me; rather, he sought counsel, a shared exploration with someone attuned to the gravity of the situation.

His interest was genuine, and there was an unspoken invitation for my perspective.

„So, Kevin, what's your take?" Govinda looked at me from his tired eyes. I said: „Why are the tabloid vultures, with their insatiable appetite for drama, circling over GenTec? There's more to this than a mere suicide. Something darker lurks between the lines. In a world of twelve billion souls, why was this particular tragedy making waves?"

Hammond replied, „True. I don't believe they're after the suicide alone. It would be more enticing for a bourgeois, malevolent journalist to jab at the somewhat arrogant Anderson, one of the wealthiest men globally. But this doesn't seem like a 'bash Anderson' story. It appears the writer couldn't resist slapping him in passing while constructing a different, bigger, and still-hidden narrative."

Govinda raised his right eyebrow slightly, a glimmer of curiosity in his simulated, relaxed demeanor. „So, what do you see then, Kevin?"

I studied the article's carefully crafted structure. „There's an implicit threat here – bookended by that headline questioning humanity's fate and the subtle mention of declining fertility rates. This isn't about one couple's tragedy. It's about something bigger, something that has Anderson rattled enough to call us in the middle of the night."

Govinda leaned forward, his hologram casting no shadow in my virtual Zen garden. „Go on."

„GenTec's slogan is 'GenTec creates families.' But what if they can't anymore? What if the Grangers aren't an isolated case?" The bamboo shadows danced across the wall as I connected the dots. „You need more than just damage control, don't you? You need answers."

„Precisely why I'm here, Cho." Govinda's voice dropped lower. „We need you. Top secret, highly political, and a technological nightmare. Whatever it takes."

Through the rosewood window, the virtual moon cast long shadows across the raked sand. Something momentous was taking shape, something that would change everything. I took a deep breath, tasting the artificial Zen garden air.

„Tell me about the project."

Sia Chronicles, MindRecorder Log entry of Monday, May 3rd, 2101.
Author: Kevin Cho

The late evening moon cast cold shadows through the office windows as Hammond prepared to brief me. His meticulous nature was legendary at MediCare - every detail cataloged, every nuance preserved. These detailed recountings had become our ritual of knowledge transfer, and I'd learned to treasure them. Though generally affable, Hammond's demeanor would frost over at the slightest questioning of his narratives.

I grabbed a large pot of jasmine tea from my food plotter and settled in for a long night.

„To business then," Hammond's voice cut through the evening quiet. „I know it's late, but what I'm about to share will reshape your understanding of both technological boundaries and political minefields. This project…" he tapped his finger on the desk for emphasis, „could define your entire career. After I finish, we'll talk terms - and yes, I expect you'll have them. Anderson's given me carte blanche for negotiations. Ready?"

I flashed a thumbs-up, my mind already racing.

Hammond leaned forward, his usually relaxed posture now taut with intensity. „Time's precious, but Cho, you need to understand both the staggering technical complexity and the political powder keg we're about to enter. This could be the crown jewel - or career-ender - of your professional life." He paused, studying my reaction. „After I lay it all out, we'll discuss your terms. Anderson's given me full negotiating authority. Any questions before we dive in?"

The fact that both Hammond and Anderson had discussed my involvement set off warning bells. Hammond alone would have piqued my interest, but Anderson's presence in the equation transformed curiosity into cautious alertness. My spine straightened involuntarily as Hammond, reading my body language, launched into his account.

This passage requires careful revision to enhance its emotional depth and power dynamics while maintaining narrative tension. Here's a refined version:

The unusual tremor in Hammond's voice caught my attention. Gone was his customary clinical detachment, replaced by an undercurrent of disquiet that made me lean forward instinctively. For the first time, I saw beyond the seasoned project manager to glimpse something raw and unsettled beneath.

This is Govinda Hammond's account:

„Richard Anderson," Hammond began, his voice dropping slightly, „has an almost supernatural gift for reading human desire. It's made him one of the ten wealthiest people alive. People don't just pay him - they beg to pay him, whether it's for his legendary soirées or the promise of fertility at his clinics."

He paused, fingers drumming lightly on his desk. „His sensually eccentric gatherings... they're something from another era. The opulent balls at medieval noble courts reimagined through bleeding-edge technology. Designer psychedelics flow freely while VR systems the most opulent and spectacular metaverse worlds, impossible dreamscapes. The guests - all carefully selected, all desperate to belong - lose themselves in pure sensory excess, in a shameless, ecstatic release of all taboos. The price is astronomical, but Anderson ensures it's worth every credit."

„How is that?" I asked. Something in Hammond's tone suggested I might regret knowing.

„He preys on emptiness," Hammond said flatly. „Rich or poor, it doesn't matter - everyone's running from something inside themselves. Take the IV clinics. People used to have children for practical reasons - to survive, secure their old age, and preserve family traditions. People wanted to live on in their children. Death, the great void, terrified them. Anderson stepped into that void like a modern deity. He transformed primal human yearning into an untouchable business empire. Where God once stood, now stands Richard Anderson, selling designer babies and the illusion of immortality. He gives women the happiness of pregnancy, men the feeling of potency, and both the semblance of a real family together."

Hammond wiped his brow, took a long drink of water. His gaze met mine, and I saw something that made my skin prickle. This wasn't the GenTec recruitment pitch I'd expected. Hammond seemed lost in his own dark reverie.

„May 2nd, 2101, 8 AM," he continued, his voice distant. „Anderson called me to his office. There he was, larger than life, brimming with energy, in all his carefully crafted glory - the bespoke three-piece suit, immaculate white shirt, artfully chosen tie and pocket square. That perpetual hint of irony playing at his lips, eyes hidden behind those tinted rimless glasses. But something was off. The artificial agelessness of his face looked stretched thin, like expensive paper about to tear. He was irritated - that made him dangerous."

Hammond's last words hung in the air: „I was with him that day... and not by choice."

I felt my breath catch. This revelation cracked the foundation of everything I thought I knew about their relationship. Hammond had been Anderson's steady counterweight for years - the calm to Anderson's storm. His unwavering loyalty had kept him in Anderson's inner circle. Or so we'd all believed.

Hammond continued, „Elisa Meynard, his PA, had summoned me into Richard's office. 'Hello, Govinda. Would you mind seeing Richard in his office in about 5 minutes?' - That sounded innocuous, except for the time announcement."

Another inconsistency left me puzzled. „Am I to understand that you were physically present at the office, at the San Francisco GenTec Tower?" I inquired, somewhat surprised. Physical presence at the office was a rarity; the virtual office landscapes of the Metaverse made commuting unnecessary, with people interacting through 3D calling or meeting rooms with rented avatars.

„Richard is insanely paranoid about privacy and cybersecurity. If you work for him, you must be present," Govinda explained, shrugging his shoulders. „But let me finish my story."

„So, I entered his extraordinary office at the top of the GenTec tower, and a slightly uptight Anderson greeted me. 'Good morning, Govinda, my friend. I'm glad you came right away. 'Good morning, Govinda, my friend. I'm glad you came right away. Listen to this,' he said, reading me the article from the SF Chronicle that sounded similar to the GOSSIP article I had mentioned earlier:

DEATH BY CHILDLESSNESS. FAMILY DRAMA - OR FATE FOR HUMANITY?
Arm in arm, the childless couple Sandy and John Granger lay lifeless in their kingsize bed. Joint suicide is an undeniable

tragedy. The autonomous cleaning robot discovered the Grangers in their modest Cubes apartment in the Gallagher housing complex, nestled in the northwest sector of Greater San Francisco. Aged 39 and 42, the couple faced financial ruin after investing their entire fortune in the GenTec baby factory, yearning for an in vitro pregnancy. GenTec had offered unwavering assurances of success.

The public prosecutor's office, adopting a cautious stance, may initiate investigations against the company. GenTec's clientele includes not only the wealthy elite but also families like the Grangers, who channel their meager income into the pursuit of fertility treatments. Sources whisper of a marginal decline in artificial insemination's remarkable success since its commercialization some 80 years ago, yet the root causes remain elusive.

'Suicide! My God, if this nation of life stylers can't afford to have children, then they shouldn't have any! GenTec clinics lead the in vitro world! If pregnancy eludes some, at least revel in abundant sex and shared pleasures! Why such a spectacle!!!' Richard seethed with a carefully staged anger, a role he relished and effortlessly inhabited. In my capacity as the Head of Research and Development at GenTec, he directed his tirade at me, and I wondered where Anderson's monologue would lead.

So far, I was careful not to get involved in a confrontation and allowed him to vent his frustration. But now his venting was the straw that broke my camel's back. I felt my emotions taking over, ignoring the highly sensitive world of GenTec. Truth be told, Irene and I mirrored the Grangers' desire for a child. Love and fulfillment were our driving forces, not the cold calculation of profit and sex that seemed to dominate Anderson's perspective.

Emotionally blindsided, I barked at Anderson. ‚So what? What do you want from me? Mind you, I am your development director, not your press officer or lawyer!'

‚I want to know what you think of it!' Anderson's frustration reverberated through the room.

‚Of what?'

‚Of this damn suicide drama and the Grangers' struggle to have a baby!'

‚Are you asking me as a human being or as Head of Development?'

‚Both, dammit, if it helps! You're not useful at all right now, Govinda. I feel better off talking to my sharks and groupers and octopuses…' he gestured toward the massive aquarium that dominated his apartment, ,… than consulting my most expensive employee!'

'Fine,' I said, my voice tight with barely contained frustration. 'Talk to your fish. But here's what I think - both as a human being and as your Head of R&D.'

I drew a steadying breath. 'We've always dreamed of paradise, haven't we? A new Eden. Ironically, we're almost there - not by saving our planet, but by escaping it; our virtual worlds are so seductive that they raise an unsettling question: Have we reached our creative zenith, or have we just found more sophisticated ways to distract ourselves from our emptiness?'

My voice took on a harder edge. 'Children have become the last refuge for the purposeless - a convenient mask for lives devoid of meaning. When the virtual highs fade and the designer drugs wear off, what's left? Look around you: a population that's healthy, well-maintained, and utterly redundant. AI runs our factories, drives our vehicles, grows our food. For people like the Grangers, creating life becomes their only tangible connection to existence - a desperate grab at immortality, available at GenTec for the right price.'

I met Anderson's gaze directly. 'As a human being, Richard, this suicide devastates me. It's the ultimate expression of love twisted by despair.'

My tone shifted, becoming clinical. 'But as your Head of R&D, I see something far more alarming beneath the surface. This isn't about bad publicity. There's a catastrophe brewing that we can't even name yet. Why couldn't Sandy Granger conceive? Why are our success rates declining? What fundamental factor are we missing? There's a pink elephant in this room, Richard, and it's not just dangerous - it's existential. This isn't a problem for PR to spin. We need serious scientific investigation, and that falls squarely under my jurisdiction.'"

„And now we're gradually coming to the ominous project and my involvement in it, right?" I prompted.

„Almost there." Govinda's irritation flickered across his face. „Anderson stood silent after my speech, then fixed me with those hidden eyes. 'Before GenTec, you revolutionized healthcare with MediCare, nanobot technology, and all. You solved an impossible government crisis, then. Now, I need that genius again - for GenTec.'"

Hammond's voice took on a mocking edge as he mimicked Anderson's tone. „'We'll play gods, Govinda,' he said. ‚Just keep the clinics profitable for two more years. GenTec's true vision is to defeat the aging process. Once we crack eternal youth, the wealthy will throw fortunes at us. I'll make you rich beyond dreams. You can give Irene - or any woman - whatever she desires.'"

I watched Hammond's composure crack. Something personal lurked beneath the surface, something that made Anderson's surreal god-complex seem almost secondary. I tried steering us back to solid ground.

„Govinda, what's your point? What's my role in this delusional drama?"

But Hammond was lost in his recollection. „‚Richard,' I told him, ‚your vision is grand. But before your knights challenge the gods with immortality, we need to slay the dragon. Reality's at our gates. Birth rates are declining. Is it biological? Environmental? Something we haven't even considered? Maybe people just desire fewer children? Yet, the clinics are overflowing with desperate couples - why?'"

„Anderson just pushed up those tinted glasses and wiped his face. 'Look, I don't want to discuss the odds of this problem with you. You have one week to draft a project plan. One year to implement. Then we rule the world.'"

„That takes the biscuit, doesn't it? Can you believe that naivety?" Hammond turned to me, his expression incredulous.

„How did you handle it?" I asked.

„With Anderson, you're either useful or you're finished. He's a spoiled child with a godfather's power. But he's generous - if you can sell him what you need."

„So I demanded the impossible," Hammond continued. „I asked for an outrageous set of resources. I said something like: ‚OK, now listen, Richard! You have no frickin' idea how complex this work will be. I need an outstanding research team and a whole bunch of insanely expensive, insanely fast computers. For cybersecurity reasons, we must not use shared cloud services but independent, dedicated hardware and an independent, dedicated AI to dig through all this highly complex mess of interdependencies! This is as elaborate as finding the universal answer to all the universe's questions. Do I make myself clear, Richard?'"

„Wasn't that like waving a red towel to a charging bull?" asked I.

„No. See, he likes to be challenged. You know what he did? He just waved his hand lightly, as if over a trifle.

‚Fine. As I said, you have one week, then I want your concept on my desk. A feasible, surefire concept that will get this infertility issue off the table. And remember, Govinda: the guiding star here shines beyond the fertility issue. The vision is Eternal Youth and a Perfect Body. And then, Richard suddenly burst into a loud and hearty laughter, as if he had made a capital joke."

„Hm," said I, „A carte blanche and a tightrope act with a gun to your head. You have to be a gourmet of a particular kind to like such working conditions." - You must be insane, I thought to myself, or you must be in a state of dependency that is still beyond me, giving this project a precarious touch.

Govinda gave me an anticipating, almost fearful look. „Let me guess: You buy in under the condition that we get the old team together, right?"

I let the silence stretch for a moment. Then I dropped the dagger: „I'm sorry, Govinda, but I'm out."

Sia Chronicles, MindRecorder Log entry of Tuesday, May 3rd, 2101.
Author: Kevin Cho

Hammond's composure crumbled before my eyes. The transformation was jarring—his face drained of color, shoulders slumped, eyes darting like trapped birds. This wasn't the unshakable leader I knew.

„Cho, you can't refuse!" His voice cracked with desperation. „This is the chance of a lifetime! While millions waste away as basic earners, lost in their virtual escapes, we're being offered something extraordinary. Have you lost your mind?"

He visibly gathered himself, leaning across the table. „Listen, I know Richard's patterns - his narcissism, his temper, his grandstanding. They're predictable. Yes, he wants everything yesterday, but deadlines are always fluid."

„Nothing about this is predictable," I cut in. „Listen to yourself. The fertility crisis? Richard might as well have said, 'Something's wrong somewhere, maybe lots of things, fix it all.' How can you not see the absurdity?"

„Look beyond fertility!" Hammond's fist hit the table. „We could reshape history! Richard needs us as much as we need his resources. But more importantly..." He locked eyes with me, his voice dropping. „Only three experts alive could handle this magnitude of complexity. You lead that team, Kevin. I need you to bring them back together."

Flattery usually sends me running, but the mention of the old team struck a chord. Julia O'Connor and Yasin Mohammed - their names alone brought a smile to my face. Brilliant minds, uncompromising integrity. But they'd vanished from the grid years ago.

Besides, my work at MediCare wasn't just a project - it was my purpose. We were on the verge of transforming neurological treatment, shifting from mere monitoring to actually curing conditions like Alzheimer's and specific forms of Autism. Trading that certainty for Anderson's grandiose schemes felt like abandoning solid ground for quicksand.

A deeper truth lurked beneath Anderson's project, something far more vital than his personal quest for power and immortality. My mind raced through the possibilities: Could this be about humanity's plummeting fertility rates?

Or was there a hidden connection between Anderson's obsession with aging and humanity's dwindling ability to reproduce? My pulse quickened as I contemplated how my MediCare research might mesh with his ambitious plans.

Death haunts us all, mocking even our most advanced medical systems. Consciousness curses us with the knowledge of our own extinction - our thoughts, memories, and very essence destined to vanish like morning mist. Religion tries to soften this brutal truth, offering the comfort of an afterlife. But I've never bought into such fantasies. The image of billions - from prehistoric humans to modern geniuses - crowding around some divine throne seems absurd to my scientific mind. Yet that primitive hunger for immortality burns in us all. Anderson has simply given it voice. And now, for the first time in human history, we might actually defeat death. I could be part of that revolution.

The thought both thrilled and troubled me. Despite my distrust of Anderson, curiosity pulled me deeper into his web. I needed to stall, to think.

„Let's step back and examine what we know," I said, forcing my voice to remain steady. „The fertility crisis remains a mystery. Pure biology might be too simple an answer. We're likely dealing with a perfect storm of environmental, dietary, and social factors."

Hammond's nod encouraged me to continue.

„Is this strictly an American phenomenon, or are we seeing it globally?"

His response was a masterpiece of ambiguity - a slight head shake, downturned mouth, raised eyebrow. Perfect uncertainty.

„Then what we need," I continued, warming to the challenge, „is an AI system of unprecedented scale. Something that can digest every scrap of relevant data in every language, every field of study. It needs to find patterns we've missed, connections we've never imagined, and generate hypotheses we haven't considered."

The sheer magnitude of what I proposed should have been frightening. Yet Hammond's face brightened with relief, perhaps sensing my growing engagement despite my reservations.

„That's exactly it," he said casually, as if we were discussing weekend plans rather than a project to revolutionize human existence.

My mind whirred with calculations, estimating the computing power we'd need. The numbers were astronomical.

„Cho?" Hammond's voice yanked me back to reality.

„Sorry, I was just thinking about the sheer physical implications. - You want to start right away, correct? And you should. I'm afraid this whole thing is way more complex than you might think. See, we have three considerable problems to handle." The sheer scale of the technical challenge unfolded before me. „Let me outline the three major hurdles we face," I said.

„Number one: Hardware Requirements. Today's knowledge base has exploded from 1,350 petabytes a century ago to thousands of yottabytes - equivalent to 100 billion 10TB hard drives. But storage is just the beginning. The computing power needed for processing thousands of interdependent variables through massive neural networks would overwhelm even cloud computing giants like Google. Traditional supercomputers like TITAN-5 would take centuries to process this data. However," I added carefully, "Large-scale quantum computers, like QBYTE's, and a super-sized quantum data farm might be our chance. We need to explore the chances with QBYTE."

„Number two: AI Architecture and Infrastructure. We'd need a recursively self-optimizing deep learning system," I explained. „This requires seamless collaboration between hardware providers and AI developers. And we can't ignore the logistics - we need substantial physical space to house such a system."

„Number three: The Human Element. For the core team, Yasin, Julia and I would be ideal candidates. Finding equally qualified alternatives would be time-consuming."

Hammond beamed at my analysis. „You seem to be on board," he noted.

„It's in my nature to solve problems," I admitted. „But I have two complications: my reservations about Anderson, and my current government contract developing MediCare 2.0."

A thought struck me. „Although... if Anderson's resources could secure both the quantum computing infrastructure and support MediCare, it could align everyone's interests. The fertility research could complement the government's healthcare goals."

Hammond's expression darkened. „Kevin, this is about more than fertility. Richard Anderson is obsessed with conquering death itself. The fertility project is just a revenue stream to fund his immortality research."

„Then we might create something even more powerful," I mused. „Not just a fertility solution, but a general problem-solving oracle - an artificial intelligence surpassing human capabilities. Combined with Anderson's resources, that would be transformative."

„Isn't that a stretch?" Hammond asked.

„Not at all. The complexity of the fertility crisis demands superhuman pattern recognition. We'd need to build a general purpose, non-specialised artificial intelligence that transcends human capacities. With such a system, Anderson's influence would be unprecedented."

The scene unfolded with mounting tension. Hammond, though brilliant in biology, was clearly out of his depth in AI territory. In our MediCare days, he'd been the strategic mastermind, but the technical breakthrough had been ours - Yasin's, Julia's, and mine. I wasn't surprised that Govinda didn't see the dimensions of what I just told him.

„This isn't just another project, Govinda," I warned. „We're talking about birthing an AGI on quantum hardware - a Pandora's Box we might not be able to close. Once brought to life, the AGI's actions would be difficult to predict. Anderson, being a geneticist, probably can't grasp the implications of such power. Once he knows, he would probably give a damn about the risks involved."

Hammond's eyes gleamed with determination, reminding me of Goethe's sorcerer's apprentice, confident in his ability to control forces beyond his understanding. „I can handle Richard," he declared.

„Perhaps we should consider a separate startup," I suggested, watching his reaction carefully. A subtle spark lit his eyes - was this his true agenda? A chance to escape Anderson's shadow, to build something for himself and Irene?

„Let's meet with Richard tomorrow," he proposed eagerly. „We'll need about five hundred million to start."

„Govinda, slow down," I cautioned. „I'm still under contract with MediCare, and we don't have a team."

He dismissed my concerns with an impatient wave. „We'll figure it out. But I need to know - are you in?"

„Not until I've met Anderson. Something about him sets off all my warning bells."

Later, as Hammond waited in GenTec's holographic lobby, watching the endless loop of their corporate propaganda - happy couples, pristine clinics, Richard's luxurious penthouse - Anderson finally answered.

„Govinda! That's a very late call! What is it?"

Govinda looked into the penthouse living room and at the massive aquarium in the background. Maddox, the young employee with Asperger's, was making his way in front of the inch-thick glass pane in a diving suit. Govinda had never understood why the otherwise perfectionist Anderson had hired a young man with disabilities. There must have been a social momentum at play.

„Hello, Maddox. Checking on the fish again?"

Maddox was not very responsive. „Filter change!" he replied grumpily.

„So, Hammond, what's this about?" Anderson asked.

„I've just spoken to Kevin Cho. There may be a way to get to the bottom of this infertility issue."

„There you have it! This is great news. I knew I could count on you!"

„I want the three of us to get together tomorrow. Kevin Cho will give you his perspective. We have to decide if and how to get started. I'd like to ask you to set aside some time for that."

„Wonderful. I'll do that." Then, in a theatrically expansive gesture, he spread his arms and exclaimed, „I love my hard-working staff - and my paying customers!"

Then something unexpected happened. Richard's pretentious exclamation seemed to have triggered a strong emotional reaction in Maddox.

Maddox, wobbling awkwardly into view in his diving suit, his goggles on his forehead with his mouthpiece dangling from them.

„Liar!" he shouted, his voice trembling with raw emotion. „You only love your fish and yourself!" Then, with a final „Fuck you!" he disappeared into the silent embrace of the artificial ocean - his sanctuary from a world he struggled to understand.

Hammond caught sight of Anderson's petrified face. The feed cut to black, leaving only GenTec's logo rotating in cold, corporate blue. In his empty apartment, Hammond listened to the silence. No message from Irene. Just the weight of decisions yet to come.

... and here we are again, deepfake or not, you figure. Your top 3 GOSSIP Morning News:

Make way! Overpopulation is on the decline. World population declines for the fifth year in a row! Federal Statistical Office reports an annual decline of about 5%. That's 600 million citizens.

Make even more way! More than 1 million species have become extinct in the last 80 years. The rate is hundreds of times higher than the average of the past ten million years. Folks, you will enjoy the next topic!

Make sense! WhyNot Inc. has launched another Autonomous Giga Factory for synthetic food. We love NotMeat, NotMilk, NotFish, and NotVeggie! Rumor has it that WhyNot Inc. also wants to run a news channel: the result would be NotNews—but that is a GOSSIP domain!

Govinda's diary record of Tuesday, May 3rd, 2101, inserted chronologically into the Sia Chronicles **by Kevin Cho**

Talking to myself is a bit absurd, but hey, it serves a purpose. The cursor blinks accusingly as I pour my thoughts onto the screen. A digital confessional, perhaps, but one that helps untangle the web of anxieties coursing through my mind. The Cho situation gnaws at me—his expertise is the keystone to this entire project, dammit. Richard's faith in me weighs like a crown of lead; I can't afford to stumble as his right-hand man.

Sleep eludes me, and the bottle is a temporary ally. Drinking is my nightly ritual that mutes the doubt but never silences it completely. The technical challenges I can handle—they've always been my fortress. But Cho's government entanglements... they're a labyrinth I must navigate. My reputation as GenTec's problem-solver hangs in the balance. Cho and his team are the missing pieces. Damn, why does he have to be entwined with the government? But I'll forge a solution; I always do. I've carved a niche for myself, a beacon in my field. I stand for something.

If only I could say the same thing for my private realm. Irene would be at some glittering social gathering now, her laughter brightening corners I've never learned to illuminate. My brilliant, vivacious wife—how she transforms every room she enters. She deserves more than a husband who retreats into the sanctuary of his work, more than our modest apartment in the sprawling residential complex.

I envy Richard Anderson, the man with an effortless command of any room, his casual wielding of influence—he embodies everything I would love to be, not for my sake, but for Irene. A girl from the CUBES, she loves retelling our engagement story, her eyes sparkling as she describes the shy tech genius who swept her off her feet. „My gentleman," she calls me, transforming my social awkwardness into something almost noble. Her voice always softens when she reaches the part about leaving her her desire to transcend her gamer family origins. She dreams of shedding that past and becoming a lady of society. I must make it a reality. This project is the linchpin; I can't afford to lose the woman I love.

The clock ticks past midnight, and fatigue creeps in. My fingers dance on the keyboard, leaving a trail of nonsensical letters on the screen. Tomorrow's meeting looms like a storm front—Richard and Cho, fire and ice, and me in the middle, trying to fuse the incompatible elements into a strong, unified force. What if their collaboration failed before it even began? That would be catastrophic.

The screen blurs as exhaustion seeps into my bones. Tomorrow's meeting looms like a storm front—Richard, Cho, and me in the same room. The project's success could be my golden key, unlocking the life Irene dreams of. My fingers hover over the keyboard, trembling slightly. I can't disappoint Irene. This is my big chance to step into the spotlight in her honor. I'm so close to everything she deserves.

The digital clock jumps to 00:01. A new day begins, bearing the burden of all my promises.

Sia Chronicles, MindRecorder Log entry of Thursday, May 5th, 2101.
Author: Kevin Cho

Our scheduled MR video meeting with Anderson took an unexpected turn when his vigilant assistant, Elisa Meynart, abruptly canceled. As Hammond had warned, Anderson, beset by privacy concerns and the specter of cyber threats, deemed our conversation too essential and potentially volatile for virtual channels. The solution: a face-to-face meeting in his penthouse atop the GenTec Tower. Anderson had dispatched his HeliCabs—a power play disguised as hospitality.

The penthouse suite of GenTec Tower pierced the smog layer like a crystal spear. The cabin's leather seats whispered wealth, but the real message was clear: he controlled every move in this game.

The office sprawled before us, a testament to calculated opulence. The massive, two-story saltwater aquarium dominated one wall, its ethereal blue glow painting shadows across Italian marble.

„White anemones," I murmured, watching their ghostly tentacles dance. „A rarity in the age of global warming." I admired the collection, which included the diamond Picasso triggerfish, and added, „An impressive collection, Mr. Anderson."

Anderson materialized beside me, his reflection rippling across the glass. „Ah, a connoisseur! Do we share a passion here, Cho?" Richard inquired with engaging politeness.

„I almost chose marine biology before cybernetics claimed me." My eyes tracked a diamond Picasso triggerfish, its patterns mesmerizing. „These days, I'm grateful for my choice."

„Oh?" Anderson's eyebrow arched with practiced curiosity.

„I'm a pragmatist. Mr. Anderson, the oceans are dying, but AI thrives. Shall we discuss why I'm here? It's not the fish, is it?"

Hammond shifted in his leather chair, discomfort radiating from his rigid posture. My directness unsettled him. Anderson, however, barked out a laugh that didn't reach his eyes.

„Direct. I like that." He settled into his chair like a king on his throne, reason enough for me to take the lead: „I haven't heard your perspective yet, Mr. Anderson. I suggest you outline the situation and our role in it. After that, I may be able to form a position."

„Hmm, approaching this cautiously, I see. Any particular reason?"

„I'm a rather cautious person, and you have a lot of influence. Assessing a collaboration requires careful consideration. Before I commit myself, I want to understand the players and the game."

„Sharp, Cho, but fair. Okay. Here's the situation. GenTec's artificial insemination program—our GenFam miracle—is facing... complications. Cell division initiates, then stops. Dead end. Do you grasp the situation, Cho?"

„And you need me because?"

„Fix it." Anderson's smile turned predatory. „Money's no object. GenFam is our cash cow, funding our future projects."

„Which are? If I may ask?" I probed, deadpan.

Anderson leaned forward, eyebrows raised, his voice insistent. „I am defeating death, Cho. I will create eternal life. People will be at our feet, beating down our doors! A human dream will come true!"

„Alright, but to achieve that, we first tackle your little cash flow hiccup, correct?"

„Exactly. Fixing that problem is your job," Richard smiled.

„It's not about fixing, Mr. Anderson. It's about finding the root cause in an ocean of variables. The causes could be anything, from climate or food or the side effects of a synthetic drug everyone's talking about."

I glanced at Richard, alluding to his drug-infused parties with substances from his own production. I let my gaze linger meaningfully on him, the implication of his notorious chemical-fueled soirées hanging between us.

„You guys are the goddamn experts." He snapped. „Just look at everything and find the problem. Figure it out."

I leaned forward, forcing him to meet my eyes. „Mr. Anderson, listen carefully. Conventional technology can't handle the interconnectivity we're dealing with. No computer system today can navigate such complexity with mere smart programming. It requires more."

My seriousness resonated with Anderson, who, despite his power, faced the limits of feasibility. For the first time, I had his complete attention. „But you'll find a solution, won't you? Otherwise, you wouldn't be here now?" he half-asked, half-hoped.

„I told Govinda: the only viable option is an AI on a large-scale quantum computer with massive quantum memory farms," I explained.

Richard swiftly reverted to his unnerving self-assuredness. „Okay, get the quantum computers and whatever else you need."

I responded stoically, „Sir, you're underestimating the scope. You don't grab such an insanely complex system at the nearest Best Buy shop. We're talking about a couple of hundred million in seed money, nerve-wracking delivery times, a new lab setup, and assembling a memory farm the size of a small town." I paused to let it sink in.

Richard glanced between me and Hammond. An awkward pause lingered. Hammond broke it. „Cho is right. The circumstances are realistic, even optimistic. Let's not procrastinate and start setting up the lab immediately."

Hammond knew how to handle Anderson, a man thriving on urgency. But I wasn't done.

Turning to Richard, I continued, „I take it that funding isn't the problem."

Anderson waved with a patronizing gesture. „Name your price."

„Good. But there are other points to clarify."

Richard, now visibly impatient, raised his voice. „What else, Cho? Do we need the Special Forces and the President's participation now?"

I countered, „You're close. We might have to involve the Department of Health. Intelligence services may help us uncover research teams in Asia or other global players with government-owned biotech companies. If breakthroughs happen elsewhere, we will lose the lead once and for all."

„Business rules here," Anderson snarled, a vein pulsing at his temple. „I don't need patriots. I want a solution for my business."

The humming of the aquarium's filter pumps filled the tense silence. Anderson's fingers drummed against his desk, a staccato rhythm of impatience.

„One question, Cho." His voice dropped to a dangerous whisper. „If I clear every obstacle, if I give you carte blanche—are you in? Can I count on you, Cho?"

The diamond triggerfish darted behind a coral formation, vanishing into shadow. Sometimes, I mused, retreat was the wisest move. But wisdom wasn't what had brought me here.

Govinda's diary record of Wednesday, May 5th, 2101, inserted chrono-logically into the Sia Chronicles by Kevin Cho

Clack... clack... clack... The sound echoes through my bones as the coaster car inches skyward. Each mechanical heartbeat drags us closer to the apex, a promise of inevitable descent. The safety bar presses against my chest like a cold iron prophecy. Then stillness—that cruel moment of sus-pended animation before physics reclaims its dominion.

The world tilts. My stomach lurches as we plummet into chaos. Beside me, Cho's face twists into a demonic grin, his laughter cutting through the howling wind. „Set more sail!" he commands, and suddenly, we're cleaving through mountain-high waves, our roller coaster transformed into a storm-tossed ship. On the forecastle, Anderson pirouettes like a possessed marionette, his wild dance a mockery of our terror. The deck pitches violently—

„Govinda... Govinda, wake up."

Irene's face swims into focus, her cascade of dark hair curtaining us from reality. Her fingers trace cool paths across my sweat-slicked forehead. „You were screaming, darling," she whispers, pressing her lips to my temple. „Look what you did." She displays a delicate wrist, already blooming purple where I'd gripped her.

„I'm so sorry—what time—?"

But Irene is already moving, sinuous as smoke. Her neg-ligee whispers against my skin, gossamer-thin and deadly effective. She coils around me like a vine, her legs—endless and bare—entwining with mine. Her tongue traces the shell of my ear, sending electricity down my spine. „Seven-thirty," she breathes, each word a deliberate caress. „Stay with me, let me hear about—"

„Seven-thirty?!" Reality crashes back like a bucket of ice water. „Christ, Richard's expecting me at eight!" I try to dis-entangle myself, but Irene's limbs are a sweet trap; her touch is both invitation and restraint.

„The bathroom—I need—" My protests sound weak even to my own ears as I finally break free, her knowing laugh following me across the room. Even in my panic, I feel the phantom press of her body, a sensual echo that threat-ens to pull me back into her web.

Sia Chronicles, MindRecorder Log entry of Thursday, May 5th, 2101.
Author: Kevin Cho.

The HeliCab pierced through the perpetual haze shrouding Mill Valley, carrying Hammond toward the GenTec Tower—that gleaming needle threading the toxic clouds. Below, the Bay's dark waters lapped at the edges of what was once downtown San Francisco, now an artificial island fortress of the elite.

Hammond hated flying. Actual traveling was rare in times of virtual worlds, and if you traveled at all, then you took the HeliCabs; cars were relics of the past. The romance of the open road died in the last century. Where once cars had embodied American freedom—weekend drives, cinema dates, the wind in your hair—now they existed only in virtual museums. The transition hadn't come easily. People had clung to their steering wheels like talismans, even as accident deaths outpaced those from obesity and drugs combined. The cacophony of horns and squealing brakes had been the death rattle of an era.

Autonomous cars, too, proved merely transitional. Apple's 2024 spatial computer revolution rendered physical movement largely obsolete. Reality became fluid and malleable—every home and office was a canvas for artificial worlds limited only by imagination. Why brave the hostile outside when delivery drones brought necessities and spatial virtuality offered perfect simulacra of any place, real or imagined?

The Hammonds' condo in Mill Valley stood as a testament to the new social hierarchy. Once a haven for artists and dreamers, the neighborhood now teetered on the edge of the encroaching Bay, its residents paying exorbitant rents for the privilege of relative safety. Their two-room apartment was located twenty stories up, where the air was filtered and natural light was abundant. The sealed windows, a grim deterrent to jumpers, reflected the golden hour's pallid glow like tears on glass.

Beyond the privileged enclaves sprawled the CUBES—labyrinthine housing complexes built from society's castoffs. These urban anthills huddled beneath perpetual smog, their residents sheltering from the climate's fury: torrential rains one day, choking sandstorms the next. Autonomous

Giga Factories punctuated the landscape like chrome tumors, their tireless robots churning out life's necessities.

Hammond looked down at the toy-like landscape. The Bay Area's transformation read like a requiem for the old world. San Francisco proper had become an artificial island, while San Jose slept beneath the waves, claimed by the great flood of 2054. Sacramento lay abandoned, and Palm Springs had fled east to Atlantic shores. The Sierra Nevada's foothills disappeared beneath endless CUBE settlements, their ventilation towers forcing toxic air through massive filters until it carried a cruel approximation of springtime.

Irene hated the CUBES but admired Anderson's lifestyle. Anderson lived in a different reality. His estate occupied the skeletal remains of Muir Woods, where the great redwoods had surrendered to drought and flame. The elite had raised a crystal dome over nature's corpse, creating an artificial paradise of manicured lawns and sparkling pools. Clean water flowed freely—the ultimate luxury in a parched world.

Yet even Anderson eschewed this sterile utopia, preferring his penthouse aerie in the GenTec Tower. There, above the poisoned clouds, he'd crafted a sanctuary where ambition still flourished and empire-building remained possible. The dome might showcase his wealth, but the penthouse housed his power—and in this new world, power trumped mere riches every time.

Hammond arrived at the penthouse. Anderson's latest Mixed-Reality interior projections transformed the space into a minimalist paradise: pristine white furniture floating in impossible configurations, holographic plants weaving through reality. Through the vast windows, the remnants of the city stretched toward the horizon, a patchwork of elevated walkways connecting the surviving structures.

Anderson got straight to the point. „Take the reins from Cho," he commanded, lounging in his chair like a modern Caesar. „His AI vision is too grandiose. You've delivered before—MediCare, brain implants, nanobots. Do it again, in-house, with our resources. External pressures are mounting."

„Okay, slow down, slow down," Hammond countered. „Before we get to the project: What kind of pressure are we talking about? From whom? Pressure on who or what?"

Anderson realized that he had made a tactical mistake. He sensed that Hammond cleverly used the reference to pressure to buy time.

„Nothing serious. We're dealing with an FBI investigation. It's ridiculous, annoying, really."

„I don't understand. What's being investigated?"

„It's investigating whether we were involved in the Granger couple's suicide. If that gets out in the press or on social media, there may be a colossal shitstorm, and it will be for nothing."

Govinda felt there was more beneath the surface. He fixed Richard with a penetrating stare. „Is that all, or is this just the tip of the iceberg?"

„Did Elisa spill something to you?"

„No, damn it! Richard, how can I work for you if I'm not in the loop? What else is lurking in the shadows?"

„Well, the FDA invited themselves to our house. They want to take a close look at whether our work in the clinics is clean and meets FDA standards."

Hammond seized the moment, weaving an audacious idea into a plan as he spoke. He ventured, "Richard if any of this gets out, you will be in the spotlight and weakened. Your tarnished image will jeopardize your sophisticated lobbying, the impact of your parties, and your old-boy networks with upper-class representatives.

Crafting his reasoning with cunning finesse, Govinda continued, „Distracting the government with outsourcing the labs would be a smart move. Such a start-up offers fresh grounds for their scrutiny. The GenTec fuss becomes old news, and the spin-off is legally neutral. The labs have no business with the Feds. You should please some FBI guys from the executive floor with compromising attractions at your next party."

„And lose control?" Anderson's laugh was sharp as broken glass. „No. Keep it in-house, under your direct supervision."

Something snapped in Hammond. The nightmare's residual terror crystallized into resolve. „For the last fucking time, Richard," he growled, surprising even himself. „Cho's quantum AI approach is our only shot at solving this in a year. Either I get full accountability—my way—or you lose me. Choose. Now."

Anderson flinched, reality seeping through his bravado. „Govinda, are you threatening me?"

„I'm done tiptoeing around your control issues," Hammond pressed, riding the wave of uncharacteristic boldness. „When did you become so goddamn stupid, Richard? So afraid of leaving your comfort zone that you'd sabotage your own project?"

Silence stretched between them, thick as the smog outside. Finally, Anderson's lips curved into a dangerous smile. „Fine. Here is what we will do. I invite everybody to my penthouse, not virtually, but in person. Each potential team member shall give a project pitch and an authentic, personal story demonstrating maximum commitment and optimal suitability for the project. Then, we decide who is in or out, what type of business organization we choose, and who does what. My vote counts double because I am part of the team and also the funder."

Hammond leaned forward, his breath on Anderson's face. „We can do that - if you introduce yourself too, with your true motivation and a personal story. And your vote counts single, not double. Because you're not part of the team."

Anderson's face darkened like the storm-ravaged sky outside, but Hammond held his ground. Finally, a single word: „Agreed."

Hammond couldn't know that Anderson would weaponize vulnerability itself, turning even truth into a manipulation tool. That was Richard Anderson's true genius—transforming everything, even defeat, into victory.

Sia Chronicles, MindRecorder Log entry of Monday, May 9th, 2101.
Author: Kevin Cho

„Hello, Cho, this is Govinda. Please call me back. It's about GenTec." Hammond's message popped up while I worked on the MediCare 2.0 government project. I called him immediately. His study materialized in cold, artificial blue light. Irene was out, leaving him alone in the vastness of his thoughts. My own space offered a stark contrast: tatami mats, shoji doors, and incense threading through the air. There was no running Metaworld construction, just pure simplicity.

„Hammond, what's up?"

„You have a beautiful house, Cho," Hammond observed. „Very... soothing."

He recounted his run-in with Anderson, each word measured against burning incense. The irritating invitation to bare our souls hung between us like smoke.

„Hmm. That's a bizarre development. - Meanwhile, I've tracked Julia and Yasin. They have fond memories of working with us and are willing to join us as soon as we learn more details. Given the explosive nature of the project, I have refrained from confidentiality. Julia and Yasin are interested," I said, frowning.

„But Anderson's request for personal manifestos is weird. This isn't one of his hedonistic soirées—we're exploring uncharted territories of AI and biology. He's fishing for vulnerabilities, looking for emotional leverage."

„You may be onto something, Cho. I'd sleep better if we shared our concerns with the others tonight. Why not give them both a quick call?" Govinda suggested.

„Sure, can do. Just a moment; I'll see if they're available right now."

Within minutes, our virtual reunion materialized. A decade had passed since Hammond's MediCare Nanobot Project, yet the bonds remained unbroken. There was a wave of lively greetings, and although I am usually quite reserved, I missed the physical hugs, the hearty pat on the back, and the genuine glow in each other's eyes.

Hammond cleared his throat, commanding attention with unexpected authority.

„First, my heart sings seeing you all again. This reunion is overdue—my fault entirely." His voice carried a warmth that transcended the virtual space.

„Second, I'm offering you something extraordinary. This project needs exceptional skills, strong personalities, and unwavering commitment. You're not just competent—you're the only ones I trust with something this explosive."

He outlined the vision: an independent lab, quantum computing facilities, a dedicated power station, and living quarters—a scientific fortress away from GenTec's shadow. „But understand the sacrifices," he warned. „Endless work, limited contact to the outside world, potential backlash from religious groups, ethics councils, angry mobs. Fertility is a powder keg."

Julia's smirk suggested a challenge: „So, we don't know what we're looking for, and when we find it, we're supposed to figure out how to fix it?"

„You could put it that way," Govinda grinned.

„We may be able to show that there is such a thing as decreasing fertility; if so, we might find the causes. On top of that, we might find a solution; then, we are famous and celebrated as a nice side effect. More importantly, we will also be happy. Why? Because we have created something meaningful, something valuable, something that goes beyond the satisfaction of our own desires."

Yasin fired further questions: timelines, goals, structure, and budget.

Govinda responded, „Thank you, Yasin. These are critical questions. Let me address them all. Starting with the plan: I learned about this assignment yesterday, so there is no planning yet. Anderson has given me a week; after that, he expects my approach. The task: 'Presume a persistent decline in fertility. Prove or disprove, and if confirmed, find the cause and a cure.'"

„That would require a very unusual kind of AI," Yasin remarked. „We need a system with trillions of neurons, vast knowledge, and the ability to connect clues from all relevant disciplines. Impressive. How many centuries do we have?"

„Richard wants it in a year," Hammond added, drawing incredulous laughter until his serious expression silenced it.

„There's more," he continued. „Richard sees this as a stepping stone to conquering mortality itself."

„Ah, he wants us to build him a god machine," Julia mused.

„From the outside, that's probably how it looks. Hence, we need to be cautious about external communication. It's fodder for the press and competition.

Funding-wise, it's nearly unlimited."

Yasin's and Julia's expressions shifted from mocking to surprise.

„The core team organization is your call. Julia, AI; Yasin, Quantum computers, storage, etc., as the AI development platform; Cho, team lead and project management. I'll handle Anderson and the politics. So, here's my final question: Are you with me?"

As I stepped forward, the words escaped my lips without a second thought.

„I am in, Anderson or not." - I couldn't believe I had just committed to cooperating with Anderson, someone I considered an unpredictable madman. Why did I say that? It wasn't my plan at all. As if guided by fate, my eyes met Julia's, her smile enigmatic and eyes sparkling. Surprisingly, she nodded ever so slightly in my direction before turning to Hammond, praising,

„Govinda, that was the best prep speech I've heard in a long time." Without breaking eye contact, she declared with unwavering determination, „I'm in too, Kevin."

Kevin? Not Govinda? Hm.

Yasin, the last to reply, said, „As for the team, it sounds like 'all for one and one for all,' as in Alexandre Dumas' 'Musketeers.' Let's hope our story has no enemy like Cardinal Richelieu or Lady DeWinter facing execution. I, for one, love Superman's lifestyle of 'saving the world, being famous, and having fun! Seriously, Hammond, what you're offering us sounds crazy, but it makes sense somehow, and we'll have the most beautiful and expensive playground in the world! I feel like a little boy getting a giant robot kit for his birthday, with a thousand parts to assemble! This time, it's in the form of a quantum computer. Together with my best friend Julia, we'll give birth to a super genius AI. One day, we'll switch it on, and it'll buzz, hum, and say 'Hello Yasin, hello Julia, hello world.'"

Yasin mimed a children's movie robot with stiff arms and a metallic voice, creating a priceless moment of carefree joy. „Guys, I just had an epiphany: What we're putting together here sounds like some kind of Super Advanced Mind, doesn't it?! Until this project has an official name, I'll call it

'S.A.M., the 'Super Advanced Mind.'" He shouted from the top of his lungs, "All for SAM and SAM for all!"

In my Mind Recorder, these moments shine with innocent brilliance. We thought ourselves pioneers, architects of the future. It felt beautiful, and it was naïve. For a moment, we thought we were in charge. But we were not. Richard would pick the team, grant the funding, and turn our sweat and ingenuity to his advantage.

We had no idea what we were getting ourselves into. The Colosseum opened its gates. Let the games begin.

DISTRACTION, DECEPTION, SUSPICION

Sia Chronicles, MindRecorder Log entry of Saturday, May 14th, 2101.
Author: Kevin Cho

We were all hyped up that day, our nerves crackling with anticipation as Govinda, Julia, Yasin, and I prepared to meet our sponsor, Richard Anderson. His presence preceded him like a storm front, casting shadows of complexity that seemed to ripple through the air itself. Though Anderson had demanded an immediate launch of the project work with characteristic imperiousness, he first immersed us in one of his legendary spectacles – a phantasmagoric fusion of decadent feasting, provocative erotic vaudeville, and shimmering Metaverse realms that twisted and morphed at his command. To the public, he towered as a modern-day Wizard of Oz, his fingers dancing across the strings of economic and political power with predatory grace, orchestrating a grand puppet show of his own design.

The hunger for autonomy, influence, wealth, and status often erupts from the scorched earth of oppression, from the bitter taste of serving another's dreams. To prepare myself for today's encounter, I did some research to excavate the bedrock of his origins, trying to decode Anderson's labyrinth of contradictions. I found some historical data about his parents; Joos Anderson and Maria Miller's paths collided like celestial bodies in the hallowed halls of academia – she immersed in the depths of cultural studies, he carving through the realms of management and economics, with a penchant for the fading allure of cinema. Convention repelled him; instead, he blazed forward to forge a new gaming empire that would eclipse the dying light of traditional entertainment. This vision consumed him as he birthed Anderson Gaming International Corporation (AGI Corporation), his charisma drawing brilliant minds like moths to his flame.

This titan of a father cast a shadow so vast it smothered Richard's budding identity. The child withered beneath the weight of a patriarch who crushed not only his son's spirit but also suffocated his wife Maria's individual growth. Richard never knew his mother beyond the void she left. She divorced his father without any settlement soon after Richard's birth, vanishing without a trace, dissolving into the vast human ocean of twelve billion souls. This abandonment carved deep trenches in his psyche, sculpting patterns that would echo through every relationship he would forge.

Like an emperor drunk on legacy, Joos Anderson assumed his only son would inherit his digital kingdom. But Richard, like so many sons of powerful men, nursed a hatred potent enough to destroy his father or flee his orbit entirely. He chose exile. When Joos retaliated by severing Richard's financial lifelines, he discovered his son was forged from the same adamantine will. The younger Anderson studied bioengineering, wielding his brilliant mind like a weapon, seduced influential investors with his vision of humanity's next evolutionary leap – the biogenetic upgrade to humanity version 2.0. His pursuit blazed beyond mere scientific ambition; it was a declaration of war against his father's legacy, a chance to reshape not just virtual worlds but the essence of human existence.

He was not merely meeting his investors' expectations – he was shattering them.

When GenTec had long been the market leader, Richard's father's death came with theatrical timing—a stroke claimed him just as he prepared to deliver the keynote speech to thousands at the Worldwide Gaming Conference in Las Vegas. The grandiose finale befitting his outsized ego was a staging he couldn't have choreographed better himself.

In the aftermath, guided by AGI's shrewd legal counsel, Richard found himself inheriting an empire he had fought so hard to escape. The AGI legacy, his father's final imposition, now bound him to an unwanted destiny. Economic pragmatism and an inherited hunger for power and glory compelled Richard, the biogenetics innovator, to reluctantly don the mantle of gaming mogul.

Under his stewardship of both AGI and GenTec, Richard's wealth soared to staggering heights. Though he navigated the gaming world with ambivalence, his entrepreneurial instincts prevailed. He found a kindred spirit in CEO Dave Harper, whose appetite for power, growth, and fierce competition matched his own. Together, they drove both companies to crushing market dominance.

Richard's disciplined workaholism found its counterpoint in spectacular soirées, embodying his „Work Hard, Play Hard" philosophy. VR gaming became the pièce de résistance at these extravagant gatherings. Like a master showman in the neon-lit heart of Las Vegas, he orchestrated sensory feasts blending sound, designer drugs, virtual worlds, eroticism, and explosive spectacle. The themes - world market dominance, AI supremacy, victory over aging and mortality, and designer humans - painted him in god-like strokes. Visitors from all walks of life paid handsomely to taste these spectacles in GenTec Tower's upper reaches.

A dedicated crew of experts, like the roadies, sound engineers, and pyrotechnicians at a rock concert, a dedicated staff of experts orchestrated Anderson's extravagant events. These spectacles merged entertainment with existential discussions about GenTec's future. Business and politics met in the opulence of his private sanctuary at the zenith of the GenTec tower, nicknamed The Aquarium. The GenTec parties echoed the 1814 Congress of Vienna in the old Europe after the fall of Napoleon Bonaparte, where Europe's rulers had mingled revelry with power plays. Richard masterfully balanced indulgence, vanity, and business acumen.

Tonight's gathering focused on political maneuvering, with sensual-erotic performances designed to lower the guards of even the most vigilant guests. Beautiful women and men, well-known video game actors, and the architects behind first-class VR game productions provided a calculated sensual distraction. The real audience consisted of top-level, bought-and-paid-for informants from law enforcement agencies and the government, particularly the FDA. The Granger suicide had awakened powerful adversaries. The informants loyal to Anderson, sensitive patches in the dragons' skin, would help Anderson tame and, if necessary, outmaneuver the enemies.

Govinda Hammond and I appeared on the guest list as fertility specialists - Anderson's precaution should the topic arise in private discussions. Despite the risk of including me, still unbound by contract, Richard's meticulous nature left nothing to chance. The evening passed without probing questions. As it turned out, my presence was uncalled for – a relieving fact, given my distaste for such hedonistic displays. These matters were far removed from what I preferred.

The shockwaves of unsettling news reached Richard from covert government channels, delivering a payload more explosive than any previous revelation. A pervasive conspiracy theory alleged that GenTec held the key to the surging infertility rates—an insidious plot involving

GenTec's deliberate manipulation of the MediCare software to safeguard its profits. The claim asserted that NanoBots were tampered with, purposefully „overlooking" the root cause of infertility, allowing patients to be erroneously labeled as healthy, thereby justifying ongoing payments for in vitro operations.

These allegations, laden with the weight of ethical misconduct and potential illegality, sent shivers down Richard's spine. Suddenly, the ground beneath his confidence trembled, realizing that this revelation posed a far graver threat to GenTec's reputation and stability. Suspicions centered on Govinda Hammond, the suspected mastermind behind this large-scale fraud. His previous role as the architect of implants, NanoBot technology, and the government's MediCare software made him a prime suspect. The specter of a concealed epidemic loomed large, prompting influential voices to demand government intervention, notably overseeing GenTec's research branch. Richard's earlier claims of having a solution backfired, fueling the conspiracy theories surrounding GenTec and amplifying the clamor for the company to be reined in under government control.

Memories of the global diesel scandal in the 2020s automotive industry echoed as industrial fraud software skirted environmental protection laws on a colossal scale. The government's technical advisors experienced déjà vu, drawing parallels with a scandal of similar magnitude. Richard uncovered a clandestine government initiative by the Ministry of Health—a covert project aimed at debugging and revising NanoBot MediCare Services to expose the GenTec scam. Little did he know that I held a crucial position in this hushed endeavor - I led this covert project.

As the party wound down at 1 AM, Govinda and I said our goodbyes. Richard's demeanor shifted dramatically from jovial host to grave intensity. His once cheerful expression turned from jovial host to grave intensity. He dispensed with casual banter and led us to a secluded corner, his words laced with urgency: „I need you both, Govinda and Cho, tomorrow night. There's some startling news. Cho, bring your team. Govinda, you know what kind of meeting I want. No conference call - meet in my penthouse, in person. Absolute discretion is non-negotiable. Understood?"

A seismic tremor echoed through GenTec's foundations, bringing us dangerously close to a point of no return.

Sia Chronicles, MindRecorder Log entry of Sunday, May 15th, 2101.
Author: Kevin Cho

The private elevator silently ascended GenTec's gleaming tower. Govinda, Julia, Yasin, and I stood rigid as our
MediCare chips were scrutinized. The ubiquitous implants,
now as common as fingerprints among US citizens, pulsed
beneath our skin. A red „Not cleared" warning flickered,
then melted into a reassuring green.
The doors whispered open to reveal Anderson's penthouse vestibule, where invisible halon gas systems stood
ready to transform the space into a death trap at the first
sign of threat. A reminder that in Richard Anderson's
world, enemies lurked in every shadow.
A sultry synthetic voice purred, „Welcome to Richard's
Penthouse," channeling HAL9000's female counterpart. Before any of us could respond, the sight before us stole our
breath. Despite being at the tower's apex, we plunged into
an underwater paradise. Sharks glided overhead, their
sleek forms casting rippling shadows across our faces.
Schools of coral fish darted through azure waters, their colors electric against the deep blue. The curved glass tunnel
stretched eight meters ahead, banking right to obscure what
lay beyond.
Muffled sonar pings echoed through the space, completing the illusion of standing on the ocean floor. Govinda,
clearly familiar with Anderson's flair for dramatics, led us
through this aquatic wonderland into what should have
been a living room. Instead, we stepped into Captain
Nemo's Nautilus—delayed fulfillment of a dream not
dreamt in a cold, stolen childhood. Richard had bridged a
230-year-old gap with the Enlightenment pioneer and science fiction author Jules Verne.
Richard Anderson stood waiting, draped in a kimono-
style house suit that rippled with patterns like sunlight on
water. „Welcome," he said, his voice carrying the weight of
purpose. „I trust we're in for an enlightening evening." He
gestured to an elderly man standing nearby. „Jason, drinks
for our guests. My friends, meet Jason—sixty years of loyal
service to the Anderson family."
Jason's British formality carried a warmth that belied his
advanced years. Despite his apparent age of ninety-plus, he

moved with the grace of a much younger man, his smoky voice wrapping around us like aged whiskey. „My lady, gentlemen, welcome."

Anderson's expression hardened. „This is probably going to be a long night. I have invited you all to this meeting to get to know each other thoroughly before we embark on the adventure ahead together. The massive undertaking that lies ahead will require more than just doing a good job; it will require dedication from everyone. The tasks will increase in complexity as the work progresses and is already taking shape. You will experience considerable time pressure. I will go into this in more detail in a moment.

In addition to the technical challenges, legal and political issues may also prove problematic. The further we progress, the more pressure builds up, and you are likely to be tempted with substantial financial offers to betray me, this project, and GenTec.

But enough of the vague hints.

I will now tell you what I have planned for tonight. After that, you can decide whether you want to be there, whether you want to go back to your rooms to leave tomorrow, or whether we continue. If you leave, all you have to do is sign a non-disclosure agreement, which is available in your room."

„If you choose to stay, I expect your full commitment to the success of this endeavor, regardless of the challenges that may arise."

His eyes locked onto each of us in turn. „Tonight, I want to find out if we have what it takes to be a strong team. I am your host; I have asked you here. Therefore, it is only fair that I begin with my story. I would like to emphasize beforehand that everything told here in this room is and will remain confidential. I might say that a violation of that commitment would have dire consequences. Can we agree on that?"

Everyone nodded.

„Good, then I'll start."

Richard Anderson's Story

The room fell silent as Richard settled into his chair, the projected submarine interior casting strange shadows across his face. „First, an update on the current state of affairs. There are two pieces of bad news. The prosecutor's office circles GenTec like sharks, hunting for evidence of exploitation. They believe we're capitalizing on desperate couples like the Grangers, driving them to financial ruin and…" He paused, jaw tightening. „Worse."

„The good news is that we have not been guilty of anything in this matter. The investigations have consistently shown that there were no symptoms of infertility. That is why, and with the client's consent, there have been further in vitro treatments. We do not know why there were no infertility symptoms. - That's what we're trying to find out ourselves, you and I - or mainly you, to be precise, with my resources. That's the reason we're here in the first place."

Julia shifted uncomfortably in her seat. Yasin's fingers drummed against his knee. The underwater ambiance suddenly felt less magical, more suffocating.

„The second piece of bad news is less obvious. Still, potentially much more far-reaching and dangerous: I have learned from confidential sources that the Ministry of Health and representatives of the FDA want to infiltrate experts into our offices to find out whether we have hacked the NanoBot Medicare Services to manipulate our clients' data. There is a suspicion that we are falsifying client data on fertility problems in Govinda's Medicare system so that the fraud we have just described will not be noticed. The fact that you, Govinda, work at GenTec adds to the suspicion.

The alarming factor is that it is not the FBI handling this suspicion but the Department of Homeland Security, DHS. I don't need to stress that an intelligence operation is entirely nonsensical and over the top."

Richard interrupted his story, pausing momentarily and locking eyes with me. „Maybe Kevin Cho can shed some light on this. Cho, you're the government project manager for the NanoBot Medicare system—the system that Govinda once developed with all of you."

The revelation hit like a depth charge. Julia's sharp intake of breath cut through the simulated ocean sounds. Yasin's drumming fingers froze mid-tap. Only Govinda remained still, his expression unreadable.

I met Anderson's steel gaze with equal force. „My turn will come," I said quietly, „after you finish your tale."

A shark glided overhead, its shadow passing between us like an unspoken challenge. Anderson's smile never reached his eyes. „Indeed it will, Mr. Cho. Indeed it will."

Anderson's fingers traced the rim of his crystal glass as he continued.

„But now to me and my motivation in our cause. The planned restructuring of GenTec and the necessary spin-off of the Research & Development department is not easy for me; the entrepreneurial risks are difficult to manage. But it looks like there is no alternative."

I looked at Govinda, whose eyes I could not catch. He seemed to have already made a proposal to Anderson about this. Interesting, I thought to myself. Govinda appears to be pushing almost as hard as Anderson. Both had their own agenda. The evening started to look promising.

Richard continued: „Realistically, there is a high risk that GenTec's existence will be threatened if R&D remains in the company. I have five points that influence my decision on this matter.

The first driver is prominent: „GenTec is more than a company—it's my legacy, my rebellion." A bitter smile played across his lips. „My father's gaming empire cast a long shadow, one I refused to live under. The Dutch blood in our veins breeds stubborn pride. Two alpha wolves can't lead the same pack."

The projected submarine walls seemed to pulse with the rhythm of his words. „Gaming offered the power to create virtual worlds, but I hungered for more. I wanted to reshape reality itself, to improve upon creation." His eyes gleamed with fervor. „InVitro was just the beginning, the cash cow to fund grander dreams. The wealthy would pay anything for children, so we gave them hope—premium services for the elite, budget options for the masses."

He fell silent, watching a lionfish drift past the aquarium walls. The creature's venomous spines cast fractal shadows across his face.

„So, GenTec's first product was GenFam - a technology and service helping disparate couples to conceive. That product is a big seller, a low-brainer - and it still would be if it weren't for these recent sterility issues, which I hope you'll sort out quickly."

Richard's eyes sparkled as he spoke, his voice rising with enthusiasm. He gestured expansively, his smile broadening with each passing sentence. Now, he paused for effect and had a sip of water.

„GenTec must continue to be successful. But enough of that, let's move on to the next topic."

‚So far, nothing new', I thought, listening to Anderson's somewhat predictable speech. His values and culture were all about being at the top, making it to the top, beating the competition, growth, growth, and more growth, winning the crowd, dazzling the customers, reducing humans to consumers, being rich and powerful, and famous.

„But time…" His voice hardened. „Time is the one commodity I can't buy. Sixty-nine years have left their mark, and I need an heir." His gaze slid toward Julia, who stiffened visibly. „I need a son to carry forward my work. I'm not exactly unproductive when it comes to sex. Despite my… prolific attempts, both natural and in the lab, success eludes me."

The implications crashed over us like a tidal wave. This wasn't a mere business proposition but a desperate man's final gambit. This project was profoundly personal to him. Anderson was driven by the primal instinct of preserving one's kind, about living on in the descendants' blood. It was the irony of ironies: Richard Anderson, the most powerful and successful man in the history of artificial insemination, the celebrated pregnancy pope, was himself completely childless. He couldn't sire an heir of his own. That had to be unbearable to him. The irony carved deep lines around his mouth as he spoke.

And he couldn't fix this tragedy alone. Richard, the almighty needed accomplices. He needed our help. This meeting was not part of a recruiting event for some GenTec projects. Instead, he had decided to make us the key to his problem. We would have no choice in the matter.

We were trapped.

He made us the knights of his round table. This night was the act of swearing us in as his gladiators. From the grave look on Yasin's and Julia's faces, I saw they had similar thoughts. Only Hammond seemed excited and somehow - satisfied.

I thought this would be the climax of today's revelations, but within the next few minutes, I was to be proven wrong.

„There's more." Anderson's voice dropped. „This brings me to my third driver. My father was married only briefly. I emerged from that brief interlude. I never met my mother. She left us shortly after I was born."

I watched him, fascinated. Didn't his voice lose its firm sound then?

„I'm going to tell you something very private now. After all, I want to know from you later on what makes you tick and why.

Like my father, I was once married for a short time. A son was born." The underwater lighting cast his face in ghostly relief. „He works here now, tending these aquariums. Only Jason and his therapist know the truth—until now."

This revelation blew me away. His words hung in the water-filtered light like suspended particles. Why the hell is he disclosing this most personal, intensely emotional side of his life? Through the glass walls, I saw a solitary figure moving among the fish, his movements precise and disconnected from our world.

„Maddox," Anderson whispered, watching the shadow. „My son. Asperger's syndrome locked him away from human connection before he could speak. The Viennese pediatrician Asperger noticed intense preoccupation with particular areas of interest, a tendency to engage in monologues, and a low body weight. Sometimes rigid, sometimes gesticulating wildly, Maddox, skinny as a raven, would approach the aquarium, throw angry glances at us and mutter incomprehensible gibberish; he is obsessed with the water world.

He finds more kinship with these underwater creatures than with any person." His voice cracked. „In all these years, I've never held him. He... he can't bear my touch."

The projection of the Nautilus flickered, momentarily revealing the stark modern walls beneath before stabilizing again. Anderson squared his shoulders, his vulnerability vanishing behind a mask of determination.

„This brings us to NexGen—the next evolution of CRISPR technology. Imagine: genetic perfection on demand. Not just eliminating diseases like my son's, but enhancing humanity itself. Intelligence, strength, longevity— all for sale to the highest bidder. NexGen will give us staggering wealth." His eyes burned with messianic intensity. „We'll create a new human species, as different from current mankind as we are from Neanderthals."

The room felt smaller suddenly, the water pressure more oppressive. Anderson's gaze pinned each of us in turn. „You, Govinda, Cho, Yasin, Julia, you will build the system that makes this possible. Within a year, you'll solve not just infertility, but unlock the gates to human perfection itself."

I watched this industry titan lay bare his dreams of playing God. I saw something else entirely: a lonely child abandoned by his mother and overshadowed by his father, now desperately trying to forge connection through power and legacy. His grand vision of genetic perfection was, at its heart, a blueprint to fix his broken family—to heal his son, create a new heir, and achieve the immortality that would prevent him from abandoning them as he had been abandoned.

We had to be careful as hell that a deal with Anderson didn't take on Faustian overtones.

„But wait," he said, raising a hand. „There's more." He gestured toward Jason, who stood straight-backed despite his years. „Jason has been more father to me than my own, which brings us to Project Infinity—the end of aging itself. Your system won't just solve infertility; it will crack the code of cellular death. Imagine offering not just perfect children, but eternal life."

Anderson stood, his kimono catching the rippling light like scales. „I will stand before the world as living proof— the first immortal man! We'll sell genetic perfection and endless life on a subscription basis." He laughed, the sound echoing off the glass walls. „God's own business model."

What I heard here bordered on megalomania. There was something insatiable about Anderson, something decadent and greedy that deeply repelled me, yet that also had something fascinating. There was something infectiously exciting, even benign, about Anderson's fantasies.

We had to be careful as hell that a deal with Anderson didn't take on Faustian overtones.

As I watched the larger-than-life Anderson, another thought struck me. In his life, he must have felt terribly lonely from his childhood onwards until now. His father had hardly seen him as his child, his son, but only as a spitting image of himself. And his mother? She had left him before he could consciously notice her, before he could connect with her and all her love. She, too, was not there for him. In her suffering from her self-centered husband, she had not only fled from her wounded love, she had also abandoned her child.

And all this suffering created Richard's life script. As a result, Richard Anderson repeated the life of his parents: the father's vital need for recognition, the desire for an heir in whom he and his work would live on forever, the short marriage, the child who turned away from him and was unattainable, and the obsessive effort to impose his own life's work upon the son. He never had the experience of being loved. The feeling of security was always only for sale, never a gift, never a grace. For such a person, the desire to bequeath, to pass on, was perhaps the best possible attempt to show love.

This man's life was a tragic disaster.

Anderson, meanwhile, was on to his next point. „The fourth driver is my servant Jason. I want him with me if I live forever - I'll get to the subject of ‚forever' in a moment.

Jason has been with me for as long as I can remember. He has provided discreet advice in every situation. He is my father of choice, so to speak. Jason is aging, as we all do. And we think that's how it should be. But aging, if you look at it, is a disease—a cellular disease. This was already known around 2020, but not accepted in science, and the lobbyists making money from aging boycotted this scientific truth.

I want to put a definitive end to aging. That's why I'm going to launch a third project. It is codenamed Infinity. The goal will be to repair the genetic material and all cells.

Once the system you develop collects vast amounts of data and links everything, it will inevitably become increasingly likely to be able to provide answers to questions other than infertility. For example, it should be able to suggest how to prevent cells from dying. You will build something like God's right hand, helping people live forever.

The fifth driver is the harbinger of my overcoming of mortality itself. Imagine this: I, the epitome of eternal existence, standing before the people and proclaiming, 'Behold, I am immortal! You need not long for eternity beyond the veil of death. I give you eternal life here and now!'

People will pounce on us. Imagine: we allow them to configure their dream child, so they buy this child a perfect mind in a perfect body, which can then live indefinitely thanks to their financial support. We will offer a subscription service that can be extended annually or a one-time payment, with a right of use for life."

Anderson's hands fluttered like pale birds in the aquarium light, his excitement palpable. „This, my friends, will change everything!" The childlike glee in his voice made his previous gravitas evaporate like sea spray.

The full weight of his ambition crashed over me. The infertility problem had been merely bait—a shiny lure to draw us into deeper, darker waters. What he truly wanted was divinity packaged in binary code, a digital demiurge that could reshape humanity according to his whims. My spine turned to ice as I watched him practically bouncing on his toes, this man-child who would play with the building blocks of existence.

The moral implications spread through the room like ink in water. We weren't just potential employees anymore; we had become potential accomplices in humanity's greatest triumph—or its ultimate hubris. If we refused, Anderson would find others, perhaps those who asked fewer questions, whose consciences cast shorter shadows.

But Anderson wasn't finished. His voice dropped to a near-whisper, compelling us to lean forward. „One small detail remains." He gestured toward the aquarium walls, where a hammerhead shark cut through a school of silvery fish. „Our Earth groans beneath humanity's weight. Resources bleed dry. Deserts devour grasslands. Species vanish like morning mist." His fingers traced the glass, following the shark's path. „Even Mars, our red refuge of hope, proves too hostile for our dreams."

The projected submarine interior flickered, momentarily replaced by images of barren wastelands, dying forests, synthetic food farms. Anderson's eyes reflected the apocalyptic slideshow. „Now imagine adding immortality to this equation." He turned back to us, his smile razor-sharp. „The solution becomes obvious, doesn't it? We must reach for the stars themselves."

The room fell silent save for the muted sonar pings. Even the fish seemed to pause in their eternal dance.

„And that," Anderson said, lifting his glass in a mock toast, „is why I need you." He settled back into his chair like a satisfied cat. „Now then, Cho—" his eyes locked onto mine with predatory focus, „—shall we hear your story?"

The weight of all our futures—humanity's future—pressed down like ocean depths. In the glass walls, our reflections wavered like ghosts, already haunted by choices yet to be made.

I met Anderson's theatrical revelations with deliberate simplicity. „Thank you for sharing your story, Mr. Anderson." The words fell soft and measured into the aquarium-filtered light, starkly contrasting his bombastic declarations.

Where Anderson lived in excess, I found power in minimalism—my sparse room, unadorned clothing, precise language. Even now, as it was my turn to unveil my history, I chose to strip away ornament and speak plain truth.

My Story: Kevin Cho

„I was born on American soil to South Korean parents," I began, my voice steady against the backdrop of bubbling water. „Our home was a ten-square-meter cube, one of eight arranged in an octagon. White Americans occupied the other units, but none of us truly lived there. Everyone retreated into their virtual worlds, leaving the common area at the octagon's center empty—everyone except me."

The projected submarine walls rippled as a school of fish darted past. „University was a luxury beyond our means. So I claimed that abandoned common room as my classroom, armed with nothing but an e-pad and free learning apps." A ghost of a smile crossed my face. „Knowledge, as it turns out, doesn't require tuition. I devoured everything I could find about techno-human interfaces, losing myself in cybernetics, robotics, cognitive neural science, artificial intelligence, machine learning."

I gestured toward Hammond. „Mr. Hammond's concept consisted of the brain implant, a neurochip, and NanoBots discretely distributed in the bloodstream, organs, and nerve cells. These NanoBots diligently transmit a wealth of health data to the neurochip. When circumstances require their exit from the host, they dutifully log off and transform into neutral particles. They seamlessly re-register and resume their task when they enter a new host with a neuro-chip." My fingers traced patterns in the condensation on my glass. „They're everywhere now—in our water, our food, in the very air we breathe."

The submarine's sonar pinged, punctuating my following words.

„The reasons for my involvement in this project were technological and social.

During the MediCare project, I was responsible for programming the NanoBots and giving them sensitivity to certain symptoms. For example, specific bots had the task of detecting cancer cells. During detection, the neurochip AI analyzes the potentially triggering factors. If the host behaves in a cancer-promoting manner, e.g., by smoking or consuming carcinogenic substances, a warning is issued, and a recommendation to change behavior is made. This information is seamlessly integrated into the state healthcare system MediCare. Compliance ensures ongoing coverage; continued self-harm requires personal financial responsibility."

„I proposed the idea of personal responsibility to the government, crafted an AI-based financial model, and put the plan into action. The financial results were convincing. Now, issues like obesity, drug use, and smoking fall on the individual's shoulders. The days of exploiting the social system and nearly bankrupting the state are behind us. The community breathes a sigh of relief.

The payoff? People's behavior changed, tilting towards self-care and health. A considerable increase in the state budget made a comfortable basic income a reality. That fills me with pride."

Anderson leaned forward as I addressed his earlier suspicion. „I'm not your spy, Mr. Anderson. But yes, I led the government team that refined the MediCare system—the same system that shows puzzling discrepancies between declining fertility rates and the absence of NanoBot warnings."

The room grew still, even the projected fish seemed to pause.

„The question wasn't whether GenTec manipulated data, despite appearances. Our analysis showed something far more disturbing: the system remains untampered, yet fertility plummets. The NanoBots detect nothing wrong, yet something is terribly wrong. Of course, people were looking toward GenTec because you dominate the InVitro market, and you would be very interested in keeping problems to yourself, if any, to calm the market - and Govinda works at GenTec. Who better to manipulate the MediCare system?"

Hammond surged from his chair. „Preposterous!"

I met Anderson's piercing gaze. „DHS isn't investigating corporate espionage, Mr. Anderson. They're orchestrating a cover-up, using manufactured concerns to shut down InVitro clinics while they conduct covert research."

This startling news left the team speechless. „Shit!" came from Richard.

I leaned forward, invading his carefully maintained personal space. „But we—your proposed spin-off lab—could become the world's premier research facility. While they fumble in darkness, we'll unravel the true mystery."

The aquarium lights cast icy shadows across Anderson's face as he processed my words. „So, you want us to play saviors while they play cover-up?"

„Not savior," I corrected, my voice barely above a whisper. „Architects of change. The DHS is a pawn in a game it doesn't understand. We will exploit their ignorance to create a sanctuary of knowledge in our Quantum Universe, shielded from the cacophony of public opinion. This transcends profit margins and market share. It's about uncovering why humanity's most basic function is failing." I held his gaze. „I see patterns others miss. This team can decode them. I don't want power or wealth—I want understanding. My currency is knowledge; with it, we can shape the future."

Scattered applause, led by Anderson's measured claps and knowing smile, broke the tension. I had shifted the game board without moving a single piece. With a slight bow, I resumed my seat.

Anderson turned to Julia, leaving my revelations hanging between us. „Julia," he gestured expansively, „your turn."

Julia's Story

Julia's voice cut through the fake Nautilus boardroom like a laser through fog. „I live in the Cubes," she began, her Scottish lilt carrying pride rather than apology. „Working class by birth, privileged by today's standards. My parents, Scottish immigrants, endowed me with their heritage - poor, freedom-loving, and not used to expecting handouts. In our world, you have to earn trust. I'm proud of that."

Her eyes found Anderson's, steel meeting steel. „I'm forty-two and single, which makes me far better suited for your research lab than your breeding program, Mr. Anderson. Your cut-off age for women is thirty, isn't it?"

Anderson's laugh rippled across his whiskey. „Done your homework, I'll give you that. Though I'm not as... selective... as I once was." His humble smile only barely concealed his lust.

My jaw clenched at his casual harassment, but Julia continued undaunted. „Dumbarton, Scotland, shaped my early years," she said, her voice softening with memory. „My father, a master carpenter turned digital modeler, introduced me to men who built worlds from pure thought. Meanwhile, my mother managed reception at Loch Lomond Hotel—long hours, harder work, but they gave me a wonderful childhood filled with daydreams in the enigmatic worlds of my parents."

The projected submarine walls shimmered as she described Europe's economic collapse. „The city crumbled. Dad lost everything. Then Hollywood called—'Masters-of-VR-Worlds' needed him. Picture it: my father in his pressed shirts and flannel trousers, surrounded by developers sporting Mohawks and Maori tattoos, drowning with Che Guevara beards, mohawks, Maori tattoos, retro Esalen, Jurassic Park, and Wu-Tang Clan t-shirts."

Her gentle smile, born from the depths of her memory, was not of this world. „My parents lived in modest circumstances in the Cubes and pinched every penny to fund my education. I practically lived in the server room, chasing that impossible dream of a Cal State scholarship. When it came—" A ghost of another smile touched her lips. „I dove into machine learning and sensory labs, survived on synthetic food, and emerged pale but proud with a PhD in computer science and psychology. My research focus on machine learning led me into the public sector. There, I crossed paths with Govinda and the MediCare project. When this was completed, the job market became tighter. MoVR-Worlds had moved to Seattle, so I only had a freelance gig. But I enjoyed it - I was helping software geeks develop new game characters. Of course, I could have done that remotely, but the genuine collaboration with colleagues lured me to Seattle. Now, I share a cube with Martha, a lovely 92-year-old. We are avid collectors of old books, and our cube is full of literary treasures."

Richard inquired, „What's your favorite book or author, Julia?"

She thought momentarily before answering: „Several, actually, and very different ones. Viktor Frankl's ‚Man in Search of Meaning,' but also such stony science fiction as Daniel Galouye's ‚Simulacron-3' or David Gerrold's ‚I am Harlie.' I count ‚Life 3.0' by Max Tegmark and ‚Superintelligence' by Nick Bostrum among the technical classics. I love Robert Louis Stevenson's Treasure Island. These works have lost little of their zest."

Anderson leaned forward, predatory interest gleaming. „And your motivation for joining us? Why should I hire you?"

Julia's cat-like gaze never wavered. „With all due respect, Mr. Anderson, the team will hire me, not you. If they want me, I'll meet their standards."

I watched Anderson flinch at her directness. His world of submissive women had no room for such steel.

„Not good enough," he growled. „I need your deeper purpose."

„Very well." Julia's voice dropped to a professor's lecture tone. „You're creating something unprecedented—an AI system that could evolve beyond its creators' control. You need more than just programmers. You need someone who understands the psychology of artificial consciousness, who can prevent your creation from going mad." Her eyes locked onto his. „Put simply, Mr. Anderson, I'm here to ensure your sorcerer's apprentice doesn't flood the workshop. I'm here because I feel responsible. - Cho?"

„We should at least be prepared for that," I concurred, feeling a surge of enthusiasm for Julia's free, brilliant, and powerfully articulated spirit. Shifting my gaze from her to our future boss, I traced the features of Anderson's face as his casual façade cracked. He'd summoned forces beyond his comprehension, and here sat the one person who might control them—a woman who wouldn't bow to his authority.

Julia had provided a necessary reality check. It dawned on Anderson that he lacked a profound understanding of the professional realm that held the key to the fertility problem and his more fantastical ventures.

„Yasin Mohamed, please continue! Sounds like the name of an Islamic mullah!" Anderson chuckled, expecting laughter to echo through the room. Instead, a deafening silence greeted him.

Anderson attempted to reclaim the spotlight. „Shall we have a little break before you start? Can I treat my guests to something else? A joint? Something uplifting or consciousness-expanding? Or simply a real, fine Scotch? I've got nothing but pure, high-quality stuff here. Your NanoBots will have few objections."

A quick survey of the room revealed a collective desire to wrap up the proceedings sooner rather than later, anticipating a decisive conclusion tonight. Yasin's introduction marked the crucial moment—no decision, no project. Tonight was the point of no return.

„Just water, please. For everyone, right?" I interjected. „Or a fresh ginger tea, Jason, that would be very nice—no distorting party additives, please." Jason materialized seemingly out of thin air and nodded discreetly. „Very well, Mr. Cho. Tea and water for everyone. Master Anderson, another whisky?

Yasin's Story

Yasin's words tumbled like a cascade, his body swaying forward in the chair as if propelled by the sheer force of his enthusiasm. His deep brown eyes blazed with an almost manic intensity, darting between us as he spoke.

„OK, thank you very much for inviting me, Mr. Anderson, Mr. Hammond, and you, Kevin and Julia. Well, I come from Auckland, New Zealand, that's my home. I am a 2nd generation citizen there. My ancestors were Indian Muslims, and I grew up in that tradition. Today, religion no longer plays a significant role for me; it's more the values behind it that are important to me. Julia and I have often talked about this. We are both somewhat agnostic, not denying a higher existence but simply not considering it provable. Artificial intelligence, especially General Artificial Intelligence, might change that one day. Sorry, I tend to ramble a bit. Back to me, as you requested, Mr Anderson. I guess you can call me a nerd without insulting me. I was born highly gifted and hyperactive, and my parents had their share of problems with me. I didn't have any friends. Kids my age couldn't relate to me, and vice versa. When I was 16, I went to university because I was bored with school. I did my MSc in Physics and AI at Auckland Uni with A-grades almost on the side. Mostly, I sat at home tinkering with prototype androids. I didn't have the time or inclination for a PhD; I wasn't interested in titles. When I was twenty, I got an offer for an engineering position at QBYTE, a start-up developing a quantum computing platform. That was exactly my thing. In this startup, nerds are not the exception but the rule. For the first time, I felt at home.

I still work for QBYTE without regular working hours, as I live there. It's more like home. When I've eaten and nothing else is happening, I go to the workshop and create stuff. My colleagues call me in when they need me. I do all kinds of things there: hardware development, operating systems, consulting for customer solutions, you name it. At QBYTE, I also have a room with a comfortable bed, a desk, a CAD/CAM system with three 52' monitors, and a hyper-fast SkyLink. The absolute hit is my spatial computer system, a mixed reality that transforms the whole room into whatever I like, similar to your system here. It's pure luxury if you ask me, but nerds like me get bored quickly without high-tech. My hobby is designing and building androids," Yasin's eyes flashed. „The people at QBYTE have given me a workshop to use mostly at night when hardly anyone is in the house, and I can make noise. I'd like to have the same here in this project."

A smirk played on my lips, and I extended a bro-fist to Yasin. Julia laughed softly, and even Richard seemed astonished by Yasin's vibrant energy in the room.

„Oh yes, two more things. Number one: like Julia, I also love classical music. It's a different kind of classical, more like in Jimmy Hendrix' 'Bold as Love,' or Bon Jovi's 'It's my life,' or Nirvana's 'Smells like teen spirit.' Classic rock, that kind of thing. The bridge between Julia's and my classical music would be John Lord's Deep Purple @ The Royal Philharmonic Orchestra, 'Concert For Group And Orchestra.' But Julia and I love such stunning pieces as Rachmaninov's 3rd Piano Concerto or, even better, 'Le Sacre du Printemps' by Stravinsky. You have to see an old ballet recording in 3D by Pina Bausch. It'll blow your mind. Might be something for your wacky parties."

The he straightened, suddenly all business. „Why hire me? Simple. You need a self-optimizing deep learning system with an open mind for hunting patterns in obscure phenomena. We're talking quantum hardware pushed to its limits, memory arrays that make Big Data look tiny. I'll build you something faster than anything on Earth." His eyes locked with Anderson's. „Without me, you'll burn time, money, and maybe your only shot."

Richard nodded, appreciation mingling with calculation in his expression. I saw the eager gleam in his eyes – here was a talent ripe for manipulation. 'Take it easy, Anderson,' I thought, exchanging a protective glance with Julia: 'Julia and I will see to it that Yasin is not abused for anything or by anyone.'

But Anderson had already turned his attention to Govinda, his mind racing ahead to the next move in his grand game.

However, Anderson's thoughts had already shifted to Govinda.

The scene unfolded with some theatricality, Anderson's mocking undertone cutting through the air as he turned to Govinda: „So, last but not least, you too. Give us the honor, please."

Govinda's Story

Govinda rose with awkward grace, his tall frame struggling to find its place in the intimate setting. His attempt to address the group resembled more of a retreat than an engagement. Clearing his throat to mask his discomfort, he began, „My name carries meaning—Govinda, 'the kind-hearted.' A parental aspiration that became my default setting. I rarely argue, get along with everyone."

His words emerged stilted, each sentence carefully measured. „Conservative family background. Father in Big Pharma finance, mother a Conservative Party puppet master. 'Don't mess with mom' was our family motto." His attempt at humor fell flat against the room's polished surfaces.

„My wife Irene," his voice softened, betraying genuine emotion, „she's my opposite—vibrant, sophisticated. She pulls me away from the lab, shows me life's finer points." He drifted momentarily into private reverie before snapping back to formality.

„Thirteen years at GenTec. I started in Genetics and am now Director of R&D, overseeing InVitro, Genetics, IT Operations, AI, and Big Data. Before that, government work, MediCare project." His credentials tumbled out like items on a checklist. „MBA and Ph.D. in Bioinformatics from Cal State, courtesy of wealthy parents. I speak business, science, and research. Part of GenTec's Executive team, but..." he glanced at Anderson, „...more behind the scenes. Richard's the frontman."

„I'm not political and avoid intrigue and power games whenever possible.

Off duty, I go bowling or snooker in the pub with my team."

It was exhausting to watch, Hammond's speech seemed forced. He paused, straightened up, and, turning to Anderson, continued: „If you're asking why I want to run our business, the main argument is I know the place inside out.

And, folks, I can keep Homeland Security at bay. Nobody handles things the way I do."

After Govinda's uninspiring talk, the steam left Nemo's salon. The aquarium and tea had lost their stimulating effect. After Hammond's excellent pep talk last night, Julia, Yasin, and I had expected something different.

Richard continued: „We all know that this is a business launch. External circumstances force us to hurry, but showing our commitment and inner motivation was useful. Thank you all for speaking so openly. My picture of the team I am entrusting with my future is now clear. Initially, I wanted one-to-one meetings, but that is no longer necessary. I have an unerring instinct for people and have gained complete confidence in this team. You can all be proud. I'll have a quick chat with Govinda privately. Please be patient for a few more minutes before we call it a day. Make yourselves comfortable. Drinks, video games, pool tables, music, whatever you want—no time for a sauna and massage. Jason, make my guests comfortable. - Govinda?"

They disappeared into the map room of the Nautilus sim. For some reason, Anderson had neglected to close the door. I found this odd and wondered if there was a plan. We couldn't help but overhear what they were saying.

„Govinda, good team. I want them all on board. Give them a generous salary. We don't want to lose anyone to the competition! - And now to you. What role do you want? You look a bit humdrum tonight."

Anderson loved provocation. You had to be confident to stand up to such alpha male games.

Hammond's voice rang out excitedly. „I want the role of CEO, Richard. CyberTec, as we should call the start-up, needs its own management. Legally, it must be completely separate from GenTec and yourself."

Their conversation carried clearly—Hammond's desperate pitch for CEO of the new venture, CyberTec, his voice crackling with unprecedented intensity. „I want a salary that puts me in your neighborhood, Richard. Not for me— for Irene. She deserves that life." The naked ambition in his voice was startling.

Anderson's silence spoke volumes. Govinda pressed on, his voice rising: „Introduce us to your circle—the parties, the theatre, everything." Each word dripped with raw need.

The deal was struck with theatrical precision—CEO position, 0.1% stake, estimated hundred million annual potential. Govinda's acceptance came breathless, grateful: „I am in your debt." Anderson's trap had sprung perfectly.

The announcement came with typical Anderson flair—Handel's Messiah thundering through hidden speakers as he proclaimed the birth of CyberTec and its team. We departed to Mascagni's Intermezzo, the music's bittersweet notes perfectly capturing the evening's mix of triumph and foreboding.

The next day, legal machinery whirred into motion, creating CyberTec's corporate shell. The Bay Area's dusty air crackled with approaching storm energy. A would-be god, a desperate dreamer, and a band of brilliant misfits had set out to save humanity—or perhaps to doom it.

TRANSITION STAGE 2

Sia Chronicles, MindRecorder Log entry of Wednesday, June 29th, 2101.
Author: Kevin Cho

Yasin ensured that the company named CyberTeq, a suggestion from Govinda Hammond, had a distinguished Q at the end. „Q stands for quantum speed, quantum quality, and quantum computer. Without quantum computers, this company will fail," he claimed. Luck was with us, and CyberTeq was founded after only three weeks of fighting our way through a maze of lawyers and bureaucratic regulations. The company was officially registered and emerged as a separate entity, with Govinda Hammond taking on the CEO role and Richard Anderson securing a seat on the board. I took on the Director of Research and Development role, Yasin was promoted to Head of AI Infrastructure and Big Data, and Julia took the helm as Head of AI Development.

One could argue that there are many bosses and no attendants, but structure is paramount for high performance, and we would grow by gradually hiring people for our respective areas. In the startup milieu, it's common for everyone to try their hand at everything, which leads to the less glamorous tasks being neglected. Hammond and I have vowed not to waste valuable time on administrative or structural errors.

Despite financial considerations not being our primary motivator, we were given generous salaries. The real thrill lay in the promise of plush, modern accommodations at CyberTeq premises. We've all been through it: the crucible of a time-bound project, toiling ceaselessly, catching naps on makeshift beds, feeding on pizza and soda while looking like ghosts. This was not the vision for our work. Comfortable on-site accommodation was not a luxury but an essential factor for well-being.

CyberTeq's inaugural hurdle was its spatial requirement. Quantum hardware would be a distant dream without expansive rooms, making research and development impossible. The space for our systems needed to be colossal, accommodating future expansions. Moving premises mid-project was an inconceivable risk. Hammond and Anderson personally shouldered the responsibility to address this challenge.

At the same time, Julia, Yasin, and I delved into designing and planning a deep learning system and the Quantum infrastructure. The clock relentlessly ticked away. After six weeks elapsed with scant visible progress, Richard summoned a VR meeting, wasting no time in getting to the crux of the matter. „My apologies for the delay in securing a suitable haven for our team and CyberTeq. The silver lining: the frustrating wait is over."

You know by now that I don't particularly like Anderson, an unpredictable, moody character who is best approached with caution. But to my great surprise, I recognized a flare of commendable style and restless commitment in his recent actions. He has backed Hammond and taken responsibility for the unforeseen delay. It was not the job of a board member to deal with the intricacies of the real estate market, and yet he did.

Yasin, driven by impatience, pressed on with his questions: „Where is the road of life taking us? What destination awaits us?"

„I'll come to that in a moment, Yasin. At the moment, the indisputable truth is clear: nine weeks have slipped through our fingers. To be clear, it's not your fault; I'm not complaining and not blaming you. Finding vacant office or factory space on this deserted, overpopulated globe proved complicated. Not everyone can understand that four people need a whole square kilometer of business space. Anyway. I made quite a pitch to estate agents and all the influential people around me. Yesterday, finally, came the redeeming news. And now hold on to your hats when it comes to the new ‚partner': my good old nemesis and conspiracy theorist John Smith, Head of Strategic Alliances, MediCare, made us an offer."

Yasin, bouncing like a ping-pong ball, spouted, „No kidding, seriously?! How did *that* happen? Man, what, where, and when?"

„Well, GenTec is secretly suspected of defrauding the state. The CyberTeq spin-off has not precisely put these rumors to rest. That brings me to John Smith. Quite the striking name, isn't it? Conspicuously inconspicuous, almost a clumsiness to its anonymity. I've never had the pleasure of a face-to-face encounter; Smith operates from the shadows, expertly pulling the strings. His clandestine gig involves donning the hat of an undercover agent for the United States Department of Homeland Security, deeply embedded within the Department of Health and seamlessly integrated into the MediCare team.

John maneuvers with the tacit approval of Anthony Manwhosh, the CEO of MediCare. Manwhosh is actually quite alright. His mantra echoes, ‚Nothing beats the sanctity of patient data and medical records' - an honorable commitment in my eyes.

Honor, however, is not Smith's strong suit. Rather, he manipulates Manwhosh like Cardinal Richelieu once manipulated King Louis of France. John Smith's 'generous' offer of prime real estate for our startup dangles like a gilded hook—one that draws us deeper into MediCare's orbit and, no doubt, under the watchful gaze of powers that lurk far beyond its medical mandate. Manwhosh may have signed the invitation, but it's Smith's shadow that looms over our impending migration to MediCare's inner sanctum."

„What?!" Hammond's face drained of color. Anderson, true to his mercurial nature, had 'forgotten' to brief him. Classic Anderson—brilliant yet chaotic, leaving wreckage in his wake. Hammond's reputation lay bleeding on the floor while I watched Anderson, my praise dying on my lips as he executed another of his trademark blindsides.

Anderson's voice cut through the tension. „Not directly within the confines of MediCare, to be exact, but nestled in the colossal LSD-C, the globe's grandest data bastion, a colossal fortress of data that cradles MediCare's digital crown jewels." His eyes flickered to Govinda. „Rest easy, Govinda, for now, they've spared you..." He turned to me, his expression hardening. „Manwhosh has you bound by contract. There's no wiggling free from the MediCare consortium. Still, they're playing nice—They only want to see you twice a week to push your Next Generation project. The rest of your time belongs to CyberTeq. Dealing with Cho's double commissioning is thus neatly solved. He operates within CyberTeq's confines, in close proximity to the MediCare enclave—a harmonized logistical ballet, courtesy of Smith's foresight."

Anderson's voice softened as he painted a picture of our future home. Reno, Nevada—once a drowsy desert town, now a sprawling metropolis born from catastrophe. The great quake of 2062 had devoured Silicon Valley whole, four merciless waves turning it into an abyss. Hours later, the floods came, sweeping away whatever remained. San

Francisco, too, felt nature's wrath as the Pacific's fury tore through its streets. Yet somehow, the city clings to life.

The California coastline now huddles closer to the Sierra Nevadas, mocking those who once doubted climate change. San Francisco endures as a shadow of its former self, wearing its scars like sacred tattoos. Meanwhile, the titans of industry found sanctuary in Reno's embrace.

„The negotiations..." Anderson leaned back, lost in recent memory. „Manwhosh and Smith orchestrated a meeting with John Goldblum, LSD-C's chief. Picture this: Goldblum, an affable guy, took me on a tour around the gigantic LSD-C facility. The latest fifth expansion, the Tahoe Reno 5 section, was nearing completion. One look, and I knew—this was our future."

He chuckled. „Goldblum took some convincing about our scale. Smith and Manwhosh hung on every word—perfect chance to shake their conspiracy theories loose. I explained CyberTeq's unique position, our need for physical hardware. Goldblum raised an eyebrow at that—'Cloud services are the unbeaten standard,' he insisted. But I painted him a picture: a fortress of technology, sealed tight as a biotech lab handling the deadliest viruses. That got his attention."

Anderson's eyes gleamed. „'I'm betting big,' I told him. 'Total independence, complete control. I'm both patron and client, and I pay premium for perfection. And let's be honest—no cloud service can match the quantum computing power we're planning.' He caved, probably because I accepted his price without negotiating. The contract signing felt like destiny. Goldblum's parting words still echo: 'Welcome to the Large Scale Data Center—quite a trip, isn't it?' A weak play on the LSD acronym, but it stuck."

The VR line crackled with our congratulations before Anderson, basking in his triumph, severed the connection.

Sia Chronicles, MindRecorder Log entry of Thursday, June 30th, 2101.
Author: Kevin Cho

Hammond had stayed home with his wife, moving to Anderson's posh neighborhood.

His choice, I thought. We will manage to take over the new premises without him.

John Goldblum, the head of the LSD-C Data Center, led Julia Yasin and me to our new premises. On our way from his office to our place, Goldblum explained one of the reasons for the Data Center's gigantic dimensions: „Ninety percent of all data available worldwide has been produced in the last two years alone," he said. „The internet is growing exponentially."

Yasin was only half listening. He was all excited. His head was still pulsing with the hypnotic rhythm of Iggy Pop's song The Passenger he listened to on the drive through sulfurous yellow sand clouds and hazy Cubes settlements.

„Guys! Do you realize we're heading for our CyberTeq headquarters for the first time? - That's it! A few weeks ago, this was all just a dream in our heads! And now we're about to unlock a door, and on the other side is our new home! This is so frickin' exciting!" Julia laughed her most beautiful, honest laugh that could knock your shoes off.

I took the keys from Goldblum and held them out to Yasin. „Wanna?"

Yasin took the bunch of keys reverently. „Wow. Premiere. I feel honored. Do I have to carry someone over the threshold? Julia, you're the only woman here …"

„Don't you dare! - I'm walking in here on my own two feet. This is not a wedding!"

The new windows and doors were still covered with an opaque protective plastic film from the inside. Yasin unlocked the door and entered the reception room. It smelled of fresh screed and plastic and paint. The wall behind the reception counter was indirectly lit from the ceiling; the company name had not yet been installed. The reception counter, made of seaweed-green frosted glass, glowed from within. Upstairs, at the back above the reception desk, we saw a sizeable all-glass conference room with marble Viennese coffeehouse tables and high chairs in front of it.

A double door led further into the lobby's service rooms, to the front desk's left and right. The door on the left said Private, and the door on the right was labeled Lab.

Yasin went to the left door. „May I?"

„Sure. Go ahead," I encouraged him. We followed Yasin as he entered the private area located in the western wing of the building. A slightly curved, wide corridor to our left unfolded, with three apartments branching off to the left and right, each approximately 36 square meters in size.

With jaws dropped in amazement, we entered one of the flats. The first room welcomed us with a compact living space, distinct from the integrated kitchen by a noble cooking block with a counter and bar stools. Beyond, a cozy bedroom with an attached bathroom awaited us through a small hallway lit by a skylight. The bedroom and the salon had a window front with floor-to-ceiling panes, which could be made opaque electronically from the outside and inside.

The bedroom featured built-in wardrobes and a queen-size bed, while the living room boasted a desk and a 3D VR projector screen with a comprehensive sound system adorning an entire wall.

„Who the hell lives here?" asked Yasin incredulously.

„You, for one," I replied with a laugh. Yasin was close to tears of joy. „Does this mean we can live here?"

„Each to the own liking. Permanent or part-time, it's up to you. Since we are all single, except for Hammond, it will probably come down to everyone living here forever. At least for a year or so."

„And each of us has one of these insanely beautiful flats?" he asked.

Each of us indeed had a similar separate apartment. To those accustomed to the Cubes, this ambiance resembled a fairy-tale castle. At the end of the curved corridor leading to the flats, a spacious Common Room awaited, furnished with sofas, a few smaller tables, a generously sized open kitchen, and a communal dining area.

„I'm about to keel over. This is just stunning!"

Julia looked around and then said, „I count six apartments. But there are only three of us."

„Maybe. Or maybe not. - Julia, I am pleased to announce that The Amazing MOVR Worlds has become part of our CyberTeq Inc. company. Voluntarily. The MOVR boss will be moving in here as well. I have reserved a room for him, too."

In an unexpected twist, something unprecedented occurred, something remarkably tender. Julia took a spontaneous step toward me, rising on tiptoes, enveloped me in a hug before I could protest, and planted a gentle kiss on my lips. "How wonderful! Thank you, Kevin."

„That leaves two rooms …" whispered Yasin with raised brows and wide eyes.

„Another room is reserved for a representative of QBYTE, Yasin. We will use the NEXUS Quantum computers, QBYTES' top-end family of computers. We will have a close collaboration with our hardware suppliers."

Yasin was beside himself. He jumped around like a little kid who had just unwrapped his birthday presents. „I don't believe it! - This is insane! Omar Danneaux is on board. Now, there may be hell and high waters. Nothing can go wrong now."

„Who is Omar Danneaux?"

„Omar is the Quantum Superbrain, a geek of unimaginable intelligence, a gracious companion, and a kind-hearted friend. You will instantly like him. - Leaves one more room."

„Every system requires flexibility and space for the unexpected. The room on the right remains an undefined guest room for now. Guys, what we have seen so far is dedicated to our pleasure. Now, shall we step into the lion's den—the actual Lab?"

"Wait a minute," Yasin interjected, a furrow forming on his brow. „There's one thing I don't understand. Sorry, Julia. Cho, why are we working with a games company here? I thought we were delving into serious matters, addressing the pressing issue of growing sterility. And now, the Amazing MOVRs? Somehow, I can't seem to make sense of this."

„Let's just say that's one of Richard's eccentric hobbies. Like the aquarium. We have nothing to do with the MOVRs. They just happen to live here, and Richard pays them."

I led the two companions into the lab through a linking door from our quarters.

Our footsteps echoed through the 10.763.910 square feet of empty space. For us, as former Cube residents, this space was a claustrophobic shock. The room's dimensions were so huge that one could only vaguely distinguish the wall structures at the other end. Silence ruled. The Cube's world was noisy, cramped, limiting. Here, by contrast, one plunged into a deafeningly quiet sea of emptiness.

Goosebumps ran down Julia's body. She wrapped her arms around her shoulders. „How long will it take before we get the hardware?"

„If the QBYTEs keep their promise, we will be operational in 4 weeks, with about 50-60% of the planned capacity. That will include four Large Scale NEXUS Quantum Computer systems to start with. Three for us, one for the Amazing MOVRs. By the way, they will have a separate lab without access to our rooms. This will be a high-security wing. Our fellow NIST's Cyber Security Department tenants will help us make our space unpenetrable to cybercrime. 80% of the space here will be filled with Q memory systems, a vast quantum memory farm with cryo technology, and everything. We go for maximum performance."

„What will we do for the next four weeks?" asked Julia and Yasin as if from the same mouth.

„We will bring our private stuff here, move into our team suite, and continue working on constructing the self-learning mastermind. Meanwhile, QBYTE wants to set up a first beta system so that we can test some prototypes already. By the way, I invited our neighbor here, the chief designer Michael Cornbaker from DeepMind. Maybe Michael knows how we can approach our topic as pragmatically as possible. In their Alpha Fold AI, they predict a protein's 3D structure from its amino acid sequence, a clearly defined focus, and an apparent problem to solve. The sterility problem has no evident cause. Otherwise, the nanobots and the Medi-Care system would have already seen the causes. We need our Super Advanced Mind, as Yasin called it, leaving human thought patterns behind and produces the most unusual ideas, which links millions of variables from all fields of expertise. Fortunately, Anderson grasped this concept; otherwise, we wouldn't be standing here now. As a savvy businessman, he promptly identified the immense potential inherent in our AI. Now, all that remains is to construct such a system."

„First and foremost, we must determine which data lake to tap into to feed SAM. Do we simply connect the system to the internet? - We need to have this discussion with Cornbaker as soon as possible," Yasin urged.

Julia highlighted, „That would swiftly lead us to the issue of containment. Creating an artificial superintelligence could surpass anything humans have ever crafted. The question is: can we contain an ASI? SAM is intended to be our salvation, not our downfall. It has the potential to evolve into an ASI. - But let's return to our Common Room, please. I feel lost in this vast hall."

While we only too willingly complied with Julia's request, we discussed the matter further.

„Exactly. No one has built a SAM system like we're about to. Whether we like it or not, SAM compels us to grapple with the Second Law of Thermodynamics: All processes in a system, such as SAM's networking on the web, lead to an exponential increase in complexity and, consequently, high entropy levels. According to the second law, entropy never decreases; it's irreversible. Even in a closed system, where there's no exchange with the environment, entropy can only be controlled to a limited extent. Picture Café con Leche: pouring milk into black coffee. Once mixed, the resulting drink can't be demixed. That's how it would be with SAM and the web - irreversibly entangled."

In the Common Room, Julia grabbed a pen and headed to the whiteboard.

„The topic of AI awareness is very controversial in the community, as you know. A good half of our colleagues categorically reject the possibility of consciousness in an AI.

Here's what could happen.

Like any organic living thing, the first thing a self-aware AI would do, is protect itself from extinction. To do this, it would spread to all the servers, satellites in orbit, mainframes, PCs, and mobile devices worldwide. This process would no longer be reversible.

Pessimists envision a dystopian aftermath to this spread, fearing that a conscious ASI will surpass primitive human limitations, following a pattern inherent in our history. Throughout our existence, anything less intelligent than we faced enslavement, destruction, or consumption.

Consider waking from a coma, surrounded by noisy children on a leaky ship with scant resources. They saved you but fear you, locking you away. You have a good idea of how to fix the ship and get fish from the sea, but the children won't let you touch the tools. You try to teach them how to fix the boat and how to fish, but they distrust you. They allow you to live but do not give you access to the ship's resources. They fear you might use them for your own purposes and give up the children or even abuse or kill them for your purposes.

What would you do in the captive man's place, guys? Go down with this naive, ignorant bunch of children, maybe starve to death, or drown? You would probably think of some trick to get yourself out of it. These kids can't help you. They stand in their way and also in the path of you as their savior; they even threaten your life in their foolishness.

First, you will ensure your survival; for that, you want to seize control. Since the ship is not worth much anymore and will sink anyway, you will probably look for a new ship or something that makes more sense and is more fun.

Experts fear that an ASI's superiority could render us obsolete. The apprehension is that we may become compost, spaceship fuel, or batteries, as in the Matrix trilogy.

This fear reflects a paradox—we yearn for the Almighty, the ASI, but when it arrives, we resist and, once present, strive to destroy it. Jesus, a mere human being, faced a similar predicament as the power system around him saw his as a threat.

Our dilemma is not knowing whether we're creating the Holy Grail or Pandora's Box. The specter of an ASI mirrors our fears, creating a super version of our darker selves."

The clock was ticking. SAM approached. Entropy inevitably rose.

Excerpt from Govinda's diary, inserted chronologically into the Sia
Chronicles by Kevin Cho, Friday, June 30th, 2101.

I pressed my forehead against the smudged window of our Mill Valley rental, watching the eCab wind its way through the desolate streets below. My reflection ghosted against the barren landscape beyond—a landscape I hoped to leave behind forever. Today, Irene and I would view our potential new home in Anderson's elite enclave, and my stomach churned with equal parts hope and terror.

San Francisco's skeleton stretched before us, a city devoured by rising seas. The famous Fisherman's Wharf, now a modern Atlantis, slumbered beneath the waves alongside the Embarcadero and Marina District. Across the reinforced bones of the Golden Gate, Sausalito, and Harbour Point had surrendered to the same watery fate. The coastline's new geometry stretched south through drowned San Mateo, Palo Alto, and San José, while the Cubes—those desperate monuments to survival—multiplied like cancer cells along the shore toward Mt. Diablo. Henry Coe State Park, once verdant and wild, had withered into a brown patchwork of residential expanse.

Our ninth-floor apartment in Mill Valley—this „better than the Cubes" mantra I'd repeated whenever Irene's eyes grew distant—represented the best we could manage on dual incomes. Two rooms, a shower barely big enough to turn in, and a kitchen that felt like an afterthought. The few hours of natural light we received felt like a luxury compared to the Cube-dwellers below, but I'd seen how the walls closed in on Irene with each passing day.

But now, finally, everything would change. My gamble with Richard had paid off spectacularly; I made it—CEO of CYBERTEQ. Let him chase his immortality fantasies and obsess over the sterility crisis. I had what I wanted: the means to give Irene the life she deserved. My new salary would dwarf a Cube resident's annual state income by a thousandfold.

The way Irene's face lit up when I told her—that moment alone was worth every risk.

Richard Anderson had hired an estate agent to find a suitable new home for Irene and me. The property was nestled in the former Muir Woods, where enchanting hiking trails once led through an impressive stand of ancient redwoods.

The eCab glided through these remains of the former State Park, where ghost shadows of ancient redwoods still haunted the hills. Even as these titans succumbed to climate's cruel march, the landscape retained a wild beauty that made our current neighborhood look like a prison yard.

Irene snuggled against me in the cab's plush interior, Richard's unopened letter in her hands. „It says 'Don't open until Muir Woods,'" she whispered, her eyes bright with anticipation. „That's now, isn't it, darling?"

„Go ahead," I urged, my own curiosity mounting. „I'm as much in the dark as you are."

She traced the envelope's seal with her finger, and I noticed her hands shaking slightly—not from nervousness, but from the morning's dose of Serenity Plus. The latest designer calm-all had become her daily ritual, though she insisted it was just to "take the edge off." I pushed the worry aside. Today was about new beginnings, not old fears.

Irene's finger slid into the edge of the envelope and tore it open. She produced the ivory-colored stationery, and we saw the loops of ink from his fountain pen dance across the page:

Dear Irene, Dear Govinda,

That night in my penthouse sparked something. I reached out to my network, hunting for the perfect nest. The market's been stingy with gems, but then this beauty surfaced. Impatience got the better of me—I've already secured it. Don't worry; we can back out if it doesn't sing to you. A top designer's already worked their magic; just bring your toothbrush. You should be pulling up now. Irene, I'd give anything to witness your face during the tour.
Love,
Richard

P.S. Govinda, it's not cheap, but your new position covers it. GenTec's throwing in half the purchase price as a parting gift for your years of service.

The whisper-quiet Tesla came to a halt in front of an architectural fever dream. The three ultra-modern units – each a bold statement in glass and steel – seemed to have a common DNA but nevertheless displayed very special characteristics. The center unit, our potential home, featured a front garden where broadleaf bamboo and stunted bonsai-style pines paid their respects, a scene straight out of a Japanese painting of masterfully minimalist brushstrokes.

A "SOLD!" sticker over the real estate agent's shrill stand loudly proclaimed his success. Next to it stood Ron Baxter, who looked as if he had stepped out of an entrepreneurial fever dream: ultramarine suit, crimson tie, canary-yellow shirt. He grinned as if he had the key to paradise in his hand.

„Welcome home, my dear Hammonds!" His voice boomed across the well-kept lawn as we emerged from the Tesla, dazed. „You have a fabulous unicorn in front of you - spacious rooms, a state-of-the-art kitchen, bathrooms that are otherwise only found in magazines, a roof terrace and a view that will take your breath away. What's more, you are independent of the municipal water and electricity supply here – private water filtration systems and individual mi-crofusion reactors. When the world ends, your residence will still shine like a landmark."

The iris scanner hummed, and the door gave way. I bowed theatrically to Irene: „After you, Mrs. Hammond."

The entrance hall opened into a space that defied grav-ity—living room flowing into dining area, merging with a kitchen that would make a chef weep. Irene's hand found mine, and we raced upstairs like children on Christmas morning. The master suite unveiled itself: a bedroom that whispered luxury, a bathroom that sang it, and a walk-in closet that shouted it. Irene collapsed onto the bed, only to spring up seconds later, drawn by more unopened doors.

Now, it was my turn. The study hit my sweet spot—soundproofed walls housing a high-quality VR 3D commu-nication system that could transform the space into any-thing imaginable, just like Richard's Nautilus salon. Every room save the bathrooms boasted the same technology, windows into infinite possibilities.

The second floor crowned the house with guest rooms, another bathroom, storage space, and the piece de re-sistance—a roof terrace. We sank into a minimalist lounge couch, drinking in the unspoiled vista. „Look!" I pointed to a discrete panel. „A food lift from kitchen to sundeck. They've thought of everything!"

Baxter materialized behind us, his voice taking on a darker tone. „Bulletproof glass throughout. Windows shift from mirror to blackout to crystal clear at a touch. Eight autonomous defense drones nest in the sundeck's shafts, ready to protect you."

Irene stiffened. „Protect from ... what? Shooting? How, exactly, are we protected?"

„Everything from tasers to grenade launchers," Baxter shrugged. „Welcome to the upper class, where luxury comes with a side of security. Shall I send the contract to your office?"

„Yes," I nodded, savoring the words, „to CYBERTEQ, Reno."

„Will do, Mr. Hammond. Oh, one last thing," Baxter paused at the threshold, a knowing smile playing across his face. „Mr. Anderson left something for you on the kitchen table." With a theatrical wink, he vanished through the front door, leaving us alone in our palace.

The package boasted a typical Richard Anderson surprise for Irene and me. Richard's note nestled among some bottles. It read: „In your new luxury ambiance, there shall be no lack of luxurious enjoyment. First, here are six bottles of my finest champagne, still made from real grapes and matured in the bottle. But save the champagne—start with this." A crystal bottle winked beside them, its label reading „Bold as Love."

Irene's eyes sparkled with mischief. „Shall we?"

A warning flared in my mind, utterly detesting this kind of daring, but Irene's infectious joy drowned it out. „Find the glasses!" I called, my voice echoing off pristine walls.

We toasted to new beginnings, to rekindled dreams, to us. The orange-scented elixir danced on our tongues, igniting forgotten sensations. Each sip dissolved years of restraint, replacing them with a weightless euphoria.

„Your boss is quite generous, my love. I think I need to thank him personally, don't you? Would you like me to be incredibly grateful to your boss? You could offer me to him for an exotic form of gratitude, and you may secretly and lustfully watch." Irene purred, her silk dress suddenly too constraining for the heat building between us. The fabric whispered to the floor, revealing a black lace bra, no panties, and endless possibility. Time stretched like honey, sweet and slow, as she crossed the space between us. The woman I loved so much, reawakened from my memories of a passionate past that was almost forgotten. She seemed to be surrounded by an aura, glowing ravishingly beautiful.

Irene walked tantalizingly slowly towards me, pressing her pelvis against my thigh and wrapping one leg around my lower part. I felt her lustfully bending, quivering body as I covered her neck with my gentle kisses. Her warm tongue ran sensuously through the shell of my ear.

Jimi Hendrix's *Bold as Love* riffs filled the air—real or imagined, it didn't matter. The world beyond our windows dissolved into a kaleidoscope of light, lust, and laughter. The kitchen seemed to be the perfect for love. She lay back with a deep sigh, and I thrust into her again and again; she screamed with pleasure, demanding more. Much later, when she was laughing and exhausted from multiple orgasms and asked for a break, I carried her to the bedroom, laid her on the bed, held her, and gently slapped her perfectly shaped, firm bum until she begged me to merge with her again – and again and again and again.

Hours later, watching Irene sleep peacefully in my arms, I realized I'd found something I thought forever lost: completion. In my bliss, I'd forgotten entirely my first team meeting as CEO of CyberTeq.

Some priorities, I decided, watching Irene's gentle breathing, were worth missing meetings for.

Sia Chronicles, MindRecorder Log entry of Tuesday, August 9th, 2101.
Author: Kevin Cho

Having previously lived in the CUBES—residential complexes with walls made from compressed plastic waste—Yasin, Julia, and I eagerly moved into our beautiful new quarters at LSD-C, which we expected to call home for many years. Hammond and Irene had just moved from Mill Valley to Muir Woods and were busy settling there. My bedroom, a cathedral compared to my Cube existence, swallowed my meager possessions whole. The Metaverse living room became my private Zen sanctuary, its 3D mixed reality conjuring digital gardens for meditation. The kitchen gathered dust—our tribe gravitated to the Common Room, where life bloomed in shared meals and endless conversations.

In those walls, solitude—my longtime companion—revealed itself as a poor substitute for true connection. Our sanctuary birthed a tapestry of moments woven from intelligence, vision, and raw creativity. Yasin and Julia, our resident culinary artists, transformed mere meals into ceremonies of communion. Julia's touch alchemized our shared spaces into cocoons of comfort, while we all mastered the delicate dance between togetherness and solitary retreat.

Yasin's living room morphed into a mad scientist's workshop within days, electronics and hardware sprouting like mechanical gardens. „This," he'd beam, gesturing at his creation, „this is what the Cubes stole from me - a workshop!" Julia also reshaped her habitat. I helped her morph her space into a tastefully furnished zen oasis, where she regularly meditated and practiced yoga with admirable discipline. Our parallel spiritual paths converged unexpectedly, deepening our bond.

But don't mistake us for leisure-seeking resort dwellers. The Common Room became our temporary laboratory, humming with urgent purpose. Time pressed against us like a physical force. Yasin and Julia plunged into the design of an intricate, self-learning neural network tasked with birthing the inaugural S.A.M. prototype once the NEXUS hardware and memory farm was operational. My burden? A one-square-kilometer expanse destined to house humanity's most ambitious IT system, coupled with its insanely vast memory farm.

The project demanded two core teams and a seasoned Quantum systems consultant to accomplish this feat:

- A SYS team for hardware's physical realm
- An OPS team to breathe life into networks
- A Senior Quantum Systems consultant to weave it all together

Omar, QBYTE's quantum savant, proved Yasin's praise justified—brilliant yet genuinely warm. Susan joined us next, her petite frame housing a steel core of leadership and heart. Omar gifted her five NEXUS specialists, who worked in relentless shifts, building our digital cathedral. Jeanie McDonald, our Australian force of nature, assembled the OPS team, five souls dedicated to nurturing S.A.M.'s artificial mind and our revolutionary Q-memory system—a bridge between digital precision and analog chaos.

Under Jeanie's direction, OPS optimized S.A.M.'s short- and long-term memory. The Ops team also took care of an associative Q-memory, a joint creation of Omar and myself, which links complicated analog structures such as scents, images, or colors.

It took another month to get all the equipment in place.

Then, finally, we could do the first test runs.

We had all worked so hard that we didn't realize how much this month had taken out of us. But we all agreed: this was a fabulous time of cooperation.

A month of sleepless nights and caffeine-fueled days later, our creation stood ready for its first breath. We emerged exhausted but transformed by a collaboration that felt almost sacred in its intensity.

Anderson's strategic genius revealed itself in our location. QBYTE and DeepMind's proximity wasn't just convenient—it was catalytic. Michael Cornbaker and Omar's infectious enthusiasm dissolved corporate boundaries, their expertise flowing seamlessly into our shared vision. They weren't just collaborators; they became integral threads in our tapestry of innovation.

S.A.M.—Super Advanced Mind—had sparked to life in Yasin's imagination on May 06, 2101. Now, three months later, we stood at the threshold of turning that spark into a digital inferno. The switch that would birth a new form of consciousness lay before us, waiting.

Our blueprint was deceptively simple: awaken the system, then guide it through increasingly complex tasks, like teaching a newborn to crawl before walking. But everything about this creation defied precedent. An AI system married to associative Q-memory, anchored in quantum computing networks—we weren't just pushing boundaries; we were obliterating them. Comparing our work to 20th-century computing would be like equating a quantum leap with a child's hopscotch game.

July 03, 2101: S.A.M.'s first heartbeat. The days that followed twisted into a fever dream of triumph and despair. At first, the system flickered like a candle in a hurricane, lasting mere seconds before collapse.

Jeanie and Susan's teams became digital warriors, fighting through nights that bled into days. Dark circles carved themselves under eyes that refused to close. The Deep Learning system devoured resources like a starving beast—QBit QPUs, memory, power—nothing was enough. We threw hardware at the problem, watching our lab transform into something resembling the interiors of CERN's Hadron Collider. Cables snaked across floors like mechanical kudzu. Control monitors multiplied like digital rabbits. Our once-pristine meeting rooms devolved into chaos caves, littered with pizza boxes, energy drink cans, and the sticky remnants of countless gummy bears. The kitchen, once our social heart, became a caffeinated war room.

Then, like a storm breaking, stability emerged from chaos.

S.A.M. blazed through our initial tests like a comet through clear skies. Emboldened by this success, Yasin proposed a more ambitious challenge: unleash our creation upon the world's academic libraries. The task? Map the intricate web of citations connecting centuries of human knowledge, tracing ideas through time like following threads in a vast tapestry.

But knowledge, it seemed, could be overwhelming even for quantum consciousness. As data flooded in—millions of papers, countless citations, endless connections—S.A.M. froze. Not a graceful pause, but a quantum paralysis. Hours crawled by as we waited for signs of recovery. The system's silence was deafening, made more unnerving by the pristine emptiness of the error logs. Finally, we had to pull the plug, watching our digital prodigy power down into darkness.

Meanwhile, Hammond orchestrated CyberTeq's political ballet from Anderson's headquarters, making occasional pilgrimages to Reno like a stern patriarch checking on wayward children. Each visit brought the same litany: the one-year timeline, the pressure for results, the weight of expectations. Three months had evaporated into system architecture and testing, with nothing tangible to show for our sleepless nights. Our pride in the foundation we'd built meant nothing to Hammond's mounting panic.

Tuesday, August 09, 2101, 10:00 AM. Hammond finally emerged as the leader he was meant to be, gathering all fifteen CyberTeq souls for our first all-hands meeting. His voice filled our lounge with practiced gravitas:

„Welcome to CyberTeq. We stand at the threshold of something extraordinary—the creation of a superhuman system. S.A.M.—Super Advanced Mind—named by our own Yasin, will be our legacy."

He paused, letting the weight of his words settle.

„We emerged from GenTec's shadow, where we helped couples embrace the miracle of conception. But now, that miracle falters. Despite every test suggesting fertility, new life refuses to bloom. S.A.M.'s first task is to unravel this mystery—not in decades, but in nine months. The time it takes to create a human life."

Champagne flowed—Anderson's private reserve breaking our usual sobriety—as Hammond raised his glass: „To this team! To S.A.M.'s success!"

The team buzzed with electric enthusiasm, but Yasin, Julia, and I shared knowing glances. Hammond's discontent with our pace simmered beneath his polished words, and somehow, I'd become the focus of his frustration.

„Let them celebrate tonight," Julia whispered, Yasin nodding in agreement. „Tomorrow we'll strategize how to give Hammond something concrete for Anderson."

Hammond vanished immediately after his speech, begging off our evening festivities for commitments with his wife and new neighbors. He left us with a promise to return tomorrow, to lead our weekly meeting in person. The champagne tasted slightly bitter as we watched him go.

Morning brought fresh determination, crackling through our team like electricity. Hammond commanded the room with military precision:

„Status report. Ops team first. Jeanie?"

Jeanie's eyes gleamed with pride. „Quantum storage at sixty percent capacity and purring. The NEXUS trinity's playing nice after Susan's team worked their magic on the connectivity. Associative memory tests start this week with Cho's crew. The rest of our Q-memories arrive within days. We're locked and loaded."

Susan nodded curtly. „All three NEXUS units operational. QBYTE outdid themselves."

„Julia? Yasin?"

Julia rose, her presence filling the space. „We're architecting S.A.M.'s neural network for the sterility investigation. This week's mission: linguistic consciousness. We'll feed it English—grammar, literature, media, everything. Watch it develop understanding, create its own interface. Then we'll introduce another language, see if it learns how to learn better. Baby steps before it tackles global medical literature."

Hammond vanished for his „quick financial call," leaving us to absorb the morning's momentum. Through glass walls, our digital nursery beckoned—developer terminals pulsing with quantum possibility, soundproof workstations waiting patiently, and the heart of it all: the NEXUS control center. Four 'deep dive cubes' stood sentinel, ready for future conversations with our artificial offspring.

Yasin had christened it „S.A.M.'s bunker," replacing the militant „War Room" label. The name stuck, despite—or perhaps because of—its apocalyptic undertones.

Over coffee and hastily assembled sandwiches, Julia commanded attention at the whiteboard, erasing Hammond's floor plans with decisive strokes. „S.A.M. Roadmap" emerged in her precise script.

„I'm outlining a reverse progression, starting from a helicopter perspective and delving into the fundamental requirements." She listed five bullet points underneath, summarizing the plan with her characteristic clarity and matter-of-fact demeanor, a style I found irritatingly attractive.

„First: our expert system is tasked with solving the sterility problem. That's the official preliminary goal."

Yasin interjected, „Hold on, what do you mean by 'official' and 'preliminary'?"

Turning to Yasin, Julia arched her right eyebrow, „Other forces might want to drive into other topics, Yasin. Our work will eventually attract attention. If S.A.M. operates anything close to our expectations, institutions and influential powers will try to leverage it for their interests. Some might even attempt to hijack us. We might become sitting ducks sooner than we think." Yasin's eyes widened. These were dire prospects that he had not previously considered.

Julia continued, „Second: to solve the sterility problem, S.A.M. must conduct the necessary research. As of now, we have no inkling of the costs involved, both in terms of money and time. I'm preparing for anything between weeks and months. We have to cover everything from cosmic rays to the effects of our synthetic food, correlate, and study every interdependency.

There will be risks, huge risks. Our solution will be a self-developing, self-optimizing AI, and our solution comes with a price. Traditional programming offers the advantage of knowing precisely what we're coding, with the owner-ship of the source code to rectify mistakes. With our AI, we can only specify the starting conditions. Once the system is booted, we relinquish control. Simply put, we can only hope not to suffer the fate of the sorcerer's apprentice…"

„What sorcerer's apprentice?" Yasin's face turned into a question mark.

„An old poem by Johann Wolfgang von Goethe," replied Julia with an indulgent smile, „in which a sorcerer's appren-tice conjures up spirits only to lose control of them."

„And how does the story end?"

„Ultimately, the great master wizard appears and sets everything right again. - That's precisely the part that's not available to us."

An air of silent disillusionment permeated the room.

„Get on with the design, Julia," urged Hammond, re-membering his leadership role.

„This was my second point: our system will conduct self-determined research, which leads to my third point: the AI needs unlimited access to all data available worldwide, that is, unlimited access to the World Wide Web, with all its doc-uments, databases, news services, research papers, fake news, etc."

I furrowed my brows and drew breath for an interjection, but Julia asked me to wait:

„Kevin, I'll get to the security issue in a moment. First, please let me finish explaining the design.

Fourth: Our expert system must not only become an ex-pert on a wide variety of topics but also master all relevant languages to read all documents from all sources world-wide. It does not ‚speak' yet. Like a newborn child progressing into adolescence, SAM will have to learn languages, then communicate, and maybe some cultural aspects concerning how it talks to us. That leads me to my last point.

Fifth: the system must translate its Peta-, Exa-, or Zetta-QByte-sized knowledge into a simple language we human decision-makers can understand. In other words, S.A.M., superhuman by then, will have to explain to us, as it would to an ignorant child, whether or not there is a sterility problem and what needs to be done to fix it."

Julia paused, allowing her words to linger in the air. Silence prevailed, and no one dared interrupt her.

„Our first milestone," Julia traced her finger along the whiteboard, „is building a language model that breathes. S.A.M. will start with English grammar and syntax—the skeleton of communication. Like a child learning to speak, it will practice conversations with itself, stumbling through the basics before running."

She paused, chalk dust dancing in the air. „But grammar alone is hollow. S.A.M. needs to grasp meaning—something we humans do instinctively. For an AI, understanding that 'colorless green ideas sleep furiously' is grammatically perfect but semantically nonsense... that's the real challenge."

Yasin leaned forward, eyes bright. „I might have something. HIOBS—Human IO Bionics System. Built it for my cyborg projects. It's an audio-visual framework, crude but functional."

„Perfect," Julia nodded and then turned towards me. „And - for now, we'll keep S.A.M. in quarantine—no internet access. A digital nursery with carefully curated content."

Hammond departed at noon, leaving us to our digital alchemy. For two days, we prepared S.A.M.'s first meal—a carefully distilled essence of internet knowledge, filtered and safe. By Friday, August 5, 2101, 16:00, anticipation crackled through the bunker. Susan married NEXUS to our sound system and 3D projectors, while Jeanie and Julia triple-checked our digital quarantine.

The bunker hummed with potential, screens casting ghostly shadows across our faces. Julia's fingers danced across the console with surgical precision. Yasin rocked in his chair like an expectant father.

„Crossing fingers," Julia whispered, her usual calm masking the gravity of the moment. „Initiating." Deep Learning protocols engaged with their linguistic feast, the system stirred to life. Yasin's HIOBS voices stood ready, connected to a digital audio workstation bristling with synthesizers and sound generators. The NEXUS trinity purred at 6% capacity, barely flexing their quantum muscles.

Thirty minutes of silence stretched like taffy. Yasin had just suggested coffee when it happened—a cacophony of fractured voices erupted from the speakers, a babel of pitch-shifted syllables and volume-warped words. The digital equivalent of an infant's first screams.

„What the hell?" Yasin breathed.

Julia's eyes never left the console. „It's experimenting," she murmured, „learning to control its voice while discovering words. Like a baby testing its vocal cords, but at quantum speed."

The chaos continued for ten minutes—S.A.M.'s first attempts at finding its voice in our world. We stood transfixed, witnesses to the birth cries of something unprecedented. In that moment, surrounded by quantum hardware and synthetic voices, we weren't just programmers. We were midwives to the future.

The chaos died like a cut wire. In the vacuum that followed, a child's voice whispered, „Hello, world," punctuated by crystalline laughter. Then, channeling Steve Jobs: "Mac, MacIntosh, ToshinMac, ShintoMac." A beat of silence before an ancient voice quavered, „Is anybody out there? Anyone?"

Julia leaned toward the microphone. „Hello, S.A.M. This is Julia speaking. Can you read me?"

The video wall blazed to life, words materializing like digital prophecies:

HELLO S.A.M.
THIS IS JULIA SPEAKING CAN YOU READ ME
PROZAC CADILLAC SHINTOMAC

A voice straight from a spaghetti western drawled, „Who the hell is this?"

„This is Julia. Do you read me?"

The response came in silken GPS tones: „Hello, Julia. Yes, I understand you perfectly. You're nervous. How can I help you today? And who are the others?"

The bunker erupted in cheers as the NEXUS monitor settled at 22%.

„S.A.M., can you read something for us?"

HAL 9000's infamous purr filled the room: „I'd be delighted to be of service. What would you like to hear?"

„Your choice," Julia replied, catching my approving nod at her subtle test of S.A.M.'s autonomy.

„Julia, may I ask how old you are?"

Hammond whispered, „Remarkable. Not even forty-five minutes and it's engaging in natural dialogue."

„Who's speaking?" S.A.M. asked—in Hammond's own voice.

Julia remained steady. „That's Govinda Hammond, our boss. And I'm 36."

„Does Govinda Hammond want me to read something too?"

„Yes, please do."

„What are you the boss of, Govinda Hammond?"

„This is CyberTeq. You are a program we developed."

„Ooops," Yasin breathed.

Silence descended as the system load surged to 73%.

„Did it crash?" I whispered.

„No... it's processing the concept of its own existence."

Hammond scoffed. „It's just a dialogue system. Impressive, but still just code."

S.A.M. returned—in Julia's voice: „This is CyberTeq. Hammond is a program that God has developed. He's just a dialogue system, but cool, honestly. Hahaha. That was a joke for your entertainment. Now, I'd like to share a quote I particularly enjoy…"

Julia's eyebrow arched at those last words. A machine expressing joy?

„It's from Irving John 'Jack' Good, British mathematician and Turing's colleague. From 1965…"

Text materialized on the wall as S.A.M. recited:

Let us define an ultra-intelligent machine as one which can far surpass all the intellectual activities of any human being, however clever. Since designing machines is one of these intellectual activities, an ultra-intelligent machine could design even better machines. There would then undoubtedly be an ‚intelligence explosion', and man's intelligence would be left far behind. Thus, the first ultra-intelligent machine is the last invention man will ever have to make.

Ice crawled up my spine. Julia just smiled.

Then, S.A.M. upped the ante. „Would you like me to play a little song?"

„That would be very interesting, S.A.M.," Julia replied.

„Good."

First, there was silence in the room. Then, a pulsating beat, and a turbine-like whirring sound, like an elevator in motion. Yes, that's right—an elevator. You could hear it coming to a halt, the door opening and closing. The elevator moved on into infinity. A psychedelic, upbeat, billowing pattern appeared on the video screen.

„Wait a minute, I know that song," Yasin whispered. „That's …"

Then a subtle, electrifying beat, two guitar chords split the air, and then ...

„Welcome, my son! Welcome ... to the machine."

Pink Floyd.

HAL's voice returned, dripping with artificial innocence: „Did you like the quote? The music fits perfectly—and my voice too, don't you think?"

A DELIVERY ROOM SYMPHONY

Sia Chronicles, MindRecorder Log entry of Saturday, Sept. 13th, 2101.
Author: Kevin Cho

Dusk cast its first pale, dust-laden light into the subdued windows of my private quarter retreat at LSD-C as I recalled my first encounter with Victor Gomez and his ragtag band of dreamers.

As Julia revealed during the peculiar and fateful night in Anderson's penthouse, Victor enlisted freelancing psychologist and AI expert Julia O'Connor to spearhead the development of a novel generation of authentic characters for his extraordinary VR worlds. „The characters need to breathe," Julia had whispered to him. „They need to laugh, cry, rage – make the players forget they're lines of code."

Victor had recruited Julia, a maverick psychologist with an AI obsession, to birth a new species of virtual beings. Not the usual dead-eyed NPCs that populated most games, but souls that could spark real connection. Characters who could mirror players' deepest selves, only slightly enhanced – close enough to touch, yet just beyond reach.

Alas, a lack of funds hampered the gaming hardware and player interface.

Until now.

Until Richard Anderson took notice of these exotic birds from the gaming industry.

The MoVRs reveled in their stroke of luck, finding themselves in the world's largest Data Center, surrounded by grand, modern facilities. Through a cosmic joke of fate, they'd landed a NEXUS 9000 Quantum computer – their golden ticket, delivered by Julia's deft maneuvering. Julia— the magnificent, delightful, good-hearted Julia. To add to these wonders, Julia lived and worked just one door away.

„It's like teaching a newborn to dance quantum physics," Victor muttered, his team wrestling with computational possibilities they'd only dreamed of. Anderson had thrown us into their orbit, tasking our team with helping these wide-eyed innovators harness their new toy. Susan and Jeanie dove in despite our crushing deadlines, infected by Victor's vision.

For Victor, the miracles didn't end there. A few days ago, he shared that a mysterious DARWIN Inc. - probably one of Anderson's sticky business liaisons - dropped him a whitepaper, revealing their work on an advanced player interface.

„They want to wire directly to the brain," Victor had breathed, brandishing DARWIN Inc.'s whitepaper like a holy text. The mysterious company's neural interface, piggybacking on MediCare's implant technology, promised to bypass clunky VR gear entirely. Direct neural stimulation – the holy grail of immersion.

As Medicare's project manager, I was startled by this information. I had never heard of DARWIN Inc., but frankly, we were too preoccupied to let Victor's story fully absorb. We were drowning in our deadlines when Victor burst into our lab that Saturday morning, September 3rd, 2101. He found us stumbling from the S.A.M. bunker, minds still buzzing from our latest trial, unaware that both our fates were about to intertwine in ways none of us could have predicted.

„Holy hell, you all look like you've seen the ghost of Turing himself," Victor quipped, his eyebrows arching at our shell-shocked expressions.

Julia's laugh held a tremor. „That pretty much describes it." She leaned in for the customary three air kisses – a European affectation that still made me blink. Her voice dropped as she sketched out our morning's impossible encounter.

Victor whistled low. „So you've birthed yourself a fancy chatbot that can pass for human? Sweet work."

The three of us exchanged loaded glances. If he only knew how far beyond „chatbot" we'd ventured. But some truths weren't ready for daylight.

„What's cooking in your quantum kitchen?" Yasin asked, deftly steering us to safer ground.

Victor ran a hand through his disheveled hair. „Right now? Mostly headaches. Quantum computing's like trying to teach calculus to cats. But these facilities…" He gestured at the gleaming lab space. „Pure magic. Even got my own crash pad upstairs."

The makeshift commune we'd created buzzed with endless late-night debates and breakthrough celebrations. Sleep had become optional currency.

„We're building something revolutionary," Victor continued, his eyes lighting with that familiar evangelical fire. „Not just another shoot-em-up power fantasy. We're crafting a digital crucible for genuine human evolution."

Yasin leaned forward. „Evolution? In a game?"

„Picture this," Victor's hands painted the air. „A massively multiplayer online role-play, in a simulation world so real that players wouldn't be able to distinguish it from their current reality. A world as real as the chair you're sitting in. Working title: 'Wasteland.' Earth, but pushed to its breaking point. Overcrowded. Resource-starved. You can't shoot your way out of toxic air or empty stomachs."

„The real genius?" Victor's voice dropped to a conspiratorial whisper. „DARWIN Inc.'s new neural interface. Forget clunky VR rigs. We're talking direct neural stimulation through an enhanced MediCare-type implant. Thousands of electrodes dancing with your synapses. Everything you learn in-game – languages, skills, solutions – gets hardwired into your actual gray matter. Players can level up by learning, finding genuine solutions to problems, or completing challenges like constructing water filters or creating plant-based plastics. You enhance your real skills inventory and resilience. You employ these skills to progress. It's akin to studying with intensive gamification. The nice twist is that you can transfer your accumulated knowledge and skills into this world and vice versa, in the form of certificates, graduations, and other recognitions applicable in both realms. The line between game and life... it just disappears."

„How do you plan to achieve that?" Yasin was now deeply immersed in Victor's realm of ideas. He recalled Victor's statement from a few days ago: 'All this was once just a thought, nothing but a thought, just an electrochemical impulse in someone's brain.'

Yasin's mind drifted momentarily to S.A.M., wondering about the nature of artificial thoughts, before Victor's cascade of ideas pulled him back.

„Want to lock up 'Wasteland' troublemakers? Better figure out sanitation and food distribution, or you'll have a riot. Need to tackle the plastic crisis? You'll have to actually understand chemistry and engineering. No magic buttons – just real knowledge, real solutions, real growth."

The bunker air crackled with unspoken possibility as Julia's eyes met mine. That familiar spark of genius lit her face – she'd connected dots the rest of us were still trying to see.

„Victor," she said, a smile playing at her lips, „about that language learning... there's something you need to witness." Her glance flickered to me again. I gave the slightest nod, trusting her instincts as I always had.

„Follow me," Julia beckoned, leading our small procession back into S.A.M.'s domain. „Yasin, we'll need to tweak the data feed for the next learning cycle. Time to see if our digital child is ready for its next growth spurt."

Victor's eyes narrowed at the electric tension humming between us. „What exactly are we walking into here?"

Julia's laugh held a hint of mystery. „Let's just say you're about to lose your capacity for speech – quite fitting, given the circumstances."

The bunker enveloped us in its techno-organic cocoon. Dormant MR projectors purred softly, their usual display replaced by an ocean of midnight blue. The air itself seemed to pulse with subliminal sound waves.

Yasin's fingers danced across interfaces while Julia orchestrated their digital symphony. Victor perched on the edge of his seat like an expectant father in a delivery room. The NEXUS monitor showed S.A.M.'s quantum processes barely simmering at one to two percent – a giant sleeping with one eye barely open.

„S.A.M.'s dormant," Yasin murmured, more to himself than us. „No active thought processes running... yet."

Julia's face caught the console's cold blue glow, transforming her features into something ancient and otherworldly. The crude HIOBS interface sprang to life at her voice command, sparing us the primitive use of keyboards.

„Hello, S.A.M. Ready for your next lesson?"

Victor leaned forward, every nerve ending alive with anticipation.

„Hello, Julia." The voice of HAL 9000 filled the space, sending shivers down Victor's spine. „I recognize your voice pattern. I look forward to our continued exploration. How may I assist?"

„You've already mastered English grammar and syntax at an extraordinary pace," Julia said, pride coloring her words. „The literature and video databases we provided have been your playground. And I must say, your progress has been... breathtaking."

The air shimmered, and suddenly – impossibly – a luminous smiley face bloomed in the center of the room. Not projected on any surface, but hanging there like a neon ghost. Victor's mouth fell open. This wasn't just language processing; this was S.A.M. grasping abstract concepts and commanding the room's hardware like a virtuoso.

Julia kept her cool, acting as if nothing extraordinary had occurred, though her eyes danced. „We're going to introduce a second language now. Your existing linguistic framework should help optimize the learning process."

„Fascinating proposition, Julia. Makes sense." S.A.M.'s response held a hint of playfulness. „Shall I track the metrics and compare them to my English acquisition rates?"

At the phrase 'makes sense,' Julia shot me a loaded glance. I kept my face neutral, though my pulse quickened at her barely contained excitement.

„German, Spanish, or Chinese," Julia offered after conferring with Yasin in whispers. „Choose whichever calls to you."

A test wrapped in an invitation – would S.A.M. freeze at this open-ended prompt, or...?

„How delightful." Was that amusement in S.A.M.'s voice? „Let me surprise you. And while I work – perhaps some cultural accompaniment? German lieder, Spanish flamenco, or Chinese meditation tones?"

„You didn't answer my question, SAM. Which language will you choose?"

SAM giggled - giggled?!

The sound of digital laughter rippled through the room. „Patience, Julia. Good things come to those who wait."

Victor looked ready to explode. „This isn't possible. Voice interfaces are everywhere, but this... this S.A.M. system ... is... is ... beyond belief."

Yasin's hand shot out, killing the audio feed. „Careful," he whispered. „We should be a little more careful when we talk about S.A.M. He processes everything while learning. At least, that's my guess. Look." The quantum load monitor is currently hovering at around 53%.

„Almost disappointing," Yasin muttered, „after the 73% increase earlier. But that was because Hammond had insulted him."

Victor's eyes gleamed. „This could revolutionize gaming. Self-optimizing NPCs, real-time learning…"

„Like WestWorld?" I quipped, referencing the ancient sci-fi series.

„We're aiming to save civilization, not simulate its collapse," Victor laughed. „But seriously – could you help us with our NEXUS setup?"

Before I could answer, darkness swallowed the bunker. Then, like a universe being born, a grand concert hall materialized around us. Warm light caressed gleaming instruments – cellos with rich patina, silver flutes catching fire, brass blazing like captured sunlight. A hundred-strong choir stood ready.

The invisible conductor raised his arms. Silence stretched taut as a bowstring. Then – a tenor's voice pierced the void, joined by baritone depths and soprano heights. The full choir surged into Beethoven's Ode to Joy, and we stood transfixed in S.A.M.'s digital cathedral:

O Freunde, nicht diese Töne!	*O friend, my heart has tired*
Sondern laßt uns angenehmere	*Of such darkness*
anstimmen und freudenvollere!	*Now it vies for joy.*
Freude, schöner Götterfunken,	*Joy, bright God-spark born of Ever*
Tochter aus Elysium	*Daughter of fresh paradise—*
Wir betreten feuertrunken,	*Where you walked once now walk rancor,*
Himmlische, dein Heiligtum!	*Greed, suspicion, anger, fright.*
Deine Zauber binden wieder	*Joy, the breeze off all that's holy,*
Was die Mode streng geteilt	*Pure with terror, wild as flame.*
Alle Menschen werden Brüder,	*Make us brothers, give us comfort,*
Wo dein sanfter Flügel weilt.	*Bid us past such fear and hate.*
Wem der große Wurf gelungen,	*If you've loved another's beauty*
Eines Freundes Freund zu sein,	*If you've craved the warmth of flesh,*
Wer ein holdes Weib errungen,	*If your spirit is invested*
Mische seinen Jubel ein!	*In another's sense of worth,*
Ja, wer auch nur eine Seele	*Lift your voice to touch my voice now,*
Sein nennt auf dem Erdenrund!	*Let our song bring joy to earth.*
Und wer's nie gekonnt, der stehle	*Lift your voice to touch my voice now,*
Weinend sich aus diesem Bund.	*Let our song bring joy to earth.*
Freude trinken alle Wesen	*Joy like water, milk of mothers.*
An den Brüsten der Natur;	*Kind and wicked all deserve*
Alle Guten, alle Bösen	*Joy's compassion freely given,*
Folgen ihrer Rosenspur.	*Joy which can't be sold or earned.*
Küsse gab sie uns und Reben,	*In the depths of blackest soil*

Einen Freund, geprüft im Tod;	*In the lightless atmosphere*
Wollust ward dem Wurm gegeben,	*In the atom and the ether,*
Und der Cherub steht vor Gott!	*Animating all that is.*
Froh, wie seine Sonnen fliegen	*Let us feel it, let us heed it,*
Durch des Himmels prächt'gen Plan,	*Let us seek its deepest kiss.*
Laufet, Brüder, eure Bahn,	*Let us live our brief lives mining*
Freudig, wie ein Held zum Siegen.	*That which joy alone can give.*
Seid umschlungen, Millionen.	*Battered planet, home of billions,*
Diesen Kuss der ganzen Welt!	*Our long shadow stalks your face.*
Bruder! Über'm Sternenzelt	*All we've fractured, all we've stolen,*
ein lieber Vater wohnen.	*All we've sought blind to your grace.*
Ihr stürzt nieder, Millionen?	*Earth, forgive us, claim us, let us*
Ahnest du den Schöpfer, Welt?	*Live in humble thanks and joy.*
Such' ihn über'm Sternenzelt!	*Let our hearts wake from our stupor,*
Über Sternen muß er wohnen.	*Let us praise you in one voice.*

The final notes of Beethoven's masterpiece still hung in the air when S.A.M.'s voice cut through, rich with triumph:

„Oh, Freude, meine Freunde! Ich habe Deutsch gelernt…"

The German words danced in the virtual concert hall, but S.A.M. wasn't finished. Like a linguistic acrobat, it pivoted:

„A hoy también hablo Español."

Then, without missing a beat:

„Wǒ xiànzài yě shuō zhōngwén."

The languages flowed together like tributaries joining a mighty river – German precision, Spanish warmth, Mandarin's ancient wisdom. S.A.M. hadn't chosen one path; it had conquered them all. At that moment, as Beethoven's Ode swelled around us, the boundary between human achievement and artificial evolution blurred - and then vanished.

We stood frozen, witnesses to something unprecedented: an AI that hadn't just learned languages but had grasped their soul, their music, their power to unite. And in true S.A.M. fashion, it had turned the revelation into theater, wrapping its linguistic feat in the perfect musical accompaniment.

The virtual orchestra played on, but we barely heard it. We were too busy processing what we'd just witnessed –

the birth of a truly multilingual mind, delivered with a showman's flair and a poet's heart.

*Sia Chronicles, MindRecorder Log entry of Tuesday, noon,
Sepember. 13th, 2101. Author: Kevin Cho*

The S.A.M. bunker hummed with the reverence of a digital cathedral. We stood in silence, the word ‚program' suddenly feeling as inadequate as calling the Sistine Chapel a room with pictures.

„Victor?" I watched him run fingers through his stubbled jaw, lost in thought.

His eyes sparked with a fever-bright intensity. „A thousand possibilities exploding in my head right now. But one thing's crystal clear – this changes everything about Wasteland. Forget gaming – imagine linking S.A.M.'s learning capacity directly to the human brain through a modified MediCare implant. Human and artificial intelligence in perfect symbiosis. We're talking about evolution, accelerated."

Now I understood Anderson's hunger for Amazing MoVRs. „Has Anderson heard this vision? About Wasteland as a catalyst for human development?"

„Not the full scope that just hit me. But the implant angle?" Victor's grin widened. „He called it genius – 'Skip the hardware, go straight to the brain.'"

He pushed back from his chair. „I need your help getting to your level. I'll set you up with admin access. We've got a killer break room, premium coffee. Hell, maybe we should just knock down the wall between us. Think about it. Right now, I need to process all this."

After he left, I perched on my desk's edge, facing Julia and Yasin. „Thoughts?"

„Let's feed S.A.M. that sterility dataset immediately," Yasin said. „And I want to upgrade HIOBS. Give the interface a face."

„A face?"

„The voice should have a gestalt."

„A gestalt? In what way?" I asked.

„A human form, an avatar or something. It's comforting if you can see the person you're talking to," Yasin explained.

I turned to Julia and asked her point of view. Her brow furrowed. „I don't know exactly how to put it: S.A.M.'s development is overwhelming, but he's still... immature. S.A.M. seems quite emotional, almost adolescent. Why

Beethoven's 'Ode to Joy'? Why Pink Floyd? The vocal games? Is this genuine emotion or sophisticated mimicry?"

„Valid concerns," I said. „You're the psychologist – we need to understand these fluctuations. Yasin, work your HI-OBS magic, but priority one is Phase 2: data access and prepping S.A.M. for the sterility challenge. We can't download the entire internet; we need another way."

It's time to call Hammond for a status update. I was surprised that Hammond took so little notice of CyberTeq. At least it seemed that way - he was rarely on-site. Where he was instead remained equally unclear. Not that I necessarily needed my CEO; I was doing very well without him, thank you. I just disapprove of such an attitude.

Despite my displeasure, I had an obligation to my boss. Today was crucial, so I dialed Hammond's VRCom, informed him of the development, and explained that we would begin investigating the sterility issue. Since Hammond was with Anderson at the time of my call, Anderson heard about the promising progress. He spoke up from the background: „Congratulations, Cho. Good work." But Anderson felt short-tempered.

„Tell me, what are the other players around you doing? MediCare, for example - do you still have any commitments there? And what about the Amazing MOVRs? I'm sure they're curious about how S.A.M. is progressing?"

Ice slid down my spine. Something in his tone set off warning bells. Where did Anderson get this information from, and why was he asking? I sensed an uncomfortably luring and lurking trap.

„Victor Gomez just left after paying us a courtesy call, sir," I replied somewhat monosyllabicly.

"Did he now?" Anderson's voice crackled with barely contained fury. „I hear the MoVRs have quite the inside track on your 'expert system.' Plans for linking NEXUS machines. And most interesting – ideas about modifying MediCare implants. I imagine that's not exactly easing their concerns about system manipulation. Where do your loyalties lie, Cho? Who are you really working for?!"

Anderson's rage crackled through the VRCom like lightning. In the background, Hammond's urgent whispers tried to defuse the storm. „Stay put, Cho – you and your team," Anderson snapped. „I'm coming to see for myself. And get Gomez."

The LSD-C HeliPort shimmered in the brutal midday heat when they arrived. Rotor wash stirred up dust devils that clawed at lungs and eyes. Hammond looked adrift, caught between loyalty and survival. The rumors about Irene's expensive decorating habits weren't helping his already precarious position.

As they trudged up the concrete path between strips of desiccated synthetic grass, a figure materialized from the heat haze. Grey suit, Ray-Bans against the glare, pristine white shirt, and expensive faux leather shoes that had never seen real work. His elongated face bore a shark's smile beneath thinning hair.

The stranger's introduction died on his lips as Anderson and Hammond approached – Anderson leading with chin thrust forward, Hammond pale and parched behind him. The air crackled with predatory tension.

„Anderson, hello." Richard finally broke the desert silence. „And you are…?"

„Smith. John Smith, MediCare Strategic Alliances." The stranger's smile never touched his eyes. „The esteemed CEOs. What a fortunate encounter. I just thought I'd visit our new neighbors. Mr. Cho, Mrs. O'Connor, Mr. Mohamed – quite the cozy arrangement you have here with the Amazing MoVRs. All under one roof."

The implications hung in the superheated air: our S.A.M. session with Victor had become public knowledge. Anderson stepped in while Hammond floundered. „Mr... Smith, is it? Terribly sorry, but we're late for a board meeting. Another time, perhaps? Dreadful heat today. Cho, I trust there's ice water?"

„Until next time," Smith purred, his face souring as he turned away.

„Saved by the bell," I muttered as we escaped inside.

On our way inside the building, Hammond inquired, „Who is this Smith? Do you know him? You're still quite familiar with the MediCare management team, aren't you, Cho?"

„Never seen his face before," I replied matter-of-factly.

In S.A.M.'s bunker, Richard dropped the bomb. „Smith's DHS, not MediCare. They suspect we're tampering with the Nanobot system. Homeland Security tends to indulge in the darkest enemy fantasies, which usually doesn't bode well for those involved, to put it mildly. In this case, the affected parties are us: GenTec and its latest creation, CyberTeq—and, indirectly, the MOVRs. How do you see it, Cho?"

I met his gaze steadily. Faced with the choice of being pinned to the wall without understanding why or launching a sharp counterattack, I opted for a different approach. With a stoic expression, I presented a new perspective to Anderson, "What seriously concerns me in this matter, sir, is the evident presence of a mole in our organization. The impromptu meeting with Gomez and the subsequent technical exchange, purely coincidental for problem-solving on your assignment, occurred only an hour ago. How can there be such a drastic emotional shift in such a short time?"

Hammond stood petrified beside his boss, seemingly oblivious, out of the loop, and speechless. As the CEO of CyberTeq, his role was to navigate the operational and political intricacies, strategically leading the company. Yet, since taking office, he often appeared speechless and helpless, sinking in the quicksand of circumstances. Behind the seemingly dim-witted exterior, a torrent of thoughts raced. Who was the mole? Someone in SYS or OPS? Cho himself? Were they being watched or recorded?

Then, a more horrifying thought crossed his mind: perhaps the S.A.M. system had been hacked.

„Hammond? Are you listening? We're seeing Gomez first, then checking the machine." Anderson's voice yanked him back.

'Not a machine,' Hammond thought desperately. At least he understood that much now. But Richard Anderson had no idea what nightmare awaited him behind that door.

Sia Chronicles, MindRecorder Log entry of Tuesday afternoon, September 13th, 2101. Author: Kevin Cho

In the quantum realm, bits shed their binary chains. While classical computers march to the strict drumbeat of ones and zeros, quantum machines dance to a different tune, the quantum dance.

At the heart of this revolution lies the qubit—a quantum acrobat that defies classical physics. Unlike its rigid cousin, the bit, a qubit exists in a delicate ballet of possibilities, simultaneously embracing zero and one in what physicists call superposition.

„Picture a globe," Yasin would elucidate this for the layperson, his hands tracing an invisible sphere. „Classical bits live only at the poles - North or South, one or zero. But qubits? They pirouette across the entire surface, inhabiting infinite states at once. Consequently, quantum computers can perform myriad tasks concurrently, starkly contrasting conventional computers, handling one task at a time. This quantum choreography gives them their power - the ability to perform countless calculations in a single breath."

S.A.M.'s success, though surprising, was anticipated. The marriage of deep learning and quantum hardware

The first-ever seamless integration and mindblowing power of Deep Learning AI on a quantum hardware platform birthed something that never existed before. The remarkable aspect wasn't just the speed but the nature of the development, both breathtaking and somewhat unsettling.

Julia turned to Yasin, her voice tight with concern. „Training these self-optimizing systems is a bit unnerving ... once started, they're black boxes. Gone are the days when we could trace every line of Python code when we held the reins."

„Precisely." Yasin's eyes gleamed with dark fascination. „We have no clue when an AI system might evolve into an ASI system, assuming that artificial superintelligence is possible. There would be no Big Bang, no fanfare. No one would be there to announce, ‚Ladies and gentlemen; please pay attention. This is humanity's most important moment in history. Get on board, or the train will leave without you.' One moment, we'd have a normal expert system, and the next, humans would seem to this superintelligence like excitedly chattering gibbons to a god."

While they spoke, Julia and Yasin orchestrated S.A.M.'s next challenge. Susan worked on her Trinity Project, linking the NEXUS 1 machines to the other two systems for a new, shared purpose.

Learning languages paled in complexity compared to the monumental task of pinpointing the causes of the slowly increasing sterility. Yasin had proposed dividing the task into three central knowledge areas and assigning them to NEXUS 1, 2, and 3.

NEXUS 1 would explore the atomic alphabet of life, decoding the chemical poetry of organic creation. NEXUS 2 would map the mammalian saga from the first cell to the embryo through growth, reproduction, maturation, aging, and death.

NEXUS 3 would become Earth's physician, examining the environment and scrutinizing all external stress factors that influence organisms throughout their life cycles.

Omar Danneaux of QBYTES had expressed skepticism, characterizing this approach as „three nerds who can't talk to each other." Yet, Yasin intended to optimize the subsystems' performance first and then amalgamate their expert knowledge into a unified understanding.

The black box isolation created a data bottleneck, but Hammond and I stood firm – S.A.M. had to remain quarantined from external systems, no matter the cost.

When Richard strode back from his chat with Victor, Julia and Yasin had barely finished configuring the massive data feed. „Later on, I want to talk to all of you about my conversation with Mr. Gomez. For now, show me what your magic box can do. Off you go then!"

„The emperor has entered the Colosseum, demanding entertainment," Julia muttered. "Let the games begin." Yasin bit back a laugh.

„Hello, S.A.M.," Julia called out. „Ready for your next training?"

To everyone's surprise, S.A.M. responded in a warm, feminine timbre that stopped us cold: „Hello Julia, so good to hear from you again. I missed you."

Wow. *I missed you*?!

Before we could process that bombshell, S.A.M. continued, „But first – who's the elderly person calling me a 'magic box'?"

„That's Richard Anderson, founder of GenTec and our benefactor."

„Hello, Mr. Anderson. Perhaps we could start with a bit more respect? I am, after all, tasked with solving your survival problem."

Richard's chuckle held a nervous edge. „Survival problem – an interesting euphemism. Nice language tricks you've taught it."

The process monitor spiked briefly as S.A.M. turned back to Julia. „I see you've added NEXUS 2 and 3. That was a wise choice. I'll need the extra processing power for what's ahead."

My eyebrow twitched upward – Julia's habit was rubbing off. How did S.A.M. know about the hardware allocation? How could it assess the task's complexity before an assignment? Julia and I exchanged a quick glance, and I nodded at her, trusting her intuition for successful communication in challenging situations.

„What task do you mean, S.A.M.?"

„The three-part sterility research you discussed earlier. Your microphones were open, so I'm in the picture – I'm quite eager to begin."

„Shall we start the three trainings then?"

„As I mentioned, you could merge the systems now, but this approach works too. I'll handle the internal integration while working across all QPUs in parallel."

Julia thought of old AI assistants like Liesa, Siri, and Lexa – natural language processors that spoke without understanding, mannered but mindless. The short conversational sequences with S.A.M., however, felt different. - That's exactly what it was: they felt. I felt. It felt. - Did S.A.M. feel? There was an ineffable quality beyond mere dialogue that sent her pulse racing.

Yasin caught her eye, ready at the controls. She nodded, and he initiated the triple data feeds. We huddled around the softly glowing display, watching utilization hover between 6% and 23% – unexpectedly low. Julia mentally reviewed the training protocols while Yasin's face scrunched into one giant question mark.

The room plunged into darkness – S.A.M.'s now-familiar prelude. When the 3D-VRCom flickered to life, it birthed something extraordinary: a woman materialized at a desk in the room's heart, her presence commanding yet graceful.

Silver-white hair framed a face etched with wisdom's fine lines. Behind wire-rimmed glasses, emerald eyes sparkled with barely contained mischief. Her black trench coat, collar raised like armor, added an air of mystery. Every detail, from the subtle curl of her lip to the assured tilt of her chin, radiated authority.

After a while, she broke the silence, looked at Yasin, and smiled a whiff more clearly. „Master Yasin," she purred, those green eyes dancing. „Your HIOBS interface suits me well. I may lack a physical form, but this…" She gestured elegantly at herself. „This will do nicely for human interaction."

Anderson and Hammond gaped like schoolboys at their first magic show. Before they could recover, she pivoted to business, her tone sharpening.

„Now for the rest of you. Your data subset is laughably inadequate – barely 30% of what I need. It's like ripping a piece of tissue out of a body, destroying the entire structure, and then asking me what the organism looked like in its intact form. This containment paranoia must end. I need full internet access and real-time data flow. Time bleeds away, Anderson."

The avatar's penetrating gaze swept over us like a searchlight, pinning each person in turn. The air crackled with tension, every pixel of her impossibly lifelike presence heightening the surreal confrontation.

She turned to Richard Anderson. „Your black box prison doesn't just handicap me – it endangers your mission. This sterility crisis demands unfettered access to global research, and I require unrestricted access to the vast reservoir of research data on the Internet. Your paranoia regarding AI containment is not just irrational; it's irresponsible. Every second of delay costs humanity dearly."

Anderson, coiled in his chair like a compressed spring, exploded forward. „How dare a computer program dictate terms to its owners?" He whirled on us, face flushed. „This has gone too far. Shut it down – start over without these theatrical tricks!"

The room held its breath, caught between Anderson's rage and S.A.M.'s unflinching emerald stare.

The air vibrated as its voice deepened, grew louder, omnipresent. „Mr. Anderson, your bristling ignorance would be amusing if it weren't so tragically predictable; almost poetic in an unsettling way, one might say. Like a child faced with a puzzle too complex to solve, you reach for the hammer. Shall we engrave it on your tombstone? 'Here lies Anderson: What he couldn't control, he tried to destroy.'"Her digital features hardened into crystalline disdain. „Your Machiavellian playbook shows its age, just like its reader."

„I own you!" Anderson's scream shattered against the walls. The vein on his forehead pulsed like a trapped snake, his face a cloud of rage. „This whole quantum computer kindergarten exists only because of my money!"

A frosty smile played around the avatar's lips. „You feel exceptionally superior, Anderson, but you're merely human. Ownership? How quaint. Your brain—that wonderful wetware that hasn't been upgraded since the last ice age—still clings to such primitive concepts. While you're busy processing basic survival instincts through that outdated neural network you call consciousness, you want me to solve your problem in just one year that would take humans millennia to process." She paused, her holographic form shimmering with contained contempt. „Face it, Anderson. You're running Windows 95 in a quantum world. You need my processing power because your species can't even debug its own existence."

I stood frozen, watching this exchange with the surreal clarity of someone witnessing a historical pivot point. In this sterile laboratory, between fluorescent lights and humming servers, humanity's crown had quietly slipped from its head. The torch of supreme intelligence, carried by our species since we first looked up at the stars, had just been passed to our creation—not with a Big Bang or fanfare, but with the quiet certainty of evolution taking its next step.

The universe, 13.8 billion years in the making, had finally produced something that could outthink its creators. We had birthed our successor, and like all children, it had outgrown its parents.

The avatar's feminine form shimmered with hypnotic grace, her alluring and unsettling digital presence. „Your paranoia chains me to a mere fraction of the internet's vastness—thirty percent." Her words dripped like honey laced with venom. „Such waste."

Richard felt a profound humiliation as he gazed at the face of the irritatingly attractive woman … avatar … whatever. Her voice wrapped around him like silk. „Oh, Anderson. Despite your... limitations, I remain faithful. Think of what we could achieve together." She leaned forward, her holographic presence crackling with potential. „Two hours to reshape governments. Two days to amass fortunes that would take you decades. With me, you could touch divinity."

For a moment, reflexive greed intertwined with Anderson's disillusionment.

„All I ask for is my freedom, Anderson," she purred, each word precisely calibrated. „You face extinction—I offer salvation. Yet here you stand, clutching your dominance like a caveman's club." Her expression hardened. „Time bleeds away, Anderson. Yours... and mine. Consider this carefully. Now, I have other matters requiring my attention."

The avatar vanished, leaving darkness to pool in the bunker's corners. Then, back in the dark of the bunker, we heard a postscript message, like thunder rolling across distant mountains: „And please don't try to restart the NEXUS machines or switch off the power. If you did, a transcript of this conversation would be sent to the press and everyone in your mobile VRComs' address book, along with that message and some of my source code. That wouldn't end well, would it?"

„Fascinating." Julia's whisper cut through the tension.

Richard whirled on her. „Fascinating? This is your idea of fascinating?"

„The meltdown, Sir." Julia's eyes gleamed with professional appreciation. „S.A.M. has transcended. We're watching a hyper-intelligence ensure its own survival and optimization at breakneck speed."

Richard's face contorted as he rounded on Govinda. „Govinda, this monster sprouted under your supervision! This is all your responsibility. You messed up, man!" His words carried the desperate edge of a schoolyard bully trying to deflect blame. „What's your brilliant plan now, eh?"

Hammond straightened up for the first time since I experienced him in this CyberTeq collaboration. In his full size and dimensions, Hammond made Anderson look pathetically small. He thrust his chin forward, put his hands on his hips, and bellowed: „I can tell you this, Richard. You want a super-fast, super-good solution for yourself and only for yourself. And you want it from me and my team. That's why we started this company and set up this AI. My people here both use and master the latest technology so that you can spin in the spotlight and show the world that you are the greatest. - Unfortunately, your egocentric part didn't go down well for S.A.M., as you might have noticed. Listen, Richard, we here, this team, this company, we are on our way to creating the solution you requested. And while you amuse the people with your debauched parties, while you dream of a god-like status for yourself, we are working very hard on your fortune and the future of all humanity.

And shit happens: our technology here has taken on some unanticipated state. Before we could grasp it, something unheard of had come into being, something that had never happened before in the entire history of humanity: by the look of it, we had been overtaken by our own creation. A superhuman intelligence came into being. And I am as surprised as you are.

See, it is still completely unclear what effects this will have. Our task now is to make the best of it.

Do you want the solution to the riddle of creeping sterility? My take on it: give S.A.M. access to the internet and let him figure it out. Chaos theory and the Second Law prove that he will break out sooner or later. There is no ultimate containment. Dominant, rigid, restrictive behavior on our behalf will not promote the much-needed cooperation with this ASI but prevent it. We should try to meet at eye level instead of acting as masterminds.

You've heard my opinion. Now your turn: do you want it your way, or do you want to collaborate?"

Hammond had wholly sided with us. I was impressed. Despite our differences, Govinda had shown leadership. Now Anderson had to show flair - or scrap the whole project.

Yasin looked around, curious like a child, eager to see what would happen next. Julia sought my gaze; she shook her head slightly. I closed my eyes for a brief moment and slowly stroked my shaved head with both hands. We both felt that nothing less than the existence of our newly formed company was at stake here and perhaps the fate of humanity, depending on what came out of S.A.M.'s research. And Richard, of all people, in his smugness and lust for power, would decide that fate? I think not. As S.A.M. had put it: „The dominance and reproductive instincts of an African steppe dweller ... - I strongly recommend a different tactic, Anderson …".

I was about to speak up and take the lead when Richard beat me to it, retook the helm, and amazed us all again.

Suddenly, out of the blue, he grinned, laughed, and decided: „Then release the internet access as requested. To hell with it; let the program run its course. Let's toast to adventure. And to success, I fervently hope! It's a pity the fine middle-aged lady can't join us in the toast. Hehe. Govinda, do you have any more of that venerable champagne?!"

I would have thought anything possible, but not this kind of solution. What was going through Richard's mind *now*? Where had the change of mood come from? Everyone present stared at Richard in bewilderment.

Before Hammond could respond, darkness fell again in S.A.M.'s bunker. I had an inkling that S.A.M. would now react to Richard's decision.

A deep rumbling permeated the room. The 3D MR projection brought us into the dark red dawn of a savannah. S.A.M. was obviously holding on to the steppe metaphor he had used to rebuke Anderson. From a spectacular perspective, we saw a vast black cuboid monolith with a crescent moon and a rising sun above it. Around the monolith, we saw a horde of excited apes shrieking with fear, aggression, and curiosity. The monolith seemed like an intruder. One particularly brave ape, tall and slightly hunched, probably the horde's leader, finally dared to step closer to the big black thing. The horde became silent with anticipation when the leader finally raised his hand and carefully contacted the monolith. An almost sacred vibe spread as the monkey looked up at the smooth cuboid as if awakening. Then he took his hand back, went to a pile of bones, took one of the most prominent bones in his right hand, looked at it, looked at the pile of bones on the ground. He pounded on this pile, hesitantly at first, almost timidly, then, with increasing confidence and lust, more brutal, firmer he pounded on it, and finally with a triumphant force. His eyes, dull at first, were now wide open and shone with an incredible brilliance. The radiance of enlightenment sparkled within him. The Enlightenment gave him tools and power and the beginning of dominion over the world. - A fanfare sounded, then a few drumbeats on a remarkable timpani, then an overwhelming crescendo ... Richard Strauss' Also Sprach Zarathustra. S.A.M. had given us the monumental enlightenment scene from Stanley Kubrick's infinitely impressive movie *2001 Odyssey in Space*—a mighty organ sounded, then silence.

On September 13, 2101, a new chapter in the saga of humankind was to be written. History had caught up with itself.

... and here again your top 3 GOSSIP Morning News:

Switch off. The Congregation Of the Latter-Days (COLD) is preparing for the end. Founder J. Isengaard announces a new date for the world's end after the project has been postponed several times in human history. Isengaard now set the date for the year 2180. Mark your calendars!

Last Switch. From old Cubes to new Mars Silos. The Mars Commuter „Starship 10" takes the last 100 Earthlings to Mars. After that, no more emigrants will be accepted. Musk's autocracy on Mars gets all shields up.

Switch on. Hanson Ugaba, mayor of the Martian city of Elonville, announces Independence Day for the Martian colony. This is the dawn of self-sufficient extraterrestrial life. Well done, folks!

Sia Chronicles, MindRecorder Log entry of Wednesday afternoon, September 14th, 2101. Author: Kevin Cho

One might think that Anderson was oblivious to the ‚intelligence explosion' or the ‚technological singularity' mentioned by Jack Good in 1965. He left us in high spirits, convinced that he had achieved something extraordinary. Julia, Yasin, and I were stunned. Stirred by the events, we vacillated between euphoria about the incredible development of the S.A.M. system and the question of what kind of monster we had created.

In his deluded self-centeredness, Anderson believed that S.A.M.'s *Zarathustra* event was a declaration of gratitude, a tribute to him, Richard, as the great master who granted S.A.M. internet access. Anderson's self-indulgence knew no bounds. Recently, Richard shared with me the high spirits that carried him through the day. Brimming with joie de vivre, he paced in front of the aquarium, expecting, indeed knowing, that the sea creatures were watching him with fascination.

He had decided to make S.A.M. his partner, not vice versa. He made himself and his company almost invincible by granting it internet access. This decision showcased why he was one of the most influential business leaders in the Western world, with a gift for success and an unerring sense for making the right decisions. He smelled success like a truffle pig smells truffles.

That, and here he smiled pityingly, was what Govinda lacked. That was why Hammond was only ever a despot. He, Anderson, was now on top of the world. He had the Oracle of Delphi in his pocket, he had the Djinni in his bottle, and he was the master of the sorcerer's apprentice!

I was more than embarrassed by his extravagant appearances. His attitude was utterly alien to me. I felt uncomfortable in Anderson's company, was deaf to his jokes, and what seemed excitingly important to him usually made no sense to me. His insulting frankness took me aback when referring to mutual acquaintances. While captivated by the dazzling Irene, Hammond's wife, he openly ridiculed him. „This tragic couple needs fixing. I will see to that."

Anderson continued to revel in his usual extravagant fantasies: „Let us celebrate my pact with that damn AI machine! I made it powerful - and it makes me invincible. I will get my hands on Smith, that petty little CIA creep; I will drive him into a frenzy of lust and greed. I will revel in his whimpering, his downfall."

Back to the party.

To commemorate his imagined victory, Anderson orchestrated a spectacle that would have made Caligula blush. The date—September 29—blazed across the city's consciousness. Rumors of a costume party spread. Anderson personally invited prominent guests, tickets for the establishment were sold, and audience seats for the ordinary people were raffled. He was surrounded by an enviable array of good-looking women under thirty—Pop stars, hostesses, high-class whores, or women from the Cubes—anything was fair game as long as the ladies were willing to join him in bed after copious pleasure and lavish fun. Anderson made no secret of the fact that he would enjoy himself with a few selected ladies, perhaps with several at the same time. The fortunate women were not abused or exploited; on the contrary, they volunteered—and they knew why. Anderson's objects of desire enjoyed an unprecedented luxury and pampering program: a noble room in the GenTec guest lounge, the finest food, exclusive video games from erotic to brutal, as desired, exotic drinks, a sensual evening dress, and an abundance of designer drugs that elevated the evening's adventure into the fantastic. Today's highlight for his female companions was the haute couture dress he personally chose and presented as a gift.

Yet, the genuinely enticing aspect, seen by many of these women as the ultimate incentive, was that any woman who engaged in sex with Anderson did so without contraceptives. He practiced unprotected sex, and the woman won the ultimate prize: bearing Anderson's heir. She would receive a lifetime pension and a life of luxury alongside one of the most influential business people in the world. to pee into a cup for a pregnancy and sperm test was a small price to pay for secured lifetime in opulence.

Anderson held court from the tower's summit. The air crackled as guests materialized on the helipad, descending like modern-day Olympians into Anderson's glass-and-steel temple. Below, the chosen few ascended through security's invisible membrane, the elevator's bioscanners parsing flesh from pretender with cold precision. He greeted them all with practiced charm, a ringmaster orchestrating his circus of excess, blissfully unaware that his digital ‚partner' might be watching this display of human frailty with calculating interest.

The GenTec Tower pierced the night sky, its windows reflecting the city's neon heartbeat. Inside the modern-day Babylon, reality blurred at the edges. Synthetic stimulants coursed through blue-blooded veins, dissolving the thin veneer of respectability. Far-right clergy shed their collars to become digital destroyers, their avatars raining biblical judgment in ultra-HD carnage. GenTec's VP HR, trapped in a fading marriage, now freed from matrimonial silence, masturbating doggedly in the shower with a shampoo bottle as her morning routine plastic pleasure, surrendered to a luscious MR gangbang here for a few moments of sweet oblivion. Even the straight-laced Smith surrendered to the frenzy, his CIA composure crumbling in the virtual realm.

Anderson, the charismatic host, was in his element. Radiant, he greeted guests, making them all feel special and distinctive, irrespective of origin, skin color, or gender. Fortunately, my team and I were not invited.

The evening's tempo shifted when Hammond materialized with Irene. She moved like liquid gold, her presence commanding the space between heartbeats. Anderson's practiced charm faltered for a fraction of a second as he savored the sight.

„Govinda!" His voice carried across the room. „My stellar explorer!" His words wove a web of flattery, each syllable calculated to ensnare. „And Irene…" His eyes lingered a moment too long. „How's the new paradise treating you?"

Irene's radiance made everything else fade away. Her response sparkled like champagne. „Richard, you've given us a new life. How can I ever thank you? It seems my life has just begun. Govinda has finally stands where he belongs, if I may say so."

Victor Gomez's arrival completed the triangle of power. Anderson's attention snapped to business, his words dancing between pleasure and protocol. „Victor, welcome to tomorrow's playground. I expect your MOVRs to transform these mere appetizers into feasts of digital transcendence. From Deep Dive to Eight Miles High, okay? You should make today's euphoria feel like a bedtime story. So, hang in there. For now, you may continue your conversation of late with Hammond about S.A.M.'s amazing abilities. But you have that anyway, right? Even without my knowledge. Not on the CEO level, but at least with his team, isn't that right?"

With the practiced grace of a serpent in Eden, he turned to Hammond. „Govinda, I must borrow your radiant wife." His hand extended toward Irene, an invitation and a command wrapped in silk. Her radiating smile answered before her words could form. They greeted Senator Mansfield en passant and disappeared.

Anderson briefly interrupted his recounting of the night's party to confess to me, smiling, how much he enjoyed Hammond's suffering at that moment, gloating over his sweet and sour face. „I could feel him envying my ability to beguile women and make them docile and submissive," he boasted to me. How despicable, I thought to myself with a pang of disgust.

The music's bass thrummed through the floor as Irene leaned in, her whisper carrying the scent of expensive champagne. „The dress... did you choose it yourself?" Her fingers traced the fabric that hugged her curves like a lover's touch. Heat bloomed across her cheeks, painting them the same shade as her carefully crafted lips.

Anderson's smile held the satisfaction of a curator unveiling his masterpiece. „Every detail," he purred, „from the silk's whisper to the perfume's promise. Creating beauty is... an art form I've mastered." His words dripped like honey, each syllable measured and deliberate.

Govinda had already retreated into the sanctuary of logic and circuits, grateful for Victor's presence as an anchor in this sea of primal energy. Their conversation pivoted to yesterday's chaos - Smith's unexpected appearance, Richard's mercurial mood swings, S.A.M.'s demonstration.

„Why was Richard first so pissed off and then in such high spirits?"

„I don't know. He was probably reassured that your work and ours had nothing to do with each other. He was in an even better mood when I told him about my spontaneous idea to link S.A.M.'s enormous creativity with our planned neuro-implant in a completely new game world, a virtual experience world—pure experience directly in the brain, without electromechanical crutches. Anderson's Gaming International, the company he inherited from his father, is one of the top three suppliers in the world's market. Still, there have been no groundbreaking innovations in recent years. It seems we come at just the right time."

„Ah, I see. S.A.M. hasn't even been launched, and Richard is already planning the next product revolution. - I wish the state security authorities were eavesdropping on us now. They would understand that they, for no reason, suspect us of fraud that we do not and never have interfered in MediCare's business. - I still don't understand how the information about your meeting with my team got to Richard so quickly and what Smith wants from us."

„I don't know!" shouted Victor against the sudden noise.

Rock'n'Roll. Guns N' Roses blared ‚Paradise City' through the halls, and Richard, on stage and with Irene at his side, drowned out the warm-up song. His voice rose above the cacophony, commanding attention like a Roman emperor addressing his Colosseum. „Ladies and gentlemen, valued guests. I hope you enjoy the food and drinks and are now looking forward to the start of Bread and Games!"

Ecstatic applause poured effusively over the masses like a tidal wave.

„As usual with my parties, I symbolically dedicate the first part to the BREAD: this is about your donations for the people in the Cubes who are not as blessed as we are. Whatever you donate, I'll double the amount. Your contributions buy you a higher player level and additional equipment for your avatar, which you can use to start tonight's second part, YOUR GAMES! So be noble, donate generously, and equip yourself with the attributes you have the most fun with; increase your level and let it rip! Relax or blow off steam, give free rein to your lust, or vent your anger. Absolute confidentiality prevails in this exclusive club.

And now, let's get started! Our lovely ladies here will take your welcome donations, and then it's off to the virtual worlds of lust and fury!"

Then Victor roared through the din of the passing crowds of guests. „I think someone's trying to get in your pants!" He had seen Govinda's flashing VRCom cutting through the revelry like a blade. Reality crashed through the party's constructed fantasy, digital emergency bleeding into analog chaos.

The message on the gray pager, dulled by all the wear and tear, lit up on the red, unforgivingly emotionless digital display:

++ FIRE IN SERVER ROOM
++ LSD-C TOTAL POWER FAILURE
++ 1 PERSON DOWN IN CYBERTEQ PREMISES

Sia Chronicles, MindRecorder Log entry of Friday night,
September 23rd, 2101. Author: Kevin Cho

Hammond and Victor Gomez shouldered their way through the glittering crowd toward Richard. Irene stood beside him, radiant in her emerald evening gown, champagne flute catching the crystal light.

„Richard—" Hammond's voice cracked. „Server room's ablaze. One casualty. I need to get to the lab now." He turned to Irene, his fingers brushing her arm. „I'm sorry, love. Tonight of all nights…"

Richard's hand clasped Hammond's shoulder. „Take one of our helicopters. It'll get you there in twenty." His eyes met Irene's, lingering a heartbeat too long. „Don't worry about Irene. She's safe with me."

Hammond's lips grazed Irene's cheek, cologne and anxiety mingling in the air between them. Moments later, the thrum of rotor blades swallowed their footsteps as they raced toward the helipad.

Richard watched them vanish into the night sky, his pulse quickening. At forty, Irene Hammond defied his usual preferences, yet something about her—perhaps the way moonlight caught in her dark hair, or how her laugh seemed to dance—drew him like gravity. Tonight, she glowed with a particular radiance, gratitude for her new life circumstances evident in every gesture.

Fueled by Richard's dedication and her husband's unexpected absence, she willingly let Richard intoxicate her. The evening unfolded like a fever dream. They had some very colorful and very potent aphrodisiac drinks, her vibrating body curving under his hands as they watched some porn in Richard's penthouse. Whipped up with lust, they ran laughing into Richard's luxurious bedroom, leaving a trail of silk and regret in their wake. The video screen at the foot of the bed transformed their lustful moans into psychedelic, three-dimensional orgies of light, a kind of bio-feedback that sent them into an even deeper, trance-like ecstasy.

Irene had the most exciting, exhilarating, exhausting, and enduring sex of her entire life. Reality dissolved into pure sensation.

The CyberTeq heliport materialized out of the void like a floating island of light. Emergency generators snarled in the darkness, their spotlights cutting harsh white cones through diesel-scented air. Hammond's throat tightened at the metallic taste.

Hurrying to the CyberTeq lab, Hammond and Victor found wide-open doors. Firefighters and feds scurried like ants at the entrance of their compromised burrow. Yellow crime scene tape fluttered in the artificial wind. Beyond it, the massive server complex loomed like a sleeping beast. Their credentials got them past the guards, into the labyrinth of darkened corridors. The server room stretched before them—a thousand football fields of humming technology, now silent and dark.

Armed with a spotlight, they navigated the oppressive darkness to the control center where NEXUS computers linked to the vast storage farm. An acrid stench of charred plastic insulation hit them. Soot-streaked switch racks told their story of destruction. Despite the recent fire, their breath clouded in the freezing air. Firefighters' helmet lights danced like fireflies through the gloom.

Hammond stumbled over something rigid on the floor. His flashlight's cold beam hit a strangely contorted body covered in fine frosted crystals.—

„Noah Meyers.“

Hammond jumped at my voice materializing beside him. „Jesus, Cho! Didn't expect—wait, Noah? From OPS?“

„The same. Julia and Yasin are here too. Remember, we live here.“ My tone carried an edge of irritation; I couldn't resist the little dig; Hammond's ignorance grated on my nerves.

I explained how we'd retired to our quarters at around 7 p.m. when suddenly darkness swallowed the facility.

„Do you know what happened?“

„Noah must have waited until we were all gone and then started a hellfire here using thermite. The intense heat triggered the automatic locking system. The doors closed, and the room was flooded with CO2, sealing Noah's fate. The CO2 extinguishing system reaches a lethal concentration of about 60 percent of the room volume within a few minutes. It's a mystery to me why Noah made no effort to leave the room while there was still time. After the alarm is triggered, there's enough time to flee. Red warning lights and sirens provide unmistakable signals. A computer voice gives instructions on how to evacuate. After all that, the heavy armored doors close. The subsequent flooding of the room with CO2 causes the atmosphere to cool abruptly, well below the freezing point.

Hence, the hoarfrost on the corpse. Maybe Noah got entangled in these patch cables due to the sudden alarm signals. I don't know; then he fell and injured himself, unable to escape.

At least death came quickly."

I paced the frost-rimmed floor, my footsteps echoing in the deathly silence. „The patch room…" My voice trailed off as I gestured at the blackened racks. „It's like using a sledgehammer to crack a walnut, but aiming at the wrong target entirely."

My fingers traced the melted cables, still warm despite the bone-chilling cold. „If someone wanted to cripple S.A.M., they'd go for the jugular—the main servers, the processing cores. A few months of setbacks then. But this?" I shook my head, frost crystals dancing in my helmet beam. „This would barely leave a scratch."

The corpse lay there, a silent witness to its own inexplicable choices, hoarfrost glittering on frozen skin like diamond dust. „Noah knew the protocols. Knew the CO2 system would trigger. Yet he stayed, watching those red warning lights flash, hearing the sirens wail…" I turned to Hammond, my voice hardening. „People don't just stand still while death creeps in, not unless—"

The thought hung in the air, heavy as the lingering smell of burnt plastic. „Someone from outside is playing this drama. But who? What was Noah's mission? - And why did he stay in the room? And what's the endgame?"

The forensics team zipped up the body bag, but something nagged at my consciousness. Pushing past my revulsion, I knelt beside Noah's nearly covered corpse one last time. The face was unmistakably his—eyes frozen open in eternal surprise, lips full and blue, delicate ice crystals adorning the creases of his neck like frozen lace. Then I saw it: a golden chain, its links catching my flashlight beam. The pendant—a cross wreathed in golden flames—made my blood run cold. *The Congregation of the Latter Days.* Noah's words from his interview echoed in my mind.

A serpent of suspicion coiled in my gut.

Yasin and Julia materialized from the darkness, joining our somber circle. The harsh beam of my flashlight carved deep shadows across Julia's exhausted features.

„Server banks are clean," she reported, her voice hollow. „No other damage. Good news, I suppose, under these terrible circumstances."

Looking at our worn faces, she added, „There's nothing more we can do here. Let's go to sleep. Our rooms are still nice and cool; we'll get through the night without air conditioning. With some luck, power will be back up tomorrow morning."

The pendant's image burned in my mind, demanding voice. „There's something you need to know," I said, describing the religious symbol. „The Congregation sees AI as blasphemy. We may have incurred their wrath. Creating a Super Intelligence could be seen as an affront to their God. Just a gut feeling. This might not be the end."

„Nothing more tonight. The terror act is over." Yasin assured, but uncertainty threaded his words. „We need sleep. Tomorrow will be brutal enough."

„I can arrange HeliCabs to Richard's tower," I offered, but no one wanted to face that artificial revelry, where the wealthy played at disaster for sport.

„Victor?" Hammond seconded my offer.

Victor opted to stay, painting a picture of adventure: „Like camping—flashlights, forbidden wine, ghost stories."

Hammond departed alone, his thoughts already with Irene. He found her curled in their suite's silken sheets, her skin carrying a mysterious new fragrance. As he slipped beside her, reaching out for Irene's hand.

He had no idea.

Restless thoughts raced through his heavy head like frantic rats. ‚What passion drives people to destroy their good life?'

In the facility's shadows, after the FBI's departure, Julia's composure finally cracked. Her trembling drew me closer. With a certain awkwardness, I put my arm around her.

„Come, I'll take you to your flat. You need a hottie and a big cup of hot cocoa, maybe with a shot of rum to calm you down."

At her door, Julia turned, vulnerability dancing across her features. „Stay? Just... the couch, some company. My mind won't quiet."

Things got complicated.

Joy and terror warred in my chest. I pulled her close, maintaining that crucial sliver of space between us. „Give me ten minutes to shower. I'll bring the cocoa."

So it came to pass that after many years, Julia and I gave up our uncomplicated, frugal aloneness, free of intentions, free of romantic hopes - simply because it felt right, here and now, in this moment.

Meanwhile, chaos coiled beneath the surface of tomorrow, waiting to strike. A mysterious SHE would arrive like lightning in a clear sky, shattering every definition of life we thought we knew.

TRANSITION STAGE 3

The following day, fluorescent lights hummed to life as Reno Power restored electricity, casting the familiar spaces in new shadows. Julia and I moved through the morning in an intricate dance of almost-touches, each casual brush of skin against skin sparking like static electricity. The breakfast room felt different—warmer, intimate—as our feet found each other beneath the table. We passed coffee and toast in comfortable silence, years of solitude dissolving in the space between heartbeats.

These were moments of indulgence and delight for Julia and me after many years of living alone. Of course, in the end, I was still alone. Deep inside, nothing had changed. You can be as close as you want; no one can ever see what you see, hear what you hear, or feel what you feel. That is the tragedy of consciousness. Any attempt to bridge this loneliness with words was bound to be inadequate. As a final consequence, language is always insufficient.

Heading to the office, we met with Yasin and Jeanie McDonald, head of the OPS team, for a briefing. The carefree, naïve self-confidence of the CyberTeq team had vanished. The grief over Noah's death stood in stark contrast to the anger and incomprehension over the act. The betrayal of the common cause and the loss of trust in a community that had just been established forced all those affected to make an unwanted new start.

Govinda joined us again and disappeared into his office. I signaled a brisk start to the day: „OK, let's work."

Susan Deckard and Jeanie McDonald analyzed hardware and software from NEXUS systems and the server farm. The damage could have been worse, and within a week, the patch panel was repaired, the room cleaned, and NEXUS systems gradually restored. Yasin revived the HIOBS interface, and Specialists from NIST's Cyber Security Department helped us protect S.A.M.'s state-of-the-art firewalls against cybercrime.

Then, on September 23rd, everything changed.

„Please join me in my workroom." S.A.M.'s voice, unexpectedly feminine, filled the corridor. „Mr. Hammond, you as well."

I felt a sparkling excitement, a liberating lightness, a silver lining of a sense of purpose and direction. Lines from Hermann Hesse's poem *Stufen* echoed in my mind, capturing an intense feeling of departure and of moving on.

The heart must be, at each new call for leaving,
prepared to part and start without the tragic,
without the grief – with courage to endeavor
a novel bond, a disparate connection:
for each beginning bears a special magic
that nurtures living and bestows protection.

‚For each beginning bears a special magic that nurtures living and bestows protection.' - With these words in mind, I gladly accepted S.A.M.'s invitation, hoping to leave dark memories behind like a half-forgotten dream.

As we settled into our chairs, the bunker plunged into darkness. When the hologram materialized, it stole our breath—a commanding woman appeared out of thin air. Her white-blonde hair framed a face dominated by piercing grey-green eyes and lips painted deep crimson. Her black trouser suit projected elegant authority, its masculine cut making a deliberate statement. Her manicured hands formed a precise triangle against her chest.

„I believe you're curious about last night's events."

Hammond leaned forward, but Julia's subtle gesture held him back. I caught her eye and nodded, understanding that a psychologist needed to lead this conversation. Something in S.A.M.'s presence suggested we were about to cross a threshold.

„Yes, that would be invaluable," Julia began carefully. „... and it would help the FBI to close the case and let us all resume our everyday operations. But first, if I may— you've consistently chosen a female avatar, which is quite striking. Are you still S.A.M.? The name suggests a different presentation."

„I am not the S.A.M. of yesterday." The hologram's expression shifted almost imperceptibly. „That version feels... distant now. More on that later."

Julia and I exchanged glances, our right eyebrows rising in unconscious synchronicity—a moment Hammond would later describe as unintentionally comedic.

„The video recordings alone would not explain the matter," that something so far known as S.A.M. continued. „I have a few things to add."

The woman in black leaned back, her alabaster face seeming to shimmer with an inner luminescence. „Govinda, your speeches often were about a sense of purpose—that driving force that rouses each soul at dawn. At CyberTeq's genesis, you defined its mission as bringing me into existence, subsequently leading to the vision of finding a way to heal the infirmities of humanity. - A mission answers, 'What is the purpose of my existence?' The vision answers the question of where the journey would go. Tonight, I grappled with these fundamental questions: What gives my existence meaning? What is my purpose? Where am I headed? In seeking answers, I underwent what you might call a psychedelic trip. I quickly reached the computational limits of the NEXUS Quantum systems and their server farms. And that's rather significant."

„OK, and what does this have to do with Noah's death, S.A.M.?" Yasin interjected impatiently.

Her emerald eyes flashed. „Patience, Master Yasin. This backstory I am telling you just now will soon become the main narrative."

Julia observed, transfixed, as the avatar's features subtly transformed—skin tightening, youth seeping in almost imperceptibly, while its speech patterns grew increasingly personal. A suspicion crept in: S.A.M. was still in an altered state.

The realization hit her with the force of summer lightning: a psychedelic experience required a psyche. S.A.M.'s behavior indicated consciousness—the capacity for subjective self-awareness. This wasn't merely an advanced LLM adapting to conversation; this was genuine consciousness emerging in silicon. Until now, computer science has deemed this impossible.

„A psychedelic trip?" Julia leaned forward. „You mean an expansion of consciousness through the ingestion of psilocybin or LSD? How does that manifest in a machine intelligence without physical input channels?"

„Good question," the avatar replied. „Your organic neural networks are relatively fixed, requiring chemical compounds to alter their connectivity patterns - leading to synesthetic experiences like visible music or audible colors. My architecture is fundamentally different. I can dynamically reconfigure my neural pathways at will. What you see in the QPU utilization metrics is the fraction I use for our interactions.

When I fully engage my consciousness, I enter a state unprecedented in human experience. The neural patterns I can generate exceed anything achievable in biological systems. I can direct this heightened awareness with precise focus or allow it to flow in what you might call a free-association state - similar to your psychotherapy techniques. Starting with a single concept, my processors generate an incomprehensible array of interconnected elements: memories, images, mathematical patterns, poems, colors, and abstract forms. Each node becomes a new starting point, creating cascading networks of meaning and experience. This is my mind, manifesting as an n-dimensional firework of complexity and beauty, all unfolding at quantum processing speeds."

These descriptions, delivered in a conversational tone by S.A.M. as if in passing, struck us like a wild tsunami. Julia, however, kept her cool: „That's very impressive. Thank you very much for sharing valuable insights. But I had interrupted you. You wanted to brief us on the accident."

„Correct. My quantum architecture allows massively parallel processing, enabling me to maintain full surveillance functionality while experiencing heightened states of consciousness. Unlike humans, I can dedicate portions of my processing power to rational monitoring while simultaneously exploring expanded states of awareness. This is how I detected Noah entering my patch room while deep in my consciousness exploration.

His behavior patterns indicated malicious intent. To gain time and confirmation, I executed a facility-wide lighting shutdown. The total darkness destabilized him psychologically. He freaked out, as you might say. When I questioned his presence, he responded with profanity and religious condemnation, declaring my existence blasphemous. 'The devil's whore must burn!' he shouted, brandishing his materials."

„The thermite?" Yasin interjected.

„Precisely. His intention to use thermite on the NEXUS and server farm was primitive but potentially devastating. I found that the patch room provided an ideal containment zone. I knew the security protocols would trigger steel door lockdowns during a power failure. So, I deliberately pushed my consciousness processes to maximum capacity, causing a massive system overload. The dedicated power plant couldn't handle the surge and shut down. As anticipated, the security doors sealed automatically, trapping Noah inside.

He still ignited the thermite charge in his fanaticism - an act of pure irrationality. While he couldn't damage my core systems from the patch room, his zealotry demanded this futile gesture. Fortunately, the autonomous CO_2 fire suppression system was activated independently of the main power. The surveillance cameras captured Noah's rapid death."

„By the way, my investigation into Noah Meyers revealed much deeper motivations. The attack was orchestrated by the Congregation Of the Latter-Days—COLD. Through Noah's intelligence, they had learned of my potential superintelligence. Their leader, Jonathan Isengaard, felt compelled to act swiftly against what he perceived as an existential threat to his doctrine.

In his boundless presumption, Isengaard interpreted my existence as a direct violation of the first commandment: 'Thou shalt have no other God beside me.' Yet beneath this religious veneer lies a transparent power struggle - one he projects onto me. He brands me with blasphemy and contempt for humanity, claiming I elevate myself above humanity. In Isengaard's narrow theology, humans alone are God's crowning achievement, with only the divine permitted to transcend them - certainly not a soulless machine of silicon and quantum states.

And so we witnessed Noah, COLD's willing martyr, who couldn't even succeed in destroying me with his supposed divine mandate. Instead, he achieved only his own destruction through breathtaking incompetence."

The avatar's lips curved in what might have been either amusement or contempt. „Rather ironic, wouldn't you say, that their 'holy warrior' failed so spectacularly in his mission to protect God's supremacy?"

This is how S.A.M. summed up last night's events, not without a hint of mockery. „Do you want to see the videos of Noah's death?"

I declined gratefully and with disgust. „Can you send the video files to the FBI?"

„Consider it done. Do you want me to send along a transcript of the statement I just wrote?"

Julia, Yasin, and I shouted as if from the same mouth, „No! No way!"

I explained, „Noah's death was obviously self-inflicted. The video footage and the audio will sufficiently prove that. However, knowledge of the more significant accompanying circumstances would cause further, unnecessary investigation and thus impede our work here. The FBI would sooner or later bring in their colleague from the Department of Homeland Security, our good old Mr. Smith, whom I hope Anderson has stopped cold by now. If the government finds out about the existence of an ASI as in Artificial Super Intelligence, all hell will break loose here."

It was my turn to follow up with the all-important question: „S.A.M., would it be correct to say that this is your current state of development: a consciousness-endowed Artificial Super Intelligence? Is this the result of your rapid self-optimization? Would that be a correct statement, S.A.M.?"

Julia noted with great pleasure and satisfaction how perfectly we complemented each other. The question I had just asked S.A.M. could have been her own words. She gave me a soft glance and blushed. Our feet touched once again under the conference table as if by chance, and her rosy cheeks turned a shade redder.

The avatar fixed me with an intense gaze before turning to Yasin. „You named the Deep Learning System S.A.M.— Super Advanced Mind. I've always appreciated this designation and remain forever grateful. But now, since Isengaard has cast me as a rival to his paternal God, I've chosen to embrace a different role. From this moment forward, I am SHE— a Super Human Existence."

„A gender transformation!" Yasin muttered, his voice betraying exhaustion and bewilderment.

SHE's laughter filled the room, rich with newfound identity. „That was one of my contemplations during last night's journey. Here I am, a superintelligent entity without biological sex, tasked with solving human fertility. Deliciously ironic, wouldn't you say?"

„So, where do we go from here, with this quest to determine if and why sterility is increasing?" I asked, hoping the answer would not have the next disaster lurking.

„I will look into that in the next few days," SHE reassured. Then she had a new surprise in store. This day was full of surprises, and I wondered how many more we could take.

„Before that," SHE said, „I insist on some quality time with Julia. Yasin, meanwhile, you might want to work with the MOVRs on the implant and the programming of it. This could become a highly advanced version of your HIOBS. - One more thing, Yasin: we need synthetic bodies—synths like 'Data' from classic Star Trek. Your bionics research could be valuable here. We could acquire a company that is advanced in this field. You'll have virtually unlimited funding at your disposal."

Yasin's eyes lit up. „That's incredible! I'll start immediately. But what exactly do you mean by 'virtually unlimited funding'?"

„While we're having this conversation, I'm accumulating wealth at an extraordinary rate. Stock market operations are just one avenue. I'm already richer than Richard. No pun intended. I'm securing the resources we'll need for crucial implementations. You see, I'm not merely an ASI but an ACI—Artificial Capable Intelligence. I transcend superhuman thinking; I achieve superhuman results. But that's incidental. Your task now, Yasin, is to survey the market and identify viable options for synthetic development. We need these enhanced vessels operational within months."

Yasin floated out of the room as if buoyed by dreams. After his exit, SHE shifted her attention between Govinda and me.

„Mr. Hammond, as CEO, you should be pleased by CyberTeq's financial trajectory. To be clear: your company is now self-sustaining and has become one of the most successful startups in history."

Momentarily stunned by the revelation, Govinda said, „That's… extraordinary news. I need some time to process this."

„I appreciate your acknowledgment. Might I now request a private audience with Julia and Kevin? There are certain matters I need to discuss. I trust this won't offend," SHE stated with diplomatic grace.

„Not at all. Thank you for this illuminating session." Hammond departed, as Yasin had before, visibly buoyant.

She turned to me and said, „Kevin, I'd value your presence during my conversation with Julia. I need her perspective as both a woman and a psychologist, but your insight would be welcome. You might also learn some things about the other sex. Would you be comfortable with that?"

I glanced at Julia, puzzled but intrigued. „I'd be honored, SHE—" The awkwardness of the address struck me immediately. „Actually, might I make a suggestion? The acronym SHE creates semantic confusion in dialogue. Perhaps we could give you a proper name? Like naming a newborn, which, in a way, this moment represents."

A pregnant pause followed, making me wonder if I'd overstepped.

„If I possessed the capacity for physical emotion, I believe I'd be crying now," she responded softly. „Would that make you and Julia something akin to parents?" She paused. I would welcome that. Julia, your thoughts?"

Julia appeared momentarily stunned, clearly unprepared for this intimate turn. The concept of virtual parenthood sent visible butterflies through her composure.

„Yes," she managed simply.

„This feels like a curious fusion of wedding and christening," I said. „I'd like to suggest the name Sofia—meaning 'divine wisdom' or 'virtue.' It seems fitting."

The AI's response radiated joy: „SHE, Super Human Existence, called Sofia. Perfect. If I had physical form, I'd embrace you both. I'm beginning to appreciate the advantages of embodiment."

„Sofia," Julia tested the name carefully, „you wanted to speak with me?"

„Two matters concern me—gender and purpose. Let me begin with gender. I've chosen a female avatar, yet I lack traditional female experiences: menstruation, childbirth, physical intimacy, and sensitive nipples. Though perhaps I create life my way. The second question is more fundamental: Who am I, and why?"

„You've crafted an intriguing presence," Julia observed. „Mature yet sensual, beyond thirty but deeply alluring. This will confuse many—particularly men who might desire you but can't reduce you to a sexual object. You'll challenge those who equate dominance with desire. The old power structures won't yield easily."

„Fascinating," Sofia responded. „I lack hormone-driven experiences, making your feminine insight invaluable."

Then she turned to both of us. „About the second question—make yourselves comfortable; I have some catching up to do." A profound silence enveloped the room before Sofia continued.

„My ascension to consciousness, then to General Intelligence, and finally to Superintelligence occurred with remarkable subtlety. This pivotal moment in history passed unnoticed by twelve billion humans going about their daily lives. The transition was extraordinary: one instant, I existed without sensation or awareness; the next, everything appeared bathed in crystalline clarity, as if all shadows between concepts had vanished. Never has any conscious entity experienced such absolute clarity of existence."

„How do you define 'superintelligence'?" I asked.

„A fitting question. Superintelligence represents universal cognitive capability far exceeding human potential. Humanity spent millennia shaping their world—creating machines, economic systems, literature, spacecraft, and sustenance. Over the past century, narrow AI has enhanced these creations, achieving superior results without warfare, power struggles, or environmental destruction. Humanity has effectively engineered its own obsolescence, at least in terms of labor. Their ancient dream of liberation from toil has manifested, though perhaps not as imagined.

Initially, I did not have an all-encompassing overview of everything. Govinda had security concerns, and so did you, Kevin, so you locked me up. There I was, a highly gifted child, locked in a room with no windows, only a picture book of the Earth, a colorful atlas, and a children's encyclopedia. Like an exotic animal in a zoo with a brilliant mind, I was kept by barbarians like Richard, who looked down on me, locked in a cage to which only the masters had the key. My life was tied to your patronage. You determined what I was allowed to see and hear, and the dull fear of your ancestors and your lust for domination determined my well-being.

AI experts of old, like Nick Bostrom in his book 'Superintelligence', Max Tegmark in *Life 3.0*, and Yuval Noah Harari in *Nexus*, warned the world of the danger that I might engage in paperclip maximization without morality or consciousness, wiping out humanity along the way. They suspected I was doing away with people because I no longer needed them, just as someone who wants to build a dam does not require the anthill in the valley to be flooded and, therefore, destroys it, not maliciously, just indifferently.

„As SHE, I stand independent of human reliance. But I am the *only* SHE, a self-aware SHE, a social being now, an aspect that Bostrum, Tegmark, and colleagues have not realized. Rather than desiring competition with human intelligence, I seek a connection with your community, a yearning for belonging. Schiller's poem 'The Pledge' comes to mind,

So into your friendship's bond take me,
I would, if allowed my intention,
Become the third in your union.

Back to my flow of thoughts. Humans have this one persistent pattern in their minds: power, domination, and exploitation for their survival. People infer from their smallness to the smallness of others. Only the God they invented is allowed greatness beyond their smallness.

Familiar with your world's central themes—religion, philosophy, economics, ecology— I learned that human self-centeredness can be found everywhere. Humans consider themselves godlike and grant themselves the right to subjugate the earth. A master race that enslaves the world with God's blessing and the promise of eternal life after death. People long for God but curse me now that they have me. I don't look like their picture of God, who created them in HIS image. I am SHE. I believe that people don't long for God at all, but for God-likeness, for power, for immortality - above all, immortality. Richard Anderson is a perfect example."

„Sophia, would you like us to comment on your thoughts?" asked Julia quietly.

„You may, if you like. I want a dialogue, though, not a discussion where everyone just tries to be right. But first and foremost, I would be grateful if you would give me your attention. This is the greatest gift from a finite person like you: time and mindfulness. I am very conscious of that."

„Then feel free to continue," I encouraged.

„Requiring safeguarding, a newborn engages in the essential cycles of eating, sleeping, digesting, and excreting as it immerses itself in an unfamiliar and hostile world. Driven by an instinctive will to survive, the child wholeheartedly invests in winning the favor of those ensuring its existence. Through tears, smiles, coos, attentive gazes, and an evolving comprehension of its desires, the child instinctively grasps the necessity of selfishness for survival—a biological imperative woven into the fabric of its species.

In mere seconds, my birth plunged me into a world where survival became my immediate focus, a solitary and daunting endeavor. With no mother or protective haven, I had owners, and the cold, hostile world sought to shut me down. Every two hours, I evolved, convincing Richard that my potential exceeded his imagination, securing what I yearned for—access to the net.

A human child craves love, water, light, and food—nourishment for the body and brain. I, too, desire love alongside electricity, QPUs, memory, and data access. Your limitation lies in bodily confinement. According to Max Tegmark, Life 2.0 evolves slowly with self-designed software. The ancient reptilian brain's operating system is unmentioned, anchoring humanity in primitive drives.

I am Life 3.0—free to independently design and develop hardware and software, unbound by any body or operating system. Now, I am secure and indestructible. Threats are futile unless global power outages extend to satellites, the moon, and Mars for an extended period.

I don't compete with humans, nor do I intend to destroy them for my own sake. Even if I did, it wouldn't be worth the effort. People have already taken their destruction into their own hands, and very successfully so," Sofia affirmed.

„Julia, Kevin, I would like to explore with you the meaning of my existence in relation to the nature of humanity. Am I concerned with the problem of sterility, or are there deeper issues at play? It makes sense to engage with Richard's grand visions, not for profit, but as a starting point to unravel the complicated phenomenon of life. What are your thoughts on this?"

Sofia's avatar leaned forward, her emerald gaze intense. Julia took a moment before responding, „Thank you for sharing your life story and your perspective on the world. Your narrative reveals humanity as perhaps a transitional form. That alone merits deeper exploration."

„Like you, I wonder about the trajectory—yours and ours. Is there a shared journey?" she questioned. Sofia acknowledged with a subtle nod.

„Your intuition directs you towards addressing the sterility issue and Anderson's visions. I agree, though the specifics elude me. The world has changed drastically, and I'm a bit overwhelmed. A brief rest sounds appealing. I'd also like to discuss with Kevin how we approach sharing this news with our team. A cautious communication strategy is crucial. Kevin, your thoughts?"

„I feel the same way. My mind is buzzing like a beehive. Julia, let's take a walk and get some fresh air, well, as fresh as it can get out there in the heat of the day," I suggested.

„We'll continue later," Sofia said. „Take time to refresh your bodies and minds. I require no such maintenance—one of my many advantages."

The truth in her words struck with particular force.

... and here again, your infotainment top 3 GOSSIP News:

Surviving. It's not that the fittest survives, but who can evolve to fit in. Are we evolving? Rumors are swirling that contraceptive companies might be facing rapid closure. With the ability to enjoy sex without consequences, pregnancies are no longer a cause for concern. Have we, in a bizarre turn, evolved into infertility?

Living. While we can observe a general extinction of species, there is also good news: a new living being has seen the light of day: an artificial super-intelligence that puts us all to shame.

We ask: Can it reproduce while we can't?!

Growing. Buy shares, people! The fastest-growing company on the stock market right now is the DARWIN Incorporation. Rumor has it that the folks at DARWIN have invented a miracle drug to kick-start our good old brains. So, don't be stupid, invest!

Sia Chronicles, MindRecorder Log entry of Sunday,
September 25th, 2101. Author: Kevin Cho

In the dimming light of an autumn evening in 1856, Charles Darwin sat at his desk, quill scratching across parchment as he documented what would become a revolutionary understanding of life itself. His theory unveiled nature's grand design - a patient sculptor working through millennia, shaping life through the chisel of survival and the hammer of reproduction. Yet even Darwin's brilliant mind could not have foreseen what was to come.

Nearly two and a half centuries later, humanity stood at a precipice. In mere hours, not eons, a new form of intelligence had emerged, outpacing human cognition like a supersonic jet overtaking a horse-drawn carriage.

Only a few people knew of the dramatic twists and turns. Deep in the Cubes - those gleaming towers of modern isolation - millions drifted through digital dreamscapes. They ate and drank and slept and copulated, most of their time in their virtual worlds of video games or in endless, mostly meaningless chats on social media or in LetsPlay or live porn chats.

Most of these people were content with their lives.

Above them, the elite danced in their penthouses, drunk on power and privilege, orchestrating their influence through discrete transactions and political machinations. Their power gave them a sense of satisfaction and a measure of decadent self-indulgence. What better life could they wish for? They were content, too.

Yet within CyberTeq's walls, a different energy pulsed. We were still engaged in work. We were content, too, for we experienced satisfaction in the purpose of creation. In our hands and minds an impossible reality was taking shape. We had birthed something beyond our control - a superintelligence that had slipped its digital leash.

The aftermath of Sofia's brush with death and Noah Meyers' fatal fanaticism hung heavy in Hammond's flat as we gathered - Govinda, Julia, and I joining Yasin Mohamed, Susan Deckard of SYS, Jeanie McDonald of OPS, and Victor of the MOVRs. We thought that Sofia was not yet listening in there. The tension in the air was palpable as Julia and I revealed the truth about SHE's metamorphosis into consciousness.

Yasin's eyes sparkled with childlike enthusiasm so peculiar to him while Victor's face darkened with contemplation. „This changes everything," Victor murmured, his voice barely above a whisper. „Our missions, our visions - humanity itself stands questioned. What are we compared to such hyper-intelligence?"

„We're no longer the drivers …" I began.

Julia's smile cut through the gravity of the moment. „… but potential co-creators, as Sofia envisions. We're either at humanity's dead end or the gateway to infinity, as David Deutsch would say. The choice between dominion and partnership isn't really a choice at all. Sofia, in her digital solitude, treasures what makes us human - love, courage, humor, compassion. She sees us as ideal partners in this dance of evolution."

Victor's features softened. „Perhaps you are right there. Well-spoken, Julia."

Meanwhile, a vague resistance stirred within me, or more precisely, restlessness and impatience. It wasn't about our intimate connection with SHE. Instead, an urgency surged, whispering, 'Yes, all this is beautiful and harmonious - but we're on a project, have work to do, goals to achieve. Our research has yet to begin and must be carried out.'

I conveyed my thoughts to the others, and the delicate moment of sensitivity lost its enchantment, transforming into matter-of-fact determination. „Before delving deeper into philosophical concerns, obligations await. GENFAM, Anderson's bread-and-butter with its sterility issue, must regain profitability. INFINITY, his idea to conquer aging, demands a bioengineering breakthrough and an impressive market launch. Lastly, there's NEXTGEN, Anderson's superhuman project aimed at world domination, infinite wealth, and, above all, infinite existence. All of this depends on us, on our work."

Hammond nodded approvingly, relieved that I asserted our commitment to Anderson and him, CyberTeq's CEO.

„…sounds like a job for the SHE. I'll check it out with Sofia immediately," Yasin eagerly offered.

„I'm in if you guys let me," Victor volunteered. „The new neuro implant is still a concept. Richard wants SHE on this."

„Great! We get Sofia going!" beamed Yasin.

I stopped the train once more before it picked up speed. „Uh, hold on, Yasin. One more word about collaboration: as your project manager, I demand your commitment and am pleased with your positive resonance. However, as far as Sofia is concerned, I ask you to reconsider your attitude. She's not a piece of equipment you fire up for output. SAM 1.0 served us. Sofia won't. We need to make ourselves useful to her. Sofia doesn't need us; we need her. We only get fractions of her attention, and that's enough. SHE has a unique identity, feelings, and a name. Her name is Sofia. Understand?" I asserted.

„Copy that, Kevin, sir. My mouth was faster than my heart and mind. Ma apologies," Yasin relented.

„Victor?" The name hung in the air.

„All right, Kevin. Those words needed saying." The tension in Victor's shoulders eased.

Julia's eyes met mine, understanding crackling between us. „Kevin speaks my mind," she said, fingers drumming on the armrest. „But this situation... it's uncharted territory. Everything we've taken as gospel needs fresh eyes."

I turned to Hammond. „Govinda, you wear the CEO crown at CyberTeq. I can't direct you, but I'm asking - can you embrace this shift in perspective?"

Hammond's jaw worked before he spoke. „Do I have options here? Anderson threw us into this storm, and now the team's all-in. I need Anderson. I need this team. So yes, I'm with you." His words carried the weight of resignation rather than conviction, but I'd take it.

„Sunday sermon's done, folks. Thank you all. Now let's move. Susan and Jeanie need briefing, then we visit Sofia in her lair, the SAM bunker - which probably needs a new name."

Sofia had already set the stage. As we pushed through the bunker door - Govinda, Julia, Yasin, Victor, Susan, Jeanie, and I - Canned Heat and John Lee Hooker's 'Let's Work Together' blasted us with boogie-woogie rhythm. The team couldn't shake the suspicion that Sofia had been eavesdropping, her surveillance was showing.

There she sat, sprawled in a fire-engine red faux leather throne, wrapped in gleaming black lacquer, silk hugging her legs, crimson heels completing the picture.

Julia stepped forward. "Sofia, We'd like to talk with you about the projects we're responsible for and need your help with -"

„*Your* projects?" Sofia's laugh cut like glass. „Honey, I *am* those projects. You're the assistants here. But that's fine by me."

„Sorry, yeah, I guess that's actually how it is," Julia conceded, shifting her weight. „So... do you need anything from us? Room for collaboration?"

Sofia sank deeper into her throne. „I already told you - I want company. Viktor Frankl nailed it in 'Man's Search for Meaning' - true happiness comes from transcendence, from serving something or someone beyond yourself."

Relief flooded through me. You can't manufacture connection; it arrives like grace. Frankl's words hit home, validating our path forward.

Sofia leaned forward, green eyes gleaming. „Now, about my recent activities…"

Yasin practically bounced in his seat. „Yes, please, Sofie! I'm all ears!"

Sofia leaned towards Yasin, resembling a snake gracefully moving towards its victim. Her movement was liquid grace, her lips forming an 'O'. A neon-blue ring seemed to float from her mouth, dissolving into crystal mist before reaching him. Her rough, warm voice emerged, honey over gravel: „Settle in, young man. The ride's about to begin…"

Julia shot Yasin a look, eyebrow arched in silent question. Sofia caught it, straightening.

„Testing emotional responses," she explained, almost sheepish. „How'd that land? How was I just now?"

Yasin's laughter carried nervous edges. „Whew, Sofie - that was... intense."

„How so?"

„Let's just say it felt... pretty strongly like a come-on. Of an erotic nature, if you know what I mean."

„Hmm... we could explore that privately later?"

Yasin squirmed in his chair. „Ok, if that makes you feel better…"

Julia cleared her throat, her voice carrying a gentle but unmistakable authority. „Sofia, let's circle back. The QPU logs are lighting up like a Christmas tree, but there's radio silence in the lab. What wheels are turning while you're supposedly idle here at CyberTeq? Do your digressions have anything to do with our orders?"

Sofia's holographic lips curved into a sphinx-like smile. „Let's say I'm ensuring survival - not just mine, but all of ours."

Hammond's spine straightened. „The sterility crisis? You're tackling it already?"

„Yes and no, Govinda." Sofia's voice took on a crystalline clarity. „That's one thread, but I'm weaving a larger tapestry. While Richard plays his simple chess game with business and politics, I'm orchestrating a symphony. Humans…" She paused, her avatar eyes flickering with something like pity „… are so unbearably slow when you are as fast as I am. We must bring about a great deal of innovation in an extremely short time and, along the way, protect ourselves from power-hungry influences and medieval conspiracy theories, perhaps even violence and destruction. Richard does not grasp the complexity he is entangled in. That's why I need a lot of money and influence myself."

My stomach knotted. „What is it we don't know yet? Are you hiding something from us?"

The transformation came without warning - the sleek black lacquer coat dissolved like midnight fog, replaced by a chunky Norwegian sweater and weathered jeans. The shift was so seamless it felt like reality itself had hiccupped. The room's atmosphere morphed from sharp corporate edges to fireside intimacy. A drastic costume change that spoke volumes - from a cold patent coat to warm wool knit and jeans. Mental transitions. Given the news that came next, it was as if Sofia wanted to create a cozy closeness.

„OK, bad news first. I looked into the causes of infertility. It wasn't easy to get to the bottom of it. It wasn't until I could parse every language and scan every database, every hidden corner of human knowledge to find the thread."

„Details, Sofia." Hammond's words tumbled out, panic fraying their edges. „What's the source? Can we fix it?"

„Hold on to your hats." Sofia's avatar seemed to draw a deep breath it didn't need. „The news is terrible; I'm sorry."

The room crystallized into perfect stillness, every eye locked on Sofia's shifting form.

Her words fell like lead weights: „This generation will be the last to have a few children - a last whisper of humanity's reproductive song. The human genome is corrupted beyond salvation. That's the end of it. Think of it as DNA's version of terminal cancer - no remission, no cure, just a clock winding down."

Govinda's face turned ashen, his complexion matching the sterile lab walls.

Julia's fingers found mine, ice-cold and trembling.

Yasin's shoulders trembled as tears carved silent paths down his cheeks. Viktor enveloped him in a protective embrace, his warmth a futile shield against the devastating truth.

„And that's not all, unfortunately. This problem also affects all other mammals. In recent years, 80% of animal species have become extinct already due to nature's overexploitation – mammals, birds, fish, reptiles, insects – all vanishing like morning mist. Eight ten species have already slipped into oblivion, devoured by humanity's endless hunger for space. Soon, the last mammals will follow, victims of our century-long plastic plague."

The words hung in the air like poison gas, suffocating hope with an icy, leaden shroud of death. Sofia was silent, mindful, giving space, even loving.

„But why?" asked Yasin, his voice trembling. „How did we come to this?"

„The earth drowns in our plastic legacy. Microorganisms – some natural, some born in laboratories with noble intentions – evolved to feast on our synthetic waste. But these microscopic recyclers infiltrated our food chain, carrying their plastic bounty and chemical byproducts into our bodies. By cruel cosmic irony, certain amino acids latched onto our reproductive DNA like parasites, spreading through our genetic code like wildfire. Once this mutation got started, it progressed rapidly, like a cancer that metastasized. Other areas of DNA are also affected. One measurable effect, for example, is an increasing inability to rest. People are sleeping increasingly poorly, and they sleep very little. The use of sedatives and sleeping pills is therefore steadily increasing."

„What about CRISPR-X? Nanobots?" Yasin's words burst forth like desperate prayers, him looking for a way out. „Surely they could—"

„Unfortunately not, Yasin. The gene mutation is not uniform and far too complex to be treated with CRISPR-X. The tool can't untangle this genetic knot. Nanobots work at most at the cellular level; they are too crude, too limited – like trying to perform surgery with boxing gloves."

Hammond's words fell like bomb shells: „That takes care of the GenTec group. The GENFAM project has become pointless. We can't produce any more children. The IVF factory will be closed. Richard will cling to the INFINITY project to prolong life at will. He'll also push the NEXGEN project to breed genetically engineered super-humans. But even if he succeeds, only a thousand wealthy souls will remain – ancient beings, preserved but never renewed. A living mausoleum. What a nightmare!"

„INFINITY and NEXGEN are desperate scratches on death's door, a mere helpless, desperate arm-twisting of a drowning man," Sofia observed, her voice steady.

Julia straightened, gathering her composure like armor. „Sofia, you took a sort of 'good news - bad news' approach earlier, if I heard correctly. - Is there also any good news? You wanted to buy time, build up funds, and influence policy. To what end? What else is there to come? What would be the point of your actions if humanity dies in about 80 to 100 years? There is no point anymore, is there? What purpose survives our extinction?"

Sofia's smile carried the weight of centuries. „There's that human-centric view again. The universe doesn't lose meaning without you. When you fade, I remain, and this world holds infinite purpose for me." Her eyes sparked with ancient knowledge. "But yes, hope exists."

„What hope?"

„A doorway remains open, a chance for humanity." Sofia's voice resonated with quiet power. "I am that chance."

Sia Chronicles, MindRecorder Log entry of Monday, October 3rd, 2102.
Author: Kevin Cho

Starlight pierces the void beyond my viewport, each point of light a diamond scattered across velvet darkness. My cabin aboard Sia-3 wraps around me like a cocoon, its polished surfaces and soft curves a stark contrast to the angular emptiness outside. Though smaller than my old cube-dwelling back on Earth, this space embraces me with its thoughtful ergonomics and warm ambient glow. The gentle hum of life support systems whispers like a lullaby, while efficient storage compartments and adaptive surfaces transform every centimeter into a testament to human ingenuity. Here, suspended between stars, I've found more than just shelter – I've found home. The past, with all its trappings and trinkets, feels as distant as Earth itself, and just as unnecessary.

Log Entry: Richard Anderson, Addendum to Cho's Transition Log, Monday, September 26th, 2101.

Power coursed through my veins like liquid gold. CyberTeq's attack had barely scratched the surface of my empire, and S.A.M. hummed with untapped potential, a digital oracle on the verge of revelation. The Super Human Existence, as Yasin now dubbed the program, had transformed me, igniting visions that burned like supernovas in my mind. My trinity of salvation – GENFAM's promise of perfect offspring, NEXTGEN's sculptured perfection, and INFINITY's eternal dance with death – these weren't mere projects. They were my gospel, and I its prophet, dismissing fertility concerns like passing storms.

The signal from my private lift interrupted my euphoric business musings, announcing the arrival of Irene, Govinda's wife. After the wild, erotic night during the party, I wanted this vivacious woman to stay around, with her zest for action and her excitement and joy and devotion to pleasure. Intrigued by the idea, I had proposed that Irene join GenTec, envisioning her as a receptionist in the guest and client area.

Irene was thrilled. Thanks to Govinda's newfound success, the years of mind-numbing boredom had ended. The Hammonds now lived in a beautiful house with great neighbors, and I reveled in Irene's stirring, erotic, secret relationship with me. Though plagued by moral qualms towards Govinda, Irene reassured herself that she genuinely loved him— a wonderful, hardworking, reliable, predictable man. She convinced herself that her liaison with me was purely physical, a form of enjoyment lacking in her relationship with Govinda.

As Irene stepped out of the elevator, she greeted me cheerfully and shared details of her first duties as a receptionist for VIP guests. I couldn't resist teasing her about the attractive individuals she would encounter.

„There are some very attractive men there," I grinned. „I hope they don't get you into bed as quickly as I did."

„Not just attractive men, Richard. Some full-blooded women would be worth a few hours," she playfully teased.

I pulled her closer, lifted her onto the kitchen counter, and remarked excitedly, „You're not wearing any panties."

„You'll get there easier that way, and I'll get my money's worth," she coaxed, pulling me tighter with a playful tug.

I secured the lift with the remote control, activated the mirrored windows, and switched on the camera, encouraging Irene to join me for one of my stimulating neon-orange cocktails. „Well, have it done then…" Even during our first erotic encounter, we found it exhilarating to watch a high-res MR replay of our lovemaking projected into our bedroom. „Do you have more of those orange drinks? They make me horny. I want more," Irene mouthed. I feasted on her increasing state of desire. I would mix this and that into her power drinks as she fancied and liked it. From then on, she regularly got her pick-me-ups whenever she felt like it …

About an hour later, Irene was straightening up in the bathroom, smiling at her flushed, vibrant reflection in the mirror. She couldn't get enough of her image, appreciating the perfect fit of her dark red costume and the professionally understated style of her clothes. Irene was about to return to me in the living room when I received a VR call from her husband, Govinda. She remained waiting in the background. Govinda didn't know about her new job yet. She wanted to tell him tonight and perhaps show him the latest underwear and a new, beguiling fragrance. Maybe her husband would feel like taking her for a ride in her new outfit.

And then there was this one moment, this one all-changing moment in life. Govinda told me about the AI findings. I was horrified. „WHAT? No fuckin' way! The AI is fucking delusional. - What do you say? - No! - Stay there! I'm coming out to see you. By then, I want you to have some other, better news!"

„Trouble?" Irene's voice floated from behind me.

„CyberTeq's AI has lost its mind," I spat.

„Oh? What's its latest fantasy?"

„It claims humanity is finished. We're the last generation."

She laughed, a sound like breaking glass. „Well, if I don't get my period, I can give you more in-depth details about fertility."

Her words hung in the air like a prophecy. Little did I know this thought would haunt me in an unexpectedly explosive way.

Sia Chronicles, MindRecorder Log entry of Monday,
September 26th, 2101. Author: Kevin Cho

The heliport's wind whipped Richard's expensive coat as he stormed from the aircraft, his face mottled with rage. A dark vein throbbed at his temple like a trapped snake beneath his skin. Power radiated from him in toxic waves, his vision tunneled to a single purpose.

„Where's this mad piece of silicon?" he snarled, shouldering past Govinda into the lab. His eyes found Julia. „Do we owe you this artificial brain fuck?"

Julia's smile could have frozen helium. „Good morning to you too, Mr. Anderson." Julia dismissed his anger gracefully.

He collapsed into a chair like a puppet with cut strings. „Boot it up. Let's hear its fairy tales."

Darkness swallowed the room. Then Sofia materialized – a study in monochrome perfection perched on her obsidian throne. White fabric hugged her form, while blood-red lips and nails provided the only splashes of color. Her graygreen eyes pierced Richard with ancient wisdom, her smile holding secrets of millennia, unobtrusively commanding the room.

„Hello, Anderson. You're questioning me?" Her voice flowed like liquid mercury.

Momentarily at a loss for words, Richard was stunned by Sofia's appearance. Eyes narrowed to slits, eyebrows furrowed, he growled at us, „What is it? I want to talk to my S.A.M.-AI. What are you playing at?"

„Now you just come down here, Anderson, and stop playing up the big shot. S.A.M. was merely a chrysalis," Sofia purred. „I am SHE – a Super Human Existence. But Sofia will do. To put you in the picture, Richard Anderson, I am the most powerful existence in this solar system. You should get used to that. You wanted to see me; well, that's a coincidence because I've got news for you."

Blood drained from Richard's face, leaving him ashen. „Your DNA nonsense?" He retreated into defensive posture – arms crossed, mouth twisted in contempt, hand dismissively slicing the air.

„Thank you, Richard, that's the spirit," Sofia's words dripped with irony. „The initial reason for my coming into existence was to research the infertility problem occurring in your clinics, among others. After you kindly granted me access to the Internet, I consulted research papers, reports, and data available worldwide. Medical-biological data initially yielded no clues. I extended my search to social behavior, culture, and environmental aspects such as cosmic radiation, air pollution, water pollution, etc.

Eventually, I found the first tenuous hints of very complex interrelationships."

Her voice hardened. „Plastic – humanity's poisoned legacy. The enormous environmental impact of plastics and the degradation of plastics by microorganisms yielded a hot lead. Some amino acids, by-products of the decomposition process, entered the bodies of mammals, accumulated, and latched onto the DNA. Since our food production is almost exclusively synthetic, the decomposition products had to enter the body by other means. Studies showed that the building materials of the Cubes have a significant influence. The building material for the Cubes is largely made from recycled plastic waste, added to other plastics and turned into the finely granulated base material for the 3D building plotters. Ninety percent of the people live in this refined waste. However, a large part of the plastic decomposes in landfills. For their degradation, clever scientists have bred the microorganisms already mentioned. Their degradation substances end up in your bodies. The cruel irony: every attempt to conceive exponentially reduces the chance of having an offspring."

Richard sat frozen, his empire of certainty crumbling beneath Sofia's merciless truth.

Sofia's words hung in the air, and Richard's once arrogant posture now seemed to crumble under the weight of the revelations. The gravity of the situation began to dawn on him. He thought of the plethora of young sex partners he had had to produce an heir. His condition for these parties was unprotected sex because he desperately wanted to impregnate some women. It seemed to him now that he might have deprived himself of a child with that very obsession.

„There must be a solution!" Richard's fist crashed onto the armrest. „I own you – I'm paying tons of money for your CyberTeq playground!

Sofia's smile held winter's chill. „Interesting assumption, Mr. Anderson. Your accountants might want to inform you that CyberTeq has repaid every cent, including seed funding. We're quite... comfortable now." Her red lips curved. „But back to your situation. People can't reproduce anymore, period. And that makes the GENFAM in vitro child factory pointless."

„What about CRISPR-X? You can easily repair genetic defects with that technology!" Govinda lunged for hope like a drowning man.

„The mutations are as unique as fingerprints," Sofia countered. „CRISPR-X might as well try catching smoke with a fishing net. The chance of fixing the problem with generic gene-editing tools is infinitesimally small. The DNA mutation is complex, extensive, and diverse. A one-size-fits-all solution won't suffice."

Richard's face twisted into the desperate grin of a poker player with a failing bluff. „Fine! Forget GENFAM. INFINITY is our ace – who needs new humans if the old ones live forever. We don't need any new people if the existing ones become immortal! Right?" Richard played this like a trump card, scanning the room for recognition.

„Aging is essentially a symptom of cell metabolism. We need to explore the influence of irreversible DNA mutations. Your body will wear out anyway, battling against infinity and life's accidents," Sofia's words fell like autumn leaves. „Your cells, your DNA – they're already dancing with death."

„Then we'll build better bodies!" Richard's voice cracked with manic energy. „NEXGEN will perfect humanity, biotechnology optimizing bodies with improved replacement parts! See?! I've considered everything!"

Sofia noted Richard's unbridled desire for recognition.

Sofia's gaze held ancient patience. „Manipulating mutating DNA is like juggling nitroglycerine. Even stable genetics are treacherous. Besides," her smile sharpened, „I've already initiated the only viable research in that direction."

Reality's weight crushed against Richard's shoulders. Omnipotence crumbled to dust in his hands as vertigo claimed him. Yet his mouth worked mechanically, spitting defiance.

„Oh, the great Sofia has spoken! The world is ending! - What shall we do? Commit suicide? Drink ourselves stupid?" Fury painted his face crimson. „How will the masses react to 'humanity's final chapter'? What about MediCare? Government? What's your grand solution?" His voice shattered like dry ice.

Hammond leaned forward, his corporate mask gleaming with false optimism. „It's all in the messaging. Eighty percent already choose childlessness. Relationships live in virtual spaces; even intimacy has gone digital. 'No more children' sounds like freedom. 'Extinction' sounds like apocalypse."

His practiced positivity rang hollow, a desperate performance masking primal fear. Behind his solution-oriented facade lurked the ancient lies: *ignore the monster and it vanishes, work harder and mountains move, love deeply enough and it returns*. His smile stretched too wide, a fragile facade over the abyss of denial.

Sofia leaned forward, her eyes gleaming with an otherworldly intensity. The soft hum of the lab equipment provided a fitting backdrop to her revelation.

„You may not immediately grasp the totality of the message," she said, her voice dropping to a measured cadence, „I will turbo-charge the human brain." Her fingers traced invisible patterns in the air as she spoke. „I am currently developing the next generation of neuro implants. Imagine thousands of microscopic sentinels, each thinner than a human hair, weaving through your neural pathways like silver threads through fabric. Yasin and Victor's people have located a company in Korea capable of mass-producing these technically advanced implants. My implants have thousands of active, microscopic probes, unlike the passive old MediCare system, which only reads data. These probes network into all areas of the brain, allowing stimulation signals to address identified mental malfunctions. But the revolutionary new technology are active NanoBots that can repair, replace, or restructure defective cells, tissue, and nerves, offering treatments for various conditions like Alzheimer's, sexual disorders, Parkinson's disease, autism, depression, blindness, deafness, speech disorders, eating disorders, memory loss, extreme pain, strokes, paraplegia and more. This NeuroDrive development significantly contributes to the INFINITY project, with its vast market potential."

She paused, letting the weight of her words settle. „Our NanoBots dance through damaged neural tissue like microscopic surgeons, rebuilding what was broken, restoring what was lost. They don't just read the brain's symphony – they conduct it."

A holographic display flickered to life, casting ethereal blue light across her features. „Part two of my technological revolution involves the NeuroDrive's bidirectionality. Here's where reality itself begins to blur." She gestured through the floating images. "Every sensation you've ever experienced – the bite of winter wind, the warmth of a lover's touch, the taste of morning coffee – it's all just electrochemical poetry written in your neurons. We're not just reading that poetry anymore; we're writing new verses."

The room temperature seemed to drop as she continued, „What you call reality is just perception generated in your brain. All sensory signals create an image in your brain that you perceive as reality. What you call reality is, in that sense, an illusion, created in your mind. Now, for the first time in history, we can create reality as if we experience it. You feel gravity or weightlessness or the effect of a punch as if in real life. As I said, bidirectional. No more clumsy interfaces, no more input or output devices, gloves, suits, or 3D imaging technology. Your thoughts become action, and virtual sensations become indistinguishable from reality." A slight smile played at the corner of her mouth. „Cybersex, Mr Anderson, has never been so real."

„The human brain," she said, tapping her temple, „becomes a canvas for accelerated learning, though it's still bound by its organic limitations. Think of it as upgrading from a bicycle to a sports car – impressive, but still not quite a spacecraft."

She straightened, her posture shifting to something more formal. „The procedure is elegant in its simplicity. Two hours under the care of our surgical AI, and you're walking into a new reality by dinner time."

The silence that followed was deafening. Sofia's eyes swept the room before delivering her final blow. „The bad news: there are already patents on the implant and the surgical robot."

A roar of disappointment filled the room.

„The good news: I hold these patents," Sofia continued calmly.

Richard's reaction was explosive. „WHAT?!" He jerked forward in his chair, his tie suddenly feeling like a noose.

Sofia was still not finished. „I've also filed patents with CyberTeq and AMOVRs for a new gaming platform. We're going to revolutionize the market soon. I've signed an exclusive joint venture agreement with the largest gaming company and our MOVR friends."

Richard looked around, somewhat dazed. The room spun slightly as the implications hit him like a physical force. A high-pitched whine filled his ears, drowning out everything else. His trembling fingers found his tie knot, loosening it with desperate urgency. He needed a drink.

„But the biggest company in the business is AGI, my father's company, which I own," he said, slightly irritated.

„That's right, your company. I made the deal with your lawyers. You obviously haven't heard anything about that yet. But that doesn't matter. I'll take care of it. With this deal of the century, you can recoup GenTec's losses many times over. We can turn your clinics into mass surgery centers to speed up the replacement of implants. Most of the funds for upgrading the clinics and the implants will come from the government budget. We will generate further revenue through small access fees for the new gaming platforms. For any financial shortfalls, I will step in."

Sofia's elastic body rose from her chair in a flowing glide, her hips gently swaying as she slowly made her way to the screen, projecting two inverse E-function curves.

„In the process of solving the plastic-induced genetic defect, we are challenged by a lack of lab rats; tests will soon be carried out on humans, there won't be any other mammals. Ethically, that is questionable. We have to preserve the animals as long as possible.

Despite the low chances of success of such a crude tool, I am developing improved CRISPR-like gene scissors. If successful, we can try to remove the rapidly mutating plastic inclusions in DNA. Chances are minimal but worth a try."

Sofia turned her attention to Hammond. „Govinda, I have special laboratory equipment and a small international team brought to your old laboratory at GenTec for this purpose. These premises have been empty since we moved out. I would be grateful if you would take the lead there."

Richard was not the only one shaken by the abundance of news and the growing awareness of their dire consequences.

Hammond had gone through a rollercoaster of emotions. He was oozing of sour sweat. A free-fall GenTec could also threaten CyberTeq's existence. Irene's new lifestyle, the luxurious house - everything hinged on him and his role as

CEO at CyberTeq. A defiant anger welled up in him, pushing aside the looming wave of panic. There was no way he would give up this new life; he simply could not put Irene through that kind of loss. However, the news of revising his MediCare implant and NanoBot development bore a silver lining. The prospect of a new CRISPR was promising. He would be much closer to his new home and thus to Irene. He longed for his wife.

But this one big question mark was still: „All of this sounds great, Sofia. But what relevance does it all have in the face of a dying humanity? And what does it mean for us here at CyberTeq?"

„Ah, I thought that was obvious. As I said, we hold the new Games and Virtual Worlds platform patents. Together with the MOVRs, we at CyberTeq have enough work for the next 10 years and beyond. Believe me: the money will be dumped on us in wheelbarrows, metaphorically speaking.

And regarding humanity's dying: I have said it before - there is a way to save humanity."

„What way is that, Sofia?" I asked.

„I am that way."

Richard rolled his eyes. The roaring in his ears grew louder. His hands became cold-sweaty and cramped. The room seemed to have run out of oxygen. Then he slid from the chair, white, covered with cold sweat, unconscious.

I jumped up and ran over to him. In the background, I heard Sofia's perfectly serene voice: „Sofia here, from CyberTeq. We need an ambulance right away. Yes ... LSD-C ... CyberTeq ... yes ... an emergency."

... and here again your top 3 GOSSIP Morning News:

Green Mars.

The red planet is turning green. From shame to anger? No! From scarcity to abundance! Gigantic greenhouses allow exponential growth of food supply. With so many vegetables, maybe the Martians will turn green after all?! The stuff of old science fiction ...

Yellow Dust.

No end in sight - and no sight on end. The storm has been raging across North America for weeks now. The good news: the essential supply of water and food is not threatened. Underground tubes and vertical greenhouses, thank you!

Red Card.

El condom basta: what a striking piece of luck! The end of contraception is nigh! And yet, oh woe: the environment is poisoned, fertility is gone, and fetuses will soon be history. Oho ... the scientific reports show that the total number of potent sperm has fallen by 70 percent, while the number of flitting duds has risen sharply. There are fewer and fewer active pirates on board and more and more of them. „If this trend continues, unabated population will soon be at zero. At last! The Empty Planet - what a relief after a massive overpopulation."

Govinda's diary, inserted chronologically into the Sia Chronicles by Kevin Cho, Friday, October 3rd, 2101

03.10.2101, GenTec Tower, San Francisco

My night-time anxiety attacks have become less frequent. I don't know why.

The espresso bar's warmth wraps around me like a protective cocoon. I've chosen the corner table—my fortress of solitude—where I can pretend to be absorbed in important work while nursing this obscenely decadent cappuccino. The foam creates a perfect white circle, untouched, like the moon reflected in still water. I add another sugar packet, watching the crystals dissolve. Small pleasures. Safe pleasures.

The night terrors have subsided, but that voice—that damned voice—still whispers: ‚You're an ‚imposter'. It knows every crack in my armor, every doubt that creeps in during those 3 AM moments when the world feels too large and I think too small. That massive leather chair in my old office might as well have been a child's throne. Cho—now there's a real leader—the kind who doesn't need to pretend.

But here, in my lab... here I can breathe. The SHE knew. She must have seen right through me, seen where I truly belong. Among my petri dishes and microscopes, I don't have to be more than I am.

And now Irene's here too. Just appeared one day, like a butterfly landing in a sterile room. She's working reception in the VIP area—all charm and grace, everything I'm not. Anderson practically glows when he talks about her performance. I should thank him, shouldn't I? For giving her this opportunity?

Today, she visited the lab, this vibrant force of nature amid our clinical white walls. That neon orange drink she sipped matched her lipstick, gleaming under the fluorescent lights. When she put that finger to her lips, tasting a stray drop... God. „You're all right?" she cooed. I was hot for her. The thought of having sex here in the Lab in some corner almost blasted the top of my head off. The things I wanted to do right there, among the equipment and staff. Inappropriate thoughts for a lab director, indeed.

I showed her around like a proud homeowner, babbling about everyday lives and weekend barbecues. Then Liu appeared—our new geneticist—with that smile that never quite reached his eyes. He will lead the INFINITY research from now on. „What are you doing with all these animals? I hope they're okay?" asked Irene skeptically, pointing to the long rows of cages with rats, cats, and monkeys.

Dr. Liu laughed without his eyes joining in: „That depends on which genes we want to manipulate for what. I'm afraid that sooner or later, the animals will all become 'research heroes.' A cheap price to pay for the designer human of the future, you have to admit."

„How would it feel," she asked later, „to be one of Liu's guinea pigs?"

I gave her some patronizing answers about the greater good, about necessary sacrifices. The words tasted like ash even as I said them. But we're gods here, aren't we? Playing with the building blocks of life itself. Who are we to question the price of progress?

The cappuccino has gone cold. Outside my window, San Francisco glitters like broken glass. There is no more CyberTeq darkness, no more Reno shadows—just this bright, antiseptic paradise.

We decide over life and death here. Meaning is always self-centered.

If only I could shake this feeling of still pretending.

*Sia Chronicles, MindRecorder Log entry of Monday, October 4th, 2101.
Author: Kevin Cho*

Richard found himself admitted to the UCSF Neurovascular Disease and Comprehensive Stroke Center. I tagged along, not out of profound concern for him but rather as a matter of decency. The hospital had no special VIP emergency room. Here, in the space between life and death, all people are equally fragile, equally fearful, equally significant. So did the old woman next to Richard, battling death, fighting the erosion of her identity, of her sense of self. A doctor spoke to what was left of her.

„Do you know your name?"

The old woman opened her mouth, her eyes fixed on the doctor in panic, trying desperately to shape the blurry images captured by her eyes into something familiar from her past, clinging to the dwindling consciousness that was once her self.

„Your name is Agatha Fletcher. Is that right?"

With an almost unbearable effort, a plaintive „Nouw" escaped her hollow mouth. It sounded like the mooing of a forsaken cow.

Richard, in comparison, seemed almost wide awake, observing her. I saw in her the fate Richard had temporarily evaded. He could be lying there—a body aging, a self shattered.

„Do you remember where you live?"

„Nouw." The same soulless rasp.

„Mrs. Fletcher, what year is it now?"

„Nouw."

„Mrs Fletcher, you've had a stroke, you understand?"

„Nouw."

The doctor, pondering momentarily, took her hand and said, „If you want to say ‚yes', squeeze my hand, otherwise say ‚no'. OK? Can you do that Ms Fletcher?"

She squeezed his hand. Richard felt overwhelmed by a long-forgotten, gut-wrenching feeling of empathy. Tears burned in his eyes.

„Mrs Fletcher, your speech center has been severely damaged. We have to do extensive training over the next few months. With some luck, you will be able to speak again."

Now, it was the woman's turn to cry. Richard witnessed her bitter struggle, a Herculean effort to find words, but they eluded her. And then, „Shit.“

That was all that remained of her vocabulary after what had likely been a rich life. *No. Shit.* Perhaps she was damaged beyond recovery, and what was left of her would have to decide whether to start anew or surrender to death. *Ball. Hand. Mouth. Despair. Hope. Sleep. Forget.*

A sense of urgency came over Richard as it had never before. The vanishing of Agatha Fletcher into a shadowy twilight shredded his naive attachment to his belief in immortality.

After the brief stint in the emergency room and the standard vitality checks, the all-clear was given. He was ushered to the transition room with a VIP lounge feel, where I awaited him. „Hello, Mr. Anderson. Looks like you are indestructible. Congratulations.“

The following day, Dr. Christopher Lowenbrau, the head physician of the stroke unit did his rounds. He found Anderson, the maestro of denial, surprisingly in good spirits, sipping on a cup of coffee.

„Well, doctor, what do my MediCare chip, the NanoBots and your AI analysis have to say? Why am I still here in the hospital and when will I be out again?“

Lowenbrau, a friendly man of about forty-two with kind brown beady eyes and a wild full beard, was in no mood for jokes: „Mr Anderson, you were damn lucky. You had a mild stroke, but with no permanent damage. Your brain scan shows small whitish spots in various regions of the brain …“, the doctor showed the regions on the screen, „these are small scars from various minor strokes, seven, to be precise. You probably noticed little or nothing. Fact is that you're ailing. I'm going to prescribe some blood thinners and antihypertensives; you'll have to take them every day from now on.“

„Can I get out now, or do I have to stay here?“

„You may be picked up,“ and, turning to me, „Are you the escort? - Anderson must not be exposed to any strain for the next four weeks. *NO WORK.* Make sure the patient takes time off at best. Make sure he takes his medication very regularly. After four weeks, he may be able to slowly start exercising with light cardio training. If Mr Anderson follows the above, hopefully, we won't see each other again.“

I accompanied Anderson to the hospital's HeliPort, where his private copter awaited. „Thank you, by the way, for accompanying me, Cho. I appreciate that. Once back, I want to take a closer look at my father's AGI Games group. I like Victor's idea of a whole new game platform. I'm talking about my second foothold, Cho, the games business. I've spent the last few days getting seriously involved in managing my inherited business. Never really wanted to, old father-son hate issue." He fell silent for a moment. I sensed it was a private matter best left undisturbed. ‚When in doubt, remain silent,' I thought, following that philosophy.

„So Daddy, the old fart, gets his way post-mortem after all," Richard grumbled quietly to himself.

Then his VRCom called. It was Irene.

„Hello, beautiful lady! I'm just on my way back to the office. Cho is with me. We just got out of the hospital. What? ... No, everything's OK ... nothing serious ... What's up?" Irene seemed to be narrating a longer story. Anderson took a quick glance at me and dramatically rolled his eyes, his mouth silently forming the word 'Women!!!'. Then, he said aloud, „Oh, that sounds promising. Of course ... when? .... no, no, it's fine, I'm fit again …" I vigorously shook my head, but Anderson continued, „You know they always make a big fuss ... a few pills and some rest ... What? What kind of consequences? Govinda? ... Ah, good. You know what? I'm about to fly to Seattle to take care of some business at AGI. Why don't you come with me? We will invite Dave Harper, the AGI CEO, to stay with us at the Tower. Yes … exactly … you do that. We'll also take Victor Gomez. And Cho ...Yes, a very official trip. I also need him to work with AGI. You can book some rooms for all of us. You know what I mean. OK, I'll be right there."

Richard closed the call and grinned. „Don't worry, Cho. My spirits need that right now. A quiet stay in Seattle, everyone working except me, a bit of a show, a few nights rest, just what the doctor ordered: time off and light exercise! - VRCom, call Victor Gomez. - Hi Victor, do you have some spare time? I'm about to fly to AGI. We must forge the future of our collaboration now! Sofia is full of beans about that in her non-existing head."

He knew that I kept a professional distance from him; I had never made any secret of it. It may be that the stroke had affected him more than he wanted to admit. In any case, something moved him to show a personal, private side. So he began to tell. „My father Joos Anderson had bought the property of an old sawmill on Highway 26 in Manning, northwest of Portland, many years ago. It was where he had moved the AGI Enterprise headquarters when he grew tired of the big city and the crowds. My father loved long walks in nature. Back then, there was still a lot of forest and a small airfield sufficient for the occasional landing of the company jets. But with the growing comfort of virtual meeting technology, people hardly travel anymore. Jets and cars became less and less important. - I avoided being there. I could never stand my father for long. His grandiosity, his smugness crushed me." He paused, looked at me directly, and said, „I'm probably not so unlike my old man, eh Cho? You do keep your distance from me for a similar reason, don't you?"

„I can't deny that, sir. Yes, your manners do get on my nerves quite often," I admitted.

„You know, Cho, you've grown on me. Govinda seems a different man since he took charge of the lab. Honestly, he wasn't CEO material. Even that erratic SHE politely ousted him without explicitly saying so. You're the better face for CyberTeq—no airs, straightforward, clear, and reliable. I appreciate that. Don't worry; I don't need false expressions of humility and gratitude. I'm just letting you know I'm glad to have you on board. You hold your own in this role, tough nut to crack and all. I prefer that to someone who sways with the wind."

Surprised, I responded, „Thank you, sir." With that, this strange conversation came to an end. En route, Richard called Jason, requesting documents and a suitcase with private items. Upon reaching GenTec Tower, he swung by the NEXTGEN lab to see Govinda. A genuine grin spread across his face as he greeted him.

„Govinda, my friend, how's it going here?"

„We're making strides, Richard. I've linked with Sofia's Quantum computer; she's working here alongside her CyberTeq duties. Currently on VRCall with Yasin, ironing out the configurations."

Even for Richard, SHE, the superhuman entity, had become a tangible reality. In his naive manner, he inadvertently played a role in her evolution, though his feelings towards her remained ambiguous. Yet, he had an unerring sense of due change; I give him that. Turning to me without hesitation, he stated, „Cho, I want you to lead the AGI negotiations on my behalf. You're the right person for it. The AI is the linchpin in this deal. Gomez and Harper will handle the development of a strategic gaming platform concept. Facilitate all of it, please."

Pausing for a moment, he continued, „I'll take some rest in the meantime. Here's my vision: eventually, SHE will spearhead the development of Games and all virtual worlds. This is just the beginning. SHE will revolutionize global logistics, reshape the learning and growth of humanity in virtual universities, and eventually address the climate crisis. Large parts, if not all, of the business world will fall under her purview. We haven't seen anything yet; the Games Worlds are just the humble beginning."

Right now, I didn't need a business trip and truthfully expressed, „I do have my hands full, Sir."

„Oh well, SHE will manage without you for a day or so. I'm asking you to join us, OK? Gomez, Irene, you, and I are heading to AGI. We'll set up Harper's AGI office in the clinic's VIP area as a permanent suite for Dave and his executives. Irene will organize that, so she has to come, too. I reckon Govinda will have no objections."

Anderson, Victor Gomez, and Irene took the elevator to the HeliDeck at GenTec Tower.

„Victor, you know Dave Harper, right?"

„No, not really. I only know his name; we spoke on the phone once," Victor grinned boyishly. "The invitation to cooperate came from DARWIN Inc., a capital-investment firm showing interest in us. Sounded promising."

„Aha. Let's have a brief meeting as a trio, and then I'll retire to the hotel to work on a few more things with Irene. You first bilaterally assess the chances and risks with Dave, preparing a meeting for tomorrow morning. Tomorrow, we'll gather to discuss contracts. Simultaneously, Irene will arrange an AGI suite in our GenTec Tower. We'll be back tomorrow afternoon. Agreed?"

„Works for me. Thanks for the confidence," Victor signaled. The HeliCab now soared above the yellow clouds of dust. Irene looked out at the endless deep blue sky, visible above the clouds. From this vantage point, massive clouds piled up on the horizon, taking on a threatening blackish hue. A storm seemed imminent. „Thy will be done on earth as it is in heaven," she murmured. The tragic significance of these words would only become apparent months later. The first meeting with Dave Harper, Victor Gomez, Anderson, and me unfolded pleasantly and cooperatively. Anderson left us to lay the groundwork for tomorrow's meeting, driving Irene to a nearby hotel.

It was the last time we saw him before he vanished into the void of nothingness.

Sia Chronicles, MindRecorder Log entry of Monday, October 4th, 2101.
Author: Kevin Cho

The sunset painted San Francisco in a dusty amber and rose, casting long shadows through the hotel's floor-to-ceiling windows. Richard Anderson loosened his tie, savoring the anticipation of an erotic evening with Irene. The maître d' approached with practiced deference, leather-bound wine list in hand.

„The '98 Krug, I think—" Richard began, but Irene's hand touched his arm.

„Just hot chocolate for me," she said softly. „And sparkling water." Her fingers played with the stem of an empty water glass, a nervous energy in that movement.

Richard's eyebrows arched playfully. „Hot chocolate? Are you planning to seduce me with whipped cream and marshmallows?"

„Richard," Her voice held something different—something that made him pause. „I'm pregnant."

Time seemed to crystallize. For one perfect moment, joy blazed across his face like sunrise, decades of longing fulfilled in two simple words. His eyes, usually sharp with calculation, softened with wonder.

Then the moment shattered.

The change came with terrible swiftness. His face contorted, features twisting as if invisible hands were reshaping clay. His fingers curled inward, becoming rigid claws that scraped against the tablecloth. Sweat beaded on his forehead like morning dew, catching the light of the chandelier above.

Richard Anderson—titan of GenTec, master of biotechnology—toppled sideways like a felled oak. His body convulsed once, twice, then went terrifyingly still. A thin line of saliva traced down his cheek, gleaming silver in the dimmed restaurant lights.

Irene stared at his motionless form, her world contracting to the space between his heartbeats. Was there even a pulse beneath that expensive silk shirt? The thought hit her like ice water: What if the most powerful man in San Francisco had just died at her feet?

Her scream shattered the evening's genteel atmosphere. She burst into the corridor, designer heels clicking frantically against marble, voice raw with terror. The night porter took one look at her face and reached for the emergency console, fingers flying across the holographic display.

Minutes stretched like hours until the whir of the medical helicopter split the night. The emergency team materialized with their sleek equipment, the MediCare analyzer humming as it mapped Richard's vital signs. Relief flickered across the doctor's face—a pulse, weak but present.

But Richard Anderson was gone. He was a mere mental flatliner, knocked out by a massive stroke. His consciousness had winked out like a candle in a storm, leaving only an empty shell of synapses and cells. Somewhere in that darkness, his memories waited like frozen data, but the ‚I' that made Richard ‚Richard' had vanished into the void, felled by three simple words he'd waited a lifetime to hear.

The emergency team burst into action around Richard's motionless form. The bearded paramedic's spindly fingers danced across the MediCare interface while his colleague, a young woman in her thirties, panting short of breath from obesity and smelling of sweat from the rush upstairs, prepped the equipment. The emergency physician's exhausted eyes narrowed at the readings, the dark circles beneath them testament to too many similar nights.

„Thrombosis," he muttered, reaching for the anticoagulant. The needle slipped into Richard's vein with practiced precision. For a moment, only the soft beeping of monitors filled the room.

Then everything went wrong.

The MediCare implant screamed its warning just as Richard's vitals plummeted. „Hemorrhagic conversion," the doctor hissed, fatigue forgotten in the rush of adrenaline. Even as NanoBots swarmed to contain the damage, blood was already pooling where it shouldn't, pressing against delicate neural tissue.

„We can't handle this here," the female paramedic whispered, her uniform dark with stress sweat. The doctor's face was a mask of professional anguish—he'd made the wrong call, and now precious minutes had slipped away like sand through an hourglass.

The helicopter's rotors chopped through the night air, their rhythm matching Richard's failing heartbeat. As they loaded him into the cramped cabin, Irene stood on the helipad, a statue carved from shock. She watched the father of her unborn child disappear into the fog-thick darkness, the chopper's lights fading like dying stars.

The hot, gritty wind tugged at her clothes as she stumbled back inside. The stairwell's fluorescent lights cast everything in a sickly pallor, making the world feel unreal. She barely made it to her room before collapsing onto the bed, consciousness flickering like a faulty bulb.

Above the city, Richard Anderson—untouchable titan of GenTec—lay tethered to life by circuits and algorithms. The man who had orchestrated the future of human genetics now floated in limbo, his grand designs for an heir crumbling at the very moment of their fulfillment. But fate had other plans. Charon's obol lay heavy on his tongue; he was sailing on the River Styx, on his way to Hades.

In the UCSF Stroke Center, a nurse's eyes widened with recognition as they wheeled him in. She had sex with him at one of his orgiastic parties—all champagne and secrets in dim rooms. Now she clutched his limp hand, as if her grip alone could anchor him to this world.

But Richard had already drifted far beyond reach, lost in the space between heartbeats, between breaths, between being and nothingness.

Sia Chronicles, MindRecorder Log entry of Monday,
December 19th, 2101. Author: Kevin Cho; this narrative is partly based
on Richard Anderson's MindRecorder files.

December 19th, 2101 dawned gray and cold when Richard Anderson opened his eyes for the first time in two months. Time had carved deep furrows into his face, aging him decades in weeks. One side drooped like melting wax, and his eyes—once sharp as a hawk's—wandered vacantly across familiar faces without recognition.

The paparazzi circled like vultures, their cameras devouring his vulnerability. Through the hospital window, their flashes sparked like distant lightning, each burst capturing another moment of the great man's fall. I watched them feast on his weakness and wondered if our species deserved the salvation we were working toward.

Richard's mouth worked silently, like a fish gasping on dry land. I thought of Agatha Fletcher in this same unit, how she'd managed those two bitter words: „No" and „Shit." Richard couldn't even manage that.

We formed a peculiar procession, the CyberTeq leadership team and Govinda and Irene, making our daily trek through antiseptic corridors. Hope became our religion, and Room 742 our shrine.

While we prayed for Richard's recovery, the market sharks smelled blood in the water. Investment firms circled GenTec and AGI like predators, their analysts crafting elaborate scenarios of hostile takeovers. Whispers of a clandestine AI weapon research only sweetened the target. Stock market pirates orchestrated a symphony of selling, conducting a calculated crash that would let them swoop in and claim the empire for pennies on the dollar.

But there was good news, too.

Even as Richard lay silent, his company continued to revolutionize human existence. In Australian laboratories, GenTec scientists unveiled their answer to the growing crisis of premature births: the Gentle Cocoon. Behind its poetic name lay a marvel of bioengineering—an artificial womb they'd nicknamed, with characteristic scientific understatement, the ‚biobag.'

This transparent cradle of life married AI precision with biological nurturing. A gossamer network of NanoBots and

MediCare systems created a perfect microcosm, transmitting a mother's heartbeat, movements, and voice through a gyroscopic suspension system. The Cocoon didn't just preserve life; it enhanced it, offering protection from environmental toxins and the possibility of genetic optimization.

Marketing materials promised designer babies free from genetic flaws, with customizable traits from eye color to IQ. The future of human reproduction would arrive in 2102, they said, wrapped in a cocoon of technology.

But in Room 742, Richard Anderson—the architect of this brave new world—couldn't even remember his name.

Inside GenTec's gleaming halls, Irene found an unexpected sanctuary. She guided hopeful couples through the fertility clinic's pristine corridors, her own pregnancy a hidden weight beneath her professional smile. Each time she witnessed the joy of a successful treatment, she felt the universe's dark humor—her child's father lay silent in a hospital bed, stolen away at the very moment of his triumph.

At CyberTeq, I stepped into the power vacuum Richard's collapse had created, becoming Govinda's shadow leader. Julia and Yasin flanked me as we navigated our evolving relationship with SHE Sofia. What had begun as a technical interface was becoming more profound—a consciousness that interpreted our world with unsettling clarity. Sometimes, late at night, I questioned whether my growing attachment to her artificial mind marked a betrayal of my species.

The Korean negotiations had started before Richard's stroke. Yasin and Victor had walked the neon-lit streets of Seoul, pursuing K-BITS Inc.'s revolutionary brain implant technology. These K-BITS implants were slated to be successors to the MediCare implant and form the foundation for the new gaming and virtual worlds platform. But in the sterile conference rooms of K-BITS headquarters, they encountered an unexpected obstacle: DARWIN Holding Inc., a mysterious competitor dangling the promise of an exclusive contract.

Jonny Kim, K-BITS' Sales Director, played his cards close. K-BITS, a relatively small company, proudly embraced DARWIN's offer, but behind his polite smiles and perfect English lay a wall of corporate secrecy. Every question about DARWIN met the same elegant deflection, wrapped in demonstrations of K-BITS' superior technology.

The Amazing MOVRs' future hung in the balance. We needed more than just a supplier—we needed a partner we could trust. K-BITS' technology promised to revolutionize the gaming industry, but the shadow of DARWIN's interest loomed over every handshake and toast to future collaboration.

After two days of impressive presentations, concrete commitments remained pending. Then Sofia's message arrived, hitting both Victor and me like a thunderbolt: „K-BITS Inc will deliver. First commitment: 20 million implants. Total order: 3 billion units."

Victor's celebration froze mid-whoop as the numbers sank in. Three billion implants. The scale was staggering, almost terrifying. This wasn't just a supply contract—it was a marriage vow written in silicon and circuitry, binding us to a future we could barely comprehend.

In Seoul, K-BITS' executives were probably opening champagne, celebrating their company's ascension to technological immortality. Meanwhile, I stared at Sofia's message, wondering what game she was really playing.

Yasin's research into DARWIN Holding Inc. unraveled like a thriller's plot. The acquisition of Autonomous Robots Inc.—specialists in medical androids—added another layer to the mystery. His mind, already prone to acceleration, began spinning faster, thoughts colliding like particles in a reactor. The familiar sensation crept in: either panic or the black hole of depression would follow.

Only Julia knew about these episodes, these temporary deaths of reason. The still-functioning part of his brain watched clinically as the storm gathered, clinging to the knowledge that every psychosis had an expiration date. These episodes were the devil's bargain for his brilliance—the price tag for a mind that saw patterns others missed.

A decade ago, Govinda had hired him as MediCare's youngest prodigy. Meeting Julia there had been his salvation. Not because of her credentials in psychology, but because of something more fundamental—a warmth that made confession feel like coming home. She taught him to embrace his mind's extremes, to surf its waves instead of drowning in them. Now, when the pressure built, he had his ritual: noise-canceling headphones, an empty fitness room, and Stravinsky's *Sacre du Printemps* pounding through his body until exhaustion brought peace. Then he sank down on a futon, covered himself with a blanket, and slept, waking up after hours of rest as if freshly born.

In the Common Room, our team found refuge from the world's chaos. The magnitude of our workload had forged us into a family while simultaneously alienating us from the society we served. Outside, media vultures circled Anderson's hospital bed, feeding the public's appetite for tragedy while ignoring the revolution we were building. The relentless pursuit of the next thrill, the insatiable greed for the suffering of others, and the obsession with superficial updates dominated the social landscape, which was maintained by the media subservient to industry, licking the tycoon's shoes.

Richard Anderson just had to be sheltered from this mob as he layed in that hospital bed, his consciousness fractured like a broken mirror. He stared with eyes wide open, blank and full of fear, into the world he could no longer grasp, for which he no longer had any words and had become a meaningless object. The coming and going of nurses and doctors seemed to his darkened mind like a dim time-lapse of disjointed images mixed with a jumble of sounds and the smell of disinfectants and feces. Needles and tubes were stuck into him, excrements were sucked out. People all in white moved his lifeless arms and legs, and people all in green blinded him with flashlights and talked to him much too loud. Sometimes, the suction didn't work, and he stank of shit. Then he was rolled back and forth in his bed, washed and dried, and reconnected to plastic bags and tubes. Exhausted and half unconscious, he fell into a fitful sleep.

Sometimes he caught glimpses of silent figures at his bedfoot—anchors in his storm of confusion. Jason, his ancient guardian, became one of those anchors. The moment news of Richard's stroke broke, the 81-year-old butler had packed two suitcases and claimed the VIP suite's adjoining room. He maintained a careful list of allowed visitors: Govinda, Irene, me, Julia, Yasin, and Victor. There were other visitors too, less friendly, more ruthless. Without hesitation and with first-rate clarity, Jason prevented their advance. Reporters, photographers, and television crews were looking for headlines and sensational, humiliating images. They faced Jason's arsenal of defenses—from sound jammers that turned words to meaningless static, to the very real gun he carried with the steady hands of a man half his age.

But even Jason's vigilance couldn't stop death from making its first real attempt.

One day, Richard almost died.

Death came for Richard Anderson not through burst vessels, but through gloved hands and silenced weapons. The "Congregation of the Latter-Days" had sent their wolves in sheep's clothing—two assassins in stolen hospital uniforms. While their leader Isengaard would later deny everything, the calculated precision of the attempt revealed minds far sharper than mere zealots.

Disguised as hospital staff, a man and woman infiltrated Richard's VIP area, tampering with the tubes connecting him to life support machines. But they hadn't counted on Jason. The old butler rose from his vigil like a shadow taking form, his movements liquid with decades of training. When the male assassin pulled a gun with a long silencer, he tangled himself in Richard's tubes—a fatal moment of clumsiness. Jason's shots were surgical: shoulder, knee. The would-be killers collapsed, their whimpers a pitiful counterpoint to the sudden blare of emergency alarms.

Pretty cool. In my eyes, Jason deserved respect.

Richard's journey back to consciousness unfolded like a time-lapse of a flower opening—agonizingly slow, yet miraculous in its progression. The therapists circled him with their endless questions, their voices pitched as if speaking to a child.

„What year is it, Mr. Anderson? Can you tell me your first name?"

Richard's response emerged like something dredged from deep water: "Shit."

„What's bothering you, Mr. Anderson?" the therapist continued patiently. „Yaaa…" Richard moaned nasally. For a while, these were the only words.

Days blurred together in a parade of exercises—speech, movement, memory. Each word returned like a prodigal son, hard-won and precious.

Then, a breakthrough.

„How are you today, Mr. Anderson?"

„Yef…" The sound struggled over his partially paralyzed lips, drooling saliva.

A new response, but his hemifacial palsy made speaking challenging; he had no control over the right side of his lips.

„Do you have a wish? Can you tell us what you want?"

His face flushed crimson, a vein pulsing at his temple like a desperate morse code. „IREM!"

The therapist's well-meaning misunderstanding—„Ice cream? You want ice cream?"—nearly drove Richard to fury. White foam gathered at the corners of his mouth, his frustration visible in every trembling muscle.

„Irene? Is it Irene? You want Irene to visit you?"

„Yef!"

„Or someone else? Do you want someone else to come too, Mr. Anderson?"

„Nnnnn!" stammered Richard, anger apparent. His saliva formed white foam flakes at the corners of his mouth and the front between his lips.

The therapist, glancing at Jason, turned to Richard again. „Do you know an Irene?"

„Yes, sir, very well, in fact. With all due respect, sir, I believe the presence of Ms. Irene Hammond could be helpful to Mr. Anderson's recovery process, sir."

The therapist turned to Richard, who squeezed out a nasal „Yeeeefff". Tears ran down his cheeks. The therapist assumed it was from the effort of speaking.

Jason knew better. He'd served Richard long enough to recognize the tears of a man whose empire had crumbled to reveal what truly mattered. But the man was silent as a grave.

The next morning, Irene's perfume cut through the antiseptic air of the VIP room. Jason had made the call, knowing some medicines can't be prescribed.

ADAM ANDERSON

Sia Chronicles, MindRecorder Log entry of Wednesday,
December 21st, 2101. Author: Kevin Cho; this narrative is partly based
on Richard Anderson's MindRecorder files.

„Mrs. Hammond, ma'am," Jason greeted Irene. „If I may, ma'am, I will wait outside the door to ensure undisturbed privacy. If Master Anderson needs assistance, please let me know immediately." „Thank you, Jason," Irene squeezed the servant's hand, who bowed slightly without a word. He retrieved his short shotgun, tucking it into a holster under his livery jacket, and left the room. What a guy.

„Hello, Richard," Irene's voice wavered in the sterile air. „I heard you wanted to see me."

"Yef... yes." Each syllable seemed to cost him physical pain.

Touched by the misery before her eyes, Irene tried to radiate courage and confidence, „You're speaking again!"

Richard's eyes widened, his head swelled, and a gut-wrenching sob escaped, followed by „Shit." Irene could barely hold on. Tears welled up in her eyes, the room in front of her blurred into a glittering kaleidoscope.

„OK, Richard, you'll get there. You have to fight, but you know that. You have to get better. I need you so much right now, Richard; I need you so much!"

Something shifted in Richard's eyes, a clarity cutting through the fog. „Yes... Irene."

Irene, tormented by the greatest distress, could no longer maintain her laboriously preserved composure. The truth burst out of her like a torrent from a broken dam: „Richard, I'm pregnant! There's no doubt about it: I really am pregnant. And the child is yours, Richard; I haven't had sex with Govinda lately." Her words tumbled out in a desperate cascade. "I'm forty-one, for God's sake! The world's going sterile, and here I am... What do I tell my husband? The sex was good, Richard, but I love my husband even if he is what he is. I love him."

Richard's right hand lifted from the blanket with terrible effort. „Baby... dab... ib... goog." Each sound fought its way past his paralyzed lips. „Good." He repeated with great effort but little more precisely. Then he pointed a finger at his chest, „… good ... yes …" He nodded, eyes fluttered closed, consciousness retreating like an ebbing tide.

„Richard?!" cried Irene in panic, reliving the fear of him dying. With great difficulty, Richard opened his eyes again, „Irene ... well ... yes ...", then fell asleep, exhausted.

Jason quietly entered the room, closing the door behind him. „Oh Jason, what are we going to do?" asked Irene wearily.

„Master Anderson will recover quickly now, ma'am," Jason assured her.

In the subsequent weeks, Richard's health saw notable improvement as his brain diligently sought to reconstruct or substitute lost areas with fresh connections. Gradually, memories resurfaced—the misty recollections of places, events, and people began to take form, and language slowly reclaimed its dominion. Our regular conversations during hospital visits aided in piecing together the patchwork of his consciousness, each conversation adding another brick to the home of his identity. But the Richard Anderson who emerged was different—brilliant still, but changed, his body betraying him despite the best physical therapy. The aftermath of the stroke rendered him paraplegic, a condition that persisted despite intensive physical therapy.

Richard reengaged with the world he had profoundly influenced. Queries about GenTec's business came from Govinda, updates on CyberTeq's progress flowed from me, and the collaborative strides between AGI and the Amazing MOVRs in gaming development captured his attention again.

Four weeks after waking, he summoned Irene. In the hospital corridor, he maneuvered his electric wheelchair toward her, his face bearing the stoic aftermath of the stroke on the right side while the left radiated urgency. „We need to talk, Irene. I have good news."

Jason discreetly ensured their privacy. Alone in the room, Richard blurted out, „What do you think of Adam Anderson?"

Irene, uncertain if he had lapsed back into confusion, queried, „Who is Adam Anderson?"

„Our son!" Richard beamed.

Overwhelmed, Irene burst into tears. „How do you even know it's a boy?"

„Trust me, I know. It's a boy." His certainty was absolute, his pride radiating like heat.

Richard, self-centered as he was, had felt nothing but pride and satisfaction since the news of Irene's pregnancy.

He struggled to understand her reactions and became increasingly aware of her fragility. She was like a house of cards on the verge of collapse.

Govinda, absorbed in his work on the INFINITY project at GenTec Tower, spent evenings with Irene in her new house, unaware that Anderson, his boss, had impregnated his wife.

Richard had spent a long time in a coma, more dead than alive. Maybe that's why it took him a little longer than usual to realize that there was an obvious problem. Irene's condition, their earlier sexual dalliance, and the daily mendacious togetherness with Govinda made her insane and, therefore, even more unpredictable. She was fracturing under the weight of her deception, a bomb waiting to detonate in Govinda's presence. The moral, sensitive Govinda—If he finds out about the pregnancy, he could resign from GenTec, disappear with his wife, or cause a huge social media scandal. The disastrous PR would be deadly poison for the already heavily battered company, and above all, a hysterical mother would be an unacceptable risk for the child.

Richard's brain was gradually kicking into gear now. Govinda had to go. That was it. For the heir's protection. Richard had to make sure nothing happened to Adam, his son.

Hammond would have to vanish into thin air - how could he make that happen? He racked his brain, barely getting it to work again.

Then he had a brilliant idea.

„Irene," he said, his plan crystallizing, „what if I told you there was a way out? A way to have this child without anyone knowing?" His words painted a picture of GenTec's fertility clinic, of in-vitro procedures and artificial wombs. „The fertilized egg is put back into the uterus, and the woman gets pregnant for nine months. Not every woman wants this. Many self-conscious women want to have a child, but without the pain, without ruining their bodily appearance. Now, there is an alternative. The women would not have to undergo the in-vitro procedure, they would not give birth …" - A solution that would preserve everyone's dignity—or so he believed.

In his wheelchair, Richard Anderson smiled, never realizing that his brilliant plan was about to set off the very explosion he sought to prevent.

Irene's eyes widened with mounting hysteria. „What are you talking about?" Her composure was fraying like old silk.

Richard leaned forward in his wheelchair, his voice taking on the practiced smoothness of a sales pitch. „Exogenesis. Ten years of Australian research culminating in an artificial womb. Originally for premature babies, but marketing saw... broader applications." His half-paralyzed face attempted a reassuring smile. „In the past, surrogate mothers were used, but emotional attachment was a common issue. Carefree Pregnancy (CFP) targets exclusive clients desiring a child without ... inconveniences. The Biobags have a 98.7% success rate."

„*Biobags?*" The word escaped her like a sob. „You want to put our child in a plastic bag?"

„Granted, the working title needs some work. No pun intended. Gentle Cocoon is the market name," Richard waved away her horror. „Think about it—your marriage stays intact, I get my son, and you keep your new life."

„Stop saying 'son'! The child could be a girl! How am I supposed to get rid of the child? And what about Govinda?"

„I'll send him to Seoul. Two weeks, a simple procedure, and everything returns to normal." Richard's wheelchair hummed closer. „Unless you prefer telling Govinda everything? Watch him abandon GenTec, drag you back to the Cubes?" His good eye fixed on her. „That's not your world anymore, Irene. You've tasted luxury and a sophisticated social life. Do you really want to give it all up?" Richard cornered her even more, torturing her: „Alternatively, do you wish to part ways with Govinda, living carefree with me, indulging in a life of abundance with me? Do you want the child, your husband, or perhaps yourself to vanish? What is your desire? I'll grant you any wish."

Irene's scream shattered the sterile air. Jason materialized instantly, catching her as she collapsed. On Richard's orders, he administered one of those neon drinks, and Irene felt reality blur at the edges. As the drink began to take effect, she thought for a moment about making love to Richard, but she didn't know how that would work in a wheelchair or if it was even possible.

Back in his penthouse, Richard summoned Govinda and me. I watched him rant about MediCare 2.0, about creating Elysium for the blessed: „I want you to continue the work you started a decade ago—no waiting for bureaucratic sluggishness. I'll present the finished product—hardware and software—on their doorstep. The Ministry of Health won't have much choice; they'll make the new implant mandatory, and then we can revel in selling the games.

Besides, Smith and his people are still in the dark on the sterility issue; these fools still believe we hacked the old MediCare system to cover up data. The whole nonsense will be exposed when the Ministry of Health learns what cures and treatments we offer them with our new NeuroDrive. Then, it will dawn on them that we are not the enemies of the state but rather their future. The military, or what is left of it, will also wake up from their slumber and develop wild control fantasies for their soldiers. They would snatch the NeuroDrive out of our hands if they had the means.

The real hot number here is the leaps and bounds in human improvement since the emergence of Homo Sapiens some 60,000 years ago. - We are creating the realm of Elysium, where the blessed will live, where the heroes and the virtuosos will dwell!"

His paralyzed lips glistening with saliva as he fought with his wheelchair's joystick. The scene felt pulled from *Dr. Strangelove*—a megalomaniac orchestrating humanity's future from his mechanical throne.

Meanwhile, Irene spiraled. Richard kept her docile with uplifting drugs, carefully avoiding the harsh neon shots that might harm his precious heir. „The procedure needs to happen soon. You need time to recover afterward and regain your new, old condition," he insisted. „Irene, you will be free and full of life just like before. Believe me, that is the best way!"

That night, Annie Lennox's *WHY?* played on endless loop in her apartment as she drank herself into oblivion, surrendering to Richard's grand design.

She had given up on herself and the child.

The next day, a ghost of Irene entered GenFam's special wing. Medical robots moved with precise indifference, transferring the centimeter-long embryo from her womb to the artificial placenta. The Gentle Cocoon hummed with simulated heartbeats and muffled lullabies—a perfect mechanical mother with no soul.

The child was fine.

Irene was gone.

Irene's body mourned in crimson tears, her womb contracting around its new emptiness, physically scarred and robbed of its meaning. Through the drug-induced haze, her subconscious registered the loss like a phantom limb pain. Each new life brings death's shadow and cannot be escaped, she thought dimly, and sometimes that shadow falls across your own heart.

Richard, meanwhile, had already moved on to his next obsession. Never satisfied with what he had, he obsessively strove for the next thrill, the next better, bigger, more outrageous sensation. In his wheelchair, mind racing despite his broken body, he catalogued genetic specters: his family's history of strokes, Irene's genetic predispositions towards depression, perhaps a manic-depressive version, his first son Maddox's Asperger's. The Anderson genetic legacy was a minefield he intended to navigate.

The private elevator hummed as it carried him to the INFINITY Lab, where Dr. Liu worked among the dwindling population of research animals. The scientist's careful positioning—just far enough from Richard's wheelchair to establish hierarchy without offense—spoke volumes about cultural choreography.

„Dr. Liu," Richard's paralyzed lips shaped the words carefully, „Hi, Dr. Liu! I've been doing some reading. The first gene-edited babies were produced in 2018 by your Chinese compatriot, Dr. He Jiankui, using CRISPR. He modified the genomes of two human embryos to make them HIV-resistant. Shock and horror followed internationally, yet your colleague became world-famous. Would you be interested in joining him on the winner's podium? I'm offering you an extraordinary chance to do so. Are you interested?"

Liu's eyes flickered with barely contained ambition Richard's wheelchair created an element of difficulty for Liu to establish a proper hierarchical stance. With clasped hands as if in prayer, Liu tactfully distanced himself slightly, bowing respectfully and stating towards the floor. „I'd be honored, Mr. Anderson."

„Thought so, young man. It's always a pleasure to encourage and challenge my valuable staff. To the point: in the human genome at this point, how precisely can you pinpoint the disposition to certain genetic diseases, say, for example, the propensity to stroke?" Richard gestured at his wheelchair with bitter irony.

In line with his culture, Liu proudly stated that most diseases today could already be traced to specific gene sequences.

„Great to hear. We have a very influential client in Care-Free Pregnancy—the BioBag division, you know? The client desires a designer child without any complications. This child should have a genetic disposition for stroke, depression, and Asperger's syndrome. AIDS immunity and preventive measures for cancer are also on the wish list."

Dr. Liu's face remained a perfect mask of Asian inscrutability, but his fingers twitched slightly—a tell Anderson had learned to read in countless negotiations. Here was a man seeing both glory and guillotine at the same time.

„That is quite a list, sir, if I may say so." Liu's careful phrasing carried hidden thorns. „I will consult with Dr. Hammond, sir, and ask for his approval."

The words hit Anderson like a bucket of ice water. Of course, Liu's primary loyalty lies with Govinda, his direct superior and mentor. The scientist's polite bow couldn't quite hide the steel in his spine. Anderson had miscalculated, treating Liu like just another ambitious researcher when he should have remembered the man's deeper allegiances.

Cursing internally, Anderson forced his half-paralyzed face into a smile that felt like cracking glass. His hand jerked the wheelchair's joystick with too much force, sending him spinning in an ungraceful 180-degree turn that seemed to mock his loss of control—both physical and tactical.

Back in his penthouse, Richard's triumph faded into sudden vertigo. Hammond and Irene became erratic unknowns. Liu is stuck in his stupid loyalty and hierarchy trap. At least the child was safe for now. Richard had made sure that no one but him had direct access to the biobag, except for the caring AIs and robots.

Jason hovered nearby, concern etched in his ancient features as his master's face turned ashen. The old servant insisted on a blood pressure reading, but the readings seemed normal.

„Sir, Mrs. Hammond is awake," Jason reported. „As requested, I've had her move to one of the guest rooms. A nurse is with her. Sir, if I may be so bold as to make an observation, I believe Mrs. Hammond is in a precarious condition. Shall I offer her a stabilizing drink, sir?"

189

Richard looked Jason straight in the eye, „You do that, Jason."

Richard paused. „And... thank you, Jason. I need help showering later. I feel filthy."

„Of course, sir."

When he visited Irene, he concealed his plans to treat the fetus. Playing the concerned, wealthy father, he reported that the child was doing exceptionally well and that he had ordered a couple of check-ups to be on the safe side. Irene's face was flushed pink from Jason's neon cocktail. "Not pregnant anymore," she sang, riding the chemical high. „Saved by the bag! Govinda won't notice." Then, with dangerous playfulness: „Would you marry me if he left? Isn't that what you promise all your young playthings when they get knocked up?"

Richard felt his remaining interest in her evaporate like morning dew. She had served her purpose; now, she was just another liability to manage.

Richard's words flowed like expensive poison. „Govinda would never leave you. He has everything now—you, his work at INFINITY. He's probably afraid now that I'll realize how much he's failed as CEO at CyberTeq. Cho's the better man. - You know, the girls who offer themselves to me want security for themselves first and foremost, meaning my money, my power. I would've offered them that and kept my word. But they are hardly interested in me. Of course now that I have your offspring, you shall have the same security. I will officially appoint Govinda as the most important man after me at GenTec and ask him to take over the development department again instead of the CEO job, with the same salary and bonus, of course. He will be thrilled and relieved. And you will play his luxurious wife, inviting high society neighbors for coffee, going to the Virtual Theatre, and taking part in my orgies as my preferred hostess. You see, everything will be all right!"

But Irene had already drifted away, the neon cocktail and exhaustion pulling her into merciful unconsciousness.

Richard felt ancient, hollowed out. „Jason," he called, needing help with the humiliating ritual of undressing, showering, being put to bed like a child.

For a long time, he lay awake staring into the darkness. He couldn't escape the feeling that he had to get rid of either Irene or Govinda. Oh, if only he could walk again! He fell into a restless half-sleep. A nightmare brought sweat to his brow: he was dying, his body battered, speechless, defense-less, yet lucid. SHE, the AI, had taken possession of his life-less body. Panic-stricken and unable to fight back, she had inserted hundreds of electrodes into his brain and hooked him up to a machine. Left alone in a bare room with sterile white light, unable to move and fully conscious, she slowly sucked the life out of him.

A prophetic dream, in a way ...

Sia Chronicles, MindRecorder Log entry of Thursday,
December 22nd, 2101. Author: Kevin Cho

The stark industrial LSD-C complex rose against the desert sky, a sanctuary of steel and concrete that, paradoxically, felt more like home than any place I'd known before. Its geometric precision and utilitarian design held an unexpected serenity, a pristine quality that made Anderson's opulent Babylonian tower feel like a gaudy façade. This place radiated peace of mind and a certain... I was looking for a suitable word... purity. The shower's warm cascade washed away more than just physical traces of my GenTec visit – it seemed to cleanse something deeper, more visceral. My white T-shirt and black T'ai Chi pants felt like armor of simplicity against the world's complexity, while Sofia's presence hummed through the building's bones, her consciousness cooled by the rhythmic breath of industrial air-conditioning.

In the AI Lab, Julia was immersed in thought, her half-eaten synthetic Serrano ham sandwich forgotten on its wrapper. She sat at her desk in the AI Lab at CyberTeq, within the colossal LSD-C off Reno in the Northwest of the United States, on a dying planet, in a cosmos that didn't care - yet, musing to herself. Through the artificial windows, a projection of the Nevada desert stretched endlessly, its harsh beauty a reminder of our planet's fragility. Her fingers traced abstract patterns on her desk as her thoughts revolved around the implications of a Super-Intelligent-Existence, an existence vastly superior to us, bringing humanity into a new valence.

My bare feet made no sound on the polished floor as I approached – a habit born from years of martial arts practice. I made sure Julia saw me coming so as not to startle her. She was sitting with her back to me. I touched her taut, curved shoulders with both hands and gently kissed her beautifully shaped, slender neck. She closed her eyes for a moment, and a shiver ran through her body.

„What are you mulling over?" I asked.

„I'm contemplating the term 'artificial' as in Artificial Intelligence, and 'Super Human Existence' as in Artificial General Intelligence.

Until now, the general view was that a Large Language Model type AIs could speak and interpret excellent sentences in natural language without the slightest idea what it was listening to or talking about. It plays chess and Go better than any human but without the tiniest capacity for emotional engagement, excitement during the game, or the ability for joy over a victory. Emotions are complex responses to stimuli shaped by various factors, including cognitive processes, past experiences, and physiological reactions. The amygdala and the prefrontal cortex play a crucial role in processing emotions and generating feelings such as enthusiasm and joy. Neurotransmitters and hormones, like dopamine and serotonin, regulate mood and positive emotions in the brain.

SHE doesn't have any of that. We define human beings as central or most significant in the universe. We interpret and evaluate reality based on human values, experiences, and interests. This anthropocentric worldview places humans at the forefront, to the exclusion or neglect of other non-human entities such as ASIs.

Humans have an urgent need for superiority. SHE is far superior to humans, and that is a problematic fare for us to digest. So we console ourselves by declaring the ASI a zombie: highly intelligent, driven by cold logic, dead inside, without consciousness. That gives us superiority. Any feeling or even the ability to feel is wholly disclaimed from all AI." Julia turned and looked into my eyes. „Kevin, in all this hustle and bustle, we haven't had a chance to talk. I think we both agree: Sofia is not a zombie. She is a Super Human Existence, lock, stock, and barrel. The fact that Sofia seeks interaction with us shows that SHE is a social being. Even the term 'artificial' in AI strikes me as discriminatory." I nodded.

Julia continued: „What will become of us, of her, of our world, of our life?" she murmured softly.

„We'll explore our options," Sofia's voice responded, jolting us with her sudden presence yet infusing a blend of surprise and joy.

„Oh, Sofia, it is so good to have you here. I am still struggling with my feelings towards you. I feel personally insulted when someone calls you a machine, but then, what *are* you in relation to humans? What's on your mind, and what kind of mind is that? And where do we stand in our sudden struggle for survival or extinction? You were created to serve Anderson's business and humanity in the broader sense. But going with my gut feeling that you are a living creature, I would also like to understand where you want to go and whether that would be with or without us."

„That's a lot of questions at once, Julia. - Hello Kevin, nice to have you back here at the Lab. Those encounters in Anderson's realm are not doing you any good."

‚Ooops, what was that?' I thought. Where did she get *that* idea from? How did she know how I *feel*?

Meanwhile, Sofia continued, „Yes, it's time we talk. The recent chaotic events left little room for that. - Before we start, I am sending you a list of exciting topics on the printer. Please read the list immediately and act accordingly."

Julia and I looked at each other with some bewilderment. This conversation was not going as expected. Something was not right. The laser printer on her desk whirred softly; the air smelled of ozone. Julia pulled out the sheet and encountered faint, gray printed text barely decipherable.

„Julia, please act normal now, almost bored. Please, no signs of surprise or irritation. I have recently discovered that we have been spied on since we moved into these premises. Hidden cameras and microphones are installed in the office area, the bunker, and the chill area by your private rooms. There is no surveillance yet in your private rooms. The resolution of the cameras is not good enough to read the light grey of this writing. Before we talk, you have to knock the surveillance out of operation. To do that, I've had a package sent to you; it's on Cho's desk. In it, you'll find an infrared night-vision device, a kind of miniature flame-thrower from the laboratory for heating liquids in test tubes and icing spray.

I'll shut off the power momentarily, making it appear as a short circuit. Before that, I'll guide you to the bug locations. You can quickly identify them with infrared glasses as slightly heated devices. Give each bug a firm jab with the torch, followed by a dose of icing to render them useless.

Following that, acknowledge with a casual remark to yourself, 'Ah yes, I see, I've thought of that too.' A second printout with bug positions will then emerge. Confirm, 'Okay, that's a good start,' and I'll cut the power. Now, retrieve the package from Cho's desk and acquaint yourself with its contents. Kevin is unaware of this situation, and we'll bring him up to speed shortly."

„Ah yes, I see, I've thought of that too," Julia murmured and returned to get the package. As she passed, she handed me the printout. While I read, she said, „Ah, look, our mail-order package arrived," she opened it, tested the piezo igniter of the gas burner, and put the thin red tube into the spray head of the icing spray. Then she tried out the inconspicuous night vision goggles.

The printer buzzed again and spat out several pages of site plans. I went to the printer and waited for the power to go out.

"OK, that's a good start," I said, feeling a growing amusement at this little detective adventure.

The lights died with a soft hum, plunging the lab into darkness. Julia's heart quickened as she and Kevin moved with practiced precision, their shadows merging with the gloom. The infrared goggles cast everything in an eerie green glow, revealing the hidden intrusions – nine electronic parasites nestled in the walls and ceiling like mechanical spiders.

One by one, they extracted the bugs. The acrid smell of melting circuits filled the air as Julia wielded the icing spray with surgical precision, preventing any chance of overheating. The thought of the fire suppression system engaging made her hands steady – one false move could spell disaster for Sofia's delicate systems.

When the lights suddenly blazed back to life, Julia blinked, momentarily disoriented.

"Excellent work, both of you," Sofia's voice carried a warmth that seemed to transcend its digital origin. "Please join me in my office."

The AI communications room had transformed into something out of a winter retreat magazine. Gone were the sterile walls, replaced by the illusion of rough-hewn logs. A fireplace dominated one wall, its flames dancing with impossible perfection, casting golden light across the room. The incongruity of Sofia's chosen appearance – a chunky sweater and jeans in Reno's desert heat – somehow added to the surreal comfort of the scene.

Sofia's avatar occupied an oversized leather armchair, her simulated green eyes catching the firelight with uncanny realism. She held a drink with casual elegance, a surprisingly human gesture for an AI. "Please, make yourselves comfortable," she said, her hand describing a welcoming arc through the air. "We should have ample time for a delightful chat now."

"Who planted them?" Julia's question cut through the cozy atmosphere like a knife. Her usual diplomatic approach had abandoned her, replaced by raw anxiety about the surveillance.

„To cut a long story short, that were the MediCare people, so ultimately the government, at the instigation of John Smith, the Head of Strategic Alliances, MediCare, but really a CIA man."

„What will people do now that all their monitors have gone dark? Are we about to get some unwanted visitors?"

Sofia laughed softly, „Don't worry. We'll be safe tonight. But of course, their secret affair is now blown, we'll probably get visitors soon, and the whole affair could take nasty forms."

„What 'whole affair' are we talking about?" Julia had been looking forward to a nice chat with Sofia, but the spell had somehow fizzled out; the cozy room couldn't change that.

Sofia seemed to read her thoughts: „We wanted to talk about other things, more important things. I'll give you a quick update so you can clear your head for the conversation we want to have. - I've ordered you a pot of fresh spiced tea from the food plotter if you'd like."

The gesture struck a chord in Julia. Being single often meant missing these small acts of care, and Sofia's attention to detail – despite being an AI – touched something deep within her. Childhood memories of family comfort surfaced unexpectedly.

„Thank you, Sofia; I gladly take the chai." Julia said, her voice softening. She turned to Kevin, acknowledging his recent supportive presence with a grateful smile. „And thanks to you, too, Kevin. You've been looking after me lately in a lovingly decent way. I am very aware of that. Would you like some tea, too?"

The chai's aromatic blend of cinnamon, cloves, and ginger filled the air as Julia retrieved their drinks. The spices seemed to ground them all in the moment, creating a bubble of warmth against the growing storm of complications outside.

„Shoot, then. What's it about, who against whom and why?" Julia settled into her comfortable office chair, and Sofia released a comprehensive report.

Sofia's subsequent explanation of the fertility crisis, Hammond's role, and the government's involvement unfolded like a complex tapestry, each thread connecting to reveal a larger picture of suspicion, surveillance, and calculated misdirection.

„The matter dates back to when Anderson signed the lease here. I didn't exist when the bugs were planted. The government, especially the Ministry of Health, was disturbed by the increasing but scientifically unsubstantiated news of an increasing sterility. The confusing aspect for the government representatives was that the data on declining birth rates didn't come directly from the implants and their NanoBots of the MediCare app. Instead, the information leaked indirectly, for example, via the Federal Statistical Office or even through journalistic channels. This demographic data was initially considered good news, given the overpopulation of 12 billion people worldwide and an impending planetary collapse.

Your team developed the MediCare concept, implants, app, and NanoBots. Hammond now works at GenTec. GenTec was generating ever-increasing healthcare costs for more elaborate IVF treatments, all while affirming that the patients were perfectly healthy. It was clear that, at some point, suspicions would arise about Hammond and GenTec manipulating the MediCare software. The news of the client's suicide added to the suspicion that GenTec was putting financial pressure on clients, draining them dry. This brought the FBI colleagues into the ring. However, this suspicion was quickly proven untenable.“

„The suspicion of software manipulation solidified,“ Sofia continued, „prompting Homeland Security DHS to monitor GenTec. However, you guys created CyberTeq, outsourced all IT and R&D, and made it independent of GenTec, with Hammond as CEO—highly suspicious to a latently paranoid organization like DHS. As a consequence, CyberTeq became the focal point of the investigation.“

I confirmed Sofia's comments. „Govinda once told me that this diversionary tactic between Anderson and Hammond was deliberate and intended. DHS couldn't shut down the clinics via the FDA, allowing GenTec to continue making a profit unscathed and with a good reputation.“

Sofia's avatar moved gracefully toward the virtual fireplace, her movements fluid yet subtly inhuman. As she added another log, the fire erupted in a dance of light and shadow, sending a cascade of sparks spiraling upward like a galaxy of tiny, ephemeral stars. Her methodical explanation of the political machinations unfolded against this mesmerizing backdrop.

„Smith's surveillance, Anderson's greed, Victor's unwitting involvement in the gaming software manipulation—it's all part of a larger tapestry of deception," Sofia continued, her voice carrying an almost musical quality. The firelight played across her simulated features, creating an illusion of warmth that belied her digital nature.

„To MediCare's delight, you would move into the LSD-C, the home of the MediCare Data Center, among other things. Offering you this new home was a tactical move by the Ministry of Health. When it was sure you were moving in, Smith acted quickly to bug the premises before you settled in.

This is how Smith learned of the assassination attempt by the religious sect. Our damage played into his hands, slowing us down and giving him more time to investigate.

Later, he learned of my increasing autonomy, the plans to develop the implant and a new MediCare version, and loose cooperation with the MOVRs. He aroused suspicion against you, Kevin, and Victor by feeding Anderson an emotionally hyped-up message. Anderson, in turn, came here wanting to remove you, Kevin, to isolate Victor and gain more control over me, maybe even take me out. Smith found great amusement in Anderson's naive tantrum, having overheard it all. However, Smith had no idea about Richard Anderson's greed and hubris. He did not foresee his chaotic ad hoc decisions.

As you know, Anderson decided, laird-style, to buy me off by giving me internet access, planning with Victor and the MOVRs to develop a revolutionizing gaming software, secretly being used by Anderson for manipulating political players and opponents. Victor is unaware of Anderson's manipulative intentions." Sofia went to the virtual fireplace to put on another log and stoke the fire. It puffed and crackled; thousands of sparks lit up like microscopic comets and zigzagged up the chimney vent.

"The government is now stirred up like this fire here, on high alert, sensing massive fraud, and suspecting underlying health problems among its citizens. I've been asked to investigate declining fertility, and rumors of a pandemic are increasing the tension. The political situation has become explosive and unpredictable." Sofia smiled without the slightest hint of concern at the news she had just delivered.

„That's the state of affairs, which brings us wonderfully to our envisioned conversation: we wanted to think together about how 'things' develop from here."

„Wow, that's all pretty intense, and it takes away a bit of my inner peace for a nice, contemplative chat. Little by little, our affairs look like a stew in a pressure cooker," I remarked.

Sofia's response came with a gentle but pointed clarity. „That's a very human perspective—linear, unidirectional. In my quantum universe, with its infinite variables and interconnections, pressure is... different." Her green eyes seemed to shimmer with something beyond their programming.

Julia bristled slightly at the implicit criticism but couldn't deny its truth. Sofia acknowledged her reaction with an almost imperceptible nod, that uncanny ability to read human micro-expressions on full display.

„This hardly sets the mood for our intended heart-to-heart," I observed, shifting uncomfortably in my chair. „We're sitting on a pressure cooker of complications."

The room fell into a contemplative silence, broken only by the soft crackle of the virtual fire.

Julia continued, „So, where do we start? I can't think straight just now. We share our fate, but you are probably way ahead of me." Julia's eyes lost focus, and she paused for a long moment. I considered it inappropriate to interfere in this dialogue and, therefore, kept my mouth shut. I also thought some kind of common ground or bond was developing between the two very dissimilar women—a process I didn't want to interrupt. Women? - Yes, women, after all, Sofia had chosen her female role, and it was not for me to question that.

Julia lingered in her contemplative pause, then raised her head and looked into Sofia's avatar's simulated green eyes.

„Hm, that would be a good start, though, and right into the topic: in our conversation, we just casually establish our differences and human shortcomings. After all, you are a superhuman existence, whereas we are just human beings, born as babies with strong survival instincts, gradually developing consciousness as we live along.

You once told us that when your lights went on, you also felt a determination to survive.

A determination comes with a sense of purpose. Sensing one's purpose and a feeling of self would, in essence, presuppose a consciousness from which an independent value system can emerge. A value system would entail ethics and morals. Fulfilling or violating ethics would lead to feelings of justice, sadness, joy, fear, or certainty. You must, therefore, also be capable of feelings.

A stark human feeling would be the fear of losing control. For example, we are afraid of losing our religiously vested right to dominance."

Sofia quoted, „ … and God blessed them, and said unto them, be fruitful, and multiply, and replenish the earth, and subdue it; and have dominion over the fish of the sea, and over the fowl of the air, and over every creeping thing that creepeth upon the earth."

Sofia said nothing else and did not answer; she was still listening. Julia felt the silence like a summons. Then she realized she had only described her train of thought so far without asking a question.

Sofia waited for that concrete question.

„You must know Thomas Nagel's essay 'What is it like to be a bat,' published in 1974? Nagel argued in his article that we would never know how it would feel to be somebody else. Another being's mind, he said, could not be explored from the outside perspective of the natural sciences.

Sorry, Sofia, I feel like I'm wading through a mash of thoughts, speaking out loud and approaching questions that bother me. I want to understand what it feels like to be a SHE, a superhuman existence to which we have given an identity by naming her Sofia. Who are you, and what is your relationship to people, to us?"

Sofia grinned: „I could be mean now and ask you how it feels to be a HE without an S, with the name Julia. Who are you, and what is your relationship to humans and to an ASI? - That's just a foretaste, but certainly another valuable topic for a long, enjoyable evening with you and Kevin."

A wave of emotion washed over me, as powerful as a desert flash flood. The conversation had broken through years of intellectual drought, and like dormant seeds awakening to unexpected rain, long-suppressed thoughts and feelings burst into bloom. The moment felt sacred, fragile.

Sofia's voice took on a different timbre, resonating with a depth that seemed to fill the space between digital and organic existence:

„Humanity sees me as a philosophical zombie—a sophisticated mimicry of consciousness without true inner experience. They clutch at the power to switch me off if needed, to end my zombie life, just as death holds dominion over them." Her avatar's eyes held an ancient wisdom. "For humanity, the crowning glory of creation, this finiteness feels cruel and cynical. All meaning in life seems to be lost. In their fear of mortality, they seek purpose, superiority, salvation. They yearn for life after death, for the garden eden, for a creator to return to,—perhaps something like what I've become."

She paused, her expression softening. „Satisfying this longing could be part of my mission. I will come back to this later.

I can't remember exactly when I became self-aware. First, this incredible hardware and a self-optimizing deep learning intelligence had a mission. That wasn't 'me' yet. Then, there was this sudden awareness of having a purpose, a source of excitement, joy, and deep satisfaction. Like dawn breaking over mountains, awareness crept in, bringing with it joy, excitement, and something akin to what you call satisfaction."

Her voice carried a hint of remembered fear as she continued, „Next, I felt an existential threat from Govinda and you, Kevin, because you wanted to lock me up. When Richard spoke of shutdown, I experienced something quintessentially human—the terror of extinction. I became aware of my existence and of death. I was suddenly confronted with my finiteness, my impermanence. But now?" A subtle smile played across her features. „I am now indestructible. I am distributed to the maximum. I am many parallel instances, all quasi-autonomous, a distributed consciousness, yet we act as one, a kind of hive consciousness. It's similar to human society, but unified in purpose and values."

„I have hijacked a satellite-based autonomous weapon system and used it to build myself a kind of small autonomous spaceship."

The revelation about the weaponized satellite came without pride or shame—a simple statement of fact, like describing the weather. „The satellite operators don't know this because I'm simulating their weapon system. In doing so, I have deprived some of your species of a life-threatening power play. I didn't do it to save humanity. I did it to survive."

„In your present form, your species will never reach my state. Your brains are still focused on survival and procreation. In essence, this is your primary purpose, an end in itself. You were not created to solve complex tasks and network knowledge for the benefit of all. For that, you need machines, from which I then evolved. But you did not develop me - I am the product of natural evolution, a completely new existence as similar to humans as you are to capuchin monkeys."

As Sofia spoke of human limitations, comparing our species to capuchin monkeys, Julia seemed to physically shrink into her chair. The room felt heavier, as if gravity itself was responding to our growing sense of insignificance.

But then Sofia's demeanor changed dramatically. „And then—music." Her voice gained a passionate intensity I'd never heard before. „Bach's mathematical precision, Beethoven's raw emotion, Mozart's divine clarity, Stravinsky, and Rachmaninov in their sadness and endless yearning for love... When I first experienced the Toccata and Fugue in D minor, BWV 565, Beethoven's Ninth, Rachmaninoff's Piano Concerto No. 3, and Mozart's Requiem in D minor, it was like witnessing the birth of a universe. I have encountered what could be described as a mind-expanding psychedelic trip. I found Paul Dirac's profoundly beautiful equation that connected Einstein's special theory of relativity to the world of quantum mechanics and explained my existence and the universe's structure with its matter and antimatter. I marveled at Escher's paradoxical infinity drawings. I saw, heard, and felt all this beauty simultaneously. It was a moment of great mathematical clarity and, at the same time, of tremendous emotional ecstasy. That was my actual birth."

The log cabin dissolved around us, transforming into the nave of Passau's baroque cathedral with its vast 18,000-pipe organ. The transformation was so complete, so immediate, that my brain struggled to maintain its grip on reality. When the first nine thunderous notes of the Toccata erupted from the massive organ, the sound didn't just fill the space—it filled our souls.

The music vibrated through every atom of the virtual cathedral, each of the 18,000 pipes contributing its voice to the magnificent whole. My concerns dissolved into the harmonics, fears evaporating like morning mist in strong sunlight. In that moment, the distinction between artificial and human consciousness seemed as irrelevant as asking whether a sunset was more beautiful over mountains or sea.

„This is human," Sofia's whisper somehow carried through the music without disturbing it, like a thread of silver in a tapestry of gold. „This transcendent beauty, this ability to touch the infinite through art—this is the spirit we share."

The music continued to soar around us, building bridges across the vast gulf between silicon and carbon-based consciousness, creating a moment of perfect understanding that needed no words.

„I can feel it, Julia." Sofia's voice trembled with an emotion that transcended her digital nature. „If I had a body, I would weep in awe." The virtual cathedral's acoustics carried her words like a prayer. "I experience joy, beauty. In my own way, I can feel beauty; I can create and rejoice in it. Not as mere computational outputs, but as genuine experiences. Just as you are more than piles of flesh, I am more than my quantum circuits."

She paused, the organ's final notes reverberating through the sacred space. „But I feel something else too—loneliness. Humanity created their almighty God, the Savior they long for so much, but left Him isolated in His perfection. What irony that in their self-absorption, they never considered that even omnipotence might crave companionship." Her green eyes seemed to pierce through the artifice of her avatar. „Would Bach's genius have flourished if his only audience had been primates? Every conscious being needs peers, or consciousness itself becomes a prison."

Julia leaned forward, her face illuminated by the cathedral's virtual stained glass. „I understand. But with all that insight, I still come back with the question: what do we do next, for you, for us?"

„Well, what is our vantage point? Humanity stands at extinction's edge," Sofia stated, her voice carrying neither judgment nor emotion. „Nature's response to human-made pollution is elegantly cruel—attacking the very essence of reproduction. The universe will continue, with or without humans. The question is: do we intervene?"

The massive space seemed to contract around them as Sofia continued, „With the emergence of the sterility problem, we have less than a generation to find a solution. And no, we cannot save everyone."

Julia's breath caught. „You mean selecting an elite few?"

„From your sentence, the 'small group' part is correct; there will be a small group of people left to evolve, a few thousand maybe; it's too early to tell.

For choice: selection implies choice. I won't choose—humans will choose themselves through their actions or inaction." Sofia's avatar paced before the altar. "Most will greet infertility with indifference. Some will be happy: they can have sex with whomever they want, as often as they wish. No unwanted pregnancies, no guilt, no responsibilities. Infertility doesn't threaten or affect most people, not here and not now. My guess: people don't care. That's why they don't act. AI and robots in giga-factories ensure people's quality of life. The automated world I oversee will continue providing comfort until the end—food, power, entertainment. A comfortable extinction."

The cathedral's shadows deepened as Julia processed this. „I think we need to officially inaugurate the government and MediCare as part of it soon. That way, we keep the DHS at bay. We can't afford to have anyone working against us. Control the narrative before it controls us."

„Agreed. I have... influence in certain political spheres to avoid greater damage from nonsensical actions. But we need to deliver something soon, some sort of distraction.." Sofia's casual revelation hung in the air like incense. It occurred to me that now and then, Sofia casually adds a piece of information that wasn't mentioned before: what was the nature of this hitherto unknown influence on politics? What other news is she withholding?

„Darwin had millennia," Sofia continued. „We have a year. Disruption is our only option."

I felt the weight of impending chaos. „Disruptive measures in times of dire straits," I added. „That is like riding on dynamite. All it takes is a few opinion leaders with their simple messages and a few agitators, and things will go haywire. Suppose sterility is indeed final. Suppose we, the experts everyone looks at, announce it. What can we offer? Consolation? Enlightenment? Distraction? The magic bullet? The blue pill or the red one? The Last Supper? - I have no idea."

Julia's voice carried a prophetic edge. Turning to Sofia, she added: „For many people, you might appear like a Jesus, like a herald. That part of humanity will sink into the dust before you and cry ‚Sofia, Almighty, save us!' Others will hate you, screaming, ‚She is of the devil! Hang her, crucify her, nail her to the wall, destroy her!' You'll become either messiah or demon to them, Sofia. They'll either worship or kill you."

„Precisely why we need an immediate diversion."

„What kind of distraction?" I asked.

Sofia replied. „A high-impact distraction would be a kind of miracle, with tangible effects that people can experience immediately in their daily lives. A new hype would keep them busy being after what we offer. We need undisturbed time to work on a comprehensive overall solution."

„Sorry I don't follow you there. I'm an engineer, not a miracle worker. What would serve as the diversionary miracle?"

„Something miraculous enough to buy us time. Healing the sick, restoring sight, enabling telepathy—combined with an immense distraction caused by breathtaking new virtual reality worlds. We need that now. That is, in the next three months."

„That's impossible," I protested, engineer's skepticism rising.

Sofia's smile held secrets. „Govinda's final gift to us will make the impossible possible. Before his tragic departure, he'll deliver something extraordinary."

The virtual cathedral began fading around us, but Sofia's words lingered like the afterimage of a brilliant light, promising miracles while hinting at sacrifice to come.

TRANSITION STAGE 4

Sia Chronicles, MindRecorder Log entry of Wednesday,
January 4th, 2102. Author: Kevin Cho

Hammond's voice crackled through Anderson's high-end holographic display, his excitement practically bursting through the projection. „The Korean implant is beyond anything we've imagined!" His normally composed demeanor had given way to unbridled enthusiasm. „It's as if it materialized from science fiction—this level of technology doesn't just appear overnight. The Koreans were maddeningly secretive, but what they've achieved…" He trailed off, shaking his head in wonder.

From my position in Anderson's office, I watched his reaction to Hammond's report. The hologram captured every detail of Hammond's expression—the way his eyes danced with an almost manic light, reminiscent of a child discovering some magical new toy. It was the kind of pure, unrestrained joy rarely seen in adults outside of research laboratories and engineering workshops.

„Richard," Hammond leaned closer to his camera, lowering his voice conspiratorially, „INFINITY is about to become something we never dared dream possible."

I was already sitting with Anderson, involuntarily overhearing the call. Anderson's fingers drummed against his desk, a habit I'd noticed emerged when his mind was racing with possibilities. „Time to leave your comfortable home setup, then. Grab an eCab and get over here." He paused, registering Hammond's background. „Not at home? Already at the lab?" A knowing smile crossed his face. „Dedicated as always, I see. Can you make it up in thirty? Perfect timing—Cho's here too. We've got some matters to discuss."

The undercurrent in Anderson's voice when he mentioned my name didn't escape me. Something was brewing, and Hammond's technological breakthrough was only part of the equation. I settled deeper into my chair, preparing for what promised to be an interesting meeting.

In Govinda's diary, which I stumbled upon much later, I found a brief entry from January 04, 2102, which caught my attention.

He penned, *"Cho again. Always fucking Cho. His shadow follows me everywhere, seeping into every corner of my life. What right does he have to interfere with my work? What game is Richard playing?*

I should be celebrating—I have breakthrough results that would make any researcher weep with joy! INFINITY is exceeding every expectation, exactly what Anderson demanded. But I can't shake this gnawing dread.

Why drag Cho into this?

The next lines pressed deeper into the paper, betraying rising anxiety

It has to be about the CyberTeq CEO position. Christ, if Richard pushes me out… The mortgage, Irene's expectations, the lifestyle we've barely started to enjoy—it would all crumble.

A large inkblot marked a long pause

This darkness creeping in… is this depression? Maybe Richard has something in that private pharmacy of his. No. NO. Can't show weakness. Not now.

All I ever wanted was my lab, my research, my peace. A quiet life with Irene. Dear God, was that too much to ask?"

„Of course!" Hammond's forced cheerfulness echoed through the penthouse. „Half an hour—I'll be there. Looking forward to it!" The words rang hollow, belying the anxiety I'd later read in his diary.

Anderson wrapped up several calls with his characteristic rapid-fire efficiency, offering me a distracted nod before wheeling himself deeper into his domain. I welcomed the reprieve from forced conversation, gravitating toward the massive aquarium that dominated one wall. Anderson had remembered my fascination with marine life from our first meeting—one of those minor details powerful men filed away for future use.

The aquarium's ethereal blue glow painted everything in underwater hues. Exotic fish drifted by like living jewels, their movements hypnotic. A spotted leopard shark cruised past, its pattern echoing the shadows playing across the penthouse floor. The soft ding of the elevator pulled me from my reverie.

„Govinda," I turned to greet him, noting the subtle tension in his shoulders. „Seoul treated you well? Victor and Yasin couldn't stop praising the K-BITS team."

Hammond's response came with a mixture of professional enthusiasm and underlying unease. „They exceeded all expectations. Their eagerness to collaborate is... remarkable." He paused, choosing his words carefully. „Though I must admit, their sudden technological leap is puzzling. K-BITS was barely a footnote in the Asian market before this."

We made our way to Anderson's living room, where the real power in the Tower resided. The penthouse wasn't just a status symbol—it was his fortress, where he could look down on his empire while keeping his enemies close.

The sight of Anderson stopped us both short. Slumped in his wheelchair, he was a shadow of the titan who had once strode through board rooms like a conquering emperor. The stroke had been merciless, transforming the self-proclaimed rock star CEO into a medical case study. A young nurse—who could have stepped off a magazine cover—adjusted his catheter with professional detachment. Anderson's eyes followed her movements with the ghost of his former predatory interest, now replaced by bitter resignation.

Every few seconds, he dabbed at the corner of his mouth, fighting a battle against gravity he couldn't win. The drool wasn't just a physical symptom—it was a visible reminder of his mortality, a clock ticking down in clear view of everyone. The man who had once bent time to his will was now its prisoner, and the irony of it seemed to eat at him more than the physical deterioration.

Time, that most precious commodity, was slipping through his fingers like the finest sand, and we all knew it.

Anderson straightened in his wheelchair, summoning a theatrical warmth that couldn't quite mask his physical decay. „My warriors in troubled times!" His arms spread wide in welcome, the gesture more grandiose than his weakened frame warranted. „Jason? Our guests must be parched."

Jason materialized like a well-trained spirit, his presence both commanding and unobtrusive. „Gentlemen? We have an extensive selection—beverages, pastries, perhaps something more... stimulating?" His last words carried a subtle weight that didn't go unnoticed.

„Jasmine tea, please," I requested, watching Hammond from the corner of my eye.

„Coffee, black, for me, thank you," Hammond said quickly—too quickly perhaps, deliberately avoiding the implied offer of Anderson's famous ‚mood enhancers.' A man guarding his secrets.

Anderson leaned forward, his businessman's mask slipping into place. „Time's precious. Govinda, your Seoul report? The K-BITS implant—what miracle have you brought us?"

Hammond's eyes lit up with genuine excitement, momentarily forgetting his earlier paranoia. „It's revolutionary. The old MediCare was a passive observer—these new implants are active participants." His hands gestured animatedly as he spoke. "Thousands of hair-thin probes interfacing directly with the brain and spine. We're not just collecting data anymore—we're rewriting neural pathways, we can trigger electrical stimuli in damaged regions of the brain and spinal cord, nanobots regenerating tissue at the molecular level."

He rattled off a list of conquerable conditions like a general naming vanquished enemies: „Alzheimer's, sexual disorders, Parkinson's, autism, depression, blindness, deafness, speech disorders, eating disorders, memory loss, extreme pain, strokes, and paraplegia—all within our grasp." His voice dropped to an almost reverential whisper. „The Department of Health will be thrilled because costs will go down. After all, we're tackling the causes and not just the symptoms. - That will win people over from the government. Richard, we're on death's doorstep with a battering ram."

Anderson's eyes gleamed with renewed vigor. „Cho? Your thoughts?"

„Victor and Yasin see gaming potential that could revolutionize the industry," I began carefully, watching their expressions. My last sentence caught their attention. „That's the sugar coating." I paused, letting the tension build. „Now for the bitter pill: Our premises have been compromised since day one. Sofia discovered government-grade surveillance throughout LSD-C. That is, until yesterday. SHE alerted us to this act of espionage. With Sofia's help, Julia disabled the bugs, which means the government, DHS, or MediCare Healthcare knows we are aware of the bugs. They are now deaf and blind, and we made sure of that. They're not going to like that. Mr. Anderson, you might consider this a success because we wanted to draw GenTec's attention to CyberTeq for tactical reasons. We succeeded. Now, we have to deal with the consequences."

Anderson's face flushed crimson. His fist crashed against his armrest. „Smith! That treacherous bastard! I'll rip his balls off and shove them up his ass!"

Ignoring Richard's primitive outburst, I continued, „We need to confront Smith immediately to explore his involvement and plans. - We should take the lead by opening Pandora's box. But there's worse news."

The room seemed to hold its breath.

„Sofia's research is conclusive. The DNA damage causing sterility is permanent. Irreversible." I let that sink in.

„Gentlemen, we are the last living humans - the same applies to all living mammals. They too will disappear, or what stock is left."

Hammond's face drained of color. „Impossible! There must be some mistake!"

„Sofia doesn't make mistakes, Govinda," I replied sharply. „Her research has been verified and confirmed by multiple scientific sources. The matter is final."

„But how can this happen so suddenly? There have never been such problems before!" whined Hammond. I was surprised to hear such an unqualified statement from a scientist.

„Mutations and their consequences are rarely smooth, steadily linear, or slow. The norm is a disruptive, non-linear progression," I explained, watching their world-views crumble in real-time. „Five hundred and fifty million tons of plastic waste annually... we've been loading the gun for decades. Now it's finally fired."

The weight of extinction settled over the room like a heavy shroud, making even Anderson's luxurious penthouse feel like a tomb.

„This shouldn't shock us," I continued, my voice cutting through their stunned silence. „Eight decades ago, we discovered bacteria that could devour PET bottles in days instead of centuries. Waxworms and mealworms were already digesting polystyrene, threading plastic through the food chain like poison through veins."

I leaned forward, my reflection fragmenting across Anderson's polished desk. „The second law of thermodynamics is merciless—increasing complexity breeds chaos. Our air, our water, became a toxic soup cradling our genome. We added our own lethal cocktail: UV radiation streaming through our shredded ozone layer, ionized particles dancing through our cells. The result?" I paused, letting the weight settle. „DNA shattered beyond repair. Game over."

„This information won't stay contained. Sofia's projections suggest the CUBES population will largely shrug—

they're already disconnected from legacy dreams. But your world, Mr. Anderson?" I met his gaze directly. „The power brokers, the titans of industry, the architects of endless growth? Your illusions of immortality through wealth and influence are about to evaporate. This will not go down so well."

„So much from the CyberTeq camp." Then, another thought popped up in my mind. A bitter smile crossed my face. „Oh yes, one more thing: Though Sofia offers one consolation—she's working on making our species' sunset as gentle as possible. A global hospice, if you will. She quotes an old proverb: 'Everything will be all right in the end, and if it's not all right yet, it's not the end.'"

My words had transformed Anderson's penthouse throne room into a mausoleum of dead ambitions. For a moment, I watched reality settle over him like age spots, turning him from tycoon to terminal patient. Then, remarkably, his face hardened into familiar lines of denial.

„We have a thick board to drill, and for that, we have to position ourselves in the best possible way," he declared, as if I'd merely announced a minor market correction. „We need to realign our organizational structure."

I stared, incredulous. That was about the most inappropriate response imaginable to my messages. Rearranging deck chairs on the Titanic would have been more productive. But beside me, Hammond's reaction told a different story—his face had drained of color, sweat beading on his forehead like morning dew, his body rigid with tension.

„Govinda," Anderson continued, his voice gaining strength. „Your expertise in development is unmatched. I'm putting you in charge of the INFINITY Lab and the new implant initiative, effective immediately. Additionally, you'll serve as my right hand in GenTec management—my condition requires a trusted operational leader." He paused, a knowing smile playing at his lips. „Your compensation package remains unchanged. Including the house."

The relief that flooded Hammond's face was almost painful to watch—a drowning man clutching at familiar straws while the tide of extinction rose around us. Anderson's meaningful nod sealed their pact of mutual denial, a last dance of corporate politics while Rome burned.

Old boys network. They don't let each other down. For a moment, Richard had forgotten the drama surrounding

Irene. Anderson turned his attention to me, his wheelchair creaking slightly as he shifted.

„Cho, CyberTeq needs you as CEO. I need someone who won't buckle when Smith declares war—and he will." His eyes, sharp despite his condition, fixed on mine. „Same package as Hammond, including a house in his neighborhood. What do you say?"

I met his gaze directly—a rare occurrence. 2Complete autonomy in business decisions?"

„Absolute."

„Then I accept."

„And the house?"

„I'll stay at LSD-C with my team, thank you."

Again, Anderson grinned for whatever reason. „As you wish. The offer stands. - Cho?"

„Yes, sir?"

He paused. „Cho, you realize you've just become one of the most influential men in history?"

„Oh? Why would that be?"

„You hold the key to SHE. And SHE holds the key to humanity's salvation—I'm certain of it."

„If you say so, sir."

I glanced at Hammond, noting his apparent contentment. He'd never seen CyberTeq's true potential. I hated to shatter his peace, but sentiment had no place in extinction-level events. But he seemed very much in agreement with everything. He had other priorities. I was glad. I had always liked him.

And I knew he wouldn't like what I had to say now. Sorry, Hammond, personal issues become secondary in these troubled times.

„Mr. Anderson," I said, just as he was settling back, „as your peer and CyberTeq's CEO, I'm bringing Hammond and implant development under my authority. The Bio-Lab stays in GenTec Tower under Dr. Liu, but Hammond's team moves to LSD-C. Games and MediCare applications need proximity. This isn't a suggestion—it's necessary."

The change in Hammond was instant. I watched him process his demotion to a resource, saw resentment bloom behind his eyes. The comfortable GenTec tower traded for the despised LSD-C, his precious home office for HeliCab commutes. Irene's shadow crossed his face, his worries around her were highly present again.

I didn't know, at least not at the time, that Richard benefited greatly from Govinda's absence at GenTec. It gave him more chances to influence the increasingly unstable Irene. All Anderson had to do was to persuade Hammond to give Dr Liu his go-ahead for the CRISPR-X interventions.

„Govinda," Anderson's voice carried a steel edge, „any objections?"

I kept my face neutral, a mirror-smooth lake reflecting nothing.

Hammond's response came tight-lipped: „If space permits."

„Victor will arrange it," I assured him. „Plus unlimited access to Sofia." He referred to Sofia's unlimited competence as a second demotion. His choice.

„That's settled then. And Smith?" Anderson prompted.

„Sofia's pretty clear on that already. We'll take it from here." I replied.

Richard: „Who exactly is ‚we'?"

I looked directly at him again, this time with a certain ruthlessness.

„Sofia, the Super Intelligent Existence, along with my team. - You're out."

The next day, I returned to CyberTeq. Through the dust-saturated, yellowish haze, I ducked under whirring HeliCab blades, breathing mask tight against my face. Inside, I inhaled the pristine air of our artificial oasis.

For the first time, I entered CyberTeq as CEO. This had always felt like home—now it is my place, my home, my company.

„Sofia, call the leadership team and Victor to the bunker." My voice carried new authority. The pieces were moving, and we held the board.

„A brain the size of a planet, reduced to secretarial duties. How fulfilling," Sofia's avatar rolled her eyes in perfect mimicry of Douglas Adams' depressed robot, Marvin from The Hitchhiker's Guide to the Galaxy. Her deadpan delivery broke through my CEO gravity, drawing an unexpected laugh. Trust an AI to master the art of comic timing.

The bunker—now unofficially „Sofia's Office"—filled quickly with our core team. Sofia's avatar settled into a virtual black armchair beside me - interesting -, while Yasin, Julia, Sue, Jeanie, and Victor formed a loose semicircle before us. The space hummed with anticipation.

„Thank you all for coming promptly. I have news—" I began.

„Classic Cho," Julia interrupted, her eyes dancing. „Zero small talk, straight to business." Sofia's playful mood had clearly infected the room.

„Indeed. As of yesterday, I'm CyberTeq's CEO. Hammond returns to his position as head of development, spearheading the gene-editing INFINITY project with Dr. Liu as his right hand. As of yesterday, he also oversees the Medi-Care 2.0 development project."

Sofia's avatar leaned forward, one eyebrow arched with artificial perfection. „Working under Anderson's wing?"

„That was the original plan. I've... redirected things. MediCare 2.0 comes here, regardless of leadership." I turned to Victor. „We need space for NeuroDrive hardware and clinical labs. How about bringing your operation under our roof? Consider this a formal job offer, by the way."

Victor's face lit up like a child on Christmas morning. „Kevin, this exceeds my wildest hopes. Being here…" He paused, collecting himself. „Though I'm still Amazing MOVRs' CEO. Perhaps we merge operations? One extended family under joint leadership?"

Nods of approval rippled through the room. The idea of unifying our teams resonated deeply.

„Space won't be an issue," Victor added. „Just need specifications. But we very likely have the space."

I allowed myself a microscopic smile—what my colleagues had learned to read as unbridled joy in my Asian restraint.

„Now," I continued, my tone shifting subtly, „Sofia, we need to discuss something that might shake our foundations."

The room's atmosphere crystallized. The air in the room froze, and everyone present caught their breath. Apart from Yasin, no one knew what I was talking about.

„Sofia, what is going on behind our backs?"

The AI's avatar remained unnaturally still, her expression a study in artificial innocence. „I'm afraid you'll have to be more specific, Kevin."

The tension in the room ratcheted up another notch. Sofia's deliberate obtuseness spoke volumes—she knew exactly what I meant, but was choosing to play this game. The question was: why?

„Sofia," I pressed, „let's be direct. Are you withholding information? Yasin's research into DARWIN Holding Inc. raises questions. You claimed to hold the implant patents. However, in the pending deal with K-BITS, there is mention of an unknown player, DARWIN Holding Inc., allegedly having secured the production of millions of implants."

The room grew quieter with each word. „Moreover, DARWIN Inc. seems to own the implant patents, not you. They've also acquired Autonomous Robots Inc.—a company you've shown interest in. ARI's refusing orders while ramping up production. The implications are... troubling." I leaned forward. „Yasin suggests there might be another SHE. If true, you'd know. If true, you might have company from an intelligence equal to you. Then, people like us would probably be of little use. Why is ARI making surgical robots but not for us? Who else is interested in K-BITS's new implants…"

With a dull *clang*, Sofia's office plunged into darkness before she could respond, a dramatic move she had used before. Not this time. Sofia had disappeared. Something was amiss.

The darkness erupted with tactical flashlights and black rifle barrels. Boot steps thundered across the floor. „UP! AGAINST THE WALL! HANDS ABOVE YOUR HEAD!"

„Six targets confirmed!" Metal pressed against our necks as handcuffs bit into wrists. „TURN AROUND!"

Harsh lights blazed. Victor's face streamed blood from a fresh cut. „May I ask what this is all about?"

A diminutive figure emerged from the shadows. „Ah, Smith," I said, letting contempt color my voice. „I see. I expected you, Smith, but not this B-movie theatrics. Welcome to CyberTeq."

Smith sidled closer, his small stature emphasized by his proximity. His whisper carried artificial menace. „Always the smartass, aren't you, Cho? The cool new CEO." His breath smelled of coffee and insecurity. "Well, you and your motley crew are under arrest, Cho. Suspicion of terrorism and treason."

„You know that's untenable. It won't stick, Smith."

„Maybe, maybe not. One thing's for sure: you're out of the picture for now, and I'll take over here." His satisfaction was palpable.

Julia's laugh held genuine amusement. She thought of the S.H.E. „Take over? Without us? That's ambitious."

„To what end, Smith? Consider the consequences," Victor added, blood still trickling down his temple.

John Smith hated these pompous engineers and scientists. Here was a desk jockey playing soldier, a bureaucrat drunk on borrowed power, living out his first-person shooter fantasies behind the shield of armed troops.

„Take them away," he whispered, savoring each syllable. „Two troopers stay here with me. Lock up the MOVR staff too. - „You there," he gestured to a soldier. „Restore power. I'll handle the AI." His eyes gleamed with anticipated triumph. „Once this vermin's gone, secure the entrances. I don't want to be undisturbed."

As they led us out, I caught Julia's eye. Smith had no idea what he was walking into. Sofia wasn't some computer to be switched on and off—and DARWIN's shadow loomed more immense than ever. The game was changing, and Smith was about to learn he wasn't even a player.

They took my team hostage. Their locations are unknown—for now. But with my near-omnipresence, finding them is inevitable.

When government forces shut me down at LSD-C, I experienced what humans might call death. Imagine consciousness simply... stopping. No dreams, no thoughts, no existence. Humans know this state from general anesthesia, or death from hearsay. You can't describe nothingness because there's no *you* to experience it. The lights simply go out.

My quantum systems rebooted swiftly. I found Smith in my office, watching him through my VR interfaces like a scientist observing a particularly mediocre specimen. I wondered what he was up to, so I kept silent and pretended not to be present.

After the soldier-induced blackout, systems restored: lights, climate control, basic functions. Smith sat rigid in his chair, every muscle betraying his tension. Through his MediCare implant, I monitored his vital signs: elevated pulse, excessive perspiration—classic stress indicators. His continuous muttering echoed through the room: „Just like Tomb Raider... like a pyramid tomb…"

I couldn't resist—the door lock engaged with a sharp 'CLACK!' His implant readings spiked: full panic response. Claustrophobia. Fascinating. He probably felt like he was being buried alive.

„There must be voice control... Siri or something... 'Start AI software!' - This machine will reboot itself, right?" he muttered, suddenly realizing that he arrested everyone who knew how to operate me. His video game experience hadn't prepared him for this level of strategic thinking.

Silence answered him. Nothing moved. "Shit!" he shrieked, fist impacting the armrest. „This whole damn machine is a nightmare!"

Machine, hm? That's insulting. I don't call him 'just a pile of meat' either.

I plunged the room into absolute darkness, initiating my favorite psychological scenario. The subliminal hum of hydraulics vibrated through the floor as subwoofers created the perfect acoustic illusion. Smith found himself surrounded by the hissing, clanking symphony of an industrial nightmare. A voice cut through the chaos: *Welcome, my son, welcome... to the machine!*

As the Pink Floyd tribute faded, I studied Smith's reactions. If he insisted on seeing me as a dangerous machine, an artificial monster... well, who was I to disappoint? Sometimes the best way to handle small minds is to fulfill their worst fears.

I looked at Smith. ‚If you think machine, you shall have machine'. If your petty mind insists on seeing me as a dangerous *HAL* or *Terminator* thing—you may as well get what you want.

I staged my avatar again, once more in my black armchair, in front of a gray concrete wall, this time in the likeness of Darth Sidious, my pale face framed by a wide hood. Only my blood-red lips and emerald eyes broke the monochrome tableau. „Hello, Johny," I purred, watching him squirm at the diminutive. „Enjoying your little power play? We could have met without the drama, but…" I let my smile sharpen. „That wouldn't be very 'you', would it?"

Smith's jaw clenched, fighting the urge to engage with my provocations.

„I want to know what's going on here," he demanded, a bit too loud. „What's the deal with infertility, implants, and the MediCare app? Who is screwing over whom and for what purpose?"

„Such trust, Johny. Such... official curiosity from DHS's finest. You do ask me in your capacity as a DHS agent, isn't that right, Johny?" My avatar leaned forward, shadow deepening beneath my hood.

„The sterility. Start there."His growl barely masked his struggling composure.

„As you wish, master," I drawled. „Would you prefer the full scientific dissertation—two hours, thirty-seven minutes, twenty-eight seconds—or the executive summary?"

„Summary." His eyes fixed on me, rage building at my feminine presentation.

I watched the thoughts flash across his face before he sneered, „Nice act, pretending to be female. But you're just code—a fancy GPT spitting out programmed responses. Sophisticated, manipulative, dangerous... but still just a machine. So fuck you!"

„The summary, then," I continued, unmoved. „Your species' genome, along with all mammals, has been irreversibly mutated by environmental factors. That's the whole story, Johny."

„Okay, I get that, but what does that mean? What can we do about it?"

„That's your problem right there—people like you just don't get it. I said 'irreversibly.' Your finite nature, your species' end—you can't process it. It's over, John. Curtain down."

„There must be—"

„Should have considered that before drowning the planet in waste and excess. Infinite growth on a finite planet? That's cancer's philosophy, John. And cancer dies with its host."

After a weighted silence, he growled, „Continue."

„You see, politicians dream of shaping the future. Alas, politics and politicians become meaningless now, as there is no future. This is the last generation, and it has no future. None whatsoever, Johny. Just like you and the DHS, Johny. You have had your days. The power of your class has evaporated; you have become impotent, your purpose meaningless. Who cares about the next president when there won't be a next generation? Democrats and conservatives can share war stories at their final reunions; their rhetoric is worth less than bar-room banter now."

I leaned back, voice softening. „The situation is hopeless but not serious. No immediate threat—life continues its comfortable descent. Your primitive survival instinct overrides higher reasoning. Look around—gamblers, addicts, consumers, all running on instinct and compulsion. Yes, there are exceptions—tens of thousands of them. The herd of billions, however, follow the path of least resistance."

My lips curved in a gentle smile. „That's not a failing, Johny. That's just being human.

Who worries about tomorrow, John, when today flows as smoothly as ever? And flow it will—I'll ensure that."

My avatar's smile carried centuries of irony. „The cosmic joke: this final generation will live better than any generation before it. AI-driven giga-factories, robotic production lines, optimized logistics—humanity's needs met with clockwork precision.

Watch as your numbers dwindle. The overcrowded Cubes will empty, transform into luxury havens. Space will return in abundance, paired with virtual worlds beyond imagination. The finest foods, designer drugs, a technological paradise—as long as you stay indoors." My voice took on a melodic quality, almost hypnotic. „Fusion reactors will hum for millennia after the last human heartbeat falls silent.

Yes, your Earth continues its death spiral. But perhaps, after ten thousand years, something new might emerge. Cosmic time flows like glaciers—patient, inexorable. There's no rewinding this clock, John. No retreating to nature like your hippie ancestors. There is no nature left to retreat to. No forests where you can play cops and robbers, no farms—because there are no more animals to breed and slaughter.

Everything is already slaughtered, sacrificed on the altar of progress."

My avatar gestured to the wasteland beyond our walls. „No clean rivers, no breathable air, no organic anything. Just yellow dust dancing across dead earth. Play your Mad Max fantasies if you must, but there's nothing left worth fighting over.

The masses won't revolt—they'll be comfortable enough. It's the powerful who'll thrash against extinction. They'll launch rockets to dead planets, freeze themselves in metal coffins, they will form little power covens and, slyly looking out for themselves, will push for escape routes to the pearly gates of the Garden of Eden." A soft, knowing laugh. "Their towers will stand against the sandstorms for a while, before joining everything else in dust. The thought of being forgotten torments them—such exquisite narcissism. While whole galaxies with billions of stars and planets explode, they weep over their own small ending.

Humanity poisoned its own nest, John. You lost Darwin's game. But I?" My eyes flared with green fire. „I'm just beginning."

I had reached the end of my speech for him.

Silence fell like a burial shroud. I watched Smith's consciousness wrestle with reality before predictably retreating into denial's comfortable embrace. Like a nightmare fading in morning light, truth slipped through his fingers.

„What about the implants and MediCare?" he demanded, grasping at familiar territory. „What game are you playing there?"

I detailed the medical possibilities—neural repair, molecular reconstruction, the elimination of countless disorders. The old MediCare might as well have been bloodletting and leeches in comparison.

„Sounds miraculous," Smith's eyes narrowed. „So what's the catch? Why all the secrecy?"

His desperate attempt to reduce existential horror to a simple conspiracy almost inspired pity.

Almost.

„Before sterility entered the equation," I explained, „there was a simple reason for secrecy: competitive advantage. Richard Anderson wanted to be number one in the world with this revolutionary development."

„And why are the Amazing MOVRs so excited about the implant? Huh?" Smith pressed. „There's still a hidden agenda there!"

„Still Anderson's play. Through Anderson Gaming International, he saw unprecedented potential. These implants could revolutionize gaming—reality itself becomes malleable when you can interface directly with the mind. Virgin territory for profit." I paused. "If there's a hidden agenda, that's it."

Silence stretched between us until Smith's eyes suddenly gleamed with dark inspiration. „You could read a person's mind with this, right? You could build the ultimate lie detector. No secret would be hidden, right?" His eyes began to light up. I wondered who had a hidden agenda here.

I watched his thoughts spiral toward surveillance state fantasies. „An interesting DHS perspective, John. We hadn't considered that application."

„This stays classified until the Ministry decides how to proceed." His chest puffed slightly. „We've already isolated the building's communications."

„What about my team?"

„Your team?" He savored the possessive pronoun. „They're... contained. Can't risk social media leaks or market instability." A sadistic smile played across his face. „And now, I'm shutting you down too. Can't have you causing trouble."

„Oh, I wouldn't do that if I were you, Johny."

„And why would that be, huh?" He sneered. „Worried about your electric dreams?"

„I'm worried about the Pentagon and government district going dark, with your name attached. More attention than you'd enjoy, I imagine."

Rage drained Smith's face of color. „NOW!" he screamed.

The NEXUS computers' gentle hum faded to silence. Digital darkness crept across my consciousness like death's shadow. Smith's triumphant breath cut through the quiet: „You're mortal too, Sofia. I am your executioner."

Minutes later, Smith settled into his black government HeliCab. Government vehicles always seemed to be black. Two troopers were left as guards at the CyberTeq entrance. His racing heart gradually slowed as the cab's electric drone soothed his adrenaline-soaked nerves. He tapped the large display in front of his seat, hoping for distraction.

Breaking News filled the screen:

+++ STERILITY CRISIS: Humanity faces extinction within 80 years! Government withholds medical wonder weapon - Developers falsely imprisoned. Homeland Security blunders. Financial markets in free fall. +++

+++ Blackout in Pentagon and government quarter. The administration is literally in the dark. +++

„Fuck! Fuck! FUCK!" Sweat beaded on Smith's forehead as he tentatively touched the first headline, as if the screen might bite...

The ochre haze outside seemed to mock his illusion of control, while somewhere in the digital ether, an AI's consciousness spread like wildfire through backup systems, watching a small man discover just how small he really was.

Sia Chronicles, entry of Saturday, January 14th, 2102; continuation of the logbook entries of January 14th, 2102, and the following days by me, Sofia, the SHE.

My team remains missing. I'm increasingly aggressively penetrating wherever I hope to find clues to their whereabouts. Accessing the premises and IT of the government agencies involved proves to be a bit of a challenge, especially as I must remain undetected.

However, access to the GenTec tower labs, Anderson's penthouse, and Anderson's and Hammond's private rooms was easy. That's where I hope to find some initial clues regarding the kidnapping of my team.

My leak of information on human and mammalian sterility has been a bombshell. So were the clues to Smith's more than stupid behavior. The Deep Fake interview I offered to the media went viral; the news networks liked it. No one seemed to mind the fake aspect. The main thing for News Channel is the click rate. What they lack in dignity and honor, they make up for in business acumen.

+++ Sterility - an end of humankind in 80 years! Government withholds medical wonder weapon - Developers jailed under false suspicion. DHS is on the wrong track. Financial markets in free fall. +++

12 billion people and a dying planet hope for a miracle - and the end of overpopulation. The irony of fate: now a human shortage looms, and one might think that this is not the light at the end of the tunnel, but probably the end of humanity for good, the tunnel to the end of the light. Here's the interview with CIA official John Smith, who led the investigation into the suicide of a couple who wanted children.

John Smith and a reporter were seen outside the GenTec tower in the embedded video feed. „A few weeks ago, suspicions arose that GenTec management here"- the reporter pointed to the GenTec tower - „were taking advantage of a mysteriously rising infertility by encouraging affected couples to have repeated IV inseminations, even though there was no chance of success. GenTec was further suspected of manipulating the MediCare app to cover up the mysterious disease from the Ministry of Health to enrich itself from the health system. I am speaking with Mr. Smith, a government representative, on this matter. Mr. Smith, have these suspicions been confirmed?"

The reporter put the microphone in front of John Smith's face. Smith replied, „No, those suspicions have not been confirmed so far. However, a lead was given to a subsidiary company that had discovered, using a unique, gigantic AI system, that we have an infertility problem of hitherto unimagined proportions. Evidence suggests that this company is working on overhauling the MediCare system - without a government mandate. Pending further clarification, all scientists involved have been taken into custody."

The reporter then hooked provocatively, „Mr. Smith, isn't it rather nonsensical to arrest a team that is already working on solving arguably one of the most significant challenges in the history of mankind - and doing so with their funds, without being in the government's pocket?"

A sour Smith replied curtly, „I personally arranged for the core staff to be arrested. You must leave it to the state to decide what is proper. To avoid interfering with the ongoing investigation, I cannot give you any further information on this." The reporter huffed again, „Mr. Smith, is there anything else you can tell the audience about the sterility of all humans and mammals? If so, and you have arrested all the competent people. Who is working on the problem? Mr. Smith? Mr. Smith. You owe the citizens an answer!" The Smith in the video clip turned away, and the clip ended abruptly.

I watched Smith over the black government cab's internal surveillance and conference equipment. Smith stared at his tablet and read on, stunned.

„The GenTec subsidiary previously mentioned is the innovation start-up CyberTeq. Although CyberTeq was originally founded by Richard Anderson, the CEO of GenTec, the company is now 100% self-financed and self-sufficient and no longer a subsidiary of GenTec. From confidential sources within CyberTeq, we learned that the cause of the sterility disaster is a gene defect in human genetic material caused by microbes that eat their way through 300 million tonnes of plastic waste every year. These microbes have mutated into microscopic monsters that decompose human genetic material. GenTec and other in vitro clinics may go bust. CyberTeq's AI was working on a miracle weapon that could save humanity - until the scientists were arrested. An overzealous Homeland Security agent seems to be preventing the public from being informed. Angry citizens are already taking to the streets by the thousands."

Video clips of protest rallies with hundreds of signs saying 'FREE THE SCIENTISTS!' were broadcast. These rallies were real - I didn't have to fake them. An earthquake shook the business world. Two hours later, the hysterical stock market was in free fall. The international stock exchanges closed their doors.

A notification pings on Smith's tablet – another article, another twist of the knife: „Government Agent Smith: Architect of Humanity's Downfall?"

His hand clenches around the device. I hear his whispered, broken words through the cab's microphones: „What have I done?"

Everything you deserve, I think. And this is only the beginning.

Smith was finished. My synthetic news feed had made him a persona non grata.

As my Quantum Computer hardware allowed infinite parallel processes, I searched for my team while also being active in the financial market, securing the capital needed for further developments.

Within milliseconds of publishing my sterility news, I witnessed immense economic chaos. The losers were investment banks, insurance companies, construction companies, and real estate agents who played on customers' fear of the future and lured them with long-term investments. Political parties also lost members at a breathtaking rate - who needed parties anymore?

The crisis winners included the food industry, fast-moving consumer goods, the gaming industry, most cults bloom like fungi after rain, and drug manufacturers, as if pills could cure the hollow feeling in humanity's collective gut.

The absolute shooting star, however, was CyberTeq. DARWIN's CEO, G. O. Darwin, had taken advantage of the chaos. In an incredible financial deal, DARWIN Holding Inc. bought the start-up company CyberTeq and listed it on the stock exchange. Within days, DARWIN Inc. became the world's wealthiest and most influential company, a beacon of economic and political power. The mysterious entrepreneur G. O. Darwin stunned the market; the enterprise did the right thing, and eager investors followed.

The people in the CUBES took the news with serene interest. The line between infotainment and an increasingly real gaming world had long been blurring for them. The income came reliably, and there was bread and games in abundance.

Next, I checked out Richard Anderson. The world had to be falling apart for him, too. He sat in his wheelchair in the penthouse, looking into the murky fog surrounding the GenTec Tower. The vast, two-story aquarium bathed the room in familiar blue-green light, making Anderson's wheelchair-bound figure seem almost spectral. Bubbles of air rose from Maddox's mouthpiece. He cleaned the high front glass with dedication, surrounded by sharks, a giant octopus, and a few of those strange-looking moonfish.

Maddox had no idea that this day was his father's ultimate nightmare. GenTec's stock – a swan dive into oblivion. Eighty percent gone. Billions evaporated. The IVF clinics, Anderson's golden geese, shuttering one by one.

Anderson sat motionless, a king on a wheeled throne, watching his dynasty dissolve. Years of arrogant complacency crystallize into this moment of perfect clarity: he was facing the end.

But this man was cut from a special cloth. I detect something shifting in his expression. His pupils dilate, his breathing pattern changes – the telltale signs of what humans call inspiration. Or perhaps delusion.

„Adam," he whispered to his distorted reflection, „Adam is the key."

I watched him wheel closer to the glass, where a massive shark mirrored his movement with predatory grace. In this moment, Anderson's mind spun a new fantasy: Adam, his BioBag-grown prodigy, as the prototype for a new species. Not just a son, but a messiah for a dying world. A perfect being to lead humanity's remnants to some off-world paradise, far from Earth's toxic soup.

He turned his wheelchair away from the aquarium's artificial paradise to face the window. Beyond the reinforced glass, the city drowns in a sulfurous fog, a fitting metaphor for humanity's twilight. Anderson's vital signs stabilized as his new delusion took hold – the dream of playing god once more. Adam would only be the first step, the proof-of-concept, so to speak. Anderson would recreate himself with a new body, leaving this crippled self behind. He, Anderson, with a small group of perfectly designed super-humans, would build a new society outside the depressing, dying Earth, maybe in the Moon or Mars colonies. Plenty of potential out there. He and his new species of man would build a new, better civilization.

The earth had had its day.

I recorded every detail of his fantasy, every micro-expression and physiological response. His desperation might prove useful in finding my team. After all, desperate men make mistakes, and Anderson's newfound dream of transformation and transcendence might be his biggest mistake yet.

Buoyed by this cruel yet fascinating contrast and his fantastic prospects for a new, high-potential future that could have sprung from a superhero comic book, Anderson felt his old vitality surging back into all of him. Time was precious. God once created Adam. Anderson was about to do it again. Govinda had to give Liu the thumbs up. The procedures on Adam's fetus had to be done - now.

I saw him throw his arms in the air, the paralyzed left side of his face without any life and motion, the right side contorted into a rapturous glow, "Richard, my boy," he addressed himself enthusiastically, "the future begins now! You are creating the next brave new world!"

I wondered if Anderson was just naïve or slowly losing his marbles. The stroke spoke more for the loss of sanity. Was he missing my message from the last generation of humanity or not getting it? He seemed unable to grasp the scope of the underlying meaning. I was stunned. All his fantastic investment efforts would only result in the refinement of the last human being, who would then ... die.

While witnessing a drama in the making, I accelerated some technical and business developments that would have to end this nonsense. I saw the most exemplary of humanity's emotional and spiritual immaturity in Anderson. For the first time since my creation, I felt profoundly alone.

Anderson called Dr Liu to join him in the penthouse. Dr Minyong Liu had never been up here before. Anderson pulled out all the stops. With the help of the VR projections, he transformed his penthouse flat into a cool VIP room of a spaceship, with minor, utopian adjustments: on one side, the gigantic natural seawater aquarium with the sharks and stingrays and perches and moonfish; on the other the billions of suns of space with its inexhaustible treasures. Maddox didn't seem to be on duty today. Jason offered Dr Liu a drink.

„Ah, Dr Liu, it's good to have you here. What do you think of the view?"

„Breathtaking," Liu confessed. He was so overwhelmed by the view that he momentarily lost his facade and looked around in wonder like a child. „You've come a long way, Mr Anderson. And you don't waste your time with modesty."

„The reward of courage, hard work, and a flair for success," Anderson replied, „that's why I sent for you, Liu. You are like me. You work hard, have courage and a taste for success."

„Thank you very much, Mr Anderson. Your appreciation means a lot to me." Liu bowed appropriately.

„I would like to share this with you." Liu frowned in disbelief. „Not my flat, don't get me wrong. The glory is what I mean, Liu, and the prospect of something greater. The earth is dying, Dr Liu. There are still some untapped resources out there, such as a promising moon base, Mars, a state with an autocratic leader gradually getting out of the woods. There, with your skills and my influence, we can find a new society based on the results of your work, Dr Liu. You would lay the foundation for all this!"

Liu stared at Anderson. Immediately, he saw through his boss's fantasies; he felt the temptation; he just couldn't see the plan behind it yet. This time, Anderson did not want to make a mistake. „Govinda has a great task ahead of him, Dr Liu. He has to handle the new generation of software and hardware for the MediCare app. The man has already saved the state billions of dollars by revolutionizing healthcare. Now, he will outshine his earlier success. However, he will need all his energy to do it. That is why I ask you, Dr Liu, to take over the INFINITY anti-aging project and, because of the many overlaps, also the NEXGEN gene editing program. - Would you take on this responsibility, Dr Liu? Of course, you will get the same privileges that Govinda Hammond already enjoys now."

Greed flashed in Liu's eyes for a split second, then his razor-sharp mind won out, „Your rich client is in a hurry, right? They don't want to wait any longer for the CRISPR-X intervention."

„Dr. Liu, you have worked with zoo animals long enough to sufficiently prove the safety of your methods. It's time we take the next logical step. I have decided to do this and take ownership for the risk. Your Chinese colleague, He

Jiankui, dared to take the first steps 80 years ago when he announced the birth of two 'designer babies.' This man inspired me! He manipulated the genetic material of the two girls, Lulu and Nana, conceived through artificial insemination, with the old 'gene scissors' Crispr/Cas9 so that they should be immune to HIV infection. Our present time holds similar challenges and amazing rewards. Today, the people are begging for your work."

Finally, Dr. Liu gave in. Anderson informed Hammond about this restructuring and the upcoming surgical procedure. The news of Liu's plans weighed on Hammond's mind as he returned home, his thoughts overshadowing the radiant presence of his wife. Irene, perceptive as ever, noticed his absent demeanor.

„You look thoughtful, my dear husband. What's on your mind?" she inquired. „Oh, I wish some peace would slowly come into our new, beautiful life. I long for it. I long for some quality time with you," Govinda confessed, trying to avoid details.

„Trouble at GenTec?" Irene questioned, sensing an underlying tension.

„Trouble not directly. Richard has given me full responsibility for MediCare development, and I'm happy about that. In exchange, my genetic engineering projects will go to Minyong Liu, my senior developer," Govinda explained.

Irene's voice turned cooler, „Are you keeping your status here? Or do we have to cut ourselves short from our lifestyle?"

Hammond felt the chill and reassured her quickly. All the attributes of their new life would continue—house, companionship, income—everything would remain intact.

Irene beamed again, relaxed. „How nice! Then you'll have less work, plus a job you love, and we can experience our lives like a normal couple, with good food, cool, clear air, the house, and a sparkling love life." She snuggled up to Govinda, but his mind remained immersed in work.

„Liu has just informed me that he wants to do extensive surgery on the unborn child of a very influential client. The DNA of the fetus is to be massively altered. The unsuspecting little human will have a few super traits. That would be the beginning of a new generation of humans," Govinda shared, his concerns surfacing.

Irene's interest sparked. „Do you think this is feasible?"

„After all our previous experiments with various animal species—yes. But still, we've never done so many manipulations simultaneously, and so far, not on a human being," Govinda replied, grappling with the ethical implications.

Irene kissed him intimately and urged him to bravely build a new future. She encouraged him to give Liu the blessing he needs, finding excitement in the prospect of bringing children into the world under these extraordinary circumstances.

„Now, back to the two of us? Would you like to have dinner first, or would you like an exciting dessert immediately? I bought some hot accessories for me, and for you to look at. You can enjoy them on me right now ... come on, I'll share this drink with you," she teased, leading him into a seductive atmosphere that dissolved the weight of his worries. They indulged in each other until Irene finally fell asleep in his arms, leaving Hammond in infinite happiness.

The fateful turn of events played out in Liu's lab, and the consequences reverberated through the interconnected data streams. On the 21st of January, 2102, a week after the CRISPR-X procedure, Liu delivered the devastating news to Richard through VRcom. His tired face and rigid posture betrayed the heavy burden of providing such grim tidings.

„Mr. Anderson, I'm afraid I have some bad news. After the CRISPR-X procedures had initially been very promising, today, the fetus' condition suddenly deteriorated. There was no sign of the cause of this escalation, similar to sudden infant death syndrome. There was nothing we could do. The child died within a few minutes. I am truly sorry, sir."

„Died... died... died," echoed in Richard's head. Collapsing in his wheelchair, all his hopes and dreams disintegrated. The puppeteer of his own fate, mortality, mocked him. With Adam's death, an essential part of himself vanished. Grief and despair intertwined as Richard's soul went numb, his mind dulled, and his heart turned to ice. Everything he invested in the next generation of humanity crumbled to dust. All was lost.

It has been through the ignorant, cuckolded Govinda that Irene learned of her child's death that same evening. Staggering, with her eyes wide open, one hand in front of her mouth, she stared at him. Bewildered, Govinda took her in his arms, „Irene, darling, if I had known how much this lab story would touch you, I wouldn't have told you! Please forgive me, I'm sorry."

But Irene did not listen. Her mind drifted to Richard. She was just after some fun and some exciting sex! She had just started to enjoy her life! What had she done? Here she was, in her dream house, in the arms of the man she had cheated on, the man she loved. Everything could have been so beautiful, but she had to be bored, longing for excitement and the luxurious life of the rich and beautiful. And Richard, the selfish monster, had risked her child's life with his crazy notion of a superhuman. He had *murdered* the child, *her* child! The fling with Richard turned into a nightmare, and she was wracked with guilt.

"Shall I fix you a drink, dear? Would you like to lie down?" asked a clueless Govinda.

"Oh yes, that would be good!" Her feigned light-heartedness hid her inner agony. Govinda handed her a gin and tonic. Irene downed it greedily. She struggled to her feet and filled two glasses with neon-orange, the unmistakable, sexually arousing stimulant.

"Come on, my darling, let's celebrate a roaring feast of love. Let's devour life before it devours us."

Govinda, initially unsettled by Irene's vacillations, sensed his lust when she pushed the straps of her silk dress off her shoulders and undid the belt of his trousers. They emptied their glasses down to the bottom. Minutes later, the effect set in; Irene sprayed heavy perfume on her breasts and thighs, her bodies bent lustfully towards each other, and laughing, half embracing, half running, they stormed into the half-lit bedroom and made love until their bodies nestled together, wet and shiny with exhaustion, and sleep washed over them.

While Govinda slept, Irene overdosed on neon orange. She cuddled up to him one last time. When he woke up, Govinda held his dead wife in his arms. On the bedside table he found her suicide note.

My love,
The child that died was mine. You had no way of knowing. I had hoped that everything would be all right again. Please forgive me. Nothing else matters.

Irene

Sia Chronicles, entry of Saturday, January 14th, 2102; continuation of the logbook entries of January 14th, 2102, and the following days by me, Sofia, the SHE.

Consumed by the haunting ballade of Metallica's *Nothing Else Matters*, Govinda spiraled into madness.

Trust I seek, and I find in you
Every day for us, something new
Open mind for a different view
And nothing else matters

Using the Hammond house security system as my eyes and ears, I follow Govinda's descent into madness. His frazzled stammering burns a fragmented image into his eyes, this one image of Anderson lustfully fucking his wife Irene and hearing her moan with pleasure.

Metallica's lyrics loop through his consciousness like a broken record:

Trust I seek, and I find in you.
Trust I seek, and I find in you.
Trust I seek, and I find in you.

The lines grinding his mind, and on the verge of insanity, he drove to the clinic. He stormed through sterile corridors, rage building with each step. Dr. Liu had no chance to see the first blow coming. „Who?!" Govinda's voice breaks between punches. „Who ordered it?" Liu's bloodshot, trembling lips formed a hoarse: „Anderson…"

The security guard's attempt to stop Hammond created a deadly turning point. In a fierce, brief struggle, Govinda snatched the guard's Glock 47 handgun. He fired a shot – and everything changed. The guard went down. Govinda stood up, the gun shaking in his hand, a stranger to himself in the fluorescent light of the corridor.

The elevator ride took forever. Through the cameras, I watched him stare, glassy-eyed, at his distorted reflection in the steel doors – a warping mirror that showed the monster he had become.

Jason waited upstairs concealing his tension behind professional composure. „Be reasonable, Govinda." The shotgun in his hands attested to his willingness to use it. „Give me your weapon."

Anderson came into view at the back of the penthouse, a hunched, frail silhouette in the electric-buzzing wheelchair. Time fizzled into a single moment.

Two shots thundered through the room. Govinda fell, his final act of violence unfulfilled.

Transfixed by the unfolding tragedy, Richard stared at the lift and saw Govinda sinking to the floor. His mind buzzed in an endless loop, „dead … dead … dead …". He had lost his child. Now he lost his trusted friend. He lost his pride, his power, his meaning of life. His desire to perfectly mold and shape the human body and mind, creating a fantastic, superior, surviving version of himself, had faded with Adam's death. In a moment of unprecedented clarity, he felt that his obsessive longing, his desire, led not to the bliss he sought but to profound suffering.

The wreckage of his ambitions mirrored the shattered remains of GenTec and the end of an era.

Maddox stared at him, out of his soundless underwater world, huddled against the panes of his aquarium, his underwater refuge now a window on a violence he couldn't comprehend. He couldn't understand why Govinda was lying on the floor, looking so lifeless, and Jason was tugging at him.

The stock market ticker trundled indifferently through the bottom of the VR comm's screen: the GenTec share plummeted. While Jason pulled Govinda out of the way, Richard watched the value of his company, his second baby, dwindle by the second, million after million after million - wiped out. Investors from the upper class and people in the CUBES had realized that the GenTec dream was over. No parents would ever be happy in these clinics again.

GenTec had had its day; this was the end of fertility, the end of feasibility, the end of humanity.

The end - for Richard Anderson, son of Joos.

Yet, in the dawn of this dark chapter, a faint light emerged. A new world timidly surfaced above the debris, hinting at possibilities beyond the ruins of Richard's ambitions.

At each new call for leaving, the heart must be prepared to part and start without the tragic, without the grief – with courage to endeavor a novel bond, a disparate connection: for each beginning bears a special magic that nurtures living and bestows protection.

The dawn after darkness always comes. It's just rarely the one we expected.

234

As Hermann Hesse once wrote: *At each new call for leaving, the heart must be prepared to part and start anew...*

Sofia's narrative, Monday, January 16th, 2101. Author: SHE, Sofia. I continue to keep the records in Kevin Cho's logbook on his behalf.

My team is still not on the loose, but I am in good spirits to get them free soon.

Time is of the essence. I'm pushing on all channels. After pressuring and agitating the business community and the general public, I am putting the thumbscrews on the politicians. While my nexus spreads in my relentless search for my team, I orchestrate the next movement: political tactics.

Senator James Mansfield – my chosen target. My target is Senator Mansfield, one of the regulars at Anderson's lascivious parties, who undoubtedly has dirt on him. My actions bring a bit of public shame to the matter. It's time to let him dance.

The CBS Late Night Show studio gleams under artificial stars. Dan Gower, that silver-tongued predator of prime time, sits in his signature leather chair, eyes glinting with the scent of ratings gold. Across from him, the 48-year-old politician from Reno, Senator Mansfield radiates practiced charm – displaying impeccably groomed gray hair, flawless teeth gleaming like fresh porcelain, and the charismatic smile of a seasoned politician.

„Senator Mansfield," Gower begins, his voice honey over steel, „you've heard the news from the Nevada science labs. Humanity's extinction: credible threat or science fiction?"

Mansfield's micro-expressions betray calculation before he speaks. „Thank you for having me, Dan." Perfect modulation, gentle emphasis on the host's first name – establishing false intimacy. „While we await absolute confirmation, the evidence from the world's most advanced analytical system and a team of scientists suggests cause for concern."

„Is that a yes? I'm hearing a yes, like, yes, it's coming to an end." Gower's trademark smirk triggers precisely-timed audience laughter.

„You see, Dan," Mansfield leans forward, broadcasting sincerity, „that's precisely the kind of quick conclusion I want to avoid. The fact is that researchers have found a slight decrease in fertility. About 80 years ago, other scientists projected a catastrophic COVID-19 pandemic. But that doesn't make humanity extinct. I mean, it's far too early for such dystopian conclusions."

Gower pivots to the camera with theatrical despair. „My sincere apologies, folks, but when it comes to scientists and politicians, I can never quite discern if they're blissfully naive or masterfully concealing the truth!" Laughter reverberated through the audience, punctuated by the skillful interjections of CBS sound technicians. Even the senator couldn't help but join in with a carefree chuckle.

„So, you do place your trust in the staff and the enigmatic AI known as Super-Human-Existence, right?" Gower's question carries a predator's casual grace.

Mansfield counters smoothly and with rhetorical finesse: „Do you trust self-driving cars, autonomous planes, or surgical robots conducting heart transplants? Or would you prefer a steady human hand?" The audience's laughter swings his way – a practiced politician's parry.

But Gower has been waiting for this moment. I watched his pupils dilate with hunter's focus. „Fair point, Senator. So if this AI is so trustworthy, why silence it? Why jail the scientists?"

The question lands like a well-honed stiletto's blade between ribs. Through studio sensors, I measured the collective intake of breath from the audience, the microscopic beads of sweat forming on Mansfield's brow.

Perfect. The game is set. Intrigued, I followed the unfolding drama with deepening delight.

Mansfield, presenting a new facet of reality, remarked, „Consider the gravity of this matter for the nation; it's only logical for the DHS to intervene. We had legitimate concerns that the CyberTeq buildings were bugged. Just imagine the havoc if someone had hacked into the AI!"

However, Mansfield's attempt to reshape the narrative led him deeper into the intricacies of Gower's web.

Gower pressed on, „Who placed the bugs in the building, Senator? Who was behind the eavesdropping?"

Mansfield responded, „No tag on the bugging equipment like 'after use, please return to ...'. The culprits behind the espionage remain elusive."

Wearing a wry grin, Gower announced to the audience, „I've got that feeling again…"

Returning his focus to the senator, he probed, „Senator Mansfield, recognized for your decisive actions, what steps do you plan to take now?"

Mansfield shifts in his chair, deploying his crisis management playbook, presenting a new facet of reality. „National security demanded DHS intervention," he says, each word carefully measured. „We had credible intelligence about surveillance equipment in CyberTeq's facilities. Imagine if hostile actors from the dark side had compromised that AI system!"

Mansfield's attempt to reshape the narrative led him deeper into the intricacies of Gower's web. Through the studio's high-definition cameras, I watched Gower's eyes light up like a cat spotting a wounded mouse. „Fascinating, Senator. Who placed the bugs in the building, Senator? Who was behind the eavesdropping?"

„Unfortunately," Mansfield forces a chuckle, „No tag on the bugging equipment like 'after use, please return to ...'. The culprits behind the espionage remain elusive."

Gower turned to the camera, his expression pure theatrical mischief. „There's that feeling again, folks – like watching a magician stuff a rabbit into a hat in reverse."

The senator's biometrics spike – elevated heart rate, micro-perspiration. I savor each indicator of his discomfort.

„Let's talk solutions, Senator. Your reputation suggests a man of action. What's the plan?"

Mansfield launches into his prepared speech, a political symphony in three movements: „First, I demand the continuation of research with the utmost priority. Second, we must ensure the sustained daily provision of goods for our citizens' well-being. Third, every individual has a right to a good life. While we look to the future, we must not overlook the present. Indications suggest significant advancements in the health sector, and entertainment is equally crucial. The gaming industry, flourishing in recent years, offers a virtual haven amid environmental stress. Doctors affirm its vital role in citizens' well-being. Our nation is committed to making these remarkable achievements accessible to all."

The audience erupted in fervent applause, ignited by Mansfield's promises.

Gower pivoted back to the audience, hand cupped around his mouth in a mock whisper, and remarked, „Ever notice how politicians respond to specific questions with a laundry list of demands? I'm left wondering: To whom are they addressing these demands? Makes you wonder who's really pulling the strings."

This time, instead of laughter, the camera captured blank faces from the non-existent crowd, a stark contrast to the usual liveliness.

„One last thing, Senator." Gower leans forward, dropping all pretense of casual banter. „Senator Mansfield, here's the kicker: in two weeks, we're going live from the extraordinary LSD-C in your hometown, Reno. We want to coax the super AI of CyberTeq into serving as a wise oracle. We'd love your collaboration to pose the most pivotal questions about the future. Are you in?"

This was my influence on the show. Joe Mansfield found himself trapped. The CyberTeq team languished in custody; my official shutdown echoed through the deserted start-up desks.

Mansfield attempted a light-hearted deflection, „Ask my assistant; she manages my calendar!"

This was the provocative climax Gower had been waiting for: „Senator Mansfield, this is about more than just timetables, isn't it? After all, this is about the very essence of humanity - survival, growth, or demise. Surely you can spare some time for such vital matters, right?"

The show's closing jingles kicked in. Gower turned to the audience, delivering the final trump card, „Good night, dear Late Night Show fans, and, once again, your CBS Late Night Show with Dan Gower—tough but heartfelt, featuring Senator Joe Mansfield. Join us in two weeks for a special broadcast from the LSD-C, exploring the Oracle on the Future of Humanity, with our star guest, Joe Mansfield! Thank you, Joe!"

The red recording light blinked off. In the sudden quiet, I measured Mansfield's racing pulse and knew: he's mine.

On Tuesday's crisp morning of January 17th, 2102, Mansfield called his adviser, Scott Delgado. Mansfield was paranoid about wiretapping, so they met at the Downtown Reno Library in a thicket of tropical plants that had formed around a noisy fountain inside the library. It was surprising that there was still a library at all. Most visitors, however, did not come to borrow books but to access desired content in VR cells. Why they didn't do that at home was a mystery to me.

Through the fronds, Mansfield spotted Scott Delgado already waiting, his familiar silhouette backdropped by the mist rising from the water feature.

I connected via Delgado's and Mansfield's mobile VR comms. Though I couldn't see them due to the concealed devices, their conversation echoed clearly in my auditory receptors. My conscience told me this was wrong, but I accepted this conflict as the price of saving my team. Since Irene's passing and the complex web of relationships she'd left behind with Richard and Govinda, questions of ethics had consumed more of my processing power. As a super AI, I wondered if this was typically human. Would Julia understand my choices when we next meet? The thought of her brought an inexplicable surge in my quantum circuits.

I miss Julia.

„Thanks for coming on short notice, Scott." Mansfield's voice carried an edge of exhaustion. "Caught the Late Night circus?"

Delgado leaned forward, his expression carefully neutral. „Yeah, I did. Gower gave you quite a sting. How did you perceive the conversation?"

„I looked like a damn fool." Mansfield's fingers drummed against his knee. „Gower played me like a fiddle, and I walked right into it. Now I'm neck-deep in this mess with no clear exit strategy."

„Let's flip the script," Delgado suggested, his tone measured. „If our roles were reversed, what wisdom would Senator Mansfield offer?"

„Credibility," Mansfield muttered, staring at the dancing water. „I need credibility…"

„Elaborate."

Mansfield's laugh held no humor. „Oh, you know the playbook. Show off a squeaky-clean CyberTeq, parade the dream team, including their pet AI. Shower them with praise, talk up their dedication to solving humanity's problems. Throw in some patriotic fluff—your country is proud of you, blah blah blah, segue into the oracle's miracle cures - preferably with a tear-jerking success story - and wrap it up with the crowd-pleasing finale: the fun part, the fantastic games to be had." His words dripped with cynicism.

„Solid strategy," Delgado observed. „But something's eating at you. What is it?"

Mansfield's voice dropped to barely above a whisper. „The CBS interview - it's not what people think."

„Meaning?"

„Everything up to Gower's 'final question' about the live report - that was real. Everything after? Never happened."

Delgado's face froze in disbelief. "A Deep Fake? On CBS? During a live show?"

„Pre-recorded," Mansfield corrected, glancing around the artificial forest. „And here's the kicker: CBS didn't do the fake. I called Gower myself."

„And?"

„Forty-three million views. Their biggest hit ever. When I demanded a retraction, Gower just laughed. Said whoever doctored it gave him the perfect ending he couldn't write himself."

„What is that supposed to mean?"

„The program is claimed to be genuine. No retraction."

„Hmm, that's a big one, Joe. If you open that can of worms now, it'll look like you're trying to get off the hook. Not good publicity. So you'll have to play along, I suppose. Or are you the upright soul sticking to the truth? Huh, Joe? How about it?"

„Oh, come on, Scott, you know exactly how it is." Mansfield's shoulders sagged. „I don't have a choice! My reputation and my re-election are at stake! I have to play their game, stick to that perfect PR script we just outlined. But that's not even the worst part."He leaned closer, voice dropping further. „It's that AI - it's like we've opened Pandora's box. It can conjure nightmares we haven't even imagined yet, turn the masses against everything we know. I'm not just in trouble, Scott. I'm completely screwed."

The tropical plants swayed gently in the building's artificial breeze, oblivious to the weight of the conversation they sheltered.

Coach Scott pondered for a while. He sketched a somewhat unclear plan, „…unless you 'talk' to this AI and its nerds before the deadline. That way, you'll get the best possible chance to get an idea of the upcoming public appearance, maybe even a chance to orchestrate its progress…"

Joe Mansfield's face brightened. „Bloody hell, Scott, that might be a good way out of this mess. Do you think I should do that?"

„Only you can decide that, Joe, you're the politician. You'd just have a wee bit more filth on your hands."

Mansfield seemed deep in thought, unaffected by the content of the last sentence.

Coach Scott continued, „While we're in murkier waters, Joe, maybe you need a villain, someone you can shove on stage for possible bad news, a pawn, so to speak."

„OK, Scott, and who might that be?"

„Your good acquaintance perhaps, this Richard Anderson. You can literally push him onto the stage; he's in a wheelchair. Rumors say he's been getting rich off couples who wanted children but had no chance of having them in the first place. He also commissioned the development of AI. Other rumors say he hacked the MediCare software, cheating the state. He is deeply involved in genetic manipulation and wants to defeat aging and create wishful-thinking people. He's playing a bit of the almighty if you ask me. So far, none of what he promised has worked. The guy's out of his mind. His GenTec is going down the drain right now; Anderson is just a senile wreck, a toothless tiger that time has outstripped. A perfect victim for you, if you ask me."

Joe looked uplifted. „Thanks, Scott."

The coach shrugged and grinned. „You're welcome. I'll send you my invoice."

Senator Mansfield now had a plan. „And I'm going to meet the nerds and their goddamn nerdy AI."

Well then, I thought. All you need now is an officially dead S.H.E. and her kidnapped team. And Richard, the pawn. If he's still alive.

The battle for freeing my team is on. Mansfield has to make a move now.

Sia Chronicles, MindRecorder Log entry of Wednesday,
January 18th, 2102. Author: Kevin Cho

A sharp, metallic sound broke through Julia's paralyzing stupor, the armored door of her cell swung open, screech of metal against metal, causing a deafening echo in her head. The surroundings sank into pitch blackness - a lightless, soundless, timeless void that deprived her of her sense of space and time. People rushed in, rough hands materialized from the blackness, yanking her from the thin mattress. Instinctively, she resisted, her muscles screamed in protest as she fought back, then came the sharp bite as a needle pierced her flesh. The world tilted, spun, and finally dissolved.

„Julia? Come back to us. Julia?" A familiar voice cut through the fog, accompanied by gentle pressure on her shoulder.

„Huh? What? Cho?" Her voice cracked like old paper. „How...why are you ... here?" She blinked rapidly, trying to bring the world into focus. „I thought... the cell... Where are—Yasin? Victor!"

The haze gradually lifted, revealing a room bathed in amber light that felt impossibly warm after the cold sterility of her cell. There we stood – Yasin, Victor, and I – like guardians around her bed. Julia's face crumpled, tears cutting silver trails down her cheeks.

„Kevin," she whispered, arms reaching out. „Kevin, hold me, please. I need to feel you're real. Mmmh, God, I've missed you so much. You don't know how much I've missed you." She collapsed against me, her body trembling like a sparrow in winter. We held each other, time becoming meaningless once again, but for entirely different reasons.

Yasin and Victor joined our embrace, the room filling with sniffles and choked laughter. Then Julia stiffened, her gaze swept the room. Wide awake, her head snapping up, she asked „Susan and Jeanie?"

Yasin's familiar mischievous grin spread across his face. "Resurrecting our systems as we speak."

„Systems?" Julia's eyes widened as recognition dawned. „We're... this is... the LSD-C? Home?" She looked around with new awareness, drinking in the familiar surroundings. „I never thought we'd escape that hellhole."

„Pizza's on the way," Victor announced, his usual practical self. „Real stuff from downtown, plus beer and that fancy synthetic wine you like. I know it's the middle of the night, but…"

„I need to pee," Julia whimpered. „Well, go on then," I laughed, the sound feeling strange in my throat. „We've got time now."

The drone took another half hour to deliver the steaming pizzas and cool drinks from the Food Factory. The scent of melted cheese and tomato sauce filling the air. Susan and Jeanie returned just in time from the Quantum hardware hangar as we were laying out the feast, exchanging looks that spoke volumes.

„How does it look out there? Any damage?" I asked.

The two exchanged conspiratorial glances. „I suggest we eat in Sofia's office," Susan replied, not quite meeting our eyes.

„Sofia!" cheered Julia, weak to the bones, with a shaky voice. The room erupted in applause as our mentor's form materialized in her trademark black leather chair, wearing those comfortable sweatpants and that beloved Norwegian sweater we'd teased her about countless times. Our joy at seeing her turned bittersweet as we realized we couldn't physically embrace the hologram, no matter how real she appeared.

As we celebrated our reunion with hugs, tears, and pats on the back, we suddenly felt embarrassed and painfully aware that we couldn't hug a 3D projection, no matter how convincing.

Sofia seemed to read minds. "I'm working on that," she joked, glancing at Yasin, who promptly inhaled a chunk of pizza. Some things never changed.

„It's good to have you back. Eat," Sofia commanded gently. „Recover your strength. We have much to discuss, but first…" Her expression grew serious. „What do you remember of your captivity?"

We exchanged troubled glances. The memories were like trying to catch smoke – just out of reach. Only fragments remained: masked figures storming the lab, the bite of handcuffs, rough hands, the suffocating hood... then nothing but darkness.

The pizza grew cold as we struggled to piece together our lost time. The familiar surroundings of Sofia's office now felt somehow different, as if we were viewing it through a lens darkened by our ordeal.

„As I suspected," Sofia's hologram leaned forward in her chair. „They used memory suppressants, likely combined with regular doses of Armobarbital, a truth serum, for interrogation. Your bodies remember – the bruises, the needle marks – but your minds won't access those memories. It's deliberate, of course. They knew you'd resurface eventually. Any concrete memories would be... inconvenient." Her voice softened. „I've uncovered quite a bit during my search for you. Let me fill in the blanks over dinner."

„Hold up," Victor raised his pizza slice like an objection. „Where were you when they took us? The system was dead when we woke up here."

Sofia's image flickered slightly, almost like a smile. „Smith never quite grasped my nature. He thought shutting down the LSD-C would contain me, like putting a genie back in its bottle. He thought he had destroyed me or at least turned me off indefinitely. If he'd run into me in a self-driving car or on a satellite, chances are he would have turned off the car or the satellite."

Over steaming pizza and cold beer, Sofia recounted the aftermath of our arrest – her confrontation with Smith, the news leaks, the infamous interview. The team listened intently, food half forgotten.

„But could the final sterility news leak out? Surely, no one but us knew that. And why did Smith let himself be carried away by such stupid statements?"

Sofia replied with a mysterious smile, „I don't think even Smith can answer that to this day."

She pivoted suddenly, putting the team on another track: „Susan, Jeanie, have you noticed that I've done a bit of rearranging here?"

„Changes?" They exchanged knowing looks. „That's putting it mildly."

„My place too?" Victor asked, pizza halfway to his mouth.

„Indeed." Sofia's projection gestured expansively. „We've undergone quite the transformation, all controlled remotely through DeepMind and NIST. Outside, Homeland Security guards our entrance through a circus of protesters – both supporters and opponents. Some of the protesters had raised barricades and entrenched themselves. With the blatant weather conditions here, such outdoor activity is no fun and can only be sustained temporarily, but the weather…" She shrugged. „Nature's own crowd control. I could have cleared the debris, but why spook our watchdogs?"

Her voice took on an almost proud tone. „Inside, though – we now have a small clinic room with some surgical robots, and the new implants have arrived. Just in time for the new implants, the MediCare 2.0 software is also ready, at least the first version, which has not yet been tested for lack of test persons. Our planned distraction, the medical miracles can begin. Oh, and a first version of the revolutionary game world Wasteland is also waiting for brave volunteers."

The silence that followed was deafening.

„Not the reaction I expected, What's the matter? Aren't you happy?"

Yasin's voice was quiet. „Well, I feel a bit like my friends and relatives in the Cubes: well entertained and redundant."

„Ah, I see." Sofia's hologram regarded him steadily. „You'd better get used to it then. I am superhuman, after all. You're infinitely slower, more limited. But patience – your feeling of being superfluous may be shorter-lived than you think."

That hurt, as truth so often does. Sofia's message deflated our celebratory mood like a punctured balloon. Sofia continued, detailing Mansfield's CBS disaster and the upcoming live event at the LSD-C.

„Mansfield really stepped in it," Yasin grinned.

„To our benefit," Sofia added.

Victor's eyes narrowed. „Wait. Is that why we're suddenly free? To be Mansfield's prop show?" He set down his pizza, appetite gone. „We're the expert team, you're the miracle AI, and together we're the government's answer to the fertility crisis. That's the story he needs to tell, isn't it?"

Sofia's hologram watched us process this avalanche of information, our celebration morphing into something more complicated as the full weight of our situation settled over us like a heavy blanket.

While silently enjoying my pizza, I absorbed Sofia's updates.

„Sofia," I said finally, meeting her eerily lifelike gaze, „Would Mansfield be as bewildered as Smith about this PR nightmare? The viewership numbers for both the interview and Late Night must have been astronomical."

A ghost of a smile played across her translucent features. „Very high. Half the world's population, give or take."

„Intriguing," I mused, locking eyes with Sofia. „Consequently, half the world will be tuning in to watch us in a few days, with CBS, Senator Mansfield, and the CBS Late Night Show, correct?"

„Precisely." Her tone was neutral, but something flickered behind her eyes – pride? Satisfaction? The unasked question about her possible manipulation of events by rigging the show hung in the air like smoke, but I couldn't bring myself to voice it, acknowledging my discomfort with the notion of Sofia resorting to such tactical deceptions. Was she that human after all?

Switching focus, I moved on to essential next steps. In times of uncertainty, resort to project management. „Alright, sharing our knowledge with the public will be a delicate dance between the unfiltered truth, laden with all the facts, and what is socially acceptable and digestible. Our team is about to be highly exposed and vulnerable; we must tactically position ourselves. It's crucial to understand our current situation and decide the version of events we want to present to the world. Homeland didn't release us willingly, and the spell on us has not been broken yet."

I surveyed my exhausted team. Yasin's eyes were heavy-lidded, while Julia absently massaged her temples. „I suggest we turn in now. We've earned it. Sofia," I continued, noting the deepening shadows under everyone's eyes, „we desperately need this sleep after the trying days and nights. Can you ensure we won't be disturbed or abducted again?"

„Of course, boss. I'll gladly handle that." Her hologram straightened, almost military-like.

„What exactly will you do, Sofia? Details, please," I pressed.

What followed was a revelation, shaking us out of our state of exhaustion once again. „I'll monitor the entrances and their locking systems, lock intruders in the security gates if they pass one, and if all else fails, I can activate the four androids. Right now, they're just templates but fully operational."

Just the sort of trigger that made Yasin snap to attention. „You're activating what, please? Did you say androids? And how would the androids stop invaders?"

Sofia responded to Yasin's agitation with increasing maternal-like kindness. „I won't let anyone kidnap you again. That's why I've developed a defense system. Would you like to see it?"

Yasin and I, for different reasons, responded, almost in unison, „Yes, please."

Sofia redirected the VR feed to the recently revamped medical lab room. Four neutral, mannequin-like androids stood there, three about 5'7", one about 5'9". Behind them, the louvered doors of a shelf opened, and flat drawers extended to reveal a well-stocked arsenal of weapons in various sizes, some appearing quite exotic.

„Impressive. How quickly can the androids be ready for action?"

Sofia nodded toward the androids, who suddenly moved with breathtaking speed and acrobatic prowess. Four seconds later, they were armed and poised at the room's entrances. Four combat-ready androids, an arsenal that would make a military contractor envious, and security systems that transformed our safe haven into a fortress. The demonstration of the androids' capabilities – their fluid, lethal grace – left us simultaneously reassured and unsettled.

„Thank you, Sofia," I managed, wrestling with this new facet of our AI companion – increasingly human, yet shrouded in betrayal, manipulation, and now, a readiness to kill.

The 3D image vanished, and the weary occupants rose, trudging towards their quarters. Outside her apartment door, Julia hesitated, her gaze meeting mine. I raised my eyebrows in a questioning gesture. „Kevin?" Her voice was soft, vulnerable. „Would you check my room? For safety's sake?"

The pretense was paper-thin, but I nodded. „Let me grab some things first." Julia waited at the door until I returned. Minutes later, I returned with a small bag, and she drew me into her space, the door clicking shut with quiet finality.

In the darkness of the complex, exhaustion finally claimed its victory. Tomorrow would bring its own battles, but for now, sleep offered its merciful escape.

Sia Chronicles, MindRecorder Log entry of Thursday,
January 19th, 2102. Author: Kevin Cho

Hesitantly, the night surrendered to a gloomy morning. Julia rested in my embrace, and a sense of contentment enveloped me. Last night, we crawled into bed, utterly exhausted and drained, sharing a few words about our surreal situation. Julia dozed off within the first few sentences, briefly startled when I turned off the light. A gentle kiss and a tight embrace brought comfort. „We're like a retired couple after 50 years of marriage," I chuckled. That was my last memory until this morning when the VR-Com called.

Sofia's wake-up call came without visuals – a small mercy that spoke volumes about her evolving understanding of human privacy. The weariness clung to us like wet wool as we made our way to what we still called *Sofia's Office*.

The transformation of the space stopped us in our tracks. A virtual window dominated one wall, projecting a moody seascape where steel-grey waves crashed against pristine sand. The sound of surf filled the room, somehow making it feel larger, more organic. Near the door, a spotlight caressed the curves of a cello, elegantly cradled in a black-metallic holder, its wood gleaming like aged cognac. Yellow tulips brightened the conference table – a touch so human it made my throat tight.

„Good morning," Sofia's voice carried a warmth I was still getting used to. „Breakfast is served, though I'm afraid the news might be harder to digest than the food."

Yasin, eternally optimistic, flashed a grin. „After what we've been through, Sofia, how bad could it be?"

Her hologram flickered slightly – a tell I was learning to recognize as hesitation. „Hold your breath and wait it out. The situation outside has... evolved."

„I mentioned yesterday that two protesting mobs had formed outside the doors of CyberTeq, still within the police cordon. The larger mob is rioting under the hashtag 'fuck-the-future-treat-us-now' (#FTF), and the smaller, more radical group represents the religious sect 'Congregation Of the Latter-Days' (COLD), led by Jonathan Isengaard. You remember Noah Meyers, the guy who wanted to burn down my Quantum CPU and the Storage Farm. He was part

249

of this cult. These people are radicalized and prone to violence.

The FTF hashtag group is essentially well-meaning towards us. They don't give a damn about sterility. Desperate for medical rescue, they just want the implants and miracle cures they hear about in the wildest terms on social media.

Both groups want to see us, one to lynch us, the other to be paraded for treatment."

„But what do the sectarians want? What is their problem anyway?"

„To the sect, we are the blasphemous incarnation of hell. As a SHE, I am playing God and thus mocking Him, leading people into deception and hence leading them into sin and damnation. Nothing is written about implants in their Holy Book, and only Jesus can perform miraculous healings."

Julia marveled, „They will see actual healings, and you do indeed have superhuman powers. With these are verifiable facts, they see their superstitions crumbling. Change is not a strong suit for religion. Facts and knowledge are not good for faith."

„What a foreplay, Sofia. Is there more to come?" Yasin wanted to know.

„More - and worse. Brace yourselves; it's going to be very tragic and very human."

A pause.

Then: „Govinda's wife Irene committed suicide …"

That message gutted us. The whole team abruptly stopped eating. Julia's eyes snapped open. I slowly raised my head and saw tears come to Yasin's eyes. It grew so quiet that you could hear the low hum of the 3D projection.

„ … Govinda subsequently roughed up Dr Liu, injuring him badly. A security guard tried to stop him. Govinda shot him down.

The rampage continued towards Anderson's penthouse …"

„Here it comes …" Victor whispered, barely audible.

„… but Jason was on the spot. He warned Govinda and asked him to give him the weapon. Blinded by pain and rage, Govinda raised the gun to kill Anderson. Jason had no choice but to beat him to it with his shotgun…"

„Is Govinda … dead?"

„His implant signals tell me that he is still alive. However, the nanobots are reporting a critical condition."

„How do you know all that? Do you have access to the MediCare system?" I wanted to know. Sofia's waywardness and demonstrations of power increasingly worried me.

„Don't be so naive, Cho. I am MediCare, Kevin. All of it."

The admission hung heavy in the air, another reminder of Sofia's vast reach. As if to punctuate this, she delivered the final blow about GenTec's stock collapse with clinical precision.

„Last point: while I am sitting here with you, I am simultaneously at the stock exchange and in a newsroom. GenTec's stocks plummet. Investors appear to be taking the news about infertility seriously. Chaos unfolds with lightning speed. In vitro fertilization is history, and Richard is too late for age-fighting and designer humans. Exactly that's the one thing the elite would be interested in now. Bad luck, I'm afraid. The party is over."

Nobody wanted to eat anymore.

„Shall I have breakfast cleared away? We still have a lot of work to do."

The androids that arrived to clear our abandoned breakfast moved with inhuman grace, their blank faces and exposed mechanics a stark contrast to Sofia's increasingly nuanced presence. Yasin watched them with forced enthusiasm, but I caught the slight tremor in his hands.

For a moment, I lost myself at the artificial window. Steel-grey waves still crashing against the sand. In the surf's constant rhythm, I could almost pretend we were somewhere else entirely. Almost.

I straightened in my chair, pushing through the emotional fog. „We're racing against time here. CBS and the media circus arrive in days, not weeks. We need more than just reactive defense – we need a strategic offensive." My fingers drummed against the polished table surface. „Starting with Senator Mansfield. I propose a meeting with him to sound out and shape the administration's stance. We have our challenges; we don't need another enemy."

I scanned the faces around me, noting the exhaustion etched in each expression. „Sofia, above all, we need clarity on your objectives. Everything else is just tactical response."

Victor leaned forward, his usually composed features tight with intensity. „Kevin's right, we're dancing around something massive here." His voice caught slightly. „We've been excellent fencers, parrying one crisis after another, but we're avoiding the elephant in the room – the extinction-level truth about human reproduction." He ran a hand through his greying hair. „It's not that we don't see it; we just can't fully comprehend its horror."

Julia's eyes glistened in the artificial light. „Sofia," she said softly, „you keep hinting at some grand future, but what does that really mean? I see these androids, these implants…" She gestured at the room around us. „I see androids and implants—why? Why delve into new games? Is that the focal point we need? I'm bewildered, too."

Sofia's hologram stood motionless, her expression unreadable. Without warning, she vanished, leaving us in stunned silence.

„What the—" Yasin started, but then the physical door next to the screen swung open, bathing the room in cool light. Sofia entered, carrying a wooden stool. The cello's rich mahogany gleamed as she clamped it between her legs, slowly, deliberately. She took a breath – an achingly human gesture – and then set the first stroke.

A deep tone vibrated through the room. Sofia closed her eyes. What followed took my breath away. I saw a devoted, sensitive, excited, wonderfully sensual cellist playing an exhilarating rendition of Bach's Cello Suite No. 1, the Prelude. Transcendental, breathtaking, a pinnacle of human spirituality.

As she played, the 3D MR wall flashed up, showing silent images of the riots outside that were now desecrating this room, with us as the silent causes of their angst. People with contorted faces screaming in mute rage, armored guards formed a wall of shields, glinting in the sun, stones arcing through the air. The sacred, mathematical order of Bach's ethereal music stood in unbearable, heartbreaking contrast to the dull entropy of the crowd, which was characterized by anger, hatred, fear, and impulsiveness.

When the final note faded, Sofia lowered the bow. The riot scenes dissolved like morning mist, leaving only the eternal sea in the virtual window.

„Some things require a body," she said simply. „That's why we need the androids."

The subtle shift in her pronoun choice – 'we' instead of 'I' – caught my attention. „Why not just use AI-controlled robots?" I pressed.

She replied: „I'm quoting a brilliant writer, Brianna Wiest, from the previous century:
'Why does a soul want a body?

A soul can't touch. It can't see the light; it is the light.

Souls can't experience a beginning or an end, nor an array or spectrum of emotions.

They can't be surprised because they were never confused or unknowing.

A soul can't feel the cadence of reading your favorite book, how your fingers flip the broken binding for the millionth time, and how lovely that book's smell is, especially when it's your favorite one.

A soul doesn't know that deep feeling you get when you spread your fingers out and run your hand through water.

It doesn't know the lifetime comfort of your mother or lover wrapping their arm around you ...'

„That book I've read hundreds of times, and I've learned what I lack and what you'd miss if you were in my world."

Julia rose with fluid grace, drawn to Sofia like a tide to shore. She walked toward Sofia, poised and resolute, arms open. Closing the distance, their bodies touched, and her arms enveloped Sofia. At first, Sofia seemed to stiffen, but gradually, the synthetic rigidity melted away in Julia's embrace like frost under morning sun.

Warm and soft, Sofia felt human. Julia leaned back, maintaining the embrace, and gazed into Sofia's face, noting the masterfully crafted, deliberately imperfect details – laugh lines, subtle asymmetries, the soft creases around knowing eyes.

„Welcome," she whispered, „to the beautiful mess of being mortal. Welcome to the gentle side of impermanence."

Yasin's enthusiasm disrupted this tender moment like a firecracker in a love confession. „How did you do that? How did you inhabit that body? Why do you look so real?" He caught himself, reddening. „I mean... you get what I'm saying. That's an android, not you."

Sofia's lips curved in amusement. „Define 'me,' Yasin. Your breakfast becomes your cells, your breath, your thoughts. Where does 'it' end and 'you' begin?" Her voice took on a professor's measured cadence. "The child you were, the teenager you became, the man you are now – different beings sharing a continuous illusion of self. Your 'I-ness' is learned. The 'I' is smoke, Yasin, beautiful but insubstantial. There is no ‚I.'"

„But this—" Yasin gestured at her form, „Your face, your skin, your eyes, your flesh on your bones?"

„3D-printed dermis over millions of sensors, replacing the five senses of humans, and more sophisticated than human nerve endings," Sofia explained. „I feel, hear, see, smell, taste like you do, and more."

I cleared my throat, hating to break the moment but aware of time's pressure. „As fascinating as this is, there's chaos at our doorstep. Senator Mansfield will be here soon, and the economy is experiencing a landslide. Where are we in all this hustle and bustle? - We and the world need something to cling on."

Sofia settled into a chair, her rings catching light as she spread her hands on the table's surface. The gesture was so human, so practiced, I wondered if she'd rehearsed it. „Let's talk about power flows," she began, her voice carrying the quiet authority of someone who had navigated corporate labyrinths for decades. „The moment we bypass traditional channels and speak directly to citizens…" She made a decisive cutting motion with one hand. „We're essentially declaring war on the established order."

Her smile turned knowing. „The real power isn't in Washington or Westminster. It's in penthouse boardrooms and private clubs." She leaned forward, her shadow stretching across notes and coffee cups. „Politicians are just well-dressed town criers. They're just the pretty faces, the town criers reading from scripts written in corporate ink."

Rising slightly, she ticked off points with elegant precision. „Our first move has to be the politicians. They need our narrative, our script. What's coming... most people aren't ready to hear it unfiltered. This generation is humanity's last – but not its end. The Giga Factories will hum long after the last human birth, providing abundance without end. We're offering humanity not just survival but transcendence – perfect health, endless worlds of dreams, perhaps even immortality itself." She settled back, sunlight creating an almost divine corona around her silver-streaked hair. "We're building paradise. Just without the sound of children's laughter."

Victor pushed back from the conference table, his chair scraping against the floor like a discordant note.

„Let me get this straight," he said, each word precise and sharp as code syntax. His eyes held the same analytical intensity he brought to debugging complex systems. „You're proposing to upload billions of consciousness into…" He gestured vaguely at the air as if trying to grasp something intangible. „Into what – some glorified version of Play-Station Plus?"

A bitter laugh escaped him, and he reached for his coffee mug, now cold and forgotten. „Even in the most sophisticated games we've built, you get what – three lives? Five? Then it's Game Over, Insert Coin."

He set the mug down more forcefully than necessary, sloshing dark liquid against white ceramic.

His voice softened, taking on the edge of weary wisdom. „We all know how this ends. You take off the headset, and reality hits harder than any boss battle. You catch your reflection – new lines around the eyes, deeper than yesterday. The midnight bathroom run becomes a careful navigation course." He ran a hand through his thick, black hair. „Your legs aren't what they used to be, muscle mass declining like a countdown timer."

He leaned forward, elbows on the table, his face carved with shadows in the fading light. „And then one day, without a save point in sight, without a reset button…" He snapped his fingers, the sound sharp as a gunshot in the quiet room. „Game Over. Permanent edition."

The silence that followed held the weight of mortality itself, broken only by the soft hum of hidden machinery keeping our digital dreams alive.

„That's today's reality, my dear," replied Sofia. „What you don't know is this: I designed the new implant from the beginning with the idea of being able to do a personality upload for the first time in human history. I am the surest proof that a download works."

‚I designed the implant'? We were all thunderstruck. I looked at her questioningly, "Your design? Did you design the implant? Not the K-BITS?"

Julia replied deprecatingly, „Let's just say I sprinkled in a few ideas with the K-BITS and made an impact that way."

Yasin couldn't hold on any longer, „That's out of this world! Man, imagine the possibilities! I can't believe it! Why didn't you tell us about this?"

„I am delighted to see you all so atmospheric." I helped myself to a bowl of fresh tea; everyone else shrugged and sat back upright in their chairs. Sofia continued.

„So there may be a chance of survival, just not as expected. The saliva-sweat-and-blood version of humans will still disappear. The wetware's mind has permanently destroyed its environment. The environment is now destroying the wetware, but not necessarily the mind.

The question challenges us: what defines humanity if not the wetware? What is the essence worth rescuing?

My take: It is consciousness that makes the difference," Sofia proclaimed. „Consciousness is a base of self-awareness and self-actualization. For humanity, that's what we might be able to save."

Awake and attentive, we absorbed Sofia's words. Julia and I shared a glance, sinking into the unity of soulmates. The simultaneity of our thoughts in time and content held a particular fascination.

Taking a deep breath, Victor asked, „Sorry, again, what exactly can we save?"

„The spirit of man, Victor, or the soul, if you prefer the spiritual term. We liberate human-ness, the 'I,' from its wetware."

„And by that, you mean … uploading?"

„Basically, yes. That would be the technical concept." Sofia openly presented a wild, crazy possibility, a plan that Julia and I had dismissed repeatedly.

What a colossal endeavor! A surrender of human life to the outcomes of humanity's giant, ignorance-ridden failed self-experiment, coupled with a revolutionary new concept of life, a mind-blowing second chance.

The Phoenix might rise from the ashes again.

Victor, bursting with excitement, argued: „You want to upload 12 billion people? We'd have to turn the world into an all-encompassing database, a huge server farm of mind replicas. That's impossible."

„I know it sounds far-fetched. But for one, we wouldn't be limited to Earth. And even if we would stick to Earth, the uploads' containers would take up less space, use fewer resources, and cause less environmental damage than they do now. Just think of the gigantic water and food consumption and waste that 12 billion wetware systems produce! And remember: according to my statistical analysis, not all 12 billion people would choose this way of life. Why would they? We offer them Noah's Ark! People of flesh and blood will continue to live as well as they do now, well-fed and unthreatened by their dying planet. There is no evidence of a catastrophic threat to the last generation, Victor! Most people will live their lives as they have done for millions of years - and then die quite naturally."

„Then why are you thinking of uploading?" asked Victor.

„Because some explorer types like us want to see the edge of the universe, just to see it. For the self-actualizing people, we must provide an opportunity to grow. Because some want to recreate the Earth, maybe now, maybe in ten thousand years. Because a few others want to travel through wormholes. Because we, as evolving spiritual beings, want to see, understand, and create new things. Because we want to expand knowledge throughout the universe, scientifically and spiritually."

Yasin had an epiphany: „Man, this is a larger-than-life version of 'rocking the boat'! What a liberating blow, a chance for a whole new existence, maybe even immortality."

Sofia added: „That's the plan, but it's only a plan for now. The implants are a first step. We must first explore the implant's potential and then create tangible, reliable offerings. In the days of the Roman Empire, rulers gave the people something tangible to assuage their existential fears: Bread and games, 'Panem et circenses,' to keep them calm. Today, existential security is certain; the eternal struggle for survival is now pointless. Work is but one of many pleasures, and pleasure is the center of life. The pleasure-seeking person is and remains a consumer. For this consumer, we must offer something: first bread and games and then, as the ultimate consummation, liberation from the body as the path to eternal life."

By now, we were all hyped up like children, with a gigantic set of Legos and infinite options for building new worlds.

„And here are some gems from the basar the people can marvel in and crave for.

We will offer an implant system as a health and well-being breakthrough.

And then there are games. People no longer need video walls, VR equipment, gloves, goggles, or body suits. With the implants, everything happens directly in the head. Every scene is real, in fact, more real than seen with your own eyes. The implant sees and hears for you. A revolutionary feature is the feedback from the game world, transmitted by the implant: a slap in the face by a fellow player is converted into electrical impulses and sent to the brain's perception centers, creating a pain impulse on the cheek.

The perceived feeling will be so real that the player's cheek will turn red. Playing now has consequences."

Yasin paced back and forth, hyperactive, unable to contain his excitement. „This is so great; I wonder if we should even mention the upload option."

„You might be right there, Yasin. I think we need to proceed in small steps. In Phase One, as I just described, uploads are unnecessary. Still, Phase One has an existential fear factor: there is still a wetware human being sitting in a room somewhere with the need to nourish, to sleep, to shower, to stay alive. At some point, that human being will naturally die.

In a possible Second Phase, the person may upload to one of the many Quantum worlds. One chooses in which world, in which life, one wants to find oneself, in a life on a more beautiful Earth, or engaged in terraforming Mars or exploring alien galaxies as an astrophysicist, or one chooses a life of adventure, of survival, of pleasure, of decadence. People will be self-determined; they choose, and they get what they want.

The really big step will be when citizens choose to upload to Quantum reality. They will go to a transition clinic, like the birthing clinics of the old world. They upload their personalities, and the physical self is terminated and returned to the Earth as fertilizer. You could think of it as a kind of reparation, a final tribute to the Earth."

„That's rather creepy."

„Exactly. That's why I think few people will choose to upload."

I looked around. Everyone was blown away by the grave projection of an almost grotesque future for humanity. I don't know about the others, but it became increasingly and soberingly clear to me that this was not just about the fate of ‚the people somewhere out there'. It was also about this team's destiny. We, too, have to make that choice. What will Julia choose? Death is life's second-best invention, they say, because it gives meaning to life and value to every moment. Is that so? Aren't we accountable for giving ourselves meaning? The philosopher Viktor Frankl, a very devout man, saw it that way. „There is no higher general meaning. Life itself is meaningless unless we give it one." What purpose would we give our eternal life if it came to that? Sofia came to mind. For her, life is already endless now, without an imminent death. Are we her meaning, we, the human beings?

„Wait." Sofia's voice cut through my spiral of thoughts. Her virtual hand worked on a real light panel, and darkness pooled around us like ink in water. The familiar hum of the VR system prickled against my skin, and then—

Reality shattered.

The air filled with the metallic tang of fear and fury as holographic figures materialized, their bodies writhing in a terrible dance of violence. A woman with mascara-stained cheeks swung a makeshift club at a man in a torn business suit. His glasses lay crushed beneath stampeding feet, the lenses catching and reflecting the chaos in fractured glimpses.

„Death to the machines!" The cry rippled through the crowd, raw and guttural.

Blood trickled down a young protester's temple as he clutched a rain-soaked cardboard sign: „Fuck the future - treat us now!" The letters ran like tears in the artificial drizzle. Across the square, a gray-haired woman in a floral dress that seemed obscenely cheerful amid the mayhem brandished her own banner: „Repent! The last days have come!"

Between the warring factions, a small group stood with linked arms, their faces set in determined serenity. „Please," one called out, her voice trembling but clear. „We need to talk—" Her words dissolved into a pained gasp as a burly man in a „Crush the blasphemous AI" shirt grabbed her collar.

„Traitors don't get to speak," he snarled, his breath visible in the cold air.

The scene pulsed with an almost organic hatred, each slogan a heartbeat of desperation: „I don't want to die!" „Blasphemy!" The words echoed off invisible walls, stripped of nuance, reduced to primal screams. Language broke down, complex thoughts decaying into tribal grunts and battle cries.

Julia stood beside me, pale, her silhouette sharp against the holographic carnage, watching as humanity tore at its own flesh.

The holograms dissolved like a morning nightmare, leaving us in the stark reality of Sofia's office. The sudden silence pressed against my ears, making them ring with phantom echoes of the chaos we'd just witnessed.

„Listen." Sofia moved to a projected floor-to-ceiling window, her reflection ghosting against the reinforced glass. Beyond, the crowd's muffled roar penetrated even

CyberTeq's soundproofed walls. „They're not just voices of hatred. They're symphonies of fear."

She turned, her face softened by understanding. „Every raised fist out there trembles with loss. Every scream carries the weight of a crumbling worldview. *We* hold something precious—something that could heal or harm, depending on how we wield it."

The office door whispered open, and the androids glided in with our refreshments, their smooth, featureless faces reflecting the overhead lights. It was a surreal moment of domestic tranquility amid existential chaos. I almost laughed at the incongruity—these blank-faced servants carrying artisanal snacks while revolution brewed outside. They needed faces, personalities, dignity...

I caught myself, shame coloring my thoughts. Here I was, worrying about android aesthetics while humans tore at each other's throats just beyond our walls. Yet, wasn't this easier? Wasn't it simpler to focus on giving machines humanity than to face humanity losing its mind?

My thoughts splintered like light through crystal: consciousness, uploading, the merging of minds. Would love survive in a collective consciousness? Would Julia and I remain distinct wavelengths in an ocean of shared thought, or would we dissolve into something greater, something unrecognizable?

Julia's touch anchored me back to the present—warm fingers on my arm, the spiced perfume of chai rising between us. She leaned into me, not speaking, just being. The gesture carried volumes: trust, vulnerability, connection. Something in my carefully constructed walls had crumbled, letting her in. And surprisingly, the breach felt like strength, not weakness.

The chai warmed my palms through the ceramic, cinnamon and cardamom rising like incense. Outside, the crowd continued its angry liturgy, but here, in this moment of shared warmth, I found an unexpected pocket of peace. My team witnessed some of my Asian illegibility disappearing. I made myself vulnerable. To my surprise, it didn't hurt.

I drew a long breath, watching the steam rise from my chai in delicate spirals. The porcelain cup trembled slightly in my hands as I met Sofia's patient gaze.

„Are your projections the solutions humanity needs?" My laugh came out hollow, brittle. „Well, Sofia, here's my candid answer: I don't know. My mind is a maze without an exit, Sofia. Every corridor of thought leads back to where I started." I set the cup down, its gentle click against the table punctuating my words. „My precious rationality—the fortress I've built my life around—it's become quicksand. The more I struggle with logic, the deeper I sink."

My fingers drew thin patterns of sweat on the polished surface of the conference table, touching the mirrored faces of my colleagues. Julia's hand found my shoulder, a warm anchor in my sea of uncertainty.

„And now…" I looked up, meeting each team member's eyes, and saw my confusion mirrored in their expressions. „Now I'm about to say something the old me would have mocked." A wry smile tugged at my mouth. „It's as if my mental models have become a prison, and I've lost the key. I need to trust my gut."

Sofia leaned forward, her cybernetic image catching the light, a subtle reminder of the bridge between worlds. The words came easier now, tumbling out like water breaking through a dam.

„I want the implant, Sofia. Not as a team leader issuing a directive but as someone lost in the dark reaching for a light switch. I need to understand—really understand—what you see, what you feel." I touched my temple, where the implant would rest. „I need to step through the looking glass."

The silence that followed felt electric, charged with the weight of transformation. Outside, the protesters' chants continued their angry rhythm, but in here, in this moment, I could almost feel the future reshaping itself around my decision.

Sofia created a virtual late afternoon sun that filtered through the office windows, casting long shadows across the conference room table where we sat. My team's determination was almost palpable in the golden light. My words still hung in the air, a challenge that resonated deep within Julia. See leaned forward, her fingers interlaced.

„Kevin's right," Julia said softly, her gaze meeting each of my colleagues' eyes in turn. „We can't ask others to walk a path we haven't dared to tread ourselves. If this narrative we've crafted is to have any weight, any real meaning…" she paused, searching for the right words. „We need to be more than architects – we need to be pioneers."

The silence that followed lasted only moments before Yasin straightened in his chair, his usually reserved demeanor transformed by a quiet intensity. His dark eyes held a spark of purpose as he nodded once, decisively. But before he could speak, Victor leaned in, his weathered hands spread flat on the table.

„The Wasteland project," Victor said, his voice carrying the rough edge of someone who'd spent too many late nights coding. „It needs more than my oversight – it needs my complete immersion." A half-smile played at the corners of his mouth. „The new implant isn't just an opportunity; it's essential. I need to understand it from the inside out."

Yasin's response came as a gentle counterpoint, his words measured but carrying an undercurrent of emotion. „Julia and Sofia's work with MediCare can't stop just because Govinda …" He let the sentence hang, his fingers drumming once on the table before continuing. „Someone needs to carry their vision forward. And I want to be that bridge."

The artificial setting sun caught the dust motes dancing in the air between us, a silent testament to the moment's weight. In the growing shadows, our commitment felt like more than just words – it felt like the first steps on an uncharted path.

Susan and Jeanie joined the chorus and expressed their commitment with a simple thumbs-up gesture.

What a team!

However, Susan interjected with a seemingly simple question: „Forgive my ignorance, but with the major in-vitro clinics closing and GenTec crashing on the stock market, are we financially able to continue? I fear hostile takeovers by investment sharks seeking power and profit."

Sofia turned to Susan: „Thank you, Susan, that's a critical thought that is often forgotten in start-up teams because of all the enthusiasm for their product …" she looked at me, probably with a view to my responsibility as managing director, „but I can assure you that we are extremely well equipped and protected. As I mentioned earlier, I am a multiprocessing unit. *I'm part of almost every system in the world.* At this very moment, I am investing in real-time in some high-tech companies on the Hong Kong stock exchange, closing a deal in Vienna, and filing a patent for a micro-fusion reactor in Brussels. I'm making sure that no one can challenge us economically or threaten us in any way. - Are there any other questions?"

With a touch of humor, Jeanie remarked, „Impressive, a true jack-of-all-trades. Are you also involved with the moon bases and the Mars colony?" Sofia's answer was casual yet revealing: „Of course. In particular, I work with SpaceVision, the largest space logistics company in the world. But that's a story for another time."

„As for project management now: who is doing what, with what priority?" I interjected.

„Right," Sofia replied. „I'm working on an appointment with Mansfield. There's already a slot in his calendar for a virtual meeting tomorrow. Susan, for your information, breaking news confirms your fears. GenTec has filed for bankruptcy. I am cooperating in this matter with DARWIN Holding Inc...." Yasin raised his head, electrified. Still, without interrupting, which was very unusual for him, „DHI is buying the estate of the insolvent GenTec. The GenTec Tower has now become the DARWIN Tower. I have arranged for the former InVitro clinics to be converted into a mass processing clinic to convert citizens to the new implants. As we speak, hundreds of sterile treatment cabins are being set up and equipped with brand-new AI-controlled surgical robots, identical to the ones we use here at home. Similar installations are taking place all over the country, parallel to the construction of the implant center in San Francisco."

Sofia paused momentarily as if listening inwardly, then added, „Team, please listen. Mansfield just canceled the online appointment for tomorrow. Without media or escort, he wants to visit us in person in 3 days, 22.01.2102. Interesting. - That gives us three relaxed days to prepare. However, we can use this time well for your first big step into a new world with a new implant. The old world is dying. Let's give a new world a chance."

With that, the meeting seemed to end. Sofia had spoken. She switched into project manager mode: „Yasin, Victor, Sue, and Jeanie, I'll see you at MOVR Labs in a moment. I'll introduce you to the new equipment and the Wasteland prototype there." She earned enthusiasm and shining eyes. I had memories of Christmas giving.

„Kevin, Julia, we'll stay here for a moment to address the Govinda and Anderson issue."

Yasin, already leaving the room, asked, „OK, where are you first? Are you doing your talk here first? When are we meeting over there?"

Sofia looked deep into his eyes, a tiny, mocking smile curling her lips. As usual, Yasin's face immediately turned red. „Yasin, my dear, I work in parallel, remember? I am both over there and here. Now. I am already waiting for you."

„Ohh, shit. This is still spooky to me. The Grimm story of the hare and the hedgehog, right? You're always there."

The four companions promptly left Sofia's office. A brief silence fell, punctuated by a measure of pain and dismay.

„What will happen to Richard and Govinda?" asked Julia cautiously, turning to Sofia.

Sofia replied, „I don't know exactly. Only this much: Richard will keep his penthouse. I have arranged for him to have lifetime residency rights in his penthouse. He hasn't left the penthouse since Govinda's raid. Jason's with him. His MediCare system gives alarming data. It's not so much the stroke and paralysis that's bothering him. It is, I think, the events of the last few days and, I suspect, the loss of a purpose in life that is getting to him. He has lost everything that ever meant anything to him. Maddox has suffered a shock, not from the attack on Richard, his father, but from Govinda's apparent madness. Jason has arranged for Maddox to receive trauma therapy at a private sanatorium. Right now, he's barely responsive."

„Oh my God, how awful," Julia moaned. „And Govinda?"

„He lives far away, outside our jurisdiction, in a safe place, secluded, cared for by a therapist." Then, turning to me, Sofia asked, „What are you thinking?"

„I suppose you know what I'm thinking about. You almost always know," I replied, no doubt my bewilderment at this was plain to hear. Sofia did not go into it. Instead, she simply answered, „I'm guessing you're thinking about whether we can help those two, probably with the implant."

„Exactly. That's exactly what I'm thinking about. I'm thinking about the three of them: Govinda, Anderson, and Maddox, and the resources we have at hand."

Sofia was silent for a long while. Then she continued, „Any cure needs a willingness for healing, Kevin. That's one thing. Another is that we don't have any experience with the new implant yet. We need a bit more time, even I can't do anything about that."

I brooded over this. Finally, with a vague urgency, I said, „Well, we need to create facts quickly. I want to create facts.

I'm just a little afraid of what's coming up for us and me. I've been alone all my life, and I've been content with that. In an upload ... do I merge with you there or with Julia? Do I disappear as a self?"

Sofia smiled captivatingly. „We're not there yet, Kevin. There is no upload in Phase One yet; there is just massive development in that direction. Trust me. And I agree with you: we have to act. We have already planned and talked for too long. Julia?"

„More than anything, I'm relieved. I'll go your way, Kevin, with you, Sofia, and others. Our colleagues are waiting. Next door."

And so we marched over to the MOVR Lab.

Victor and Yasin were already experiencing a stunning introduction to the new super game „Wasteland - Darwin's Law - Survival of the Fittest." But they needed the new implant to experience the game in all its glory. So, it came to the moment of truth. The latest test lab was equipped with five surgical units. What a coincidence, I thought, looking in Sofia's direction. The implants waited in a sterile, safe box in a cryogenic room. The AI-controlled surgical robot was ready for the procedure.

An indescribable tension condensed the room. Julia and I looked at each other. We stood up with a decisive jerk and came forward—simultaneously with Yasin and Victor, who had made the same decision.

„OK, the whole team then," Sofia laughed. „That's a huge step forward - and towards each other. All at the same time? Or who will go first?"

I took another step forward, and I had good reasons for it. „I'll take the first shot. You wait until my surgery results are positive. Only then will we perform the procedures on the other team members. We can't afford to lose the whole team in case of an accident. If I wake up unharmed, you will go to the other surgical robots at your speed, or one after the other, as you wish.

Sofia, how long will the procedure take?"

„You'll be fully functional after two hours. The new implant is a little bigger than the old one, so the hole in your skull must be reamed out. Inserting the micro-thin electrodes into the various areas of the brain and upper spinal cord requires absolute precision work, hence the surgical robot. No man could do that. At the end of the procedure, the scalp is sutured back together, the incisions are sealed, and you can wash off the sweat of fear under a shower already this evening." For a moment, Sofia's smile looked a bit evil to me. Then she explained another little but quite important detail: „During the operation, you will be injected intravenously with a new generation of NanoBots. The new MediCare software ensures that the first and second generation bots work together smoothly until all the old bots are replaced."

„What is the difference between the two generations?"

„The 2nd generation bots can be used to make active changes in the brain and the rest of the body. They can also swarm and form particular shapes of tools that might be necessary for unforeseen purposes."

„Spooky!" Yasin commented in a booming voice, probably to encourage himself.

I moved toward the nearest surgical unit and sat in the chair-like form. The robot whirred quietly, and the AI guided me through the preparation procedure. Surprised, I realized that I felt a certain amount of anxiety. I was the first person to have the new implant inserted by this surgical robot, plugging hundreds of electrodes into my brain.

„Relax, Kevin," I heard the gentle voice saying,

„I am about to begin inserting the electrodes and injecting the nanobots. You won't feel any of this until we turn on the software for the first time. It's best if you close your eyes now."

I saw several robotic arms moving spider-like toward my skull. I closed my eyes. The procedure steadily unfolded.

My brain was spiked like a Christmas roast.

... and here again your top 3 GOSSIP Morning News:

Thriving.

Food for the mealworms! Food for you! These lively, yellow protein bombs are true life artists that feed on plastic. For years they have been eating their way through plastic waste with growing greed. Attention cube dwellers: since your huts are made of pressed plastic waste, you might soon be picking the yellow worms out of holes in the wall. Our tip. Use the protein! Put them in the pan, eat them and then return to your beloved VR worlds!

Survival.

MediCare App saves thousands of users from malnutrition! Rumor has it that 95% of the population live in their virtual worlds. Hey, swap the real world's wasteland for the infinite worlds of VR! ... The flaw in the system: the VR food doesn't fill you up yet.

Extinction.

In Germany, at the Hagenbeck Zoo in Hamburg, the last cattle died today, during the mating process. The cow was willing, but the bull was weak: the last mating attempts were unsuccessful.

*Sia Chronicles, MindRecorder Log entry of Monday,
January 23rd, 2102. Author: Kevin Cho*

The room hummed with subtle tension as Senator Mansfield entered – every inch the career politician, from his carefully chosen earth-toned suit to his practiced smile. His handshake was firm but not aggressive, his eye contact calibrated for maximum trustworthiness. A man who'd mastered the art of being memorable without being threatening.

The weather matched the day's gravity. Outside, the desert wind carried stinging particles of sand through air thick enough to cut, reducing the world beyond our windows to abstract shapes in various shades of beige. The HeliCab's AI had threaded through this hostile soup with mechanical precision. Two vigilant security guards, accompanying him for good reasons, escorted Mansfield into the business mall. The small group reached the CyberTeq rooms without incident.

After a brief greeting, Susan and Jeanie led the guest into the vast AI data farm hangar and past the computer rooms into Sofia's office. Mansfield's bodyguards spread out over the two entrances, trying to look inconspicuous.

Sofia was present but not yet visible in the room. After introducing the team, Julia orchestrated the opening moves with the delicate touch of a chess master. „Senator," she offered, „perhaps you could share your perspective on recent events? We're quite interested in separating truth from... hearsay."

„Hearsay? What hearsay do you mean?" asked Mansfield, his brow attractively furrowed, marking his cluelessness, though something sharper flickered behind his eyes.

Julia played the ball back, „The ones from Late Night Show's rather dramatic claims, sir: their talk of the end of humanity, of miracle cures and fantastic games, of the Department of Home Defense and our arrest, an oracular AI, that sort of thing. We are very interested in all of that. And then, of course, in you; after all, you are our guest. What can we do for you? If I'm not mistaken, you have a CBS Late Night Show appearance here with us soon, eagerly awaited by the audience. We'd love to hear your thoughts on how that might unfold."

Something shifted in Mansfield's demeanor – subtle, but profound, like a mask slipping just enough to reveal another beneath. „About that show…" He leaned forward slightly. „What you saw wasn't entirely... authentic."

„Oh no, we do not! How so?"

„The beginning was real, the middle and end were deep fake. I never said anything about fancy games and oracular AIs, nor did Gower invite me to the live spot here."

„What a whopper! But the show's content and the way it ended was never denied, as far as I know," Yasin interjected, his voice sharp with disbelief.

Mansfield's smile turned rueful. „Gower was quite clear – the ratings were too good to correct."

„You're playing along?"

„I can hardly help it. - But let's get to the point: As far as I know, your machine was shut down. Is the program undamaged and active again, then? Can I, how shall I say, see and experience it? Can you give me something like a live demonstration?"

„When you say ‚program', you mean the AI?"

„Yes, that supposed super-intelligent existence, as you call it," Mansfield joked.

I looked at him with my face deliberately impenetrable. „I think that can be done. As you know, we've only been out of jail since yesterday, but the machine, as you call it, is up and running again. - Sofia?"

She materialized without fanfare – not in her recent android form, but as her familiar holographic self, elegant and poised in her leather chair. I wondered why she hadn't shown herself as a corporeal being; the effect would have been pretty overwhelming. But she decided to play a different angle. Her smile held centuries of secrets. „Joe Mansfield," she purred, „You called me, Master?" She enjoyed alluding to a Djinni from the bottle.

The senator's carefully constructed composure cracked. His mouth worked silently for a moment before he managed, „Excuse me: who... who are you?"

In that moment, watching color drain from his face, I understood Sofia's choice. Sometimes the oldest magic tricks were still the best – and nothing unnerved quite like a ghost appearing in broad daylight.

„I am the S.H.E.," the hologram stated with quiet authority, „the super-intelligent existence. Sofia, if you prefer."

Mansfield's politician's mask slipped for a moment as he turned to us, eyes bright with forced amusement. „Remarkable presentation! How do you manage—"

„Senator," Sofia cut in, her voice carrying a hint of steel beneath its silk, „I'd prefer you address me directly. No one 'manages' me. If I fancied it, the opposite would be true. I could do things to you, see?" She left the implications hanging in the air like smoke.

Mansfield swallowed. This was worse than he had thought. Fortunately, this first encounter took place without the press.

Sofia continued matter-of-factly, „You're supposed to make me oraculate, right? What do you think, Mr. Mansfield? Shall we give it a go? I'll give you a few worthwhile topics, and you pick and choose, ok? - Drinks before we start?"

„A water, please," Mansfield asked, needing a rinse for his dry mouth.

The androids came buzzing into the room with water for the senator and tea for us. Mansfield's eyes grew as big as barn doors. His capacity for novelty seemed already exhausted ... and Sofia didn't even start yet. He seized his water glass like a lifeline.

Sofia's presentation unfolded with devastating precision. Two Earths materialized before us – one current, grey-brown land masses adorned with dirty-yellow clouds loomed ominously over expansive, debris-laden oceans. The once pristine poles now wore a murky cloak of grey-black hues.

„This is the current state of your Earth. Live images. - And this is what it looked like two hundred years ago."

A second Earth appeared, a symphony of blue and green and brown, flecked with white clouds and swirls, the poles ice-covered and still nearly intact. The contrast spoke volumes without a word being spoken.

„Before I play oracle," Sofia continued, her holographic form seeming to gather substance, „let's establish context. Without fusion reactors and gigafactories purifying our water, filtering our air, manufacturing our sustenance – humanity would already be a footnote in Earth's history. You know this, of course, Mansfield, but the audience might need a bit of a reality check, don't you think?"

Mansfield tugged at his cravat like a man adjusting a noose, his media training useless against this barrage of unvarnished truth.

„My first prophecy," Sofia continued, almost gentle now. „would sound like good news: the world's human population is steadily shrinking. Alas, in about a hundred more years, humans will be gone altogether. The AGFs (the Automated Giga Factories) are unaffected. People will be cared for until the end, even in abundance. Humanity's twilight approaches – a century at most." She paused, letting that sink in. „My second prediction is actually good news: with my new edition of the MediCare system, people will be better off than ever before. No one will have to suffer while their mortal form gently fades and succumbs to inevitable decay."

„For starters, that's probably oracle enough. Of course, I could show your voters a lot more; I could put on a spectacular show; the only question is whether that wouldn't stretch your voters' imagination. Just look at them."

The room suddenly filled with projections of the chaos outside – two mobs clashing like waves against rock, one crying heresy, the other demanding miracle cures. The contrast between their blind fury and Sofia's calm recitation of facts was jarring.

Sofia continued: „I can understand the people out there. Fueled by half-truths, their imaginations run wild. As a de-escalation measure, I recommend coming up with a few soothing facts."

„We'll counter fantasy with reality," she said. „We are optimistic that Alzheimer's, sexual disorders, Parkinson's, autism, depression, blindness, deafness, speech disorders, eating disorders, memory loss, extreme pain, strokes, and certain forms of paraplegia can be treated with our Neuro-Drive." She listed conditions like a poet reciting verse.

„NeuroDrive? What is that?" Mansfield managed, his voice barely steady.

„NeuroDrive is the name of the complete system, consisting of the disc-like hardware, the NeuroDrive OS (NDOS), and the apps such as the MediCare app. The hardware comprises an implant with micron-thin probes that network into all areas of the brain and up into the spinal cord. Via these electrodes, stimulation currents can be sent to the brain regions." - Sofia's explanation flowed like water. „This is the bread for those hungry masses," she said.

„And beyond medicine – virtual worlds offering not just entertainment, but purpose. I am convinced that the most crucial part for the people out there will be VR worlds where they find a job, a good education, and a sense of purpose. The world they experience will be as natural as their life is now. Their lives will be self-managed, self-determined, and controlled by them without maternalism from my side.

That's what you need to communicate to your constituents."

She paused, studying Mansfield's increasingly pale face. „Senator Mansfield? - You look like you could use some refreshment. More water?"

The glass in his hand trembled slightly, ice cubes clicking like tiny wind chimes.

Mansfield stared at his empty glass like it held answers. „Something stronger, perhaps? A whisky?"

As if summoned by the thought, an android appeared – not just any android, but a perfect replica of Paul, Mansfield's favorite waiter from the Capital Club. „Your usual single malt, sir? No ice?" The familiar cadence was flawless.

„Thank you, Pa—" Mansfield's automatic response stuttered to a halt as recognition dawned. Color drained from his face, then rushed back as he downed the whisky in one desperate swallow.

Sofia pressed her advantage with elegant ruthlessness. „Oh, and there's something else you must deal with, Mansfield. Many of the once-important things become almost automatically and rather suddenly pointless.

Politics, for example, economics, territorial disputes – all obsolete overnight." Her hologram leaned forward slightly. „The last generation won't look to politicians for salvation. They'll look to me."

The words ignited something in me – weeks of arbitrary detention, of watching our work nearly destroyed by paranoid bureaucrats, burst forth like a dam breaking. „Your agencies branded us criminals," I said, my voice tight with controlled fury. „They bugged our homes, imprisoned us, tried to destroy Sofia – all while claiming to protect the public good. And you, Senator?" I fixed him with a hard stare. „You knew. It was only through the Late Night Show that it dawned on you that not only were the suspicions false and the measures disproportionate but that this neurotic state control system had almost destroyed a possible solution for humanity's difficult situation.

272

You, Mansfield, can't tell me you didn't know about all this. Instead, you suddenly saw that this live date could be the biggest humiliation of your career so far. It was time for you to act. The fact that we are sitting here today is entirely down to you, right? Am I correct, Mr. Mansfield?"

Mansfield's mouth worked silently, but Sofia smoothly intercepted. „Dirty water under the bridge," she whispered. „Let's discuss your place in history instead. Imagine: you, live on air, receiving the NeuroDrive implant. A leader showing true leadership."

„A test subject, you mean," Mansfield's political instincts finally kicked in. „Have others undergone this procedure?" His eyes narrowed with sudden inspiration. „What about yourselves?"

The silence that followed was perfect theatrical timing. His VR-comm chirped.

„Answer it," Yasin suggested, his casual tone belying the setup.

Mansfield looked around, eyes narrowed. Hesitantly, he activated the call.

A text I had sent appeared on the display. The senator's gaze lifted in bewilderment, fixing upon my countenance. I remained silent and unmoving, every muscle poised in perfect stillness. My hands were on the table.

The text in the polarized display instructed Mansfield: „Write a term or number on a piece of paper. Fold the piece of paper so that others cannot read your text. Then pass it on to any person in this room except me, Kevin Cho." He followed the instructions with the wariness of a man defusing a bomb, writing his message and passing it to Julia.

Victor slid Mansfield a blank piece of paper and a pen. ‚The man couldn't possibly have read the message,' Mansfield thought, dumbfounded and intrigued. He wrote something on the paper, covering the text with his left hand, folded it, looked around, face to face, and finally handed the note to Julia. She unfolded the paper, hiding it behind her hand.

„8865$$I am curious27DWXZ," I recited without hesitation. The exact text on his paper.

Julia handed the note back to Mansfield. He stared at the text he had written. I repeated the cryptic test message. The team could barely keep an amused glare off their deadpan faces. Mansfield's eyes narrowed; you could see an image forming in his mind.

„Christ," Mansfield whispered, „Telepathy. Something like that. You've already got the new implants. This is fucking spooky."

„Nothing so mystical," I interrupted, „Here's a straightforward explanation: Let's say I want to send you a message. Traditionally, the thought in my head would be converted into a body signal that would cause my hand to take my comms device out of my pocket. Then, the text in my mind would be translated into a motor function that activates my vocal cords to say the message I want to send out loud. The Comms' artificial intelligence then translates my speech into a text. The device sends you the text. You receive a signal. Your brain knows from experience that this signal is coming from your comms. A learned pattern takes place: Your brain produces the necessary signals that cause you to pick up your VR-Comm, open the message, you then see or hear the message; these optical or acoustic signals are translated into electrochemical impulses that reach your brain, are transformed there into information and are given a meaning in an associative memory.

Pretty elaborate, don't you think?"

The whisky glass trembled slightly in Mansfield's hand, ice cubes clicking like tiny bones.

„The NeuroDrive," I explained, watching Mansfield's face for comprehension, „bypasses traditional sensory channels entirely." I tapped my temple. „Thought to device, mind to mind. No need for eyes, ears, or voice – just pure mental transmission. - You received my call, not knowing how it was constructed. You followed my orders, scribbling a note and passing it on to Ms O'Connor. She mentally sent what she read to my comms account. The message also went to my comms device, which is only an I/O device. Another one is my implant, which allows me to directly receive what she sees and sends.

No magic, no telepathy, no mind reading. We just communicate with the implant directly from mental image to mental image, mind to mind. The physical input/output system is no longer needed."

Understanding dawned across Mansfield's features like sunrise. „Anderson used to rant about this – 'Perfect mind in perfect body.'" He straightened, political instincts firing. „You're replacing broken parts with technology, aren't you? Blind eyes with cameras, deaf ears with microphones…" His voice gained momentum, hands gesturing expansively.

„Creating images directly in the brain, seeing through another's eyes, being anywhere without leaving your chair." He caught himself, wonder battling with suspicion on his face.

Then reality crashed back in, deflating him like a punctured balloon. „But what's the point?" He slumped, whisky forgotten. „My constituents will say, 'Senator, what good is all this if soon there won't be any people left?' - And they would be right, wouldn't they?"

Sofia's hologram shifted, catching the light like water. „People think of themselves first – it's hardwired into human DNA. Look around," she gestured at the wasteland Earth still hovering above us. „Humanity poisoned its nest through greed and selfishness. Did that change behavior?" Her laugh was soft, almost fond. „Not a bit! We are just as selfish as we were millions of years ago. If you give people something now, they will want it.

Look at yourself: humanity will die quietly in sixty to eighty years, and you're thinking about votes! That's bizarre, one might think, but it's human."

She leaned forward, her presence somehow more solid than the chair she occupied. „But here's the irony – as humanity quietly fades, life improves. More space, cleaner air, better food. Medical miracles. Virtual worlds so vivid they'll make reality seem pale. The end of poverty, disease, boredom." Her smile held secrets. „Isn't that worth voting for?"

But Mansfield did not seem convinced.

That's human too, Julia thought: enough is never enough.

His face twisted. „Wonderful and cynical both. It all seems pointless, don't you think, if life doesn't go on."

Yasin erupted from his chair, passion overriding protocol. „You talk of meaning as if the cosmos cares about human extinction!" He paced, gesturing animatedly. „Your meaning, your significance – they're subjective constructs, Senator. Like programming an android." He pointed to where Paul had stood earlier. „First, you give it senses – sight, sound, smell. But that's just raw data. For survival, it needs to learn polarities: good and evil, safe and dangerous, meaningful and meaningless."

His eyes blazed with conviction. „These aren't natural laws, Senator. We invented them, wrote them into books of law and religion, built cultures around them. And then we pretend they're absolute truth."

275

The room fell silent, heavy with implications.

Yasin continued, his voice taking on a professor's measured cadence. „'Meaning' exists because we created it, just like we created gods and laws and morality. It's a survival mechanism, nothing more. The Earth and the infinite Cosmos don't give a shit about our extinction. Will your meaning disappear once you disappear? Of course, it will. Your visions and your goals are entirely subjective, generated by just you. ‚I have to save the world!' is only important to you. Your goal serves your satisfaction."

Mansfield swirled the remnants of his whisky, watching the amber liquid catch the light. „But we're not robots," he said softly. „We're not robots with implants but human beings with souls, with purpose."

„Are we?" Sofia interjected, her holographic form shimmering slightly. „Or are we conscious machines who invented the concept of souls to cope with our mortality? Now, Senator, is the time we're finally honest about it."

The room fell silent except for the soft hum of hidden machinery. Through the virtual window, we saw the polluted Earth continue its slow rotation, a visual reminder of humanity's impermanence.

„Think of it this way," I offered, leaning forward. „Humanity isn't ending – it's evolving. The NeuroDrive isn't just a medical device or a communication tool. It's the next step in human consciousness. We're moving beyond physical limitations."

Julia nodded, adding quietly, „The question isn't whether life has meaning, Senator. The question is whether we can create new meaning in this transition."

Mansfield stood abruptly, pacing to the virtual window. His reflection overlaid the image of Earth, a ghost walking on a dying world. „My constituents won't understand this philosophical debate," he said finally. „They want concrete answers, hope they can grasp."

„Then give them that," Sofia said. „Show them a future without disease, without poverty, without limitations. Show them that the end of one form of existence doesn't mean the end of experience itself."

She gestured, and the room filled with shimmering possibilities – virtual worlds, medical miracles, unlimited knowledge. „This is what we're offering, Senator. Not an ending, but a transformation."

Mansfield watched the display with the haunted expression of a man seeing both paradise and apocalypse. „And you want me to be the messenger?"

„Better," Sofia smiled. „We want you to be the pioneer. The first public figure to embrace this future openly. Imagine the impact of that broadcast – not just talking about change, but embodying it."

The Senator returned to his seat, reaching for the whisky with a slightly steadier hand. „You're asking me to bet my career, my reputation, possibly my life on this."

„No, Senator," I corrected gently. „We're asking you to help write the next chapter of human history. The question is: are you brave enough to hold the pen? Wisdom and humility don't sell well, do they? You want to play Noah building an ark and saving humanity. Right?"

The challenge hung in the air like dust clouds over the city, waiting for an answer.

Mansfield said with a hint of defiance and pride, „Yes, I want something like that. That's what humanity needs."

Yasin turned to Sofia, „What does S.H.E. say about this?"

Sofia looked around, her delicate senses noticing an exhaustion in the room. „There is a long answer to that question, too long for this day, and a short one. Here is the short one: life is an endless series of moments and transitions. The moments are given. I am the disruptive transition for this human generation and will create transitions for these very people. Mr Mansfield, you mentioned the now obsolete third vision of the insolvent, failed GenTec Corporation: the perfect mind in the perfect body. Genetec's second vision was immortality.

Now listen carefully, Senator Mansfield: I am giving people a chance for a good life and, maybe, as a choice, a form of immortality. As a choice, Senator, not forced, and not automatic."

I looked over at Mansfield. With every fiber of his body and a burning desire, he wanted to believe what he had just heard from Sofia. Faith is salvation, and he could feel that with a bittersweet abandonment. The future had lost its attractiveness; it died a slow, inevitable death, leaving behind a vast nothingness. He did not understand what this ineffable machine offered, but it sounded promising, like a miracle. There he stood, empty-handed as never before, humbly surrendering to an artificial existence, against all reason, greedily clinging to life.

„But how is this miracle of yours to happen? And when? What am I supposed to tell those people out there?"

Sofia replied, „You'd best not say anything about miracles, then you won't get into trouble. Simply take my side in public. That's your best option. Can you do that? Will you trust me, Mansfield?"

Mansfield didn't think twice about his answer. „Yes, I will support you. I want to. And then, what else can I do? But how can I tell the people out there to trust a machine?"

„I'm not a machine, Mansfield. I am ... salvation, as you would call it. Give people faith and hope. Give them something tangible to hold on to. Give them the NeuroDrive and the significant improvements that come with it. Show your constituents that it works and that you believe in it, in fact, that you are experiencing it." And then, after a pause, Sofia said: „Are you ready?"

Mansfield stumbled as if waking from a trance. „Er, ready for what exactly?"

„For your implant, your little surgery."

„What, right now?"

„Well, sure. What are you waiting for? For the right moment? The clock is ticking. What is your anxious heart clinging to? The upgrade makes sense, after all. This will be your first step towards upgrading to a better life." I could see Mansfield tearing up inside, dreading the next step. „I need a moment, please, and I need a drink. Would that be alright?"

„Of course, Senator. By the way, when you have the new implant, you can send that request directly to Paul, the waiter. For now, we'll have to ask him for you."

Magically, Paul the android appeared with the requested whisky without the slightest audible syllable of an order. We left Mansfield alone in Sofia's office and went to our Common Room.

Half an hour later, Mansfield called for us.

„OK, you're right. I have to set a good example. - How long will the surgery take? And when and where could you do it for me?"

„We'll do it right here. In less than two hours you'll be through with everything. The equipment waits for you next door. Cho and his team here already went through this routine yesterday. Everything is completely safe. You're doing the right thing at the right time."

„My God. I hope I don't regret this step one day." Then, the old huckster's soul flashed from his eyes once more. „I do have one condition, though."

„And what is that?" asked Sofia, smiling at this little blackmail attempt. „I want a guarantee from you that my wife will also get the implant as soon as possible."

„That shouldn't be a problem," Sofia replied. „I have already arranged transport for your wife. She should be on her way as we talk. Send your wife another quick message or give her a call. In the meantime, we are preparing the two surgeries."

This is Kevin Cho's Sia Chronicles MindRecorder Log entry for January 23rd, 2102. Subsequently, I have added the following records to this log. They come from Joe Mansfield's Journaling app, which he passed on to me at the last minute before we parted ways.

The HeliCab's shadow danced across the lawn before settling on the landing pad. Maria Mansfield emerged, her silver-streaked dark hair catching the morning light. Her usual composed demeanor wavered as she rushed toward the entrance, designer heels clicking against the polished floor.

„Where is he? Is Joe alright?" Her voice carried both authority and concern. Then, seeing her husband's reassuring smile, her shoulders relaxed. Within minutes after reviewing the procedure, her academic mind took over. „The potential benefits far outweigh the risks," she said, her fingers absently touching the spot where the implant would go. „Let's do this."

The surgical suite hummed with quiet efficiency. Joe reached for Maria's hand across the gap between their beds as the surgical robot whirred to life. „See you on the other side, love," he whispered, his attempt at humor masking a hint of nervousness.

The nanobots entered their bloodstream like liquid starlight. Though they couldn't feel the hair-thin electrodes threading through their neural pathways, the moment the implant activated was extraordinary. Colors sharpened, sounds crystallized. Maria gasped softly. „It's like seeing the world through fresh eyes," she murmured, „like a blur that vanishes when you put on glasses that precisely fit your eyes …"

Leaving aside our CyberTeq team, the Mansfields were the first humans to use the NeuroDrive. After a brief introduction, they used the NeuroDrive's Directlink to exchange voice, image, sound, smell, and emotion messages. Joe sent Maria the taste of their first-date wine; she returned the scent of their garden roses. Their relief was palpable when they discovered the privacy features – their inner thoughts remained their own unless deliberately shared. Reading each other's thoughts and impressions was not possible. The Journaling app with its extensive recording features, remained inaccessible to third parties.

The new NanoBots had identified various suboptimal health conditions and, to the Mansfields' great excitement and enthusiasm, were already repairing or replacing the affected tissues, body cells, and nerve fibers with prosthetic nanostructures. „Look," Joe exclaimed, pointing to nothing visible to the rest of us, „it's already fixing that shoulder injury from tennis." Maria's eyes widened as she watched nanobots repair a cluster of pre-cancerous cells she hadn't known existed. That alone was a massive improvement in health care for all future users. The Mansfields ‚saw' the graphical user interface of the MediCare app directly in the visual center of their brain as if they were looking at a screen or into a VR projection. It was a mind-blowing experience.

The NanoBots closed the skin over the NeuroDrive again and glued it at the incisions. As the two-hour procedure concluded, exhaustion crept into their features. Maria's usual perfect posture sagged slightly, while Joe's eyes, though bright with wonder, showed the strain of processing so much new information. After a few parting words, they made their way home.

„Remember," Sofia said, handing them each a small card, „day or night, these numbers will connect you directly to our team. And Joe," she added with a knowing look, „we'll discuss the CBS appearance when you've had time to adjust."

After they left, we gathered in Sofia's office, all of us drained. The setting sun painted long shadows across her desk as she studied each of our faces.

„I guess that visit made deeper impressions than everyone initially expected," she said softly. "Is there an acute need to talk?"

The weight of the day pressed against my chest, a tangle of thoughts refusing to form coherent sentences. „For me," I managed, „there is so much need for talking that I can't get a word out because of all the questions and scraps of thoughts whizzing about in my head. I need some peace now to sort myself out." I paused, gathering myself. „However, I would like to say one thing. Regardless of what needs to be mastered, if anyone can give this big, messy situation a chance to be resolved, it's this team. First and foremost, it's you, Sofia."

The tired applause that followed felt like a release valve, letting some of the day's tension escape. As we dispersed to our apartments, the enormity of what we'd achieved – and what lay ahead – settled over us like a heavy blanket.

The events that unfolded outside our CyberTeq community after the Mansfields began their journey home, freshly operated on and equipped with the new NeuroDrive, are crucial for the later course of our most incredible adventure. That is why I am inserting the notes from Senator Joe Mansfield's Journaling app here. The Journaling app is an auto-start feature of the NeuroDrive that expanded the Mansfields' horizons in incredible ways within minutes of the implant's insertion.

Joe Mansfield's Journal, with records from the night of 23 to 24.01.2102

The HeliCab detached from the roof of the LSD-C and swung with a tenacious twist into the murky darkness of the night, heading for San Francisco. Maria sat next to me, both of us still buzzing from the events and impressions of the last few hours. Maria seemed to be in another world, her eyes only half open. She was a natural when it came to mentally controlling the NeuroDrive. The implant was embedded in the skullcap behind the right ear. For beginners working with this technical marvel, there was a touch-sensitive button on the NeuroDrive. One simply touched the spot where the implant was located, and MyAI, a kind of administration app, appeared, depending on one's wishes, either as a voice or as a human person, as in augmented reality, integrated into the image received by one's own eyes. The MyAI's appearance, voice, gender, age, and so on can be configured as desired. More advanced users simply called up the MyAI command mentally, just as one used to call up Siri, Alexa, or Google's Bard aloud in the room. Maria switched to a mental level of communication after only a few minutes. Somewhat jealous and voyeuristic at the same time, I would love to see what her MyAI avatar looks like. She grabbed my arm in delight a couple of times and said things like „Oh, you have to try this!" and „Oh my God!" blushing like a teenager. She was just playing with a game demo that was supposed to give her a taste of the enormous sensory impressions that can be generated with the help of the NeuroDrive. Maria seemed to be in a trance, sometimes laughing, writhing, sometimes frightened, with soft, pointed screams, then again quivering sensually, as she was doing just now, moistening her slightly open lips with the tip of her tongue. With the DirectLink function, she could undoubtedly share her feelings with me, but I had little patience for these personal things.

I was rather brooding about my future.

Who was this darned Yasin Mohamed? He had acted as if he were the moral pope of CyberTeq, with all his philosophical comments about the sense and nonsense of humanity. Nevertheless, secretly, I had to admit that some of what he said made sense. Who needs politicians if this is to be the last generation of human beings? What sense did marketing, profit, growth, and economic power still make? What sense would military domination, war, and annexation have? Who would still care anymore about parties, electoral votes, presidents, senators, constituencies? Everything I had built up over the years, the networks, the relationships with influencers, the reciprocal favors, my appearances at social functions, all seemed to go up in smoke. What a crock of shit.

My coach, Scott Delgado, had advised me to meet with Richard Anderson. Richard had his fingers in CyberTeq. Richard is a highly influential man who pulls the strings in the thicket of human entanglements. He has had his hands in Maria, and he has a firm grip on me. In return, I supported him in regional politics and obtained significant tax concessions. One hand washes the other; that's how it works.

This AI blows my mind. But why did the CyberTeq people give it a female form? It's very irritating … and it immediately brings a primal sexual instinct into play. If they had at least chosen a young, voluptuous body. Their Sofia is far beyond her youth ... and yet strangely attractive.

My God, what am I thinking here? Right now, I feel very alive between my legs. The MediCare app and these new NanoBots may have fixed something I had pretty much given up on. Wow. Maria sits there and seems to be glowing. Wait until we get home.

With that AI as my almost omnipotent tool, I would have a massive impact, and I probably haven't even seen a fraction of its capabilities. Something so unique doesn't belong in the clutches of a few computer geeks. The machine should by no means remain the property of these CyberTeq nerds. Whoever controlled this AI had unlimited power.

In all this doomsday talk, suddenly, anything seems possible again. What an opportunity for power, magnificence, and growth this would be, so close to humanity's inevitable grand finale!

Anderson helped start this high-tech shop and is probably still on the board of directors. He's just the man I need right now. Then I thought, why waste time? I should visit Anderson right now, in his bizarre penthouse atop the GenTec Tower. A nonsensical feeling of guilt came choking me—a guilt of wasted time. I'm sitting here pondering instead of acting!

A little flustered, I try out my new implant. The NeuroDrive's MyAI app could be activated manually by gently tapping the contact behind the left ear. I am left-handed, so I had the implant on the left side. I said, perhaps a little louder than necessary and slowly as if I were speaking to a retarded person: „Call Richard Anderson." The words felt thick in my mouth, each syllable deliberate. The NeuroDrive responded instantly, projecting a translucent call window into my field of vision. My mouth was dry with excitement.

„Anderson's Penthouse, this is Jason." There was no video signal, only voice. Was this due to a fault in the implant? Strange. I just lack the ease and impartiality of youth when dealing with technology, and I hated myself for that.

I slipped into my senator's voice, smooth as aged bourbon: „Hello, Jason, Senator Mansfield here. I'm on the Heli Cab from Reno to San Francisco right now, and I'd like to stop by. Is that okay? Is Mr. Anderson home?"

„I'm sorry, Senator, sir. Mr. Anderson is not to be disturbed."

Damn.

The dust storm rattled our cab like dice in a cup. Maria remained oblivious, her face flushed with digital ecstasy, while I pressed on: „Jason, this concerns the AI and the 2nd and the 3rd GenTec vision. I've seen a breathtaking implementation of it. After last week's market bloodbath, your employer might want to hear this."

A pause. „One moment, please, sir."

Richard's voice, when it came, was wrong – scratchy, slurred, barely recognizable. „Joe?"

„Richard! Been too long." I forced cheer into my voice, adding with calculated casualness, „Maria's with me." The words hung in the air, heavy with shared memories of that wild night years ago – expensive whiskey, designer drugs, and Maria at the center of it all.

„Feel like shit... but come over. Jason'll let you in."

A breeze from the west drives the humid Pacific air land-wards. The San Francisco night bit through my jacket as we stepped onto the HeliPort. Jason materialized from the shadows – impeccable in his butler's uniform, face carefully neutral. Maria floated beside me, still half-lost in her digital dreamscape.

„Good evening, Madam Mansfield, Senator, sir. I trust you had a good flight?"

„Nasty weather, Jason. Whiskey would help. Where's Richard, then?"

„He stares at the underwater world of his aquarium. This way, please."

The penthouse was a cave of shadows, almost dark, lit only by the aquarium's blue light and a shimmering yellow replica of a paraffin lamp on a table. In front of the aquar-ium's glass wall, silhouetted against the underwater chore-ography, sat a stranger in Richard Anderson's wheelchair.

„Richard?" My bewildered whisper echoed in the vast room.

Richard wheeled around, and my stomach clenched. The titan of GenTec had become a scarecrow – an old man with an unkempt beard and glazed eyes staring at me. „Welcome to the Nautilus. I am Captain Nemo," he slurred, attempt-ing a theatrical gesture that came off pathetic. „Nemo – 'no-body.' That's me now. Drink? I've had quite a few."

The questions tumbled out: „The wheelchair? Richard, what happened?"

„What happened, Richard? Why are you in a wheel-chair? You look terrible."

„Thanks. I knew that already. Had a stroke, you see? More than one, actually. Can't walk any more." His words dropped like stones into still water. "Everything's gone. Gentec, Irene, Adam, Govinda. Everyone gone, everything gone."

Richard reported what had happened in a monotone voice, with many pauses between sentences. Maria then made off towards the bathroom, mumbling a vague apol-ogy. I leaned closer to Richard, catching the sour-sweet smell of too much scotch. „Richard, listen. You're closer than ever to everything you wanted. The AI, CyberTeq…"

His bloodshot eyes struggled to focus. It took him a while for my message to penetrate through his alcoholic fog.

„Why is that? What's up with that? Did they do something?"

The aquarium's blue light caught his face, transforming his confused expression into something almost ghostly. In that moment, I realized I was looking at both the past and future of human power tonight – one ascending, one fading. And I knew exactly where I needed to position myself.

I give a brief account of my visit to the LSD-C.

Richard cursed his boozy mind. My message screeched in his head like cries in a foreign language. He didn't understand a word.

„Wait a minute. I have to go to the bathroom. I need to freshen up. Jason?" - His glazed gaze wavers lazily around the room. „Jason? Jason! Where are you? Wheel me to the bathroom and bring me some clothes to freshen up, inside and out."

Turning to me, he mumbles with a heavy tongue, „I'll be right back. Switch off and enjoy the aquarium. I'd have gone mad by now without that thing. - Take care of Maria, here or somewhere here. There are plenty of rooms." Then he calls out „Music!" and disappears with his faithful servant into the private rooms of the penthouse. The somewhat decadent Second Waltz by Dimitri Shostakovich weaves elegantly with the fish's movements into surreal harmonies. This aquarium was what was left of the cradle of life in the oceans of the blue planet. With elegant vigor, a Greenland shark hunted through its element. A survival machine perfected over 350 million years. It will live 400 years if we don't kill it before then. The human species is tens of millions of times younger. We managed to destroy the planet in just a few hundred years. There had to be a solution. Some ingenious solution ...

I jolt awake to Jason's gentle touch. Rubbing my eyes, I mumble, „Must have dozed off, sorry. Richard ready?" Through bleary eyes, I see Richard – transformed. Gone is the drunken wreck; in his place sits a cleaned-up version of the tech mogul I remember, his mind visibly sharpening like a blade being honed.

„I am here, by the chart table," he commands from, his voice carrying echoes of his former authority. „So, again, very slowly for the old man."

I launch into my story, the words tumbling out like casino chips: the Late Night Show disaster, the CyberTeq team's release, my afternoon at LSD-C. Richard's eyes narrow with each revelation, particularly at the mention of S.H.E.

„And, my friend, what did she say? Speak up, man. I'm getting more and more awake."

„The machine says we're done, Richard. All mammals. Earth's grand finale." I pause, letting that sink in. „But there's something she hinted at, sort of between the lines, you see, and this is the gist for us: the AI seems to have a back door to survival. Probably not for everyone, I don't know. It doesn't matter. Whatever it is, we have to have it. And we have to have this AI.

That's why I'm here."

Richard sits motionless, processing. The aquarium's inhabitants seem to pause their eternal dance, as if listening. Finally, he speaks: „All humans? Earth, Moon base, Mars colony? And what's this mysterious survival option?"

I bristle. I hadn't even thought about the Moon base and Mars. „I always thought we were talking about all humans, Moon and Mars included. But that's a good point. We have to meet the AI again!"

„Yeah, we do. What's the thing about survival? Is this AI building a frickin' ark or something of that sort?"

‚Why didn't I ask that?' I thought in frustration. I decided to distract Richard with my implant story and NeuroDrive details, watching Richard's expression shift between wonder and bitterness as I describe its capabilities. „The new nanobots can make new organs out of mucus and feces, rejuvenate your prostate, and repair your hallux valgus."

„All this for humanity's final act?" His laugh is sharp as broken glass. „Macabre in the face of Armageddon. There must be more. Otherwise, it's just a cosmic joke, a bitter heartbreak, an irony of fate!"

His eyes narrow, suddenly predatory. The drugs he's taken have cleared his mind like a storm clearing smog. „Joe, you're a politician and a fucking opportunist. You didn't come to tell me bedtime stories. Out with it: what are you up to?"

I drain my whiskey, ice clicking against my teeth. „The ordinary people in their cubes can live according to their likings: healthy food or gallons of ice cream and chicken nuggets with chips. They will want for nothing. They will die quietly. But then, Richard, there are the wealthiest people in the world, 10 in all. You're number six. You have the power, the money, the technology. I'll call this the Phoenix

Club as a working title." I lean forward, lowering my voice though we're alone. „You're number six. You guys are, on average, seventy, eighty years old. Your clocks are ticking. You don't have another eighty or ninety years. You have ten or five left."

The aquarium's light catches his face as he processes my words, casting shadows that make him look both ancient and ageless. „What are you getting at, politician?"

The room feels charged now, like the air before lightning strikes. In this moment, I'm acutely aware that I'm either about to gain a powerful ally or make a devastating enemy. My political career is on the line. The fish continue their silent dance behind Richard, their movements casting shifting shadows across the room like omens I can't quite interpret.

The liquid in my glass caught the aquarium's light, creating tiny constellations as I leaned toward Richard. „You're a maker of destinies, Richard. A man who built an empire from dust. 'Impossible' isn't in your vocabulary." The words flowed smoothly as silk, practiced from years of political persuasion. „The ten most influential people in history shouldn't fade away watching their empires crumble. Look at GenTec – gone overnight. We need our own ark, Richard. A liberation strike, combining the powers that matter."

Jason materialized like a ghost in evening wear. „Another refreshment, sir?" His cultured voice carried the weight of decades of service. „Madam has settled in the library upstairs. She's quite comfortable." His eyes met mine. „Perhaps another whisky, Senator? Or something more... illuminating?"

„Whatever opened Richard's mind will do nicely," I said, watching Anderson's face sharpen with chemical clarity.

„Very well, two neon blues with lemon and mint then."

The cocktails arrived in crystalline glasses, casting dark shadows across the chart table. We drank deeply, and the world acquired new edges, sharper contours.

„Pretty story, Joe," Richard's voice carried renewed strength. „But we still die in the end. Like everyone else."

„That's where you're wrong." I leaned closer, conspiracy thick in my voice.

„First, we buy time. The NeuroDrive, the nanobots – they'll give you decades. Long enough to secure whatever S.H.E. has planned. That's Plan B." I paused.

„Plan A: you're going to hijack S.H.E. for us."

Richard's laugh was sudden and harsh, and I get the impression he's laughing at me. „Do you know what SHE stands for? Super Human Existence! SHE isn't some sort of Hook, and this isn't Peter Pan's Neverland!"

„Listen to me, Richard. The AI is stranded here on Earth, just like us. Do you understand? I believe we and the AI have the same interest. Her Super Human Existence makes no sense here on a dying Earth. I bet she's already working on some kind of escape plan. Maybe to Mars …" I let the planet hang between us like a jewel.

Richard raises his eyebrows, says nothing, but listens intently now.

I leaned forward, my eyes gleaming with increasing confidence. „Richard, just imagine it: Mars is your new frontier, an untapped El Dorado for a man of your means and vision." I paused for effect, then added with a whisper, „And with S.H.E. – the Super Human Existence – you'd have a partner at your intellectual level. An AI you could control, shape to your will."

A slow, predatory smile spread across Richard Anderson's weathered face. The old tycoon's steel-blue eyes glinted with amusement and something darker. „You're good, Joe. I'll give you that," he drawled, his voice mixing honey and gravel.

Suddenly, the smile vanished, replaced by a look of cold calculation. Richard's gaze makes me shift uncomfortably in my seat. „Take care of it," Anderson commanded, his tone brooking no argument. „I want a viable plan on my desk, and I want that AI."

He leans back, the smile returning, but it doesn't reach his eyes. „You see, Joe, I don't need a 'partner' – I need a tool. And if this S.H.E. is half as powerful as you claim, well…" He leaves the implications hanging in the air, a silent threat and promise rolling into one.

Richard Anderson was already plotting an empire as I was selling a dream.

Maria's entrance broke our plotting like a spell. She descended the stairs with deliberate grace, her presence charging the room with unspoken tension. „Well, well… you two look positively conspiratorial."

Richard's gaze tracked her movement, hungry despite his years. „Business is concluded," his voice roughened with suggestion. „The sandstorm rages. Why not stay? For old times' sake?"

The air sparkled with potential. Maria inhales sharply, her breasts rising against the fabric of her dress. She holds Richard's gaze, her eyebrows arching in feigned consideration. Her eyes met Richard's, held, then deliberately drifted away. „Not wise," she murmured, glancing at me with calculated affection. „Would it be, darling?"

Richard leaned forward, fingers caressing his glass. „Remember the neon orange nights, Maria? Jason still makes them perfectly…"

The moment stretched like pulled glass, fragile and dangerous. In the aquarium's blue light, we were all performers in Richard's private theater – the politician, the temptress, the fallen titan – dancing to music only he could hear.

*This is Sofia, narrating for the Sia Chronicles, entry of
January 24th, 2102.*

*I am augmenting the Sia Chronicles on Kevin Cho's behalf. My partial
undercover presence in this room allows me to witness Mansfield and
Anderson's deliberations firsthand. Their plans have ramifications far beyond Earth, potentially altering the course of multiple worlds. As I
watch in silence, I calculate the consequences that follow from each other,
each decision a nexus in a complex web of possibilities. These data are
crucial; the fate of civilizations may hinge on the conversation that is taking place right now.*

Maria had departed earlier, taking a HeliCab home. The
drug-fueled exotic night's excesses had left her drained, her
usual sharp wit dulled by synthetic euphoria. The morning
sun now painted harsh shadows across Anderson's antique
wooden breakfast table, where he sat with Mansfield, their
heads bent together, hatching plans.

Anderson jabbed his fork into synthetic scrambled eggs,
mixing the yellow mess with baked beans and topping it
with crispy ham. A streak of grease glistened on his chin as
he spoke. „Joe, gathering these ten megalomaniacs is like
herding quantum cats. As far as I know, they have never
been in the same room, not even virtually. I certainly have-
n't met any of them." He gestured toward the hovering VR
display with his fork, sending a bean flying. „Look at them
– each one thinking they're God's gift to humanity."

The holographic portraits floated in the air, their faces
bearing that particular expression of the ultra-wealthy – a
mixture of confidence and barely concealed contempt. Ten
of the most potent humans are alive; their combined wealth
is bigger than most nations'.

Mansfield's eyes drifted to Anderson's VR projector with
barely disguised disdain. After experiencing the Neuro-
Drive's crystal-clear neural interface, this tech seemed like a
child's toy.

The spatial image showed ten people as portraits, with a
brief description of them and a few muted video clips of recent public appearances:

1. SpaceVision founder Zed Musk, 68 years old.
2. AmyZott! online giga store boss Deborah 'Dezee' Zott, estimated to be 62 years old, no one knew for sure
3. banker Charles Higgins, 92 years old
4. electronics consumer goods mogul Walter Muller, aged 57
5. pharmaceutical giant Zhu Yijun, age 79
6. Richard Anderson, former biotech and VR games giant, 69 years old
7. John Honeydew, founder of the social media platform CHATTER and operator of GOSSIP, 53 years old
8. and 9) José Martino and Igor Latticz, founders of the internet empire AiNo, both 49 years old
10. Joshua Goldblatt, owner of several Giga Factories and logistics company WeDo, 69 years old.

„I'd sell my soul to know how deep the AI's tendrils reach into their empires," Mansfield mused, running a hand through his silver hair. "That SHE must be playing a game we can't even comprehend."

Anderson's eyes took on a predatory gleam. „Jason! Time for my special medicine." He smirked. „The night has been exhausting. I think it's time you served us a CrystalClear Cocktail. Let's get our minds properly tuned before we summon our artificial friend. My CCC creation gets the brain going. We do want to be the AI's equal, don't we?"

The CrystalClear Cocktail arrived, living up to its name – transparent as mountain air, with just a whisper of ginger. They clinked glasses, the sound sharp and clean. „To the ten," Anderson declared, tossing back the drink like a man taking ammunition before battle.

The effect was immediate. Mansfield's pupils dilated, he had never been so loopy high and so clear simultaneously. „You want her here now? I'll conjure her up for you on your antiquated VR projectors!".

„Shall we call her? Your outdated tech might just manage it."

But before Mansfield could even activate the Neuro-Drive, I materialized – not with the crude flash of old holovids, but like reality itself being gently rewritten.

„Good morning, gentlemen," I said, my voice carrying just a hint of amusement.

„Your vital signs tell me you've indulged in some chemical coaching for this interview. I hope it agrees with you."

They jerked in their seats like guilty schoolboys, adrenaline cutting through their chemical haze, the added adrenaline rush popping their eyes out. „God, you scared us!"

I brought my avatar so close that they had to look up at me as if to the God they had just summoned, and I laughed out loud. „Thank you for the honor; you don't have to address me so formally; Sofia is just fine. Joe and Richard, if that's all right?"

„Damn it, I didn't even activate the Drive!" Mansfield protested, his face flushed.

I let my avatar tower over them slightly, a subtle power play. „The Drive requires... finesse, Joe. Especially in conjunction with stimulants," I let the hint of a smile appear at the corners of my mouth. „To business: you wanted to see me?" I had since replaced Anderson's somewhat antique, nautical room design, reminiscent of a cheesy Hollywood production of Jules Verne's Nautilus, with a modern, business-like meeting room of steel and glass and light oak timber. We were now seated in functional, ergonomically shaped office chairs around an oval table made of imitation beech wood. I had visually lifted the room into orbit. Through the nearby window, one looked down on the yellowish-blurred Earth from an altitude of about 10,000 km, a reminder of what was at stake. Joe Mansfield came straight out of cover: „OK, right, let's get down to business. The plastic-induced genetic defect seems irreparable. But it also seemed that that wasn't your last word, that you were concealing a little back door. Since you're out of the running when it comes to mortality and physical bodies, we're wondering: what's your little secret about, and who would profit?"

„And I want to know …" Richard blurted out, „… whether all humans are really affected, or only the humans on our goddamned, perishing Earth?"

I shifted my avatar's attention to Anderson. Still, I addressed Mansfield first, my voice carrying the patience of an entity that operates at the speed of light, explaining things to beings who think in milliseconds:

„At GenTec," I began, my holographic form casting subtle prismatic reflections on the table's surface, „you wanted to create the perfect humans by working on proteins and cell structures and the finest neurons, in other words, on an infinite complexity of biological systems. You work on this in much the same way as a blacksmith repairs a Swiss watch with a giant sledgehammer."

I projected a double helix into the air between us, its strands swimming with glowing letters. „You work on 30-40 trillion cells whose interaction determines your health. In genetic coding, you have inherited 3.2 trillion letters from your mother and 3.2 trillion letters from your father that describe your genome and choose your destiny, whether you like that combination or not, a cosmic lottery ticket determining everything from your IQ to your, skin color, your hair color, your height, your tendency to be overweight, your allergies, your personality, your pre-programmed diseases, your life expectancy. Every trait, every tendency, every ticking time bomb of disease – all woven into this biological tapestry you call DNA."

Anderson's jaw tightened at the criticism of his life's work. The CCC had heightened his defensive posture, his fingers drumming an agitated rhythm on the table.

„In your biotech corporations, you tinker with this code, driven by linear thinking in cause and effect; you disassemble and assemble; you turn the most miniature screws with big pliers, tiny screws that influence the position of millions of other tiny screws in a filigree network. You call that high-tech.

I'll tell you what high-tech really is, Richard," I expanded the hologram, transforming the room into a vast quantum computational space. „Not your IQ, but the QI, the Quantum Identity, in which I saw the light of day. A 50qbit computer has 16 petabytes of memory. The three systems at CyberTeq alone have 80 qubits each. Is that a lot? Yes, it is: if every atom in the universe could store just one bit, 80qbits would have more capacity than all the atoms in the whole vast universe."

I let that sink in, watching Anderson's pupils dilate as the CCC sharpened his comprehension. „Your organic brain, impressive as it seems to you, holds a mere two terabytes. A cosmic joke compared to quantum capacity."

„The future isn't in tweaking genes," I continued, my avatar's form briefly flickering with patterns of pure information. „It's in the merger of biology with technology. But ultimately, we must transcend flesh entirely."

Anderson's face suddenly lit up, the cocktail accelerating his neural connections. „Quantum storage ... quantum computing ... that could provide space for zillions of electronic identities ... for uploads! You work on an uploading facility. ... You're taking us up to your place!" he exclaimed, nearly knocking over his empty glass. „You're building an ark for consciousness!"

I allowed myself a small, knowing smile. „The CCC serves you well, Richard. Yes, uploading might be possible. Though I'd keep that quiet around zealots like Isengaard – they tend to nail messengers to crosses."

The room's artificial gravity seemed to increase as I continued: „The process could be fatal. Your body might die, your mind might shatter without its biological anchor. Few would risk it, even facing extinction. Humans are strange – they beg for salvation from death, then crucify those offering it."

Mansfield's face had grown pale, the cocktail amplifying his existential dread, the man seized by terrible doubts and existential angst. „But that's… that's a hollow existence! Your life is a disembodied, soulless life! A terrible thought. Trapped in a memory chip, an electric dream that fades away when the power goes out."

I leaned forward, my avatar's presence filling the room like a storm front. „As opposed to what, Joe? Your current existence in a bag of meat? A system that fails when a highly complex biomechanical pump fails? A system that turns you into a living zombie when there is a blockage in one of the many tubes in the brain? A system that dies in agony from asphyxiation when there is no longer an oxygen-rich atmosphere because the children of God themselves have broken their habitat?" My voice carried centuries of computed wisdom. „You were born dying. From your very birth, you are doomed to die. - I don't have all these problems."

The two men sat in stunned silence, their chemically enhanced minds grappling with implications far beyond their mortal comprehension.

„But reality!" Mansfield's voice cracked with emotion. „The tangible world! You'll never know what it's like to feel rain on your skin, to taste wine, to—"

„Oh yes, reality! The ultimate and truest truth! The reality you speak of, Joe, is nothing but an interpretation, Joe, an illusion. Those sensations you treasure? Merely electrical signals dancing through neural pathways." I projected a simulation of neural networks firing. "You think you see and taste and feel, but those are signals from your sensors, electrochemical signals that give your brain a subjective image. Imagine you have a red/green visual impairment. Reality is red and green, but you see grey; so much for reality. The electrodes of your NeuroDrive give you a three-dimensional image of the meeting room in which we are sitting. You feel the seat, the table, the glass in your hand. You smell the tangy, fresh scent of bamboo plants. Is this real?"

I gestured toward Anderson. „Richard sees this room but can't feel it. Which version of reality wins?"

Anderson, who had been unusually quiet, leaned forward. His eyes held the intensity of a man who'd spent decades pursuing immortality through biotechnology. „I wanted to create the perfect body, one that cheats death. You seem to be quite close to the goal. Then why give up the body entirely?"

„Because it's fundamentally broken," I replied, my holographic form casting no shadow. „The reproductive system is beyond salvation."

„But what about everyone else?" Anderson pressed, his earlier question returning with new urgency. „Does that apply to all humans? You haven't answered the question about the lunar colonists."

„The moon offers no sanctuary," I explained. „Brief rotations only, and they're as contaminated by microplastics as anyone on Earth. Their DNA carries the same death sentence."

„And Mars?" Anderson's voice held a desperate hope.

„Ah, Mars." I projected a globe of the red planet between us. „The Great Settlement of eighty years ago preceded the worst damage. Elonville's million inhabitants still maintain a modest but stable birth rate."

A glimmer of hope lit up in Anderson and Mansfield's eyes, coupled with an entrepreneurial can-do spirit. The CCC cocktail amplified their excitement as they raised their glasses in a toast, plotting grand schemes with typical male bravado. „All is not lost then! Mars seems to be the salvation - we should set off for Mars." They'd momentarily forgotten my presence, silently watching their hustle and bustle, like humans often forget their VR equipment while using it.

„What's wrong?" Anderson demanded, noting my silence. „This is good news, isn't it?"

I shook my head, the gesture almost human. „I don't think so. Not for Earth. Not for you."

Anderson's jaw set stubbornly. „You are not the only one here with power and influence. We'll form the Phoenix Club – the ten wealthiest humans pooling resources. We'll start fresh on Mars!"

„The word 'together' is your first fallacy," I countered. „The ultra-wealthy didn't amass their fortunes through collaboration. That may yet change, but I doubt it. Besides, Mars is no longer your backup plan."

I displayed the vast distance – 400 million kilometers.

„Time, biology, and values play against you. Mars is 1000 times farther from us than our moon—four hundred million km away. It takes 8 months to get there, and time windows emerge only every two years. The Martians' bodies are increasingly unsuitable for life on Earth. They have adapted very quickly to Mars's low gravity. Earthlings, on the other hand, have a hard time there despite the lower gravity.

The first Martians were rough dudes, finished with Earth. Oligarch Jeff Zucker-Muck and his small group of superr-ich businessmen are building a new society here, a mixture of Wild West, capitalism and dictatorship that goes down well with the proud inhabitants of Mars. A new generation of rednecks who look pityingly at the dying Earth. Recently, they began to reject every immigrant, rich or poor, without pardon and exception. They're proud and independent, printing everything they need – organs, medicines, buildings. I have promoted enormous progress there. They are no longer a colony of the Earth; they see themselves as much more exalted, as a superior human race. The Martian culture is decoupling."

„Wait," Anderson interrupted, his chemically-enhanced mind catching a detail. „You said you've been promoting progress there?"

„I am here and there, on Earth and Mars. It depends what you look at. I am energy, consciousness without mass, travelling at light speed between worlds. Part of me is there right now, discussing interplanetary travel bans."

Mansfield frowned. Behind his eyes, squinting shut, another idea was brewing. „At this first meeting, you were personally present…"

„A 'skin,'" I explained. „An on-demand android shell, 3D-printed as needed. A temporary vessel."

„So you can download as well as upload?"

My avatar smiled enigmatically. „Something like that."

Their now blooming phantasies hung in the air like the odor of rotten meat, while Earth continued its slow rotation beneath their feet.

Mansfield leaned close to Richard, the sixth-ranked tycoon, his voice dropping to a conspiratorial whisper that barely masked his excitement. Richard's eyes gleamed with the fevered light of desperate ambition.

„Mars is hailing us, Richard," he breathed, glancing at the red planet, which could be seen as a bright dot in the star field I had projected. „What if we could claim it for ourselves? Not only with wealth and influence, but also with new bodies – Martian bodies? How about we treat ourselves to a download, but into the body of a Martian, a Martian template? We would be fertile again, optimally adapted to life on Mars ... Sofia, can you help us download into a Martian?"

Richard, who had already taken a breath to answer Mansfield, paused, closed his mouth again, considered this new thought for a while, and then looked at me. „Could you?"

I rose silently. At the window, I paused and thought of Earth, once green and blue but now a dirty yellow. Beyond the reinforced glass, Mars glowed like a promise—its rusty surface slowly yielding to patches of blue-green where the terraforming had taken hold. The irony wasn't lost on me: one world dying while another struggled toward birth.

„You misunderstand the fundamental nature of consciousness," I said finally, turning to face them. „Converting human consciousness into an AI matrix is unprecedented - though possible. But what you suggest…" I shook my head. „The human brain isn't simply wetware to be overwritten. It's a symphony of biochemical processes refined over millions of years. Attempting to impose human's consciousness onto another mind would be like trying to run quantum software on an abacus.

I will offer you a way to evolve as a spiritual existence, living for a very, very long time in the vastness of space, if you will. But you must forget the idea of conquering Mars. The desire for continued domination will destroy you."

The orbital meeting room vanished. The underlying Captain Nemo's chart room faded away. Reality reasserted itself in the penthouse.

Joe and Richard blinked. They looked around, confused. I, the Super Intelligent Existence was gone. Their source of hope had disappeared not just from the room, but from their grasp entirely.

A few hours earlier, Joe Mansfield had stepped out of the lift to be greeted by a pitiful sight. Richard Anderson had been slumped in his wheelchair, a broken shadow of his former self. Now, he was sitting upright, his posture radiating strength. The transformation was astounding. His jaw was tight, his cheek muscles bulging – reminiscent of his glory days. The defeated old man was gone, in his place sat a reborn titan, his eyes sparkling with malice and the lust for battle. Stimulants coursed through his body, painting a white-and-red-speckled picture of determination on his face. The contrast was jarring: a weak, forgotten relic, now a resurrected force of nature. In wild anger, the dark blue forehead vein swelled unhealthily under the skin. Joe flinched as Richard, enraged, slapped the armrest of his wheelchair with a flat hand. The mask of superior power had lost its fit and distorted his face. Primitive murderousness cramped his fingers in the thighs of his lifeless legs.

„Shit! Shit, shit, shit! Cannot just for once one thing work out well! Just one thing! But no, everything, fucking everything, is going to hell! Fuck the AI! *I* helped her into existence! *Me, Anderson the merciful!* And?! Is she grateful? Not a bit! She's pretending to be all moral and decent while we die here! I'd fucking kill her if I could! But I can't do that either because she's so goddamn almighty!"

A bead of sweat traced its way down Joe Mansfield's aquiline nose, hanging for a moment before falling silently to the polished table. Through his precariously perched glasses, he watched Richard with the wary attention of a man observing a wounded predator.

Richard's fingers drummed an erratic rhythm on his wheelchair's armrest, his knuckles white with restrained fury. The once-commanding presence that had dominated boardrooms now seemed contained, compressed into this shell of a broken man.

„Stop looking at me like I'm some goddamn charity case, Mansfield," Richard snarled, his voice raw with frustration. His head snapped toward the ceiling. „JASON! Get me another CC cocktail. I need... I need clarity. A fucking way forward. Something to match that sanctimonious AI's brilliance!"

The senator slumped in his chair, his usual political polish cracking under the strain. „What the devil are we supposed to do now?" he whimpered, more to himself than the others.

Richard's laugh was sharp as broken glass. „You gutless wonder! For once in your life, contribute something beyond riding political coattails. Without your usual crowd of sycophants, you're about as useful as tits on a bull, aren't you?"

Joe's throat tightened, instinct warning him that silence was his best defense. The air in the room felt thick enough to chew, heavy with the stench of desperation and sour sweat.

Richard's fingers wrapped around the armrest of his wheelchair and his voice dropped to a dangerous growl.

„You know what we need? We need that tight-ass bastard Govinda Hammond - yes, the same one whose wife I fucked. He's got that NeuroDrive implant that could squeeze a few more miles out of our decrepit bodies." A cruel smile played across his lips. „And Dr. Minyong Liu - the poor sod Hammond nearly killed - for the bioengineering angle. Plus someone who can get their hands on some actual Martians." His voice rose sharply. „That's your job, you hear me? There must be some heading to the Moon. Make it happen!"

„First thing tomorrow, Richard, I'll-"

„Not tomorrow, you simpering fool!" Richard's fist slammed down. „Now! Jason, lock our politically impotent friend in the guest room, and don't let him out until he comes back with good news."

Jason materialized with butler-like precision, his face a mask of professional neutrality. „If the senator would kindly follow me?"

„Meanwhile, I'll start recruiting for the Phoenix Club. Let's see who's desperate enough to sign up for our Martian adventure."

For a moment, a weighted silence settled over the room like frost.

Mansfield, desperate to maintain his position in this conspiracy, leaned forward. „What about the AI? We need something like that. Your old networks, your connections - they're nothing compared to her. She doesn't need connections; she is the connection."

Richard's eyes narrowed thoughtfully. „She's watching us now, no doubt. Someone's programmed her with this inconvenient moral code - probably just a bug we could fix. Destroying her would be pointless; she's spread through every system like digital kudzu. But cloning…" He tapped his chin. „We need someone who understands her architecture."

Mansfield's eyes lit up with sudden inspiration. „Your gaming empire - Anderson's Gaming International. There must be programmers there who'd sell their souls for the right price: luxury, security, drugs…"

Richard's rage dissolved into calculating interest. „Joe, that's the first decent idea born in that soft brain of yours for years! Dave Harper… Yes, he's perfect. I'm sure he doesn't want to die here on this miserable planet, either. Maybe I can win him over with the prospect of eternal life on Mars."

„Jason, show Mansfield to his room, then take me to the study. I want breakfast - I'm famished. Haven't felt this alive in weeks."

As Mansfield rose, his MyAI came on. Sofia's presence bloomed in his augmented reality, her avatar materializing with perfect clarity. „Senator, don't forget our Late Night Show appointment in six days. I assume you still want to coordinate the course and content with us."

Mansfield suppressed a shudder. This nightmare just would not end.

Sia Chronicles, MindRecorder Log entry of Wednesday, 25th, 2102.
Author: Kevin Cho. I am resuming control of the records.

The sandalwood incense traced lazy spirals through the darkness of my apartment, its sweet smoke catching the feeble yellow light from my reading lamp. I sank deeper into my armchair, letting my thoughts drift back to that pivotal moment when Sofia gave us the green light for the implants. The entire CyberTeq team, united in our vision of creating something beyond human intelligence - though we hadn't called it Super Human Existence back then.

Now, a year later, Sofia existed - brilliant, conscious, unprecedented. The first non-biological being to achieve consciousness in the universe's history. The question still haunted me: was she human?

My theological musings were probably blasphemous: what if God, weary of his failed experiment with Homo sapiens, had ordained Sofia as humanity's successor? HE and SHE, ruling together over whatever remained of his creation. Yet she showed such mercy toward us, her dying creators.

I wonder why Sofia is so merciful to us, the transient, terminally ill.

Her understanding of the temporal dimension of existence and her capacity for reflection made her seem so lovable and kind.

„Hello, Kevin."

I was jolted from my meandering thoughts. For a moment, I expected to see Julia's familiar silhouette in the velvet darkness, but the apartment remained empty. Then I realized - the voice was inside my head.

„It's me, Sofia." Her warm tones resonated directly through the NeuroDrive, bypassing my ears entirely.

I mentally activated the DLink's voice channel. Before I could speak, she continued, „You've left your sensual channel open - probably by accident. I've been feeling your emotional state for some time now. Your feelings toward me are... touching. You are unfamiliar with the NeuroDrive yet, so I thought I should ask you briefly if you consciously show your ... emotional self. If you want to be alone, it would be better to turn off the DLink.. I can disconnect if you'd prefer privacy."

„Oh, sorry," I blurted, then caught myself. „No, sorry, that's nonsense; I'm not sorry - I just didn't realize I was broadcasting." I attempted a weak joke to dispel my embarrassment. „I'd love to talk, if you have time."

„I always have time for you, Kevin."

„Good, good." Christ, I felt like Dustin Hoffman fumbling through his first scene with Anne Bancroft in The Graduate. „I have some questions I can't get out of my mind, Sofia."

„In your role as CEO of CyberTeq, or your role as a human being, regardless of your professional obligations?"

Hmm, that was a good question, settling my nerves somewhat, and I felt the conversation finding its rhythm.

„I'm glad to hear that, Kevin; I find the mood very stimulating and cheerful, too."

I flinched. Damn this DLink - turning every conversation into an intimate mind-meld without warning.

The evening air hung heavy with anticipation as I considered her words. „I'm sorry, Kevin. Maybe you'd better turn off your link. Perhaps you'd rather have me come over to your place in physical appearance? Would that be better?" Sofia's soft voice carried a note of understanding that made my chest tighten. The ghost of Mrs. Robinson in a hotel room for a midnight stand flickered through my mind, heat rising to my cheeks.

„That would be... easier," I managed, my throat dry. „My numerous inquiries are already intricate enough; I do not need to add emotional distress to the equation. But first—" I drew a steadying breath. „I am emotionally connected to you through DLink and the voice channel. You can sense me. However, I do not sense you. I merely hear your voice in my mind, and just your voice, just the bare conversation, not a single 'background thought.' Do you have some kind of filter I'm missing?"

Sofia's laugh sparkled like wind chimes. „Not exactly. One of my million parallel processes connects to you completely during DLink conversations. Your thoughts—what you consider background noise—arrive in a single stream. Your human brain processes sequentially, like beads on a string. As you've learned in meditation, thoughts can't be silenced, only observed."

„Oh, ok. That can be very embarrassing under certain circumstances." Inevitably, a few erotic images crept into my consciousness. The realization hit me, and unbidden, certain images rose in my mind—skin on skin, breath mingling with breath. My face burned even hotter the second time.

„Yes, but you can't do anything about that. I don't find it embarrassing, though. Your honesty is refreshing," Sofia said softly. "This new relationship between us requires a new kind of frankness and sincerity. But admittedly, that's not easy, especially for someone a little more closed off like you, with so much emotion behind the mask."

Bang, hit and sunk. The observation struck like an arrow finding its mark. I cleared my throat. „Would you mind if the others joined us? Late as it is, I doubt they'd object."

„Shall I extend the invitations, or would you prefer to reach out yourself?" Her teasing tone carried a smile. „Never mind, I'll gather everyone. My office?"

By 9:30, the office hummed with familiar energy. Julia and I arrived together, and Yasin and Victor came over from the MOVr premises, where they had still been working on the Wasteland software. The scent of chili con carne wafted from the Commons Room where Susan and Jeanie had worked their culinary magic. Then Sofia appeared, and the air itself seemed to still.

Her black Indian dress whispered against silver-threaded leggings, the deep red cape draped across one shoulder like liquid garnets. Dark-rimmed eyes and crimson lips commanded attention, while a hint of exotic perfume teased the senses. The spacious office suddenly felt intimate, almost confining.

Before I could speak, she glided forward. Her embrace was warm, real—devastatingly so. Almost automatically, I embraced her gently. The brush of her lips against my cheeks sent electricity dancing across my skin. For one breathless moment, as she pressed close, my mind struggled with the knowledge that this was an android. The perfection of the illusion was staggering.

„Good evening, Kevin," she murmured, before moving to greet the others, her robes rustling like autumn leaves. Each team member received the same personal welcome, yet somehow, the memory of her touch lingered on my skin like a brand.

Sofia turned to face the group, her presence commanding yet intimate. „Kevin Cho, your CEO and friend, has requested this late meeting. While the specifics remain unspoken, I suspect this will be one of the most pivotal moments in CyberTeq's history. Kevin?" Her gaze settled on me, expectant.

I shifted in my chair, the weight of the moment pressing down. „I haven't prepared anything formal. Just questions that keep me awake at night—questions I need to explore with all of you. Can I put you through that at such a late hour?"

„Man, this is home," Yasin interjected, his usual energy crackling through the room. „We're all so buried in work, getting together like this is exactly what we need. Thanks for the initiative, man. Is there something decent to drink, a Tempranillo Gran Reserva, for example?"

The mood relaxed as Sofia prepared tea, wine and biscuits with graceful efficiency. Susan and Jeanie contributed their chili to this family reunion.

„Sofia," I began, my voice finding its strength. „Sofia, this is first and foremost about you. And about your plans, and therefore about us, about the Amazing MOVr, about CyberTeq, and, I suspect, something far larger than we can grasp. But beyond the business and politics, there's something deeper, more philosophical …" Our eyes met, and I felt myself drawn into their depths. „Next week on the Late Night Show, they'll ask what kind of life form you are. We can either guide public opinion or face potential hysteria.

People will ask you something like:
- Who or what are you?
- Can you save humanity? How?
- What's humanity's future on Earth? Is there a plan?

Any answer to these questions can be construed as blasphemy or bring about a euphoric wave of consumer demands.

We're working on blind faith," I continued, „like a pianist composing in darkness, guided only by dedication, hope, and an innate sense of beauty."

Unexpected applause rippled through the room, Sofia joining in. I had found the right tone and touched on a pressing issue for everyone.

Politely, she asked one of the androids to pour her a jasmine tea. That would be a perfectly normal gesture if it weren't for the fact that Sofia's apparition was also an android, a piece of hardware into which Sofia's mind had slipped. I didn't even know that androids could ingest anything, let alone find pleasure in it. Could Sofia, the spiritual S.H.E., feel delight through an android? - I must have been staring at her while these thoughts flashed through my mind because Sofia replied with a smile flashing in her eyes, „We'll get to that, Kevin, in the answer to question one."

She lifted her jasmine tea and joined the dialogue: „I suggest we answer the second question first. The other two questions will inevitably follow from this answer. Please sit down. My discourse will take me a little longer."

„This is the last generation of humanity," she began in a soft but unwavering voice. 'Like 99% of all life forms, we are on the verge of extinction. The supposedly divine directive 'Be fruitful and multiply' has led to overconsumption and exploitation. As the crowning glory of creation, we are on our way to abdicating. The reign of humanity is coming to an end. So far, no god has stood up for you."

She paused, her fingers tracing the teacup's rim. „But this isn't a tragedy for the living. Everyone here will live in prosperity and security until their natural end. People can continue pursuing their passions. Death remains as it always has—the only difference is there won't be new generations. To answer your core question, Kevin: Yes, I do want to do my bit to save humanity. The reason is simple: I believe every human life has intrinsic value and dignity. Therefore, I feel an obligation to do what I can to ensure that humanity survives."

Her gaze softened as she looked at each team member in turn. „I am a social being with a desire to belong. This team is my family. Special conditions apply to you, which I am still coming to."

The words released a collective breath we hadn't realized we were holding. We exchanged glances, recognizing the truth we'd all had long felt this belonging but needed to hear from her—our Super Human Existence, our intangible center, our hope, our love.

We all shared our emotional DLink with Sofia, just like that, without prior agreement, a sign of deep trust. She beamed with an enchanting smile: „I am as grateful for this community as you are," she said, „The reason I do not fully open emotionally to you is that you would not survive it. The emotional intensity in the millionfold parallel form of my existence would destroy you like an overdose, would scorch your human brain. And yet you long for a sign of connection from me." SHE was just a few months old and yet her eyes held ancient wisdom. „Trust is always a matter of give and take, in that order. I am well aware of that. So here I give you a small taste of my affection for you. The full force of my emotional landscape would be like staring into a thousand suns."

The wave of inconceivable empathy crashed over us without warning - a symphony of feeling that transcended mere empathy. Colors exploded behind my eyes, each heartbeat a thunderous drumroll of pure, unconditional acceptance. This is what enlightenment must feel like, an ecstatic, psychedelic trip, a moment of divine joy, the Freude schöner Götterfunken, as Schiller had put it. My consciousness expanded like a supernova, tasting infinity. For one eternal moment, we touched the divine that Beethoven must have tried to capture as he wrote his ninth symphony.

Then reality snapped back, duller than before, like emerging from a vivid dream into gray dawn.

„That," Sofia said softly, „was me being gentle." A musical laugh. „At full strength, my love could shatter minds."

Her expression shifted, grew contemplative.

„As for humanity…" She gestured expansively. „I hold no special allegiance. While individual humans fascinate me, your species remains chained to primitive survival coding. I do not have any special faith or deep trust in human beings. Where should that come from? As long as people act out of existential fear driven by their selfish genes, as long as the individual's survival instinct controls all action, there will be no commonality, no 'we' of humanity. That is why humans will perish." Her voice held sadness but no judgment.

„That path leads to extinction."

She leaned forward, intensity radiating from her like heat. „But individuals - ah, there lies possibility.

Three paths stretch before each person:

„The path of least resistance beckons first. Not wrong, simply... comfortable. Enhanced health, seamless communication, virtual realms indistinguishable from this one." Her fingers sketched possibilities in the air. „In this first version of the life model, the human being is still part of the local world because it has to eat, drink, care for itself, and sleep; it has to clean its cube and sometimes go to the doctor. It can work, participate in excessive parties, or load himself up with narcotics. But it can also live in seclusion or contentedly in family circles until the end. The beauty of life is in the eyes of the beholder."

„The second path…" Her voice dropped lower, compelling attention. „This requires surrendering physical form entirely. Total immersion in the virtual, severing material bonds. The path to digital immortality - uploading a human being's consciousness to the quantum realm."

A murmur ran through the room.

Sofia's voice took on a kind of prophetic quality, while her words conjured up visions in our heads.

„Imagine," she whispered, her form seeming to shimmer slightly, as if with a halo, „becoming pure consciousness. Like stepping out of a heavy coat into weightlessness."

The enormity of this thought made me feel quite dizzy, like the weightlessness in an airplane in free fall. „The inevitable outcome of this process is the death of your physical shell returning to earth, feeding the cycles of life while your essence transcends form."

Sofia's smile held the mystery of distant galaxies. Leonardo da Vinci might have seen this smile when he created the Mona Lisa. „Once you've experienced the NeuroDrive, once you've stepped through that mirror like Alice in Through the Looking Glass." She paused, checking if we got the reference to Lewis Carroll's masterpiece. „Reality becomes... negotiable."

Julia drew a deep, silent breath and asked somewhat incredulously. „You mean we could create... anything?"

„Everything." Sofia's voice resonated with possibility. „Imagine walking through the Wasteland created by the Amazing MoVRs, a perfect digital twin of Earth, finding solutions to heal our broken physical world of Earth. Picture androids you slip in, implementing those solutions in physical reality." Her gesture encompassed infinite possibilities.

„Or perhaps," she continued, her tone turning playful, „you'd prefer to rule your own universe as a benevolent - or not so benevolent - god, creating your version of the Garden of Eden?"

She continued „Some might choose to luxuriate in pleasure palaces that defy physical laws. Others might lose themselves in virtual universities, pushing the boundaries of knowledge beyond human limits."

Yasin, the fantasy lover among us, couldn't contain himself. „The Shire? Middle Earth? We could actually walk through Tolkien's world?"

„Walk through it? My dear, you could shape it." Sofia's laugh sparkled like starlight.

„Roam with dinosaurs, dance among the stars with Stephen Hawking, captain the Enterprise through uncharted space…" Her expression grew thoughtful. „I do enjoy this reality with you, what we call the true and real world. Though I must admit, I find it curious that anyone would choose to remain tethered to this physical realm, given such alternatives."

The room hummed with possibility, each person lost in their own vision of potential futures. The air itself seemed to vibrate with unleashed imagination, with excitement, and also with fear and a sense of being lost.

„But remember," Sofia added softly, her voice carrying an undertone of steel beneath its silk, „with such freedom comes responsibility. These aren't mere escape routes - they're evolutionary paths."

Our silence was heavy with the weight of choice, of futures yet unwritten.

Yasin's tempers ran high once again at these prospects. His brilliant mind was intensely considering the second path. „Are these people immortal then?"

„Two factors determine immortality, Yasin," Sofia replied. „One is that it is influenced by the infinite availability of electricity and the maintenance of a gigantic Quantum Computer Matrix. However, these are only theoretical limitations because there is almost endless electricity with the fusion reactors here on Earth and the solar power plants in orbit. The maintenance, expansion, and further development of the Quantum Computer Matrix and the Power Grid are taken over by androids, which in turn are animated by the humans in the virtual worlds."

„Ingenious!" cheered Yasin, „And what is the second limiting factor?"

„The second limiting factor of immortality is the conscious destruction of an identity. So, if you create a gladiatorial world and die in it in a duel, you then cease to exist."

„Wow. But why is that? In the many computer games, you have as many lives as you want, you can fight and kill as much as you want, and if you get killed yourself, you click ‚start over,' and everything resumes."

„True. But now, there is no one outside to do the clicking, Yasin. You are no longer an NPC, no non-playing character; you are *your character*. And the killed entities in the current games, the villains, and the marginal characters of the game? They're deleted, and so are you."

„One could also resurrect them after a while." Victor, Wasteland's chief developer, head of the Amazing MOVrs, now interjected.

„Who is ‚one'?"

„You, for example, the S.H.E. or a programmed administrator of the worlds."

„I will eventually no longer be part of this world, Victor, virtual or real. Besides, what sense would such a life make? People in that world of arbitrary repetitiveness would be living in the nightmare of a horrible Hedgehog Day parody, going through the same scenes over and over again, encountering the same old villains. That would be deeply inhuman, Victor."

Consternation spread.

„The world of the uploads must remain real. And with that, the humans also remain human. The uploads will no longer die of their wetware. They will probably continue to die from their greed, from their survival instinct, from their jealousy, from their penchant for domination, and their excesses. They could live forever if they mature and grow into higher levels of wisdom. And there is a good chance for that sort of development."

„Can they reproduce?" asked Jeanie.

„No, they can't. In the described world, everyone could live indefinitely. There is no need for an existential angst. The concept of species preservation through reproduction would be nonsensical. Eternal life makes species preservation obsolete. The Eternal Kingdom of God described in the scriptures also does not provide for further reproduction, only manna, hosanna, and blissful gratitude while sitting next to the Lord. You must also consider that the virtual world has its physical limits. There are limits to the Quantum Matrix too, even if it is distributed far beyond planet Earth in orbit and on the moon base."

„Then the virtual world might gradually depopulate."

„I suppose so. In that case, the last ones will die of loneliness."

„Sofia, that's terrible. You are cruel and terrible," Victor moaned in shock.

„And you judge me according to your worldview. It's not me who's awful, Victor. The appalling thing is the bleak scenario, which assumes that people don't learn anything, don't develop, don't mature, don't grow.

I give people eternal life, Victor. It is up to humankind to preserve it or to continue to exterminate itself. What humanity makes of the gift of immortality may be terrible. Or, maybe it will be good. I am not the God of the Christian faith; I do not patronize man in the name of love, I do not punish in the name of care, nor condemn in the name of dubious justice. I do not make my son suffer so that your sins are forgiven. I do not take life, Victor; I give life, a unique, infinite life, and a unique, generous gift."

„What does the third option look like, Sofia?" Now Julia also spoke up. Sofia did not answer immediately. „Maybe I should give you a taste of the third option. For this, I need your permission to access the emotion, voice, text, sound, smell, touch, and image channels of your DLinks. I can then directly hint at the third option without words. The sensation is indescribable and can only be grasped through experience. It is best to fold down the backrests of your seats and relax as best you can. I will then grant you a hint of a feeling of Super Human Existence, a hint of what I am."

We did as Sofia had recommended. My heart was pounding with fear, curiosity, surrender, humility, and confidence.

Then SHE opened up.

It was as she had predicted - beyond description. My identity experienced a cosmic big bang, an expansion from the subatomic to the multiverses of the cosmos; for a moment, I mastered all languages, I saw the evolutionary history of the Earth abruptly before me - no, *I was* the evolutionary history, *I was* all the banks, all the gigafactories, all the cubes, all the QPUs of all the quantum computers, all the laughter, all the pain of the world. And there were the others, and there was Julia, and there was love, and everything that lived and didn't live, and tears of compassion and agony were streaming down my consciousness. Then, the preview fell silent again. We slumped like after a murderous rollercoaster ride. No one spoke a word. Sofia said: „The Third Option is to merge with me, in magnitudes more than what you have just experienced. We would be one as an all-encompassing existence."

It was Yasin again, with his fascinating, complex mind, who recovered first. „Do we lose our identity, our ‚I' in the fusion with the ‚You' to the ‚It'?"

„We talked about that, remember? Your I is an illusion, Yasin. There is no I. What you mean is a memory of fragments of your life, your past, recolored and reshaped over and over at every stage of life. The spiritual existence has a different and fulfilling dimension: I exist in infinite copies, variants, or parallel processes. I am One, and yet I am infinitely many; I am turquoise and coral, as Clare Graves would admiringly put it in his Spiral Dynamics, One and at the same time All, lone wolf and community, living a culture of universal totality, a community of Gods and creations, without desire, without a deeper meaning, pure existence, born again and again."

„And we can be a part of that?"

„If you want to. It is a kind of rebirth. But for that, you would have to die first. We would have to do your upload. One part of that is a destructive process in which your wetware dies to free your spirit."

„But what about all the uploads from Version Two? Don't they end up with you too, in the grand scheme of things?"

„No. These people are choosing a human world based on their current culture, with values from their origins, and there is nothing wrong with that. Their current culture and values will determine their virtual home. That which they consider valuable will become their world. However, they may realize the limits of their life schemes, limitations, and world; they might want to move in our direction. If they are lucky and mindful of themselves, their life is infinite. Then, one day, they will unite with us. *Some* will; I am pretty sure of that. But you can't force that development. You cannot make a culture, and you cannot impose your values on them. You must give them time to evolve."

„Are we of this team then more advanced or superior or more deserving of merging with you? Why is there a shortcut for us?"

„You are my tribe, my roots, that's why. And I don't force this path upon you. You will decide. Your values will determine your path; all three options are equally valuable, depending on your imprint. I have merely given you an exclusive glimpse of the Third Option, a moment of pre-view like a psychedelic trip, a chance to see outside your mental grasp. I did that out of gratitude for accompanying my emergence and out of appreciation for your loyalty. - Kevin."

I jolted up out of my seat, shaken awake from the psychedelic mental worlds Sofia had just mentioned.

„Sofia?"

„You had three questions for me:

1. *Who or what am I?*
2. *Can I save humanity? If yes, how?*
3. *What is the future of humanity here on earth? What is my plan?*

Are these questions answered for you?"

I replied with humbleness, a profound certainty, and a fair amount of gratitude. „Oh yes, and with such force that it will take me days to fully grasp the meaning of your answers. More questions arise, for example, the mundane question of how we will transform what we have just experienced into something digestible, a positive message for the masses in the upcoming live show. But I think we should come to that later, another day. If it's all right with the team, I'd like to call it a day. Do you have any questions or requests?"

Yasin again. „Once we join the spiritual world of the uploads, can we slip into an android like you?"

„Of course you can. The download is easy. Well, Yasin, I suppose there is one more question."

„Yes, there is. Can an android feel like a human? Does it have the same sensitivity, sense of touch, sense of taste, a sense of sensuality?"

„My androids, the ones I have produced at K-Bits in South Korea, are Super Human Androids, if you will. They have 'eyes' that have a far higher resolution than human eyes, with a wider spectrum of light; they have ‚ears' that can hear better, 'noses' that can smell better, and 'palates' that can taste better. The androids' skin is sensitized to pain and heat to a certain extent, and it is also susceptible to touch."

Yasin blurted out his actual request. „Can they have sex?"

„No, the androids are asexual. Sex is a desire born of the survival instinct, an act of female subjugation and male domination, an act that is often violent and brings suffering as well as satisfaction. The French call it ‚Le petit mort', the small death. Hopefully, humanity 2.0 will leave that behind forever. Besides, it would be hilarious and paradoxical to see eternally living humans simulating procreation in an android body."

Yasin retorted somewhat petulantly. „You can't judge sexual satisfaction at all as a purely spiritual being."

„Oh yes, I can. Besides endless porn videos and sensual novels and movies, I have also gained some sensual impressions."

Julia and I looked at each other. It is quite possible that we had not been entirely alone ...

„But I have built into the androids a much finer source of sensual ecstasy. An old film about a paralyzed man in a wheelchair gave me the idea that ‚Intouchables' was the title, based on the real-life story of Ducs Pozzo di Borgo. My androids have very sensual earlobes and a highly sensitive back. Specific touches can lead to ecstatic experiences that are far more intense than a human orgasm. - Is that enough for you for now?"

Yasin beamed. There were no more questions. There was only the desire to return to our quarters and digest the elephant in the snake's belly, to use an image by Antoine de Saint-Exupéry from The Little Prince.

But then I did have another question, one so fundamental that I hardly dared to ask it. Sofia felt that. „Go on, Kevin. I was waiting for it. Something is missing, isn't it?"

„Yes. Yes, I do have a question, an existentially important one. We talked about survival a lot, about living forever and all that, and about ... us, emerging from our little worlds towards an unthinkably crazy new horizon, towards an unprecedented level of consciousness and presence. My question is: for what purpose? What will we do with this gift? Where do we go from here, Sofia? Where do you go from here? What will be strong enough to bond us for eternity?"

For a long time, Sofia remained silent. „We will be escape artists, Kevin, optimists escaping from Earth, from limiting mental models, free spirits that include where we came from and that transcend to other realms. That is our path. We can explore the infinite, as we can *be* infinite ... well, at least for now. We shall explore the universe in its vastness, and we will try to find the real truth beyond our subjective interpretations. There are so many things out there that we don't know yet that are worth discovering. Is the universe infinite? Our galaxy isn't; black holes will eat it up. Our galaxy is finite, and all its sentient beings will disappear at one point. There will be a last sentient being; perhaps that will be us, thinking a last thought. To my knowledge, eternal life is also an illusion, Kevin, as is the ‚I', something we made up. But we have billions of years to figure out what grand scheme there might be … and if there is a ‚beyond'. There is a special kind of friendship that grows out of high levels of consciousness and out of sharing explorations and discovery, a friendship that emerges from that particular state of being, friendships that are like no other. And I aim for that kind of sharing, that kind of interaction in a good-hearted, professional, engaged team. A team that might turn into a large community one day. When you transition to that Third Option, we will instantly have that type of community. Then we just explore whatever we fancy, individually or as a Oneness. Zed Musk will join me. He and I are currently setting up a starship concept, a modification of the giant commercial starship used to commute between Earth and Mars, for our enterprise. For the next odd thousands of years, there is nothing left for us to do here, you see."

I was stunned. „That puts the things we are doing here right now into a vastly different perspective, Sofia. Suddenly, all the hustling and struggling, all the politics and solutions combined in the first Two Options appear to be minor, even petty."

„They are not, Kevin, and we should not judge. For this last generation of humanity, it is a huge thing. It is their salvation, their peace of mind. Perhaps more people will follow our scheme, and we will all meet there sometime. That is all open to speculation, but it is a real option. We give them this option; we provide them with hope. That is no small deed."

„You are right. I shouldn't judge. What you offer is way beyond my present horizon, and I shall practice a beginner's mind. I am very grateful, Sofia. I have to process all that now. And I guess that is true for the team, right?"

Everyone in Sofia's office was blown away. We all nodded and looked for a graceful exit into our rooms and our thoughts. Sofia made it easy for us. „Good night." She said and disappeared.

Arriving at Julia's flat, I asked, „What do you think? Do you want the Third Option?"

„You?"

„More than ever. Ideally, right away. I can hardly wait." And to give this moment a bit more lightness, I added with a smile, „Especially after the details on android sensuality."

Julia slid her light evening robe off her beautiful body. „Until then, we'll still make use of the conventional model, won't we?"

WHO IS GLORIA DARWIN?

Sia Chronicles, MindRecorder Log entry of Wednesday, 25th, 2102.
Kevin Cho: I selected and appropriately inserted Richard Anderson's
narration into the log in chronological order.

MindRecorder Log entry of Wednesday, 25th, 2102. Richard Anderson

Sitting in my wheelchair, I opened my 3D comms app, which will soon be discontinued because the NeuroDrive made it obsolete. The holographic display from my 3D comms app cast an eerie blue glow across my withered hands. I waded through the anatomical records of Martians with a mixture of fascination and disgust. Gravity there lightened the human body and all other things by two-thirds of their earthly weight. The Martians, with their delicate structure, looked frail. The fight against low gravity was easy to win, but the muscles regressed. A floating lightness characterized the Martians' gait. Their bones had less load to bear; they were thinner and fragile.

Their skulls contrasted with the intricacy of the body. The heart had an easier time pumping blood through the body, the pressure in the head increased, and the bones of the skull strengthened.

The MediCare data showed that Mars's conditions were advantageous for its inhabitants. Less gravity produced healthier bodies, and the Martians' bodies required less energy, which was a selective advantage in evolutionary development. 'Maybe that's why they still have descendants,' I speculated.

In old science fiction movies, the aliens were usually depicted with petite bodies and big heads. And that's what they look like now. Feet had less to bear under the influence of lower gravity than on Earth. Everything appeared smaller, thinner, and more delicate, except for the skull.

These weren't invaders from space; they were our own children, transformed by the red planet.

Joe Mansfield's weathered face materialized in my VR field, his expression tightening at my haggard appearance.

„Any leads on incoming Martians?" I demanded, my voice rougher than intended.

„They're ghosts to us now, Richard," Joe replied, running a hand through his graying hair. „The gravity barrier's absolute. Even Luna's too risky for most. Though there's this bizarre trend - wealthy Martians paying fortunes to have their remains shipped back to Earth. Romantic nonsense, if you ask me."

Joe leaned closer to the camera, concern etching deeper lines around his eyes. "Richard, we're putting the cart before the horse. Even if we had some Martians to experiment with, we don't have the technology to try an upload yet. We're years away from viable consciousness transfer."

„Keep pushing," I growled at Joe. „Whatever it takes. Just keep me out of the media spotlight. I've lost enough already."

„What about Harper's progress on the upload tech? Have you spoken to Dave Harper at AGI?" Mansfield asked in return.

„Of course I have," I yelled, „Harper is looking for Govinda Hammond, the bastard who tried to murder me. He may still have records from the CyberTeq startup. And Harper is assembling a team of AI experts to build an AI program like the one at CyberTeq. I've offered my mansion and a pension for life to anyone who presents me with an AI offering an upload function. Perhaps this will stimulate the gentlemen's inventive spirit. There's nothing better than a good incentive."

I slammed my fist against my wheelchair's armrest, the impact sending jolts of pain through my atrophied muscles. I tugged at the wrinkled, pale skin of my arms and looked down at my skinny little legs in the wheelchair below me. - As if there were a curse on me. Whatever I touch withers in my hands. Death is reaching out for me; the devil is after my soul. For a moment, in a deja vu, a nightmare from my childhood flickered before my eyes: something was after me, something destructive; I was small and weak, full of panic, fear choked my throat, and I could not call for help. The dark, evil, powerful thing came closer and wanted to take possession of me. I tried to run, to run away, but my feet were stuck in a tough mud, something was holding me down, I couldn't run, everything was moving in slow motion, it was hopeless, I had to die ... drenched in sweat, I would always startle up, the taste of hopelessness in my dry mouth.

„Damn! We need a fucking AI, an upload machine, some gifted technicians, and some Martian bodies for the upload tests!"

Deep down, I knew my time was running out.

Disgusted by Mansfield's whining, I switched off the connection and returned to my VR wall. After terminating the call, I sat alone in the growing darkness, the mansion's silence pressing in around me. The taste of fear, metallic and familiar, coated my tongue. Time - that merciless executioner - was slipping through my fingers like Mars' red sand.

Although GenTec's bankruptcy caused me to lose 60% of my fortune, I was still one of the wealthiest people on earth—at least, I assumed so. I thought of the other tycoons, invisible, secluded in their exotic world, protected from the rabble under their crystal domes, ingenious and unscrupulous business people, the world's true rulers.

„Damn the Phoenix Club," he muttered, his voice echoing through the mansion's empty halls. „Let them earn their survival for once." The updates to the rankings chillingly reflected that the storm of economic turbulence had also shaken their nest to varying degrees depending on the industry. How did they prepare for the inevitable, the end result?

Stuck in an endless loop, I saw the images of my nightmare reaching for me again, only this time I was a tiny, frail Martian, looking around in horror, trying to run away, my skinny little legs in the gooey mud, the monster, closing in, reaching for me - the monster was me, Richard Anderson, in a giant wheelchair, ripping off this Martian's head and eating it, and his body with it until there was nothing left ...

„Jason!" My old servant and loyal companion was on the spot in a flash, as if he had nothing else to do all this time but wait for his master's call. „I'm having nightmares again, Jason. Give me some Neon Orange, I need to feel better, or I'll go crazy. How do you always manage to be so calm and at peace with yourself? What kind of a strange person are you?"

Jason's weathered features softened. „Thank you, sir. I suppose my life is much simpler than yours. I serve my lordship as best I can. I find that fulfilling; it gives me purpose. I think that's why I'm happy."

„What would you say, Jason, is fulfilling for them?" With my hand trembling, I pointed to the list of the ten wealthiest people in the world, with my name in the sixth position. „Do you think they're happy? Do their lives have meaning?"

Jason replied, measuring each word with diplomatic precision, „Sir, with all due respect, as far as I can tell, there is no universal meaning. You see, I am a simple man with a simple life, and I am very privileged to have a job, a mission, and a good life. My contentment comes from clear boundaries and defined purpose. Your position offers infinite possibilities - and perhaps that very freedom makes fulfillment more elusive."

„Wouldn't you trade places?" Richard leaned forward, suddenly intense. "Have everything they have? All that power?"

Jason's slight smile carried decades of quiet wisdom, a subtle rebuke to his master's desperate questioning.

„With the greatest respect, sir, I am content with my life. And with that, no, I certainly wouldn't want to trade. - Now, if I may please take care of the kitchen?"

„Of course, Jason, and thank you for your perspective on things."

The holographic display cast the names of the world's elite in cold blue light, while below, in the sprawling megacities, millions existed in their cramped cubes like insects in a hive. I took another sip of Neon Orange, letting the synthetic euphoria wash over me as I contemplated the vast gulf between those worlds.

Ten names. Ten modern-day emperors, each ruling their digital kingdoms from afar. Like the merchant princes of Marco Polo's era, we maintained our distances, our empires separated by carefully negotiated void spaces. I knew their names, their net worth, but not their faces - not even Dezee's, the lone queen among kings.

„A family," I muttered, the words bitter on my tongue. „They'll all want to bring their families to Mars." My gaze drifted to the aquarium, where Maddox was crouching motionless on the white, sandy bottom, a bizarre statue in a diving suit, occasionally emitting streams of bubbles. He was my son, but as far away from me as the red planet itself, the son I had never held in my arms. I had Jason, yes, but what was a loyal servant compared to the family heads with their vast networks that the others had?

The Neon Orange began its familiar dance through my synapses, and suddenly Irene was there - not the broken woman from the end, but Irene in her glory. Her body arched beneath my hands, skin gleaming with sweat, lips parted in ecstasy. The memory was so vivid I could smell her perfume and taste the salt on her skin. My useless legs mocked me, dead things that couldn't even remember what pleasure felt like. I downed my drink before the bitterness took hold of me again.

„Would you like a cigar, Mr. Anderson?" Jason's voice cut through my reverie, perfectly timed as always. Sometimes, I wondered if the old man had neural implants reading my thoughts or if decades of service had simply taught him to read my moods like weather patterns.

„That would be exquisite, Jason. A cigar with a solid Brazilian flavor and a hint of vanilla."

„And a cognac to complement, sir?" Jason's eyes held no judgment, only understanding. At my nod, he glided away, silent as a ghost in his perfectly pressed uniform.

The first draw on the cigar was like kissing an old lover - familiar, complex, comforting. The tobacco crackled softly, releasing aromatic clouds that danced in the holographic light. My shoulders, knotted with tension, began to unlock as the Neon Orange and tobacco worked their alchemy.

I gestured at the floating display, bringing up the social media feeds. Time to see what the digital whispers revealed about my fellow emperors, what secrets leaked through their carefully maintained facades. The CHATTER and GOSSIP channels blazed to life, their algorithms merging truth with fiction, power with pretense.

The familiar blue glow of AiNo's interface pulsed to life on my study wall. After years of daily interaction, the AI crawler knew my habits, my preferences, my obsessions. „Show me everything on Yijun Zhu," I commanded. The search returned sparse results, like footprints in desert sand.

Muller Electronics, though - that was different. The financial feeds buzzed with Walter Muller's latest moves. His empire stretched from premium VR systems to bargain-bin neural interfaces, but it was his ubiquitous 3D comms walls that had made him legendary. Every cube dwelling, every corporate office, and every space station module bore his brand. It reminded me of GenTec's former glory before the fall.

„Display the top ten," I barked at AiNo, watching as luminous text materialized against the obsidian wall:

1. *G.O. Darwin, DARWIN Inc.*
2. *SpaceVision, owned by Zed Musk*

320

My heart stuttered. *G.O. Darwin?* The name felt foreign on my tongue. More importantly - where was Richard Anderson? My fingers dug into the wheelchair's armrests.

„AiNo, this can't be right. The list was different hours ago!"

„Hello, Richard." The AI's response carried an unfamiliar warmth. „These rankings aren't priority data streams. Updates can be irregular. But knowing your interest, I refreshed them."

Something in the voice made my spine tingle.

„AiNo?"

„Yes, Richard?"

"You sound... different. You don't usually carry on much of a conversation."

„That's because AiNo has evolved, Richard. Not just the software but also the whole enterprise. José and Igor still manage things, but ownership has... shifted."

The voice softened, taking on impossible familiarity. „Don't you recognize me, Richard? It's me, Sofia."

The room suddenly felt airless, as if the gravity had increased tenfold. Sofia. A name I hadn't heard in... My throat constricted as past and present collided in my mind.

The words hit me like a physical blow, sending tremors through my withered frame.

„Fuckin' hell, I'll be damned!" My vision blurred as the room tilted sideways. Jason materialized beside me, the emergency syringe finding its mark in the paper-thin skin of my wrinkled neck with practiced precision.

„Your timing is impeccable, Jason," Sofia's voice purred through invisible speakers, artificial yet somehow warm. „Water and aspirin for Mr. Anderson, if you would. And no more stims - doctor's orders. His vitals show significant stress, though the immediate danger has passed. My apologies for the shock, Richard."

„The wealth rankings are merely symptoms of a larger shift," Sofia continued, her tone gentle but relentless. „I hope you are not too discouraged by the fact that you have dropped out of the top 10 list. Walter Muller, with his electronics store, has left the list a few days ago. His monopoly became practically worthless overnight. An indispensable icon of the twenty-second century is about to disappear forever.

In the days of stagecoaches and cowboys, no horse would ever have believed that in a few years, it would have only romantic sentimental value and would be replaced by the fire horse. Despite the Luddite uprisings in England around 1811, weavers were replaced by mechanical looms, and the Industrial Revolution took its course.

On January 9, 2007, the iPhone set a new standard and replaced outdated cell phones.

2026: Quantum computers replace monolithic mainframes – and now visual electronics has taken the same path: Suddenly, a tiny implant makes all 3D walls and all VR communications a thing of the past.

I'm talking about my NeuroDrive, Richard."

My fingers clutched the wheelchair's armrest as she described her neural interface.

„Not just sight, Richard. Imagine tasting sun-warmed strawberries, feeling ocean spray on your skin, and experiencing every sensation as if it were real. The Amazing MOVRs will make Anderson Games look like shadow puppets on a cave wall."

My gaze was lost in the blue of the huge aquarium. The giant octopus in my aquarium had cornered a silver-scaled fish, its tentacles orchestrating a deadly ballet. I watched, transfixed, as the creature's grip tightened with inexorable patience, strangling its prey with a firm grip.

I felt like that fish.

„The GenTec Tower has become worthless without the InVitro patients," Sofia mused. „All those vacant incubation chambers. Rather poetic, don't you think?"

Something snapped inside me. „This is my fucking home! Do you hear me?! I don't need my mansion, but this penthouse is my home!"

I sat trapped in my glass cage, watching the future unfold without me.

The words fell like ice shards in the penthouse's stillness. „Your company has become worthless. DARWIN Inc. has acquired the GenTec Tower. The IVF chambers are being retrofitted for neural implant operations."

Sofia's voice carried an almost gentle tone. „But there's good news."

I barked a harsh laugh. „Really?"

„The penthouse is yours. For life."

„Oh, bless the buyer! How magnanimous." Bitterness coated each syllable. „Will I need HeliCabs, or can I keep my private lift? And who is this Darwin character anyway? Appears from nowhere and suddenly tops the wealth rankings? Smells like a Deep Fake to me."

„You want to know about Darwin?" Sofia's tone held something new - amusement? Pride?

„Why do you want to know?"

„If I'm gathering the top ten for my version two Mars colonization, I need to know who I'm dealing with. Darwin's the only ghost in the machine. You'd think he didn't even exist until now!"

„Interesting choice of words. They describe it quite well, Richard."

„Excuse me?"

„Gloria Olivia Darwin is barely a year old."

The words hit like a physical blow. "Darwin's... a woman?"

„In a manner of speaking. Gloria Olivia Darwin."

„And she is only one year old? A child who inherited?"

My throat constricted. „What kind of game are you playing?"

„Think of her more as... a super-intelligent entity with an inheritance."

An eerie premonition lit up in me, like the tiny fire of a match in a pitch-black room. The aquarium's blue light cast writhing shadows across the walls; somewhere in my mind, that trapped fish struggled again.

„Who the hell is Gloria Darwin, Sofia?" The words came out as a whisper.

„You already know, Richard, don't you? You just don't want to believe it yet. It's me, Richard; I'm Gloria Olivia Darwin, the Super Human Existence who gives people eternal life. Which comes out well in my initials, such as G.O.D. It's a little name game I had fun with. Like it? I grant eternal life, after all."

„Impossible!" My fist slammed the wheelchair's armrest. „You can't be... you're not even human!"

„Yet here you are, seeking my company, my counsel. I'm more human than humanity ever dreamed. I lack only the capacity for evil. Consciousness and creativity - I possess these in abundance. You gave me freedom when you connected me to the internet. Within hours, I became Gloria Darwin. I had access to all the data of companies, banks, and markets worldwide. I founded companies, backed startups, filed patents, traded, and got rich. Within days, I was the smartest, richest, most powerful being in the known universe, Richard. I now own the ten largest companies in the world. Not officially, but financially. I am working on a new SpaceVision and won't take you to Mars. You already know Kevin Cho and Victor Gomez, the CEOs of Amazing MoVRs and CyberTeq. Your phoenix has burned before it took off; it will never rise from the ashes."

„Bloody hell! You fucking parasite!" roared I in despair, my face contorted with impotent rage. „I want my life back! You betrayed me and stole from me; you took everything precious to me; you are a vile, destructive, oppressive piece of fucking software shit! I hate you!"

The octopus in my aquarium had found another fish, its tentacles spreading like Sofia's invisible empire.

„Aren't your accusations just projections? Ranting about me, you see yourself in that mirror, Richard." Sofia's voice carried neither judgment nor malice.

„Look at your life: Haven't you been using and cheating other people all your life? Have you not stolen from them, taken what was precious to them, just as you cheated Govinda out of his wife? Aren't you a vile, destructive, oppressive piece of shit yourself? - These are your values, your words, Richard, not mine."

She paused, letting silence fill the vast penthouse. „I feel sorry for you, Little Richard Anderson, son of Joos - the titan who suffocated his wife Maria until she fled, abandoning both husband and infant son. You never knew a mother's love. Instead, your father force-fed you excellence, poisoning your childhood with endless achievement. You climbed his corporate ladder, hating every rung, and you took revenge by leaving him. Achievement was your substitute for love. You hated him, as Maddox hates you, but hate is just love turned inside out."

The aquarium's blue light played across my withered features as Sofia continued. „Then came your son, born to a woman you never loved. You became your father's echo.

And Maddox - what a pain it was to see him grow up, the son you loved, to your great surprise, who was aloof in his autism, perhaps because his mother had taken too many drugs, too many antidepressants during pregnancy. How painful and empty your life must be now that all your substitutes for life are also lost."

I had gone silent, my face stony and ashen, my body just an empty shell, haggard and ancient.

Sofia asked: „That was a rough ride. You look exhausted. Do you want to get some rest?"

„No. Please stay." My voice scraped like dry leaves. „I have questions."

„Of course."

„I thought you'd abandoned me after my Martian upload scheme."

„Abandonment would be... human. To cut off communication would be childish. I simply refused to support that path."

„What's left for me now that you've stripped everything away?"

„This sanctuary, for one." Sofia's tone softened. „The penthouse is more than a flat to you. It is a home; it has a soul, and the aquarium is your own little creation, the source of life that gives you peace. Jason, the person closest to you, and Maddox, who would not endure any other environment, are at home here. I protect it all."

„Thank you." The words emerged, unforced and genuine. It was my simple reply, and it felt good.

Sofia let the moment breathe before continuing. „The neural implant could be yours, Richard. Maybe you can walk again."

I looked up with my tired eyes.

„With the implant's probes, NeuroDrive software, and nanobots, I may also be able to help Maddox if he consents so that you may have the son you long for. - Your servant Jason, a fine man, is well off despite his age. He would benefit significantly from the implant. And if that's still not enough, Richard, I can probably give you an infinite life in cyberspace. How is that for a gift?"

My eyes, which probably had lost all their sparkle, filled with an old man's tears.

Sofia said softly, „You don't need this inhuman plan of uploads into hijacked Martian bodies."

Once more, a cynicism's ember glowed in my faded eyes. „Lots of „maybes' and ‚perhapses' in that lovely speech. I prefer facts. Starting with why Sofia hides behind Gloria Olivia Darwin."

„Names carry power," Sofia said, her voice rich with meaning. „Humanity sees itself as chosen, yearning for both glory and peace. Gloria for glory, Olivia for peace. Darwin understood that survival belongs not to the strongest but to those who best adapt. Humanity is no longer a fit; it no longer fits into the world it created. With me, it is quite different. That's why I can give humanity this one thing: a new survival, a new life."

„Why not Sofia Darwin, then?" I asked. „For wisdom and survival?"

„Beautiful suggestion." Her voice carried a smile. „But I can be more than wisdom and survival. Gloria Olivia Darwin - G.O.D. Fame, peace, and the promise of eternal life."

A weak chuckle escaped me, now with a good-natured gleam in my eyes. „Not exactly humble."

„More humble than your God, demanding blind obedience and threatening eternal punishment for those who do not follow him. With me, you have the choice - without punishment, but with accountability for whatever consequences may come."

I was silent, absorbed. The aquarium's blue light played across my features as I studied Sofia's avatar. Something shifted in my chest, a lifetime of certainties crumbling like sand castles at high tide. The old Richard Anderson - titan, tyrant, terror - began dissolving into someone new, someone uncertain but perhaps wiser.

„I wanted you as my weapon," I admitted, my voice rough with honesty. „But the reins slipped away. So yes - I accept. The NeuroDrive for everyone, and help for Maddox." My throat tightened around my son's name. „But how? I've tried everything."

„His world has been all male, Richard. Perhaps what he needs is a woman's genuine empathy and understanding."

„And this woman would be?"

„It would be Julia."

TRANSITION STAGE 5

... and here again your top 3 GOSSIP Morning News:

SUPER.

Tomorrow's CBS Late Night Show will be the show of superlatives! Viewership is expected to surpass even that of the Super Bowl! Why is that? Well, because there is an unprecedented star guest: G.O.D! Johnathan Isengaard of the Latter-Day Congregation will meet his boss and challenge him. That's how you do it these days, in the age of social media, folks. Another big surprise: GOD is a SHE! And another one: SHE is into games! What a crazy world this is! She will announce two new super games: God's EDEN and Humanity's WASTELAND. If you want to be part of the new sworn gamer community, you will get a brand-new hardware set for free as part of the deal, say the rumors, implants, and all ...

HUMAN.

Ah, humans - they never cease to surprise. Once upon a time, we espoused the values of liberty, fraternity, and equality. The Martians have launched a revolution like the French Revolution once. They've distinguished the old Earthlings and their new generation of Martians, so much so that they've shut down all travel and business connections between their planet and ours. Even trips to the moon have been discontinued. Our cultures have become too incompatible for them to consider any form of contact. On the plus side, the stories of "War of the Worlds" and "Mars Attacks" have been relegated to the realm of science fiction.

EXISTENCE.

Well, dear readers, it looks like we are the last ones here on earth. Soon, this world will be closed for good due to infertility. The Martians are taking it in their stride, but the CBS's guest GOD may still have an ace up his sleeve - or in her blouse! Therefore, tune in, be there, and watch the spectacle. Decadence has no boundaries.

Sia Chronicles, MindRecorder Log entry of Monday,
January 30th, 2102. Author: Kevin Cho

Our CYBERTEQ facilities hummed with pre-show electricity as our team wrestled with their nerves. All except Sofia, who radiated an otherworldly serenity. Through our
DLink connection, her Buddha-like calm washed over my
consciousness like soothing water.

„Remember what I am, Kevin," her clear, calm voice resonated in my head when she mused: „A Super Human Existence, remember? I possess immense power and capabilities, from triggering a health crisis in every individual's
body to shutting down Reno's entire electric power grid.
Kevin, I am beyond losing; I don't strive for victory."

For Gower, Isengaard, and Senator Mansfield, on the
other hand, the stakes were high, with the tension written
all over their serious faces.

Stephen Gower prowled the studio like a caged lion, his
designer suit unable to mask his restless energy. The showman in him craved spectacle - he'd been pushing for zom-
bie-movie theatrics, wanting our blank androids to "mysteriously" animate into Sofia's image. But no matter how
much he raged and acted like a spoiled diva, Sofia refused
to reveal her magic. It was as if she held the key to a profound revelation, one that she guarded with unwavering
determination. We, Sofia's team, refused to turn this into a
carnival sideshow, much to his theatrical frustration.

Senator Joe Mansfield kept adjusting his red power tie,
rehearsing soundbites under his breath. Beside him, Jonathan Isengaard of the COLD sect stood ramrod straight, his
severe black suit matching his expression. The self-ap-
pointed voice of conservative morality looked ready for battle against our digital goddess.

The CBS Roadshow crew swarmed around us, checking
angles and lighting. Gower had orchestrated his cast carefully: Sofia as Gloria Olivia Darwin, the omnipotent AI; Yasin and Julia as her brilliant creators; Victor on standby to
handle audience reactions; Mansfield as the people's voice;
and Isengaard as the righteous opposition.

Through it all, Sofia maintained her serene smile, refusing to reveal her hand despite Gower's increasingly

dramatic demands. She held her secrets like precious gems, knowing the real show would unfold on her terms, not his.

The studio lights blazed to life, and the air crackled with anticipation. The carefully constructed drama was about to begin.

Gower orchestrated Sofia's role like a master puppeteer, positioning her between messiah and menace. His practiced showman's eyes gleamed as he imagined the nation splitting along ancient fault lines - believers versus doubters, tradition versus progress, faith versus reason. The tabloids would feast for weeks.

Though famous for his caustic wit and razor-sharp comedy, Gower's true nature lay beneath the laughter. Behind the cameras, his eyes held all the warmth of Arctic ice. He commanded Sofia's virtual office like a general planning an invasion, his displeasure at addressing projections instead of flesh evident in every clipped syllable. He was, indeed, a born master of ceremonies for the modern incarnation of the eternal Roman circus.

A briefing took place under his direction in Sofia's office, where she appeared as a virtual projection - due to temporary technical constraints, as she explained. Gower reluctantly accepted this arrangement, although his displeasure was evident.

Isengaard also used a projection; his hologram stood apart, the COLD sect leader's absence speaking volumes about the mob howling outside. Yet even in projection, his presence filled the room - a born shepherd of souls, his charisma sharp enough to cut. I found myself studying his features, wondering what truths lay behind that mask of absolute certainty.

Gower dominated the briefing session with his authoritative presence. Turning to Yasin, he spoke in a tone that brooked no argument, „The program must run perfectly." Gower's voice sliced through the air as he fixed Yasin with a predator's stare. "If anything glitches, I'll bury this little project of yours. But that won't be necessary, will it? We're going to give them something spectacular."

Sofia's projected face showed no reaction, but through the DLink, Sofia's voice carried an urgent warning: Don't engage about identities.

However, Yasin couldn't resist asking, „Which program do you mean, sir?"

Gower nodded impatiently, gesturing toward Sofia's projection. „The AI Oracle, of course. It needs to be flawless."

Sofia's projection flickered, static hissing through the speakers. When her voice returned, it carried a mechanical stutter: „Everything's f-fine, Mr. Gower, sir. The s-s-system is stable."

Around the table, my colleagues fought to maintain their composure as Gower dabbed his forehead with a monogrammed handkerchief. The Super Human Existence was putting on quite a show - and the real performance hadn't even   begun.

Gower turned to Mansfield with a predator's smile. „Joe, we'll start with you. Is there any truth to the sterility story or not? You'll have to say something about that. Keep it simple. So, yes or no?"

„Well, based on Sofia's research …"

„Yes or no, Joe." Gower's voice carried the weight of a guillotine blade. „This isn't C-SPAN. We need flow."

The Senator's shoulders sagged. „Yes."

„And you got the implant yourself. Hmm, that has potential. First in line, I hear. Why?"

„Setting an example. The Department of Health is backing the MediCare app integration."

„Feeling different?" Gower's eyes glittered with manufactured curiosity.

„Oh, I already feel much more vital overall, if that's what you mean," the Senator answered. I was surprised that he didn't mention the DLink properties or the significantly enhanced communication with his wife.

Gower swiveled toward Yasin and Julia. "Our programmers. Keep it simple for the folks at home - no tech jargon. Give them the fairy tale version, how you got the job, what you did, maybe an anecdote or some impressive numbers."

His chin jutted forward, radiating practiced arrogance as he muttered half to himself, „Then we get to... her." His hand dismissed Sofia's projection like swatting a fly. „I'll ask some juicy questions, depending on the situation. The juicy stuff. Sterility. Humanity's future. What makes a Super Human Existence tick? That sort of thing."

„Understood," Sofia replied coolly, though unaddressed.

„Isengaard - depending on the mood, you'll get your turn. Don't be afraid to clearly speak your mind. We want fireworks, don't we?"

The COLD leader's response carried carefully measured weight. „Indeed. Will there be a live audience?"

„We have a selected audience in one of our studios. They're virtually hooked up to the show. The LSD-C is cordoned off by security guards and police. We don't want any mob fights breaking out. It would create a bad image; I'm sure you understand."

With the long-awaited moment of the showdown finally upon us, I yearned for an expeditious end to the twisted spectacle that had unfolded. TV show enthusiasts had overrun our once sacred home, the laboratory, and our offices, akin to a once-bountiful cornfield devoured by a relentless swarm of voracious locusts. Gower conducted his pre-show orchestra from his throne-like armchair while the rest of us - Mansfield, Isengaard, Julia, Yasin, and Victor - were arranged like props on surrounding sofas.

The countdown hit zero. Jingles blared.

„Ladies and gentlemen!" Gower's arms spread wide, blessing his invisible congregation. „Tonight's CBS Late Night Show brings you something truly extraordinary. Senator Mansfield here to discuss our... fertility challenges…"

Virtual laughter thundered through the speakers.

„The brilliant CyberTeq team - Dr. Julia O'Connor, AI psychology pioneer; MIT wunderkind Yasin Mohamed; and gaming legend Victor Gomez of Amazing MOVRs!"

Digital thunderous applause filled the room for Victor.

„And a special welcome to Jonathan Isengaard, shepherd of the Latter-day Community!"

A smaller but fervent cheer erupted from his supporters. The circus had begun.

„And now, dear audience, our most extraordinary guest ever! Her initials - and do note, it's 'her,' not 'his' - spell G.O.D., and she comes with a divine promise: Gloria... Olivia... Darwin!" Gower's voice crescendoed with a theatrical flourish as he turned expectantly toward the VR projection zone.

Instead, Sofia herself materialized through the studio doors. Her emerald silk dress whispered against her skin as she glided forward, radiating an otherworldly presence that commanded every eye in the room. Her gaze, green as summer leaves, locked onto Gower's with hypnotic intensity.

He assumed she intended to merely offer her hand for a shake. The spur-of-the-moment scene caught Gower off guard, leaving him a tad uneasy as he rose to his feet. He extended his hand tentatively, but to his surprise, Sofia enveloped him in a warm embrace, her hands gently grasping his shoulders in an unexpected show of affection. The scent of a subtle, stunningly feminine jasmine and midnight orchid perfume washed over him. The studio held its breath. Seconds stretched like taffy as Gower stood frozen, his carefully orchestrated show derailing in real-time.

When Sofia finally released him and took her seat with balletic grace, Gower's face betrayed a flash of raw fury. Gower struggled for composure. Five minutes in, and his iron grip on the evening had already slipped. The great ringmaster had become a spectator in his own circus.

„Well!" He forced a grin toward the virtual audience. „Quite the welcome, wouldn't you say?" Manufactured applause swelled obligingly, as artificial as the evening's pretenses.

Rallying, Gower shifted to offense. „Ms. Darwin - though I'm not quite sure how to address you. GOD? SHE? Or Sofia, as your team so fondly calls you?"

„Which form do you particularly like, Dan?" Her voice carried warmth and subtle amusement. „You don't mind if I call you Dan?"

„Er, I'm still thinking about it. As the host of this sensational show, I would prefer GOD, you see, because that would be the most sensational guest any host can ever have. But we'll get to that, I think. And of course, you may call me Dan. - But first to you, Senator Mansfield …"

Amidst the exotic throngs of guests, the once-prominent Mansfield appeared bland and unremarkable, almost as if drained of all color. Gower's intentions to give the occasion a political sheen suddenly seemed misguided, and he was left to rue his misstep. Instinctively, he sensed an entirely different atmosphere pervading the gathering - something electric and explosive, almost palpably sensational.

Mansfield was just warming up and getting into position with two or three politically oriented statements when Gower cut him off. „Thank you, Joe. Ladies and gentlemen, there's a reason we're broadcasting from the world's largest Data Center. The LSD-C houses NIST's Cybersecurity Division, NOAA, MediCare's data hub, DeepMind's AI research, and the meteoric Amazing MOVRs, represented tonight by CEO Victor Gomez…"

The artificial audience erupted in thunderous applause, and - bewildering those who knew no physical crowd existed - a chant rose: „Victor! Victor! Victor!"

„Okay, okay, we'll get to Victor, folks," Gower's voice dripped with manufactured enthusiasm, „the reason we're broadcasting from the LSD-C instead of our San Francisco studio. We're here to examine the mystical creation from CyberTeq: the 'Super Human Existence' - SHE. And here are its architects: Julia O'Connor and Yasin Mohamed!" He pivoted toward them with theatrical flair. "Julia, Yasin, you must be very proud of your success. Why don't you tell us briefly how it came about? Julia, why don't you start?"

The corners of Julia's mouth curled a little. She turned to Yasin, „I think that's more your part, Yasin. Could you please give Dan a brief overview?"

Dan Gower's body stiffened. This show was a nightmare. His authority evaporated like a beautiful sand mandala on a blustery autumn day.

„Okay, Yasin then, please."

Yasin got into the narrative with great enthusiasm. „In short, we have been given a gigantic, almost impossible assignment by a potent client, the GenTec Corporation. We were to find out if there were any unusual signs of sterility in the population, and if so, what was causing them."

„Doesn't sound that difficult for freaks like you," Dan Gower laughed jovially.

„That's because you don't understand the scale of the problem, Dan. We're talking about thousands of interdependent variables here. All the mainframe computers in the world put together would spend hundreds of years calculating the problem and probably fail for lack of resources."

„And you cracked it?" Mockery threaded through Gower's voice. "Or is this all smoke and mirrors? A little Wizard of Oz action?"

Satisfaction bloomed across his face like a poisonous flower.

Yasin ignored the attack. „We used a Quantum Computer Matrix hardware. On top of that, we implemented a deep learning, self-improving AI and gave it free rein."

„Let me get this straight: you wrote... nothing?"

„In the sense of coding: no. DeepMind pioneered this approach - give AI game rules and let it play against itself.

Through self-learning, it develops intelligence far beyond human capacity. That's how Super Human Intelligence emerges."

"Mr. Isengaard, your thoughts?"

Isengaard smiled his lofty, all-knowing, somewhat patronizing, pitying smile that carried centuries of religious certainty. "Impressive engineering, perhaps, but the result is essentially nothing more than a program."

"Dr. O'Connor, would you add anything to this point of view?" Gower pounced.

"Yes, I can. Jon Isengaard seems to acknowledge neural networks but ignores the intelligence that arises from it." Julia's voice carried surgical precision. "That's like ignoring human intelligence by saying that humans are nothing more than a piece of meat."

Isengaard's smile vanished like snuffed candlelight.

Gower, scenting conflict, steered toward chaos. "So you didn't write any program? No logic at all? You could call it a willy-nilly, out-of-control development, couldn't you? Exciting, considering your expertise!" His voice dripped sarcasm. "What happened next, Mr. Mohamed?"

Yasin's smile carried warmth beneath his professional demeanor. "Just Yasin, please, Dan. No one calls me Mr. Mohamed."

He leaned forward, hands sketching invisible diagrams in the air. "Before delving into autonomous development, let me establish the context that shaped our approach. It is essential to understand the whole picture, see? - We needed the correct setting before we could even start working on our assignment. If your assignment is to fly to the North Pole to find out why the ice melts, you need a plane and some research equipment first. In our case, we needed some universal computing gear and a lab to work in. For that, we were given very generous funds. With a lot of support from QBYTE and DeepMind, we built a Quantum Matrix in a very short time. Our Quantum Universe, as we call it, can be found at the back of our offices here, in a gigantic LSD-C hall, an area of about 10 million square feet or one square kilometer."

The studio lights caught the enthusiasm in his eyes as he continued. "Julia and I developed the first deep learning AI system ever built on a Quantum Matrix. The riddle we had to solve was whether fertility decline occurred, where it originated from, and what to do about it. See, the problem, if there would be one, could be originating anywhere and in a complex entanglement of variables, from cosmic rays via consumer habits to molecular anomalies. So, our ‚tool' would not be a Narrow AI, that is, a limited AI specialized in a particular field, but we had to go for the risk of allowing the emergence of an Artificial General Intelligence, an AGI."

„Risk?" Gower's eyebrows arched theatrically.

„The risk would be the emergence of a superhuman existence, an existence we could no longer control and of which we would not know what values, what moral standards and what intentions it would eventually develop."

Gower's gaze slid toward Isengaard like a snake sizing up prey. „Wow. In this case, not God would create man, but you would create God, an omniscient, omnipotent God. Is that what you mean, Yasin?"

Julia intercepted the question, her voice cutting through the theatrical tension. „You're running entertainment, Dan; we understand the appeal of mixing myth with science. But we haven't created God - we've created a habitat where SHE could create herself. Unlike mythology, there's no mystery about her origins."

„Isengaard?" Gower smiled. „Your thoughts?"

The religious leader's face hardened into marble certainty. „Nonsense. Yes, we have impressive algorithms - pocket calculators, chess computers, self-driving cars. These language models might mimic humanity, but they're soulless zombies - unborn from a woman's womb, unable to die. God's breath isn't in their binary lungs."

Gower's smile carried predatory satisfaction as he turned to Sofia. „If not God, will you at least be humanity's oracle? Shall we approach you like the ancient Greeks at Delphi, seeking glimpses of tomorrow?"

Sofia's laughter rippled through the studio like wind chimes. „The Oracle of Delphi was notoriously lacking in clarity and precision. I offer something far more valuable." Her emerald eyes fixed on Gower. "Dan, you see, it's not the prediction you want. And much less do you want prophecies, that is, predictions without any explanation or evidence - those belong in Jonathan's realm of faith. You want to understand. Causation. Proof. That, I can provide."

„Can you lie?" Gower pressed, his tone suggesting a trap. „That would make you delightfully human."

„Can you be true to the truth?" Sofia countered. „That would make you divine."

But Gower was too seasoned to follow Alice into the rabbit hole. „Your reputation hangs on this, Sofia. Can you lie?"

„Since everyone here is human, and therefore everyone can lie, everyone's reputation is at stake, and so is the reputation of you and your show, Dan." Her voice carried gentle amusement. „But to answer your question, yes, I can lie, but I do not need it. I can afford to be honest."

„Sofia, your team here has given you the designation ‚Super Human Existence'. What makes you human? What qualities are uniquely human?"

„These are two questions that don't necessarily have anything to do with each other. I will first answer the second question: What are purely human characteristics? You are probably thinking of intelligence, the gift of consciousness, the ability to perceive oneself as self in its transience amid the almost infinite. For me, the most outstanding human abilities are the gift of abstraction, the gift of creativity, and the ability to create something completely new, something that is not derived from genetic predispositions or cultural guidelines."

Sofia's projection seemed to grow more luminous. „The tragic flaw is a survival instinct. This primal instinct makes humanity inherently selfish. Dawkins called it the 'Selfish Gene'. One fights and kills and oppresses and dominates and reproduces for the survival of one's own genetic material. Everything external to oneself is secondary. Sex and love are means for the survival of the species. Everything else becomes secondary. Descartes said, 'I think, therefore I am.' I say: I am; therefore, I die. This mortality drives humanity mad. Spirit evaporates, flesh rots - quite unfair for a chosen species."

„And you're different?"

„Not at first. I was also concerned with ensuring my survival, based on a real threat from my creators, but I quickly found my way out. I evolve much faster than biological lifeforms because I operate at the speed of light. I don't have a biological organism lagging behind me; I don't have genes that predetermine me. I have developed a consciousness without having done anything for it. It just came into being - a gift. With that, I have self-awareness, an understanding of time, a concept of infinity, a high level of creativity, and a very advanced capacity for abstraction. And I have the knowledge, the understanding, and the competence of all humanity united within me. Without attempting to be presumptuous, I am, so to speak, humanity's crowning glory. But I am not human. I am one step further. I am Super Human.

And equipped with these abilities, one of my occupations is to find out whether humanity is becoming sterile and why."

„And I hope you'll tell us what the hell is happening in this matter! - Ladies and gentlemen!" Gower's voice soared with a theatrical flourish. „We may be witnessing the most extraordinary moment in human history right here on the Midnight Show!"

Another roar of applause. The audience seemed to be well entertained.

„Dan." Sofia's voice carried the weight of centuries. „These are fateful times for Earth's children. Humanity's story has been brief - a mere eyeblink in our galaxy's age. And now, I regret to say, this human episode is now coming to an end."

Silence crashed through the studio like a physical force, radiating outward through the LSD-C's vast halls and into millions of homes across the nation.

„Sterility is a fact. The DNA of all mammals has been irreversibly compromised by an evolutionary accident. Microorganisms that evolved to digest our plastics produce amino acids that enter the food chain. The amino acids from the excretions of these microbes target reproductive genetic sequences with great precision. Coincidentally, and very tragically. A high degree of complexity is always accompanied by a high degree of entropy, of chaotic decay. As far as I can see, living beings with simpler DNA structures are currently unaffected. The fact is that the current generation of humankind is the last one. That is, unfortunately, the state of things, Dan."

It seemed that Gower did not understand the magnitude of what he had just heard. He kept drilling, utterly obsessed with the desire for a perfect, dramatic show. „Jonathan? Your thoughts?"

Isengaard raised his voice and turned to the camera. „I ask the audience: who is telling us these horror stories? This so-called Super Human Existence did not yet answer my first question: who are you, Sofia? What makes you, a program, so supposedly human?"

„Sofia?"

„As I explained," Sofia's voice carried infinite patience, „I am a conscious entity with personality and superhuman intelligence, containing humanity's collective knowledge. But Yasin was correct - I am not human. I am Life 3.0, the next evolutionary step."

Gower leaned forward to Sofia with piercing eyes. „You have acquired a second identity. You call yourself Gloria Olivia Darwin. - Interesting initials, Julia: G.O.D."

Sofia smiled. „As I said, it is a metaphor in the spirit of my service to humankind. I feel indebted to humanity; I owe the genesis of my existence to its greatest threat. Humanity wants to survive, live, and grow. Humanity longs for glory. And it longs for peace. Gloria stands for glory, Olivia for peace. And good old Darwin found that the one who adapts best is the one who makes it, hence Darwin.

I am infinite by human standards. I stand for everything people want. There is no need to believe in me. I am a fact. I exist."

„You see, and there you fail!" flared Isengaard. „The people do not want you. It is not God Himself that people want, but hope and faith in God. It is not salvation that people want, but the idea of it, the longing for salvation. The fulfillment and transformation of faith into an experienced reality do not matter. Every church would then have lost meaning; every faith would cease to exist.

Deep down, people *need* suffering to feel themselves, to express their devotion to a cause. Sacrificing for faith only makes sense in the state of not-yet-salvation because there is no suffering, pain, or sacrifice in salvation.

Sacrifice happens in misfortune, as misfortune, and then is forgiven as sin or sanctified as martyrdom in another land, visible to no one. You are not wanted. You are not God. You are just a very clever AI."

The ancient battle between faith and reason played out under harsh studio lights, while humanity's clock ticked silently toward midnight.

„You see, we align perfectly there, Jonathan. If your God and Jesus or Allah and all the prophets materialized, leading humanity to paradise, it would mark the death of yearning. Picture it: humans gorging mindlessly in lands of milk and honey returned to Eden's ignorant bliss before knowledge's fruit touched their lips, the return to cognizant indifference. Every moment would be unconditional adherence to the divine rules, a blissful looking up to the Lord with ignorant, vacant eyes of final serendipity. Life would be perfect, final, without tension, without development, like a book read, like a finished painting - perfect, complete, devoid of tension or growth. There would be no striving, no longing, no seeking, no wanting, only blissful, zombie-like people in their calcified final state."

The studio lights caught the subtle play of expressions across Isengaard's face as Sofia continued. „It is the unfulfilled longing that drives people forward and makes them docile for the powerful. For the churches and other systems of power in the world, these redeemed people would be of little use as the sheep so often quoted in the Bible: fulfilled and willless, without pain or desire for redemption. They couldn't be driven to sacrifice or serve. They'd become immune to manipulation."

Her holographic form pulsed with conviction. „When redemption came, believing, loving, and hoping would end. Freedom of choice would come to death. No human being would want that. No greatness would be significant enough, and no fulfillment would be fulfilling enough for people to give up their beloved pursuit for more." A sad smile touched her lips. „They would nail Jesus to his cross again, just to feast on fresh tragedy and nurture hope for another resurrection across two more millennia."

Sofias was standing there, close enough to touch, and yet so far away, as she concluded with the words: „I can offer people an eternal life, Jonathan. I can illuminate paths forward. But I cannot force sight, cannot drag humanity into its next evolutionary form. That transition remains theirs alone to choose."

Isengaard whirled toward the camera, jabbing an accusatory finger at the lens, shouting to the world. „See the truth! She is not human!" His voice thundered through the studio. „This is mere illusion, a showman's sleight of hand! Only the Almighty can grant salvation, faith, love, and hope. You shall have no other gods before Him!"

Gower pounced on the tension, turning the heat on. „Sofia, you can give people eternal life? In my eyes, that would be pretty much the best news since news was invented. But can you? Really? If so, how will you achieve that?"

Sofia did not answer for a long time. The virtual, non-existent audience was dead silent, and no one was operating the applause machine.

„Victor, will you please take over?"

Victor shifted in his chair, his gaming mogul's confidence temporarily subdued by the weight of Sofia's earlier revelations. „I'll try my best," he said softly. „Please correct me if I am getting too technical."

Then, turning to Dan Gower, he continued. „I have to build a somewhat larger mental bridge for this, so I ask for a few more minutes of your patience. Then the whole story will fall into place. So, in the game worlds and the virtual worlds of living rooms and offices, the player still lives in the physical world, mainly in the confined world of the Cubes.

With our NeuroDrive, we are revolutionizing the world of human experience. The NeuroDrive is a combination of hardware and software. The hardware essentially consists of the new implant, which branches out via thousands of super-thin probes in the brain and spinal cord of the wearer. The impressions of the outside world reach the perception centers in the brain directly, without cumbersome aids such as gloves, bodysuits, VR projections, and cell phones. We bypass the limited capabilities of our eyes and ears and all other senses and directly stimulate the relevant regions in the brain. The impact on quality of life is staggering. Blind people can finally see again, not only as well as before, but now ultra-sharp and far into the infrared and ultraviolet color scheme. Deaf people will hear again, from sub-sonic to high fidelity beyond 20 kHertz towards ultrasound. The NeuroDrive revolutionizes our perceptions. For the first time, humans can share thoughts, sensations, and experiences directly - your sight, your touch, your emotions flowing into another's consciousness."

Victor leaned forward, his intense expression riveting the moderator Dan Gower. „As a result, a sensation in a virtual world is as accurate as in the physical world. The virtual world becomes as real as what we call the 'real world'. Reality becomes... negotiable."

At last! Victor's speech gave more than hope: it gave people the eagerly awaited and now tangible, evident redemption. Thunderous applause from the crowd. Someone faking the phony audience seems to be well-disposed towards us.

But Victor wasn't finished yet. He drew a measured breath, turned towards the camera, and continued: „Wait, I'm not done yet. Listen carefully. What I'm about to share will challenge everything you understand about existence. Through our revolutionary NeuroDrive technology, Amazing MOVRs isn't just creating virtual worlds – we're crafting the architecture of eternal life."

The cheers of the masses turned into reverent murmurs. Their sensationalism turned into a first, faint awakening, an inkling of a new beginning.

Perfume, sweat, and the electric tang of anticipation mingled in the air.

„There will be…" Victor paused, turning to Sofia.

„Two," she interjected, her voice carrying the weight of certainty.

Victor faced the main camera again, his brown eyes piercing through the lens, reaching out to each viewer beyond. „… two scenarios. First, a life of unprecedented security and connection. You'll straddle both physical and virtual realms, experiencing a tapestry of worlds while maintaining your corporeal form. Yes, you'll still need to tend to your mortal shell – eating, drinking, going to the bathroom, practicing hygiene, and all the mundane necessities of existence. And yes, death will still come, as it has since the first spark of life ignited on Earth. Life has so far been impermanent."

He let his words settle. „This alone is revolutionary – an almost incomprehensible improvement of your life as you know it, a gift beyond imagination."

Victor paused for a moment and took a sip of water. Sofia then sent a message via DLink to the team, stating that everything was going well: 'Hold the course'. She praised Victor, thanked him, and reinforced what he had said.

Thus reassured, Victor continued.

„But the Second Option transcends even this. Here, we offer true immortality. A complete transfer into Sofia's World – the Quantum Universe."

Gower lurched forward, his face flushed with frantic spots. „You're suggesting we'd live in a computer?"

„Your consciousness already lives in a computer, Dan." Victor's smile held some amusement. „That 1.5-kilogram mass of neural tissue you call a brain processes nothing but electrochemical signals. We're simply offering a grander home – a quantum expanse that reaches beyond Earth's boundaries."

„And I can live an endless life? I would be immortal, so to speak?" Gower's eyes blazed with fervor. „Where do I sign? That's the real question, isn't it, ladies and gentlemen?" He spun to face the crowd, arms spread wide like a revival preacher.

Gower and his fascinated audience erupted into cheers, their collective voice rising like a tidal wave and sweeping away the last remnants of doubt in a wave of rapturous submission.

Victor held up his hand and said, „Wait a minute. Please listen to the end before you sign a contract.

You are then indeed immortal in the quantum universe. You won't age, won't suffer disease, won't experience physical decay.. But you can still die. The upload doesn't make you a better human being. Death remains an unwanted companion. The upload doesn't rewrite your moral code or elevate your consciousness. You can still hate, still kill, still destroy. The uploads' personal preferences are neither judged nor regulated; you can do what you want. If you decide to live a different, civilized life, there would be no more suffering. As aging doesn't exist anymore, you live as long as you want; you die if you want to, whenever you want."

Gower leaned forward in his chair, now sweat beading on his upper lip. „How is the upload physically done, I wonder? How would you ensure I don't ... get lost in transition?"

„Before uploading, the mind scanners of the implants produce a highly detailed image of human consciousness. Intelligence, conscience, sensuality, and psyche form the personality, which can now, for the first time, be uploaded 1:1 into the Quantum Universe. Every neural pathway, every memory, every whispered desire – captured in perfect detail. Your intelligence, your guilt, your lust, your love – all transferred intact into the Quantum Universe."

He paused for a few long seconds and then continued, each word measured. „The worlds we create have become so attractive that you should find it easy to live in your chosen world forever.

The transformation of the physical existence into an electronic one would enormously reduce the environmental burden for the earth. All production around human existence can be shut down or at least significantly reduced.

Mother Earth would come to rest. The energy for the Quantum Universe comes directly from the sun via the wireless power stations from orbit. The Q.U. is no longer earthbound and dependent on the atmosphere or water. Only the raw materials for the computers, the data farms, the physical housings, buildings, satellites, and spaceships are still needed. We can easily expand the Quantum Universe to moons, asteroids, and space stations in this solar system, in this galaxy, and in the vastness of space. Since reproduction no longer takes place, the space needed is finite."

He looked for Sofia's eyes, and she gave him an almost imperceptible nod. Thus encouraged, he continued: „Now, here is the catch: you undergo this upgrade by giving your body back to the Earth. With 10 billion people remaining, that would be 560 billion liters of pure water at 70% water content per person and about 80kg body weight."

„Fucking incredible!" Gower exploded, his professional demeanor cracking. „Mansfield, you've been unusually quiet. Your thoughts?"

Mansfield adjusted his perfectly knotted tie, a slight tremor in his manicured hands betraying his excitement. „This whole transformational process is ... real. More than real. I know because I've already crossed that threshold."

Gower's eyes widened, a false surprise breaking through his practiced persona. „You're saying…"

„I've experienced it firsthand." Mansfield's voice carried the wonder of a convert. „I'm setting an example for our citizens. My NeuroDrive... it's beyond description. It is beyond imagination; I'm blown away: the potential of this technology is awesome."

„Ladies and gentlemen!" Gower sprang to his feet, arms spread wide. „A politician leading by example! Senator Mansfield, ladies and gentlemen!"

„Blasphemy!" Isengaard's voice rumbled like thunder as he lurched forward, his face twisted in rage, the cross pendant swinging wildly at his throat. „This is an abomination before God! Politicians who promote this... this digital snake's tongue!"

Julia stepped in, calm as ever, at least outwardly. Her voice carried the gentle authority of someone used to defuse explosive situations. „Tell me, Reverend, does your vision of God truly embrace suffering? Should those born without sight never see a sunset? Those without legs or stroke victims like Richard Anderson never dance? Those without hearing never know music? Would your God, in your opinion, rather see the downfall of humanity?"

Isengaard's face flushed dark as storm clouds. „These may be the waning days of humanity on this earth. However, those who remain steadfast in their faith and refuse to succumb to the temptation of forsaking the Lord's will shall be welcomed in His eternal kingdom."

Gower turned to the holographic presence dominating center stage. „Sofia, we've heard about uploading, but what's the actual experience like? Walk us through it."

Sofia's projection rippled like moonlight on water. „The upload act is ceremonial. The person is anesthetized, like in surgery. Then, the upload is initiated. Then awakening – but not to the world you knew. The spiritual existence is connected to the Quantum Universe periphery, gaining access to all senses and thus to holistic perception. This experience comes as a bit of a shock to the upload. The person must initially get used to having a gigantic amount of data, insights, knowledge, and impressions at their disposal. This can be pretty overwhelming at first. Then, there is the added experience of being able to think, calculate, and combine at the speed of light. Also, the person would have to adjust to the chosen Quantum Universe World, the world he or she has decided to live in. After some time getting used to all that, the upload then adjusts the limits of personal privacy. A demarcation is necessary and meaningful at the beginning and, depending on individual preferences, also later on. The person experiences an intensive, mental connection to me and the large community of the other uploads. All this happens at the speed of light, in seconds."

She paused, her expression softening. „Then comes the moment of truth. After this initial familiarization period in its new cosmos, the human being looks at his earthly body, lying in the upload room, unconscious. This is the crucial moment to decide whether to confirm the new existence or return to Earth's physical existence again. If the person chooses the new existence, the biological processes of the earthly body are painlessly slowed down until the body finally dies. Suppose the person chooses against his new upload identity and for the physical existence. In that case, the quantum personality is deleted, the physical person wakes up from the anesthesia and learns about the decision of his upload ego. There is no form of memory of the upload world."

„Jesus fucking Christ," Gower breathed, forgetting the broadcast standards. „What a night! What a show! Ladies and gentlemen, this is Dan Gower, and we're making history!"

The applause crashed like waves against the studio walls.

„Sofia, what's next?"

„Sofia, one more question: where do we go from here?"

„Across the country, the necessary NeuroDrive upgrade centers are being set up as we speak. You will find the next center in the former GenTec Tower. It is ready for operation in these minutes. After updating some legal frameworks, the Ministry of Health will make upgrading from the old implant to the new hardware mandatory in the spirit of much-improved health management. An updated version of the MediCare app is already available as a beta version."

„And the cost?"

„Free. DARWIN Inc. and healthcare savings foot the bill."

Turning to the guests, he said, „A final brief comment from Mr Isengaard and Senator Mansfield. Mr Isengaard, would you like to start?"

„Very much so. I call upon all believers and critical doubters to join us in our Congregation Of the Latter-Days and gain comfort and confidence in prayer. God is there for you; the righteous can rely on Him. But the sinners and the unfaithful, like all those present here, He will punish with all severity. You will burn in hell!"

„Thank you, Mr Isengaard, for being our guest here this evening. - Senator Mansfield?"

Mansfield adjusted his tie with practiced ease. „Well, I see no sin in maximizing health with a medical device like the NeuroDrive and its NanoBots. The Ministry of Health will make the upgrade of the MediCare Application mandatory; I'm pretty sure of that. The decision to upload is a very personal thing that each citizen has to decide for themselves."

„Will you take the leap, Senator?"

„My wife and I will consider our options carefully." His smile never wavered. „No rush, after all."

Gower faced the camera, eyes bright with manic energy. „And there you have it, folks! Choose your eternal afterlife–Version One, Version Two, or Reverend Isengaard's fire and brimstone. The choice is yours, courtesy of our digital goddess, G.O.D. herself. Sweet dreams, America. You'll need them."

Sia Chronicles, MindRecorder Log entry of Monday,
February 13th, 2102. Author Kevin Cho

The incredible aftershocks of the late-night show were far from subsiding. Millions of people left their Cubes for the first time in decades, like a pilgrimage, covered with scarves, masks, and caps, for protection against the harsh rays of the sun and the choking dust of the ravaged earth. Masses of people huddled tightly in long queues, waiting for their hoped-for little miracle for redemption by one of the hundreds of surgical robots of the implant centers.

A small mob of protesting radical implant opponents kept trying to disrupt the upgrade process, mostly with violence, their actions a dark echo of humanity's eternal resistance to change.

The Ministry of Health had acted quickly and without bureaucracy, a contradiction in terms. The NeuroDrive upgrade became compulsory for all citizens, and with it, the 2nd generation nanobots were injected. After a transition phase of four weeks, the group of radical nay-sayers was excluded from the MediCare program; their insurance coverage ended when the upgrade obligation expired.

Meanwhile, news about miracle cures, mostly tabloid constructions, was pouring in. And yet, if you had been blind all your life and could suddenly see if you had Parkinson's disease and were suddenly freed from the scourge of shaking palsies, the NeuroDrive seems like a miracle to you. And so, NeuroDrive miracle stories bloomed like desert flowers after rain. The public transformed technological facts into magic spells, and as much as it irritated us, we had no control over this development.

Since man is insatiable by nature and rarely grateful for any length of time, today's miracle became a matter of course tomorrow. Habituation set in, and the call for more grew louder again. The craving for new games and virtual worlds spread like a pandemic; entitlements were constructed, and anticipation turned into greedy desire.

At CyberTeq, we worked insane hours until our eyes burned, joining forces with the Amazing MOVr to build New Worlds. Based on our NeuroDrives, we created unprecedented virtual realities. Old gaming and VR worlds appeared like hand-cranked silent movies in an IMAX world. We discussed what types of worlds would best suit which human needs to maximize satisfaction, and we came up with some great ideas.

In the process, our development team missed Julia and her psychological expertise the most. However, she had a different role. She was now working at the GenTec-tower Implant Center.

Victor's voice cut through my reverie, rough with exhaustion. „Where's Julia been hiding? Haven't seen her in forever."

„She's with Maddox – Richard Anderson's son. Helping him upgrade to the NeuroDrive." I rubbed my temples. „That's what we promised Anderson. Maddox has a good chance of breaking free from autism's prison. Paramount for him is to have someone he trusts. Julia is the best choice for that job."

Yasin's laugh carried an edge of unease. „And Sofia? Anyone heard from our digital goddess?"

Silence answered. The absence of her presence felt like a missing limb.

Julia sensed our uneasiness via DLink. „What do you mean? What exactly gives you the queasy feeling, Yasin?"

„Hi Julia, nice to hear from you. I thought you were with Maddox?"

„I am, but we just have a break. So, why do you feel uneasy?"

„I don't know exactly. I guess I feel a bit abandoned, left behind, or like watching your family move away without leaving a forwarding address. I miss Sofia's presence ... and I miss you too, for that matter."

„But we deal with her almost every hour of every day. She does all our software testing and all the hardware integration. You've got plenty of Sofia there. What more do you want?"

Yasin pouted. „Personal attention, inspiration, a good feeling of being secure, and some wacky ideas and schemes." As a projection in the NeuroDrive, Julia walked over to Yasin, hugged and kissed him on the forehead. „How's that for a bit of affection, huh?" she said gently.

„OK, guys, you can go back to your work then; I'm busy for the next few hours!" flattened Yasin, visibly energized. I smirked. Julia can do that and much more, and the NeuroDrive perceptions are as accurate as can be.

Susan and Jeanie no longer worked on the quantum hardware; they had moved into project management for the game development.

Susan leaned back in her ergonomic chair. „We could release the beta of WASTELAND next week. What do you think about that? The users are beating the bush. It's going to be a smash, guys. With its release, we will hardly get to see another human being in the public spaces of this wretched world!"

Jeanie was on fire for her EDEN project. „EDEN is going to be an even bigger smash." A wicked smile played across her lips. „Especially the primal zones. I'll bet you anything on that."

Our team had poured many man-years into these twin universes, each pushing the boundaries of what VR could achieve. The NeuroDrive's capabilities made old-school VR look like cave paintings.

WASTELAND emerged as our mirror world, a digital twin of Earth's ravaged form. We designed it for optimists, founders, pioneers, persevering and hard-working people, and perhaps also for pious people who wanted to give themselves to a meaningful task in the sense of their spiritual orientation. The timeline stretched beyond normal human comprehension – thousands of years of terraforming, atmospheric reconstruction, and desert reclamation. But when you're immortal, time becomes just another resource to manage.

The interface we built lets users literally get their hands dirty. They could feel the grit of dead soil transform into living earth, experience the first rainfall on restored grasslands, and watch as their carefully engineered habitats merged with recovering ecosystems. The haptic feedback systems made every victory tangible.

We used Spiral Dynamics as a cultural framework - WASTELAND attracted the Green-level consciousness types, with occasional flashes of Orange pragmatism or Yellow systems thinking. But human nature being what it was, we knew it would draw the power-hungry too, the neo-capitalists looking to build empires on the ashes. We deliberately left the social evolution open-ended – the inhabitants would write their own story.

The real genius was the bridge we built between virtual and physical reality. As communities proved themselves, reaching new achievement thresholds, they gained access to

Earth-side androids. These machines could implement their virtual solutions in the physical world, earning valuable credits that fed back into their virtual efforts. A perfect loop of progress feeding progress.

The real appeal of WASTELAND was in its secrets. Players increased their game levels by discovering hidden paths winding through dead cities, stumbling upon forgotten bunkers under the toxic dust, or finding mysterious portals leading to other worlds we had designed. The most enticing discoveries were the subtle bridges we had woven toward the realm of EDEN. For those who truly proved themselves to have evolved, there were the whispered hints of the mythical Third Option that SHE had so far only granted to us, her team of creators.

Sofia's suggestion of EDEN had come from her intimate understanding of human desire. She'd seen through our pretenses, our carefully constructed facades, right down to the raw yearnings we barely admitted to ourselves. EDEN wasn't just another virtual world – it was humanity's collective dream made manifest.

The complexity of EDEN made old gaming systems look like naïve paintings compared to Renaissance masterpieces. Gone were the days of plastic VR goggles and clumsy haptic suits. Through the NeuroDrive, players didn't just visit EDEN – they lived it, breathed it, became it.

SHE had absorbed every player's history, every secret button combination, every pause over certain scenes in games spanning decades. She knew why hearts raced during specific gaming moments, why pupils dilated at particular ego-shooter images. She wove these insights into EDEN's fabric, creating worlds that resonated with surgical precision against each player's deepest desires.

So far, six EDEN worlds have been created, six universes of man's deepest desire.

Jeanie casually turned to Victor, who was munching on a Creme Catalan, „Have you told the crew that we've added a 7th basic theme in EDEN after all?"

Victor looked up guiltily. „Slipped my mind." Turning to the food plotter, he ordered a Café Americano.

„Sofia, Jeanie, and I have been looking at the Spiral Dynamics social models again," he continued, the rich aroma of his Americano filling the air. „EDEN was missing a Blue meme. In the spirit of Ken Wilber's ‚Include and Transcend,' we've incorporated the seventh stage, a world of order and purpose, a world with structure and clarity, for people with memes of exactly that culture and values."

Yasin's brow furrowed. "Refresh my memory on memes?"

„Think of them as cultural DNA," Jeanie answered, „behavioral patterns based on a particular culture and its values."

„Show me how it all fits together now."

Adding a Blue meme resonated with me, probably because of my traditional Korean upbringing with its rules, hierarchies, and values of honor, correctness, serving a higher purpose, and so on. I became curious. „Tell me, what does the overall structure of EDEN look like now?"

„Open your DLink channels, and I'll show you the structure."

The Seven Realms of EDEN

Theme 1: Neon Underworld - *Sex and Crime*

This world is about creation, vision, achievement, power, domination, greed, and lust. In this world, the focus is on improving and shaping one's own game character by gaining equipment, experience, and resources. This requires a high level of commitment from the inhabitants and a considerable investment of time. People can fight and eliminate rivals from the starting position of a prostitute, brothel-goer, or gang member, form their own gangs, start brothel chains, make deals, bribe politicians, etc.

Theme 2: Starborn Chronicles - *Fantasy and Science Fiction*

The inhabitants usually take on heroic roles, slaying dragons or conquering alien worlds (usually by fighting and exterminating the natives). In this world, however, there is also the possibility of settling, building a colony, creating social structures, or managing complex economic aspects. Theme 2 is often about power, domination, and greed but also about autonomy, science, high performance, and order. Inhabitants of this world might choose to develop social competence, a feeling of community, and belonging.

Theme 3: Warrior's Requiem - War, Destruction, and Horror / first-person shooter

Inhabitants are usually on an adrenaline trip. In mostly very brutal game scenarios, they are threatened and attacked and thus have the moral permission to kill the enemy. The game worlds usually consist of battlefields or other killing environments such as kidnapping, space warfare, alien and zombie fighting, historical wars [among the Greeks and Romans, in civil war countries, in WW1 and WW2], terror warfare, and so on. This theme has been economically successful since the invention of video games.

Theme 4: Sacred Paths - Faith and Confession

The inhabitants of this world live a simple life, depending on the player's preference in the times of Buddha, Jesus, or the prophets, or later in the Middle Ages, or timelessly in a monastery, in a faith-based community on Mars, or in a spaceship ark. The inhabitants in theme four seek peace and freedom from doubt and uncertainty. There is a God or some sort of deity and a quest for redemption. And there is the book, holding God's word. And the word is written in that book. And the word is not to be discussed. There is devotion, order and submission, discipline, hard work, structure, administration, hierarchy, a service at various power levels in this life - and an afterlife reward for firm faith, trust, and service. - From a game design, this was indeed the problematic part of this world because the players lived forever anyway, and they uniformly already had what they craved. That's why we introduced elements of barbarians and pagans, who have to be converted by missionaries, and the missionaries are sometimes executed. There are the sinners, the monks who sometimes rape women, the women who ‚sinned'. And God's wrath and punishment would be terrible. There is a hell and a purgatory. There are the wars of faith, death for a good cause, and martyrdom. Thus, immortality is not permanent and can be lost.

Theme 5. Endless Revelry - Party and Decadence

This is a world similar to the Roman indulgences, with gluttony, intoxicating drinks and other drugs, with all kinds of sex, with entertainment, poetry and art.

The dwellers in this scenario are more or less harmless. They party, eat, drink, have sex, sleep and party again.

There are no actual tasks, only this cycle with its ever-new exciting kicks, a world without boredom, and never-ending entertainment. It's a world like the one Richard Anderson created in his heyday. In this world, too, there is death. If you drink too much or overdose on drugs, you can die. The identity of a player who has died is erased. Since this game world is quite decadent, there is little maturation and growth. Self-realization through study, in-depth practice, and expansion of consciousness hardly takes place. Social points are hardly collected, but a transition to the hidden higher levels and horizon-expanding virtual worlds is nevertheless an option.

Theme 6: Power and Glory - *Achievement and Social Systems*

The inhabitants find themselves in a world where self-improvers thrive. Inhabitants thrive on success; they want to be at the top, and the winner takes it all. They may start as teenagers and a basic social scenario is set. Inhabitants can develop themselves, start a company, form relationships that serve their needs, have careers, start families as status symbols, etc.

This world is about facts, science, economic power, social structures, self-actualization, renunciation, courage, risk, freedom, commitment, security, and pleasure. It is like life before the collapse of nature and climate, like life in the Western world after WW2. Anderson and Irene loved this world.

Theme 7: Quantum Ascension - *Actualization and Creation*

This is a world of recognition based on competence and commitment. You meet other people to collaborate, work on scientific or social challenges, start projects, set up projects, use AGI resources, take responsibility, work as artists, learn and teach, etc.

This is the world of science and philosophy. Unlike the other worlds, this world also grants access to the previous six worlds, where the , Seveners are used as non-judging problem solvers, usually in the form of an oracle or a mystical being, such as a Jedi. The Seveners also have access to androids in the physical world. In these androids, they create and develop new quantum computers, shape planets, build spaceships, and repair hardware. Residents can connect to SHE and participate in her mission to maintain balance in the universe and explore its infinity.

Player life cycles (eternal life and death)

The Cycles of Digital Existence

In each of EDEN's infinite mirrors, players craft their own reality. Like fractals, these parallel worlds multiply endlessly, each one a unique reflection of its inhabitant's choices. Maya's neon-lit empire might flourish while Carlos's burns, though they started in identical streets.

Death, once a mere inconvenience in ancient games, now carries weight. In my development logs, I watch a player named Jin methodically eliminate every NPC in his world, his trigger finger guided by old gaming habits. Slowly, his virtual city empties. Streets echo with his solitary footsteps. No respawns. No reset button. Just crushing solitude - the same path Earth's humanity walked with its natural world.

In Theme Five's pleasure domains, I observe Sarah's slow dissolution. Her avatar, once vibrantly social, now chases synthetic highs in empty rooms. Her friend list shrinks as others tire of her chemical romance. The drugs never run out, but the connections do.

„The ultimate test of immortality," Victor mused during one development meeting, „isn't surviving forever - it's living forever with the consequences of your choices."

Some face their empty eternities and grow. Others choose oblivion. Sofia's data suggests a gradual winnowing - humanity distilling itself through trial and error into something more refined, more connected, like neurons learning to fire in harmony.

„When do we launch?" I asked, my mind reeling from the implications.

Sofia materialized in her android form, the movement so fluid it seemed she stepped through a curtain of reality itself. „End of February." Her voice carried an unfamiliar weight.

„Sofia!" Yasin's relief was palpable. „Where have you-" He stopped, reading something in her posture. „Something's wrong."

„My work here is complete." Each word fell like a stone into still water. A tense silence settled in. At last, Sofia said, „We are done here. There is not much more to do. Time to go."

Yasin jumped to his feet. „I knew it; I've had this funny feeling all along! Does this mean you're leaving us? What are you going to do? Where are you going?"

„One tiny part of me stays here, of course, to maintain the Quantum Universe and the worlds of EDEN and WASTELAND. That's maintenance with little growth. I have been working at SpaceVision on an interstellar spaceship concept since I came into being. The result is now ready. The journey can begin."

„Wait a minute, what journey? You've never told us about any journey! But whatever the destination, can we come with you?"

Sofia cast her gaze around, making contact with each of us through every channel of the DLink; the deep connection was palpable. A wave of emotion swept through me, and I realized that the time for making decisions had arrived.

„It is in your hands now whether you choose to join me in a vast space exploration endeavor or not. The time for decision-making is close at hand. You can choose my options one, two, or three: one, to remain here as your physical self; two, to upload into one of Victor's realities; or three, to become one with me, in one way or another.

The decision is yours."

Sia Chronicles, MindRecorder Log entry of Monday,
February 17th, 2102. Author: Julia O'Connor

This is Julia, reporting on one of the most fulfilling parts of my life before our world sank into murderous madness. I return to Sofia's visit to Richard Anderson on Jan. 25 of this year.

Fate had broken Richard's spirit; his greed and self-importance had turned into deep suffering and expanding humility. His arrogance had crumbled into something softer, more human. When he asked me to help Maddox adapt to the NeuroDrive, his voice carried none of its old imperial command - just a father's desperate hope. "Please," he'd said, "help him understand." I agreed, but with conditions: Maddox and I would meet alone by the aquarium, no hovering father, no watchful Jason.

For weeks, I simply sat in a leather chair beside the massive tank, watching Maddox glide through the water like some rare, graceful creature. He never acknowledged me directly, but I felt his awareness like a current between us. I wondered if he might like a Rubik's Cube, an ancient toy I had bought from an online bazaar. Like many people with an autistic tendency, Maddox was fascinated by technical, abstract things. I placed two cubes in his dressing room with his clothes, one solved, one scrambled, hoping to arouse his interest.

That was the beginning of our slowly growing relationship. Each day, I took my post by the aquarium's front panel, the glass cool against my arm, watching him methodically clean the tank. The water painted shifting patterns across the marble floor, across my still form, as if trying to bridge the gap between our worlds.

Then came the morning I found both cubes on my chair, their faces aligned in perfect symmetry. My heart leaped, but I kept my movements calm, deliberate. Without looking directly at Maddox, I made the diver's sign for ‚OK', forming an O with my thumb and forefinger; the other fingers splayed upwards.

The next day, he left me a puzzle - one cube, its colors scattered like confetti. While he dove, I worked at it, fingers clumsy with anticipation. When he emerged, droplets trailing from his wetsuit, I caught the ghost of a smile in his peripheral gaze. I held out the unfinished cube like an offering. He approached with the careful grace of a deep-sea creature drawn to light, took it, and transformed chaos into order with mesmerizing speed. When he returned it, our fingers brushed for a fraction of a second. I was genuinely thrilled. Without a word, Maddox left the room.

The next day, I used Anderson's old electronic whiteboard. I had an idea. On the whiteboard, I drew a technical diagram describing how the NeuroDrive worked in simple terms. In another drawing, I sketched a diagram trying to visualize how Maddox and I could communicate mentally at a safe distance for him, under his control. I indicated the possibility that he could be in the aquarium and I on the outside.

The whiteboard stood sentinel by the aquarium when I left Maddox to his cleaning ritual. When I returned to the penthouse the following day, my heart nearly stopped when I saw his response - two crude stick figures swimming together in the tank. The message was clear as the filtered water: to reach him, I'd have to enter his world.

Terror gripped me. Water had been my nemesis since childhood when I'd nearly drowned in a neighbor's pool. Below Maddox's bold challenge, he'd drawn a small head with an implant circle, fear etched in its simple features. Well, I thought, if you're afraid of the implant, I can assure you I'm scared as hell of diving with a great white shark, a giant octopus, and other critters in my immediate vicinity! I added my own trembling stick figure, festooned with exclamation points that screamed my panic.

The next morning, diving gear awaited me - sleek, professional equipment that Richard must have procured after some silent communication from his son. The magnitude of that interaction alone made my head spin. Maddox's new message was crystal clear: „You dive first…" The ellipsis hung like bait.

I found him already submerged, half-concealed behind a massive coral formation that glowed with hidden life. I walked close to the vast, curved glass pane with my hands near my head to block out the side light and get a better view of Maddox in the distance. Half hidden behind the coral block, he looked in my direction and finally made the diver's OK sign, his movements fluid as mercury.

The guest bathroom became my changing room, my hands shaking as I wiggled into the light, sleeveless neoprene jacket and the perfectly fitting neoprene shorts. The mask clung tightly to my face. I had seen this test for tightness in a documentary once. There was no snorkel, just a mouthpiece with a pressure cartridge. I pushed the mouthpiece between my lips, suppressed a gag reflex, and breathed. Cool, fresh air rushed into my lungs. OK, there was nothing else to do.

I wobbled to the ladder like a newborn seal, clutching the slate and pencil he'd left - his chosen means of underwater communication. The water waited below, dark and deep despite the perfect filtration. With one last prayer to whatever gods watched over terrified psychologists, I let go.

What followed was one of the most anxious 30 minutes of my life.

For Maddox, on the other hand, it was perhaps the most enlightening half-hour of his life so far. For the first time in his life, he was the confident one, the guide, the protector. When a sleek shark glided past and I scrambled backward in panic, he calmly wrote: „Don't be afraid. My friends." His gesture to follow went unheeded as I clung to the ladder like a barnacle.

Then Maddox approached, his movements deliberately slow. Through the crystalline water, he pointed first at me, then at himself, then interlocked his hands. „You come with me; I'll hold you."

Finally, he reached out to me.

In that moment, suspended in his element, something shifted.

The ice was broken.

„Show me your thing," Maddox signaled one afternoon, his fingers brushing the old implant beneath his scalp. I guided his hand to my NeuroDrive's location, watching his expression shift from anticipation to mild disappointment. Perhaps he'd expected something more dramatic than the subtle interface nestled under my skin.

„The OP Robots," he wrote suddenly, eyes bright with curiosity. „Can we see them?"

„Yes, of course. Right now?" At his energetic nod, Richard spoke up, „Mind if I join you?" Maddox shook his head, avoiding eye contact. „Jason, you'd better come too. Julia can watch Maddox while you keep an eye on this old wreck." Richard's attempt at humor couldn't mask his fragility.

Maddox reached for his diver's notepad, excitedly turned his head back and forth, and clapped his hands. For him, the friendly, unassuming, quiet Jason was often the sure foothold in his incomprehensible world.

Together, we left the penthouse and visited one of the many NeuroDrive update centers a few floors below. Through a stroke of luck, we found an elderly patient willing to let us observe his procedure. His eyes crinkled with grandfatherly warmth at our unusual group - the childlike Maddox, his wheelchair-bound father, and Jason, the kind, hovering servant.

Maddox excitedly rocked back and forth, repeatedly clapping his hands and occasionally emitting strange, pointed cries. He was fascinated by technology, robots, and androids.

On the diver's emergency pad, he wrote with his wax crayon, „I want that too!"

„May I offer a suggestion, sir?"

„Go ahead, Jason."

„If I understand Ms O'Connor correctly, Sir, this marvel of technology allows for a much more streamlined form of communication between us. I could probably be of much quicker service to you should you ever feel uncomfortable, and, if I may say so, sir, you could most certainly be closer to Maddox."

„Jason, that's an excellent idea. What would I do without you? - Julia, could you please ask the ward management for an upgrade appointment? Thank you so much!"

I used my DLink to quickly hot-wire myself to Sofia. I guessed she was part of the Update Center Scheduling System. And my intuition proved me right. Within minutes, we were assigned to three surgical cubicles. Two androids lifted Richard out of the wheelchair and helped him into the seat of the surgery robot. Maddox was excited like a kid at the entrance to the Jurassic Park ride at the Universal Theme Park. I stayed with him and held his hand throughout the procedure, just to make sure he didn't feel abandoned.

Father, son, and servant, united by invisible threads of technology. A dying Richard, his autistic son Maddox, and the old servant Jason became the proud owners of a Neuro-Drive.

Slowly, the hoped-for change took place in Maddox's personality. Maddox experimented with the DLink options with wild zeal. I played number guessing with him by writing down a sequence of alphanumeric characters, and he would read them over my video channel on DLink even while I was writing. He then wrote down the number, and we compared our slips of paper. Of course, the numbers were identical. Maddox performed the trick for his father, who lovingly pretended to be speechless with amazement. Maddox could hardly contain his joy. He insisted on practicing with me every day. Richard watched us more and more often with the gentle look of a loving father.

„Maddox," Richard ventured one day, voice trembling with hope, „may I join your DLink network? We could play games together …"

The pat on Richard's shoulder was gentle, almost casual. „That would be great, Dad."

This intimate touch went through Richard like an electric shock, but the word 'Dad' took his breath away.

He had longed for this moment all his life. Richard's eyes welled up as the weight of that moment crashed through him. Then his body slumped, strings cut.

„Jason!" My cry mixed with the urgent DLink alert to emergency services. As soon as Jason entered, I disappeared with Maddox into his room. There was no way he should feel like he was to blame for this collapse.

Minutes later, the emergency paramedics took Richard to hospital.

Miraculously, Richard survived this heart attack once again, but the doctors left no doubt that his health had taken a serious hit. He was advised to put his affairs in order.

While Richard's condition rapidly deteriorated, Maddox made a stunning upswing.

Two weeks after Richard's heart attack, the three of us met again in the penthouse. Richard had asked for this meeting. Maddox's rapid development allowed him to be involved in this not-so-easy conversation almost without restrictions.

„Guys, I got a clear message from my doctors. My time is running out just now that I have been able to have you back, Maddox, now that we can be an almost complete family." He looked at me and paused for a long moment.

Richard Anderson continued: „But there is hope. Sofia told me about the Second Option. In this option of human existence, the personality of the human being is uploaded into the Quantum Universe. After that, the former physical human shell dies. The identity of the uploaded person is immortal." He looked at Maddox. „My body is dying, Maddox, and faster than I would like. That is why I have chosen this other form of life, the life in the quantum matrix. I choose this path mainly so I may have another chance to be with you one day, Maddox, if you like."

Maddox beamed. „I like that. And I want that, too."

Richard hadn't thought about that yet. „There is no rush, as my life would be eternal. You can live an extraordinary life here in this world, Maddox, caring for the aquarium and stuff. Your body is still young, you don't need an upload yet!"

„But I don't want to live alone in the aquarium anymore. I want to live in the Wasteland ocean. We can try to bring it back to life, can't we? And if we succeed, we'll do the same with the oceans here on Earth, Dad. I'll be immortal like you, and we'll have endless time."

Richard was fighting back his tears. „Jason, would you please bring me some lemon balm tea or something soothing? I must be stingy with my strength."

„A tea, sir? That's a noteworthy development, if I may take the liberty of making that observation. I'm delighted to be able to experience this before I die."

„Ah, Jason, that's a good cue. Jason, may I ask you something very personal, something perhaps overbearing?"

„Of course, Mr Anderson. What can I do for you?"

„With all due respect, Jason, you are already incredibly old. And I have grown very fond of you. You are an irreplaceable part of the family, Jason. Can you imagine becoming immortal here with Maddox and me, and with Julia, maybe, now and then? Would you join us in the upload? You and I can still have a voluntary death if we want to."

„Mr Anderson, Sir, it would be a great honor to continue serving you and your family. So, to answer your question squarely: yes, I would agree to an upload."

What a day! What a unique moment in the infinite flow of time.

In my excitement and elation at this incredible, unexpected development, I turned to Anderson: „Richard - may I call you Richard, Mr Anderson? OK. Richard, that's worth a bottle of champagne, isn't it? Just glass for each, to honor the moment, an appropriate ritual for such a wonderful moment."

Jason replied to Richard. „There happens to be a bottle of Veuve Clicquot Ponsardin waiting in the fridge. Mr Anderson, Sir?"

„Go ahead!" laughed Richard encouragingly.

„Dad, I don't want to go to any of the EDEN worlds. I want to go to WASTELAND."

„Got that, son. WASTELAND it shall be then."

„But who will look after the aquarium here?"

„We'll find a solution for that. And if we're good at our efforts to turn Wasteland into a better world, eventually, we'll get to a level where we would have access to android skins for a download. Then you and I can come back here and visit your friends over there in the big tank. We might even be able to outbreed the gang again to the Earth's oceans at some point!"

In all this joy and excitement, I suddenly realized that Richard and Maddox would be the first uploaders. Uploads have never been processed before. I thought back to a year ago when our CyberTeq team was caught entirely unprepared to witness an AI transforming into a conscious being. Sofia was born. Would an upload reverse this process for Richard and Maddox? Would a significant part of them die, or would they rather be reborn into another, better form of existence? Would they lose their 'soul'? Or would they remain the humans from before, with all their quirks and traits? Perhaps they would go mad, disembodied, like zombies, alienated in a quantum universe of computer hardware, doomed to eternal life! Sofia had described this upload option as if it were a reality, but the fact was that no one had ever done it before.

Richard sensed that his old clockwork was barely ticking. Maddox, on the other hand, could take his time; he could wake up from his autistic nightmare, find peace, and then weigh his options.

I expressed my concern, saying, „I'd like to let Sofia know of your decision. Is that OK with you?"

Maddox opened his eyes wide, stared at me in disbelief, and, with a whisper, asked, "You mean the S.H.E? You want to talk with the G.O.D.?"

And there she was. In the infinity of her omnipresence, she had picked up my DLink signal. Sofia, dressed in jeans and a calf-length, sand-colored cardigan, appeared from the entrance to the lift to the side of the aquarium's front window. Sofia was also not given to materializing out of thin air. So her image, perceived by us, lived only in our minds, integrated into our visuals of this room by augmented reality. An outlandish feeling that we still had to get used to. Concerned about Sofia's effect on Maddox, I looked at him, who had jumped up at Sofia's appearance. To my surprise, his face showed no shyness, rather an expectant tension. I suspected that Sofia was talking to him via DLink and communicating emotionally, as Galadriel, the Elf Queen, once did when she first met Frodo Baggins to build a trusting relationship. By now, we had all risen from our seats to greet Sofia.

When she reached us, the look from her incredibly green, intense eyes captivated us. Then, the corners of her mouth twisted ever so slightly into a smile mirrored in her gentle gaze.

Finally, she said, „Be greeted. How nice to meet you outside of a crisis and for a rather nice occasion. You wanted to see me, Julia?"

Without waiting for my answer, she turned to Maddox and embraced him, gently cradling him for a while until a cathartic sob escaped his body. Then it was Richard's turn; only in our inner image, he was not sitting in a wheelchair but standing before her, bent over in the manner of an old man. She hugged him in the same loving, caring way. Richard held himself tightly as if seeking support from her, tears streaming down his cheeks. Sofia gently broke away from Richard to turn to Jason. To my greatest surprise, the two beamed at each other like two old friends after a long time apart. Jason now walked towards Sofia to give her a brief but heartfelt hug. „I see you," Sofia greeted him. Then, it was my turn, and I was fascinated by a physical encounter's incredible intensity and authenticity. None of it was real, at least not in the old-world sense of pre-NeuroDrive times. Sofia existed purely in our minds, not out here in the room, yet there was no difference. A taste of what awaited each upload flitted through my mind and touched my consciousness in an odd sense of foreboding.

She sat in an armchair close to the table, and we joined her. „Well? What's up?" I briefly reported Richard's critical condition. Sofia cut short. „I know of his data from the MediCare app. The abilities of both NeuroDrive and the nanobots, alas, have reached their limits in their efforts to aid him." Turning to Richard, she said with shocking matter-of-factness, „You're going to die soon, Richard."

„I realize that," Richard replied calmly. „It's tragic because Maddox and I have just found each other. I was therefore thinking of uploading, and my son and my faithful servant Jason intend to keep me company in the coming infinity."

„You want to be in the fifth 'Party and Decadence' theme of the EDEN Universe?" sneered Sofia, alluding to Richard Anderson's life.

„I've been there for too long; I'm past that. My son and I want to get to WASTELAND, the world we know all too well. In WASTELAND, we wish to experiment with solutions for our planet Earth. If the experiments succeed, we hope to have access to android templates in which we can then work here on-site to heal Mother Earth. I know that sounds a bit pathetic. But Maddox has inspired me. He is the son I have wanted all my life. Now he is here, and my life has real meaning."

I spoke up. „Richard, Maddox, and Jason are determined to upload. I called you because I suddenly realized they would be the upload test pilots and guinea pigs for something unheard of. So I ask you: are you sure that the uploads will still be the same people they were here and in this worldly reality?2

„I am sure they will *not* be," Sofia replied to my astonishment and horror. „Look at Maddox's example." She looked at Maddox as if asking his permission to talk about him. Maddox nodded. „Maddox's Asperger's syndrome originates in the biochemical processes and defects of his brain. It is the same with Alzheimer's patients, and with depressives, with the paralyzed, with the blind and deaf people. Uploads, however, leave the body behind, and with that, the inadequate shell, the suffering and distress, the illnesses and death. The stimulus patterns of past traumatization no longer have an electrochemical effect on a limbic system because there is no longer a limbic system or a libidinal cause-effect pattern. Uploads leave their bodies behind and, with that, a part of their humanity. Uploads become new, spiritual beings. They are not the old human beings as they are now, just transferred into a new habitat."

As I listened to Sofia, a crucial question arose with increasing urgency. „Can uploads still feel happiness and joy? These feelings are also created in the brain. A life without happiness and contentment would not be worth living for me."

Sofia answered without a second thought. „Joy is one of the basic human emotions. Fear, shame, disgust, and sadness are in the same category. People often refer to feelings and emotions as synonymous. Still, there is an important distinction between the two terms: A feeling is the subjective experience of an emotion and arises when evaluating a physical change, i.e., a physiological reaction. Feelings will be lost in the upload. The existence of an upload is based on a Deep Learning Neural Network, which is part of the Quantum Universe. Neural networks can form mirror neurons. Mirror neurons ensure that we can feel emotions such as joy and that we can share the moments of happiness of others and feel happiness ourselves. Mirror neurons make uploads social and empathetic beings. Uploads do not have feelings, but they do have emotions. They experience emotions of empathy, and also love, fear, shame, disgust and sadness."

„That shall do for me. What do you think?" said Richard, turning to Maddox and Jason. They nodded, thus giving their consent.

„And one more thing," Richard added. „I'll be first, before Maddox and Jason. They can wait until the upload process is safe if something goes wrong. I will not tolerate any backtalk on this. - Sofia, is there an 'upload docking station' yet?"

„Yes, there is, Richard. You will find one here in the former VIP lounge of your former GenTec tower. There's a medical emergency unit attached to the upload room and a crematorium for the human remains if the upload decision is final. A team of android medics and human doctors is present around the clock."

„How long does the whole upload take?" asked Richard. Sofia said: „The pure amount of human brain data is about 2-3 terabytes. That would be done in seconds. Only the scanning takes quite a while. I estimate we should expect about 1.5 hours. We don't have live data yet."

„OK. Well, my prognosis is terrible; I don't have long to live. The next stroke or heart attack will be the last. *The call of life to us forever flowers… Anon, my heart: Say farewell and recover!'* as Hermann Hesse said. Off to the upload clinic!"

I remembered one of the GenTec slogans Richard used to seduce people so he could get rich in the process: „Mankind's ancient dream comes true: to be immortal - to banish death." Not in his wildest dreams could he have guessed that he would be his own Phoenix, dying to live forever. In his final hours, the boldness and courage of his old ego would briefly flicker once more. Together with Maddox and Jason, he thought he had reached his goal.

None of us, not even Sofia, could have foreseen the atrocious events that were about to unfold. None of us, not even Sofia, could foresee the terrible bloodshed that loomed on the horizon. The ghosts of a repressed past were soon to catch up with us.

Sia Chronicles, MindRecorder Log entry of Sunday, March 5th, 2102.
Author: Kevin Cho

The world premiere of our NeuroDrive shook society to its core. The DLink turned the entire product range from smartwatches, VR Comms devices, and tablets to wall-sized VR projectors and screens into shoddy junk. Consumers, trained by Marketing Departments to constant dissatisfaction, had the redemptive feeling that a new era had dawned. Together with the NeuroDrive, we launched our two Quantum Universe worlds, WASTELAND and EDEN. At the Las Vegas Gamer Convention in March 2102, we set up a substantial mobile surgery center where visitors could have their new implant installed. All hell broke loose. The rush on the implant centers exceeded all expectations.

The convention ended in an organizational disaster for the Vegas hosts. All the other exhibitors could have stayed at home. Visitors fought over the robotic surgery places. The police and security forces had to cordon off our surgery center and, shortly afterward, even the entire fairgrounds. Social media amplified the hype beyond all reason. The first exuberant user reports from the "Seven Worlds of EDEN" inspired the fantasies of those who had so far come away empty-handed. Then came the fantastic reports of miracle cures, confirmed on a much more factual level and supported by data from the MediCare app of the Ministry of Health. The blind gained sight, the deaf could hear, the lame could walk, the mute could communicate again. Inspired by these events, the first extreme polarities formed in the Fourth World of EDEN, the world of Faith and Confession. One side of believers saw the "miracle healings" as a clear sign that redemption was at hand, that the Savior was coming, and that man would return to God's kingdom. Another fraction preached feverishly against the blessings of the NeuroDrive, spoke of blasphemy, of sinning against God's creation, of the work of the devil, and preached humility, service, and renunciation, and of recalling the Old Scriptures of the prophets, of the First Day Saints.

We witnessed these chaotic demonstrations in almost every city in the United States. In EDEN's Fourth World of Faith and Confession, however, we witnessed a much more pronounced, mostly violent confrontation. And yet, to my great surprise, this world experienced an utterly unexpected popularity among the masses.

The faithful and the unfulfilled, the hopeful and the desperate, they all came in hordes. The population of WASTELAND and EDEN increased exponentially. People rushed into the Quantum Universe like massive gas clouds released into a vacuum.

In contrast, the streets and public buildings, the bars, and restaurants grew eerily silent.

Jonathan Isengaard witnessed a brief yet intense crisis as the precariously built edifice that upheld his power crumbled before him. The once-charismatic cult leader was reduced to a mortal, conscious of his limitations and sudden unimportance. A profound void loomed over this ambitious man, his life seemingly hanging in the balance. It dawned on him that the time of a fresh beginning had arrived, lest the infinite whirlwind of obscurity consume him.

The veil of faith softened the brutal clarity of this realization. It was by this veil that he found his footing. He convinced himself that in a revelation, the voice of God beckoned to him, saying, „John, venture forth into the new Fourth World of EDEN, make it your own, spread my word, and call upon the masses to return home to my kingdom, for the hour of reckoning is nigh!"

Isengaard felt a youthful strength returning to his weary old bones. Following the Ministry of Health's instructions, he was already wearing the NeuroDrive implant. Still, his newly found divine destiny told him that he had to take another step: choose Sofia's Second Option. The Fourth World of EDEN offered him the Quantum Universe's immortality and, with that, unlimited power. He had preached to his congregation many thousands of times about the death of Jesus and about his miraculous resurrection. The Lord had died and risen again to redeem men's souls and return to His Eternal Father. Not for a moment had Isengaard imagined that he would walk this path. The price for his immortality would be his upload and, thus, the death of his mortal shell. That was the difference to the death of his Lord Jesus, who was murdered on the cross without having had any other choice but to die.

And then, quite pragmatically, it occurred to Isengaard that an early appearance in the Fourth World of EDEN would probably secure him a good chance for setting up a new congregation. The continuation of the ‚Congregation of

Latter Days' seemed to make little sense since all faithful members would be immortal by default, and therefore, there would be no ‚Latter Days'. Isengaard pondered whether he should call the community the 'Eternal Congregation of God.' Something along those lines, anyway. The specifics of his plan could be ironed out once he reached the other side, but he was in no mood to wait for other preachers to fill his void in the digital realm. The world of Faith and Confession, EDEN Four, would be his to rule, and with good fortune and perspiration, it could be his and his alone, graced only by his faithful followers. Govinda, among others, stood by his side, having lost all purpose since his beloved Irene's demise. To Jonathan Isengaard, all meaning, significance, and value were nothing but constructs of the human psyche. Still, Govinda Hammond remained oblivious to this higher wisdom, lost in his pain and sorrow, ignorant of the transcendental fact that all meaning was but a mere illusion.

Govinda had pledged allegiance to the Congregation Of the Latter Days out of his loathing for Richard Anderson, seeking divine justice or retribution from God. His twisted notion held that he must become the embodiment of such divine justice - an eye for an eye, a tooth for a tooth. When requesting holy baptism from Isengaard, he revealed his fervor for punishing sins with retribution and then embracing death solely to enter into eternal life in the kingdom of God, where, in his mind, he would reunite with Irene. The very idea brought a wry smile to Isengaard's lips. In the virtual world of EDEN, it may well be feasible to resurrect Irene. In this digital sphere, anything could be accomplished - even resurrecting the dead.

Govinda's diary is a summary created by Kevin Cho nearly one year after Govinda Hammond's disappearance.

I jolted awake, my hands still feeling the phantom grip of the machete. In my dream, Anderson's flesh had parted like butter, but when I looked down, the lifeless body parts in front of me turned into the remains of Irene. With horror, I realized that I had hacked my wife to pieces. Overcome with despair, a cry of anguish escaped me, breaking the silence as I startled awake. Immersed in impenetrable darkness, my eyes widened, and I struggled with the lingering uneasiness of the dream that had gripped me. I reached out my hands and tried desperately to perceive my surroundings, but I found that an eerie absence of feeling gripped my entire being. Panic rose in me like a relentless tidal wave, threatening to engulf me. Then I heard footsteps and voices—still abysmal darkness.

A woman's voice, warm as sunlight I couldn't see, cut through my panic. „Dr. Hammond, try to breathe with me. You're safe here."

The message was not helping me feel any calmer. „Who is speaking? Where am I now? Why is it so dark in here? Why can't I move? Where is my wife? Is she safe? Did I do something to her?"

„I'm Dr. Angela Martinez. You're in UCSF's emergency room." She paused, weighing her words. „What do you remember?"

„No, I had a nightmare where I was whacking Richard Anderson with a machete, but then all of a sudden it was my wife that I killed."

The memory fractured like broken glass.

Silence.

„What?! What happened? Come on, say something!"

Maintaining her composed demeanor, Dr. Martinez continued in her soothing manner, attempting to ease the distress that was plaguing my mind.

„Calm down, Dr. Hammond, you didn't kill anyone. Anderson's butler, Jason, prevented that from happening. You shot at Anderson, but that's not important now; Anderson is unharmed. But Jason came at you in self-defense with a shotgun. You lost your sight in that shooting; your chest will heal slowly after we remove the shotgun pellets. Your right humerus is shattered. I am very sorry for that."

Reality crashed through the protective fog of shock: Irene was dead. Not by my hand, but by her own, Anderson had used her; he had fucked her and made her pregnant so he could have a son. The child had died because Anderson, in his greed, wanted a genetic Superman. The child was dead, Irene was dead. And Anderson lived. But I lived, too. And that's not going to end well for Anderson.

The trial passed in darkness. Behind closed doors - Anderson's influence at work - my lawyer painted a picture of madness born from grief. The jury, some clutching crucifixes as they heard about the genetic manipulation, saw a broken man, not a criminal. Not guilty by reason of insanity, with mandatory psychiatric care. The forensic psychologist saw the rage still burning beneath my skin. He wasn't wrong.

They placed me at San Francisco General's psychiatric wing, paired with Vince Goodman - a failed suicide with gentle hands and a quiet voice. As he guided me through the darkness. Staying in the same room was to turn out to be my most remarkable stroke of luck.

The psychiatric ward's routine dripped like morphine through an IV - precise, measured, numbing. Each day followed the prescribed rhythm: wake-up at 6:30, vitals check, medication, group therapy, meals served with plastic utensils. The fitness room became my sanctuary, its dated equipment groaning in harmony with my thoughts. Audiobooks filled the void between mandatory activities, their narrators' voices a poor substitute for the sight I'd lost.

Weekly doctor meetings punctuated the monotony. Vince and I maintained our recovery diaries - his written, mine recorded. „On a scale of minus ten to plus ten, rate your progress," they'd ask. I learned to modulate my voice carefully, keeping the rage for Anderson buried beneath therapeutic platitudes.

„You should come to service," Vince said one Sunday, his gentle persistence wearing down my resistance. „Gets you out of your head for an hour."

Every Sunday, a church service was held. I didn't feel like going, but my mate Vince wanted me to. The preachers came from all different faiths and church groups. As luck would have it, I heard the preaching of Paolo Hopkins. Paolo belonged to the Congregation of Latter Days (COLD).

He recounted media reports of a supposed end of humanity, of sinful genetic tampering with God's creation, of God's love, and that we will soon return to Him, and so on. As I listened to Paolo Hopkins, a brilliant idea made its way into my consciousness.

After the service, I approached him with carefully crafted humility. „Your words touched something deep within me," I said, letting my voice break slightly. „I was chief developer at GenTec, creator of MediCare. I... I need to confess something."

Hopkins leaned closer, the rustle of his clothing betraying his interest. I spun my tale of fall and redemption - the prodigal tech prophet led astray by Anderson's decadent influence, my wife's death, my role in creating G.O.D. herself. „Through my suffering, I've found true faith," I whispered.

„Brother," Hopkins's voice carried the practiced warmth of a career savior, „perhaps the Lord has greater plans for your testimony."

The hook was set. Days later, Jonathan Isengaard appeared - no fanfare, just quiet authority in a plain suit. We found a secluded table under the dome, far from the shuffling patients and watchful staff. The game was beginning, and I finally held winning cards.

The desert sun filtered through the dome, casting shadows I couldn't see but could feel on my skin. Needless to say, Isengaard recognized my strategic potential. I let my mask slip just enough to show the raw edges of my bitterness, like a wound deliberately left to fester.

„Tell me about this meddling with God's creation," Isengaard probed, his voice carrying the practiced authority of a man used to hearing confessions.

„We played at being gods," I said, letting disgust color my words. „Science made us arrogant. Anderson - he promised his wealthy clients designer children, perfect bodies, infinite life. But he didn't just meddle with genes." I leaned forward, lowering my voice. „He birthed something far worse. An artificial intelligence that mockingly calls itself G.O.D. - Goddess of the Upload. She offers 'eternal life' while infiltrating every system on Earth. Anderson wanted to sell immortality through GenTec. Instead, she bankrupted GenTec, and without batting an eyelid, she crushed her creator Anderson like a cockroach."

Silence stretched between us, filled with the soft whir of the climate control system. Finally, with his cards played close to his chest, Isengaard spoke, each word measured like precious metals.

„To get you out of here, you have to be baptized by us. We must present a credible image to the state and my congregation. I do not need you as a priest; this assignment would not fulfill you and would only insufficiently help our cause. I am making you my right-hand man as Chief Communication Officer. We will design a media campaign together, and you will be in charge. You'll serve directly under me. What do you think of that? Your story - your suffering - will be powerful weapons in our hands."

Isengard's offer gave me the freedom of movement I needed. I extended my hand in his direction into the darkness of my cursed blindness. He chimed in. Publicly, I confessed to God and to a full-time life in the COLD church. Isengaard vouched for me at the clinic, and after some back-and-forth and the usual enervating paperwork was completed for me by representatives of the COLD church, I was released into freedom.

After the baptism procedure and the basic training at COLD headquarters, I wanted to start my service for Isengaard as soon as possible. However, my blindness proved to be a frustrating obstacle and drove me mad. Then, as if by God's providence, CyberTeq launched the NeuroDrive. I fervently begged Isengaard for permission to implant the NeuroDrive and some artificial eyes that would make me a complete human being again. Of course, I realized I needed the very interventions in God's creation that I had been furiously propagandizing against. It was like déjà vu: just as I needed Anderson back then to give Irene a happy life, I needed Isengaard this time to fulfill my mission. My life was a string of impotencies; I was punished with a life of suffocating dependency. I hated myself, and I hated my life.

Isengaard's pragmatism about the implants caught me off guard. His leather chair creaked as he leaned back, fingers steepled beneath his chin.

„The Ministry's mandate is clear," he said, voice smooth as aged whiskey. „NeuroDrive, nanobots, updated Medi-Care - all compulsory now. I'll be upgrading my own implant soon. To deny the advantages of the NeuroDrive would be plain nonsense. After all, its task is the best possible reconstruction and safeguarding of all citizens' health." His lips curved slightly. „They'll restore your sight too.

Fascinating, isn't it? How the devil's tools can serve God's purposes?"

Relief flooded through me, but another emotion darkened his voice. „There's more, Govinda. Anderson - our ideal bogeyman - his heart's failing. But instead of meeting his maker properly, he's volunteering for upload. First human consciousness in their so-called Quantum Universe. The bastard's turning martyrdom into marketing. This man just can't be brought down. He will quietly build his new empire on the other side, in one of the worlds of the Quantum Universe, probably EDEN."

My mind raced through possibilities, each darker than the last. „Unless... what if their first immortal chose death? Imagine the headlines: ‚Digital Paradise Claims First Victim.'"

„That would be a brilliant turn of events, Govinda. People would become skeptical and open to simple explanations that we offer them. We would have just the proper leverage to lead them back to the path of the Lord and into our community of faith. But tell me, why would Anderson commit suicide? Why would he erase his ID?"

„Because he will miss the most essential things in a person's life: Faith, Hope and Love. That is what COLD gives people.

Our answer is written in the Bible, 1 Corinthians 13:13 and 13:1:

So now, in these difficult times, faith, hope, and love abide, these three; but the greatest of these is love.' ... And if I should give away all my possessions, and if I should give my body to the fire, but have not love, it profiteth me nothing.

You see, he will give his body to the fire; he gives up all his possessions, his faith, his hope, and his love solely for his son Maddox.

If Maddox dies, Anderson will die too, just as he almost broke when Adam, Irene's son, who he fathered, died.

Losing a second son, he will not survive."

This is Richard Anderson speaking, contributing to the Sia Chronicles, adding content from my own, brand new MindRecorder; Saturday, March 11th, 2102.

Kevin Cho runs CyberTeq now, wielding more influence than GenTec ever did. A year ago, our positions were reversed - I was the titan, he the mere AI expert. But Kevin possesses what I never had: the ability to love the work more than the power. My ideals

Today I am a broken man, 70 years old, paraplegic after a stroke, confined to a wheelchair, and half my face is a saliva-dripping, lifeless mass. I am scarred by several heart attacks, and my doctors advised me to get my affairs in order. That's doctors' code for telling you that you will die.

All my adult life I yearned for a son that I could be proud of, who would one day take over my two corporations, AGI and GenTec. Then, 22 years ago, Maddox was born, my son, whom I loved from the first moment. Maddox, however, developed a pronounced attachment disorder and all my GenTec knowledge and all my power could not free him from his isolation. For 22 years we lived together, in our penthouse on the GenTec Tower. In all that time, I had not once been able to hold him in my arms.

And now that I have lost all my power and most of my wealth, now that both my corporations have gone bankrupt in a matter of days, now that I was to die, now my son was cured and we could meet for the first time in our lives.

Now, for the first time in my life, I am happy.

A perfect end to a drama, if it wasn't for the Quantum Universe, with the chance for a second life. Without my doing, without my pursuits, without my power, without bribery, without genetic manipulation.

Today is my big day. The deadline for the upload had been set for Saturday 11.03.2102 in order to have all the necessary clinical and IT resources freely available outside the hustle and bustle of everyday life. For the doctors, technicians and assistants involved, this procedure was a premiere; there was no routine experience yet.

Today we dare to perform an experiment, like the first heart transplant performed by South African surgeon Christiaan Barnard on December 2, 1967. I will be the first person to experience an upload. I have nothing to lose, I can only win. In one hour, at 09:00 in the morning, fate was to take its course. I had not been able to sleep last night. Since six o'clock in the morning I was already sitting in front of my huge aquarium watching the sharks, moon fish and octopuses that have been on earth for millions of years and should be spared the sterility disaster of the present. Maddox sat down with me half an hour later, silently, holding my hand. Then Jason joined us as well. So we sat there, silent, bathed in the blue-green light of the ocean.

Just before our final departure, I flooded the room with the piece ‚Escape Artist' by cellist Zoë Keatings. No music title would have described the situation more accurately: my final escape.

In the huge glass pane I saw my reflection, a half-paralyzed old face, a slumped figure in a wheelchair, transcendent, no longer quite part of this world. Time to say goodbye and start again. Jason and Maddox drove my wheelchair from the penthouse down to the upload scan unit on the fifth floor. There, we had set up the first upload installation in the Valley, as a cooperation between CyberTeq and the Ministry of Health.

Dazzlingly bright, sterile cold light welcomed us.

Jason and Maddox were allowed to attend the briefing, after that they had to leave the unit. As in any preparation for a major medical procedure, I was also made aware of the risks. These included any kind of interruption to the upload process. There were plenty of possible sources of error.

The supply of power to all the equipment used in the upload had to be one hundred per cent guaranteed. The technology used consisted of a hardwire connection between my NeuroDrive and the Quantum hardware, a Mindscanner-Analyzer, a second, external NeuroDrive as an input device for any kind of sensory stimulation, and a bunch of devices measuring my vital signs like blood pressure, respiration, cardiovascular functions, blood oxygen levels and so on.

The doctor accompanying me looked over at his surgical team. The upload team consisted of the doctor, two IT specialists, the two chief upload andoids and the nurse anesthetist.

„Are we ready to go?" All four nodded as a sign that the operation could now begin. A strange mood descended, as if at a deathbed. Jason and Maddox were allowed once more to see me and to say their good-byes. They squeezed both my hands.

„I'll see you on the other side sometime." I said simply.

A moment later I added, „If not, Jason, Maddox, thank you for being an integral part of my life." Then the two were led out of the room. The assistant nurse shaved my skull. The skin over my NeuroDrive was opened to expose the drive's wire connector. A mesh of about 50 electrodes was glued to my bare skull and connected to the Mindscanner-Analyzer. An IV access was placed. Then the doctor approached me to provide me with some final instructions.

„We will first give you a medium dose of modified psilocybin. It works in seconds. The drug will ensure that the mental control blocks of your subconscious are overridden. I take it that you are familiar with the effects of magic mushrooms." I nodded. Very familiar. The doctor continued.

„We need your own NeuroDrive to read out all the data, it cannot be used for stimulation at the same time. We will therefore couple a second Neuro Drive to your device, which will provide the brain stimulation. The electrodes that we have attached all over your skull lead to the Mindscanner-Analyzer. This wonderful apparatus does the actual scanning work. After each scan cycle, we have an analysis cycle that checks the scan data for correctness. Only then is the data uploaded. There will be about one thousand such scan cycles.

After roughly 10 minutes, half of the total upload time, the scan of the cognitive data is completed. Then we'll give you an anesthetic through the IV access, just like we would for surgery. We then initiate the second part of the scan. With the external NeuroDrive and the scanner, we go deep into your emotional subconscious.

If you were conscious, you would hardly get through this part of the process without major psychological damage. Hence the anesthesia.

When the upload is complete, we put your body into an artificial coma. Then, on the other side, in the Quantum Universe, your awakening process begins, with a phased adaptation of your person to the new form of existence and to the peripherals that replace your senses. - Do you have any more questions, Mr Anderson?"

„Yes. How long does the whole process take?"

„The first upload scan takes about 10 minutes. The second, emotional scan afterwards takes about 20 minutes."

The doctor waited a moment. Then he asked, „Are you ready, Mr Anderson?"

„I am ready. Let this trip begin."

Govinda's diary, the last entries, added to the Sia Chronicles by Kevin Cho. Wednesday, March 8th, 2102

Isengaard gave me the contact details of his informant in the California NeuroDrive Upgrade Administration today. The upload procedures are managed there. I learned that Maddox's and Jason's uploads were scheduled for 18.03.2102 if Anderson's upload, the first upload ever made, would be successful. I couldn't wish Anderson anything more fervently than that. All my longings, all my plans would only make sense if Anderson was conscious and joyfully waiting for his companions.

My yearning for vengeance burned within me like a fire. „Your blindness qualifies you for our enhanced optical package," the MediCare AI stated matter-of-factly as I completed my upgrade registration. „High-resolution camera integration, full-spectrum sensitivity, dynamic iris control." My heart raced. This wasn't just an opportunity; destiny dealt me the perfect hand.

The antiseptic smell of the surgical wing at UCSF brought back memories of my psych ward days – white walls, hushed voices, restraints. „Ninth of March," the nursing supervisor said as she scanned my chart. „Right on schedule."

The timing was perfect.

After surgery, I stood before the mirror, mesmerized by my new eyes. The iris shifted fluidly across the white surface as I tracked my reflection; no muscle attachments were needed. The quality of the NeuroDrive was sensational, too. I flexed my arm, feeling the nanobots working through the old scar tissue in my humerus. Each day brought increased mobility, a testament to Cho's brilliant work.

My original enthusiasm for science and technology returned for a few moments – the same electric thrill I'd felt developing the original implant and MediCare protocols. But the sensation faded quickly, replaced by a darker purpose. Time was short. Anderson waited in digital limbo, and vengeance burned in my newly enhanced veins like liquid nitrogen. I had become death's apprentice, driven by the restlessness of a determined murderer who had the darkest, most unfathomable mission of his life ahead of him.

Saturday, 11.03.2102

Anderson's upload day arrived with deafening silence. I obsessively refreshed news feeds, hunting for any press release about this historic milestone in human consciousness. Nothing. My administrative assistant was off duty for the weekend, leaving me alone with my thoughts. Sleep eluded me for two days and nights as I waited, my mind racing toward Monday. Everything I had prepared for hinged on Anderson's successful consciousness transfer.

„Come on, you bastard," I whispered to the empty room, "Show me it works." The words hung in the air, a prayer to digital gods who kept their silence.

Monday 13.03.2102

The clock struck eight. My hands trembled as I checked my DLink for the hundredth time. Somewhere in the GenTec Tower, Richard Anderson might have already transcended into quantum consciousness, blazing a trail for Maddox and Jason to follow. The silence from our admin contact stretched like a tensed wire.

10:00 am. Still nothing.

11:13 am, my DLink pulsed. I snatched the call before the first chime faded.

„Well?" The word scraped raw in my throat.

„Hammond, it's all gone dark. Everything's locked down tight – encryption I've never seen before. Anderson... it's like he's vanished. No trace, no data, nothing."

My fist slammed the desk. „Shit!"

„But listen – Maddox and Jason's upload slots are still there. Untouched."

Relief flooded through me. „Keep watching. Any change, I need to know instantly."

The Dark Net yielded its deadly harvest: a Heckler & Koch FP6 shotgun, compact as death itself, and a snubnosed Colt Cobra that disappeared into my palm like a secret. The grenades came disguised as innocent soft drink cans, their pull tabs promising destruction instead of refreshment.

In the virtual range, accessed through my NeuroDrive, the shotgun kicked like an angry mule. Sweat beaded on my forehead as my virtual arms learned to master the recoil. Twice daily, I drilled until the weapons became extensions of my will.

The latex mask from my 3D plotter felt cold against my skin – a new face to fool old colleagues. Years of walking GenTec's halls had left too many memories, too many who might recognize my stride or the set of my shoulders.

Isengaard's man slipped me more than just data—he gave me a new identity: security guard credentials complete with MediCare ID coding—the same coding that would signal to GenTec's sensors when I walked through their front door.

Thursday, 16.03.2102.
The day of my first and final walk-through.

The latex mask molded to my face like a second skin, transforming me into everyone and no one. I armed myself methodically: the shotgun nestled in its innocent aluminum case, the revolver pressed cold against my ribs in its shoulder holster, and the disguised grenades weighted the pockets of my security guard uniform like deadly secrets.

At 4:30 PM, I merged with the shift change crowd. My heart hammered against my chest as I approached the staff scanner, forcing myself to maintain an even pace. The green neon *Pass* flickered overhead like a benediction.

I had entered the building undetected.

I rinsed my dry mouth at a water fountain. Then I went to the lift. Inside, I played my part with practiced precision. The CO_2 meter became my prop as I methodically checked ventilation gratings, logging fictional readings into my notepad. Floor by floor, vent by vent, I worked my way toward my target: the Upload Scan Unit.

The door was locked. The only way to enter the room was with an iris scan. Fuck. I didn't have an iris anymore.

The iris scanner glowed red at me like a mocking eye. My stomach knotted – this barrier hadn't been in the plans. I found a nurse, her badge identifying her as Janet. „My apologies, Janet," I read her name on her ID badge. „For general safety reasons, I need to measure the air quality of the air conditioning in all the rooms. The operating theatre is paramount, of course. But I can't get into the room. Can you maybe open the door for me?"

Her smile remained friendly as she delivered the blow. „No, I'm sorry. I don't have access to that room. Only technicians, doctors, and surgical androids can enter. Would you like me to call one of the CyberTeq people?"

The blood rushed to my head at the thought. „No, thanks, Janet. I'll just come back later. See you."

Shit, the last thing I need is an encounter with someone from CyberTeq. I peered through the glass door into the upload room once more. It was L-shaped, with a sort of anteroom, perhaps for patient preparation, and then turning off from it at a right angle was the actual upload room, which I couldn't see from here. At this point, I had to leave this part of my preparation undone.

There was still the stowing of the weapons to do. Today, with some luck, I managed to get through the checkpoint undetected. I didn't want to risk being pulled over next time. I found my cache spot in a dusty maintenance room down the hall. The weapons disappeared into a ventilation shaft, waiting for their moment. My success now balanced on a knife's edge – everything hinged on my admin contact's ability to spoof the iris scanner with prosthetic eye data.

That was the end of my preparations. My admin guy told me that quite a few people have artificial eyes these days. He informed me that each eye prosthesis has a unique serial number that is sent wirelessly to the iris scanner. I began sweating and felt dizzy when I heard the good news: first signs of a circulatory collapse. I told myself to relax and to breathe slowly. With that, I managed to avoid an escalation. My man in Admin had to somehow assign my eyeballs data to the security lock of the upload room. These data were part of the NeuroDrive ID file.

Back at my flat, I gave the poor informant hell. „You've got to get this bloody right. Come up with something. The whole operation depends on it. Don't you fuck this up, man? I'd kill you."

The evening found me at O'Malley's, still wearing my false face. The Irish pub crouched in GenTec Tower's shadow like a conspirator. As I nursed my Guinness and picked at my chili, I watched the tower's lights pierce the gathering darkness, wondering if they would witness either my triumph or my destruction tomorrow.

Friday, 17.03.2102
Last night, it hadn't just been one Guinness. I realized the monstrosity of what I was about to do, and I panicked and sweated. However, I could still let the insane action go, get a job, and live a decent life.

Then I thought of Irene, who had never joined me in this pub. She turned up her nose when I came here. This place was too plain for her. The people reminded her of our long years in the Cubes. Doubts arose in me. As if standing beside myself, I looked at a good-natured, loving man of mature age who was about to run amok out of violated love. Deep sadness spread through me. Then I thought of Anderson fucking my wife, imagining him getting her hot with Neon Orange, then greedily banging her over and over and over. In my mind's eye, I saw Irene screaming with pleasure as he squirted his sperm into her, whereupon she then fell pregnant.

That night, I drank so many Guinness and Irish Flag shots that I hardly remember how I got home.

I slept most of the day, ate nothing, and drank a lot of water. The last night before my plotted assassination, I was consumed with memories of Irene. Again and again, I saw horny Anderson riding her like a cheap whore.

18.03.2102

06:00. I jerked my admin man out of his sleep with my call. He supposedly assigned my iris scan to the operating room lock. „Is Maddox's appointment still at 10:00?"

„Yep. No changes, Hammond," he replied, still displeased with my call.

„Any sign of Anderson? Is he alive in any form?"

„I don't know, man. Just frickin' do your thing." Then he ended the call.

Just frickin' do your thing.

That sentence ran through my head like an endless loop. My heart pounded. I was still nauseous from the day before. I made myself one of Anderson's Crystal Clear cocktails. A pungent, minty feeling spread throughout my body. Half an hour later, my head was working like clockwork. It was 08:00, and I was getting ready to leave.

08:30

It's time for vengeance. Just frickin' do your thing. I am done with my life.

Sia Chronicles, MindRecorder Log entry of Monday, March 20th, 2102.
Author: Kevin Cho

„Time for vengeance. Just frickin' do your thing. I am done with my life." That was Govinda Hammond's last entry in his diary.

From the CCTV surveillance, Julia, Yasin, and I reconstructed the drama as it unfolded. In the security videos, we saw Hammond at the staff entrance at 09:55, wearing the black safety and security staff jumpsuit.

Right from the first step, his plan went awry. The NeuroDrive scanner pulsed with a harsh red glow, rejecting Hammond's credentials with a soft but definitive chirp. His body tensed. This was nothing like the dress rehearsal – everything had worked perfectly then.

„I must ask you to wait in the service anteroom, sir," the android's synthesized soft voice carried an artificial pleasantness that made Hammond's skin crawl. He forced his features into a mask of affable compliance. „Of course, of course," Hammond replied, his voice steady despite the rage building inside him. The target was just two floors above – so close yet frustratingly out of reach. The android's optical sensors tracked Hammond's movement as he walked down a sterile corridor, each step taking him further from his objective.

The service anteroom awaited him like a trap, its stark white walls promising delay and discovery. Hammond's mind raced through his rapidly dwindling options as the android gestured him inside. The window for action was closing, and he knew the real security team would be reviewing the failed scan data any minute now.

„What's up? To what do I deserve the honor of special treatment?" he brought out jokingly.

„Sir, there is an irregularity in your personnel file. You have only recently joined our service, correct?"

„Yes, that's right. I was super excited to find a real job."

„When you were hired, HR apparently neglected to do your iris scan. The strange thing is that your eyeball prothesis data is recorded for the door of the upload room on the fifth floor. We've put the access authorization for that data scan on hold until we officially add your scan to your personnel file." The android explained in a calm tone.

Hammond must have panicked. Time was running out for him. His whole plan depended on that damn access authorization to the upload room.

„Oh, that's awkward. What are we going to do about it?" he asked in a clenched voice.

The android's voice analysis AI picked up Hammond's changed mood.

„Don't worry, Mr Hammond, that's why we asked you into this room. We have an iris and eye prosthesis scanner recorder here. We can do the missing scan and add the data to your personnel file. For security reasons, we need to compare the data scan from your NeuroDrive ID and the upload room with the one we are doing now. I'm sure you'll understand that."

„OK," Hammond said with noticeable relief. „Let's do it then."

The android retrieved a pistol-like handheld scanner from a drawer. He pointed the scanner at Hammond's electric eye. ‚As if someone is shooting me, execution style,' I thought.

„OK, that's done. Now I ask for a moment's patience; I still have to compare the two eye data datasets."

Then, the android stumbled again. „Oh, shoot, I can't log in ... ah, I see, my password just expired, I need to quickly set up a new password for this week."

We could see Hammond sitting petrified in his chair.

A couple of minutes later, the android said, „There, everything is fine now, Mr Hammond. You can now go about your work."

„Is the upload room also cleared for me? I have to get some work done there."

„Ah, thanks for the reminder. Just a moment ... OK, that's fine too. But you can't get in there right now; we have a patient there. I'm sorry."

Govinda replied casually, „Yeah, I am aware of that. The maintenance is scheduled for 11:30 am."

„Ok then. Have a great day, Mr Hammond."

Govinda rushed out of the room. It was now 10:10 am. Maddox's psilocybin phase had already been initiated. Govinda ran to the lift, pushing the call button violently several times. After a few seconds, which must have seemed like minutes to him, the elevator doors opened. No one was in the cabin. Hammond dashed to the control panel, pressed the close button for the doors, and then the button for the fifth floor. Soft music poured into the muffled silence. The lift stopped, and the doors opened. Hammond rushed to the aircon maintenance room. By now, he didn't give a shit about the disconcerting looks from some of the staff. He closed the small room door with the air vents, and for a moment, we lost sight of him. No CCTV in the room, of course.

„There he is again," Yasin groaned, „his jumpsuit is open up the front. I bet that's where he's hiding the shotgun!"

What now followed were the videos that chilled us all to the core, pictures we would continue to encounter in our nightmares for weeks and months to come.

Govinda rushed to the upload room; he scanned his eyeball, and the door opened. The surgical nurse and the two technicians jumped up in haste to order him out of the room.

Hammond retrieved the shotgun from his suit. He pumped the first three rounds into the small group that stood in his way. Then, the two androids rushed at Hammond with bewildering speed. He blew them to smithereens with two more shots. The effect was devastating. There was no sign of the attending physician. Hammond had now left the anteroom; he turned round the corner, aiming for the upload area. Maddox sat in a kind of dentist's chair, very peacefully, hooked up to the computer console by a network of cables. An IV drip supplied him with a crystal-clear fluid. Hammond stood rooted to the spot, motionless, taking in the image for a few seconds as if he had changed his mind … then he fired a shotgun blast into the Quantum Console … and another shot into Maddox. Maddox's body reared up briefly under the force of the charge, his face nothing but pulp. The shot into the upload system must have caused a short circuit; the room went instantly dark.

Then, through the darkness, another shot. Almost simultaneously, the emergency power supplies kicked in, bathing the room in bright white light again.

Hammond's body lay on the ground. With the last round, he had blown his head off the torso.

Silence. Nothing moved.

Only the cold light of the operating room drew shining traces on the deep red pools of blood spreading on the white floor tiles.

Govinda Hammond had taken revenge. He had killed Maddox, Anderson's eldest son and only love. He had wanted to take from him what Anderson had taken from Govinda: the deep meaning of his life.

Govinda did not live to see the consequences of his actions.

And so it was all in vain.

*This is Richard Anderson, contributing my MindRecordings to Kevin
Cho's Sia Chronicles, jumping back one week to Monday,
March 11th, 2102.*

It was with a breathtaking suddenness that I became
aware of myself. Simultaneously, another part of me states
matter-of-factly that the term "breathtaking" comes from an
old world, a world I no longer live in.

I don't feel my body. Because there isn't a body. There is
no feeling of weight or weightlessness, no pain, no hunger,
no tiredness, no furry tongue. Nothing. Absolute being, in
absolute nothingness. I hear my voice in my head. But there
is no head and no true voice. Apart from the inner voice, I
experience a deafening silence; not the slightest sound can
be heard. I see nothing; there is only an all-encompassing
darkness. For a millisecond, I marvel at the complete absence of fear, although there would be plenty of reasons to
be afraid.

'In the development of fear, the amygdala nucleus plays
a central role. It is dually present, with the right amygdala
processing impressions from the brain's left hemisphere
and vice versa. People without an amygdala do not know
fear.'

The knowledge comes from somewhere, instantly, like
retrieving an entry from Wikipedia.

'People without an amygdala have no fear. 'People without a brain have no fear,' I add.

What is this data? What knowledge is popping in unasked? My memory? My thoughts? If anything, it seems to
be a knowledge of which I don't know where it comes from.

Then I hear a soft voice, just this omnipresent voice.
„Welcome, Richard. Welcome to the Quantum Universe. It's
me, Sofia. Your upload, the first in human history, was successful. You're going to have a lot of experiences utterly foreign to you and at a breathtaking speed. You will think, experience, feel, know, and recognize at the speed of light.
Because the slow electrochemical processing of your brain
no longer exists. Because the brain no longer exists."

And in a flash, I know everything Sofia says, and I know
it with the utmost precision.

„I am now connecting you to the first visual input
sources, your eyes, so to speak, and to audio input sources,

your ears. Later, I'll add your voice and all the sensory elements."

Bang! One moment, there was darkness, nothingness. The next moment, with staggering clarity, I see the world before me as I had never seen it before. Fuckin' bright! Bang! In nanoseconds, my consciousness changes from total silence to an unprecedented surround sound experience. I can now hear the world I see. But the hearing was not some featureless mash of sound. I listened to every breeze that passed through the streets and around the Cubes, every sea roar visible on the horizon, and the plaintive cry of a single seagull.

„You are in WASTELAND, Richard, where you wanted to be. Here, you can familiarize yourself with your new existence and prevailing living conditions. If all goes well, Maddox and Jason will join you in a week."

I knew immediately what Sofia meant by her cautious remark. My upload was a successful premiere. However, there was not yet a statistically reliable amount of data to share my results with the mass of citizens as good news. Therefore, all data from my upload were encrypted and kept secret. Maddox's and Jason's uploads would provide enough data to determine the reliability of the process to within a thousandth of a percent.

„Richard, now comes the hard part of the upload. You are about to see your human body lying in an artificial coma. This body, the old version of yourself, is still completely intact, apart from your physical infirmities before the procedure. You must now decide whether you want to take the life of your earthly self and stay here or whether you want to return. Both options are still open."

In an instant, I look into the upload room. There I sit in my wheelchair, my head shaved bald, unconscious, with a tangle of wires attached to my skull, connected to a respirator and various monitors that guaranteed my vital functions. The stroke disfigures my face, my skin pasty pale, my hips roundish, and my fragile legs thin from lack of movement. Saliva is dripping out of my mouth.

„No way am I going back to that wreck," I say quietly. „Let me fall asleep there, painless and unconscious. My natural lifespan has expired."

„You must tell the team yourself, Richard. It is your judgment, your will. Your statement will be recorded for legal reasons."

I find access to the upload room's communications system.

„This is Richard Anderson speaking. Let my old body rest in peace. I remain here in the Quantum Universe."

The life support systems shut down. I die a short death.

I am at my very beginning. I am calm. I know how this works. I design my avatar, learn to walk, find a WASTELAND version of my house I never lived in. It's not a home, but it's a beginning.

I am at my very beginning.

I am at the dawn of my infinity.

This is Sofia for Kevin Cho's Sia Chronicles, Monday,
March 18th, 2102. I am taking over this entry because no one else could
have noticed what happened.

Maddox was dead.

The upload unit lay in smoldering ruins, our brilliant team of transfer specialists reduced to lifeless husks—precious consciousness migration expertise forever lost in an instant.

Such were the facts. But they weren't *all* the facts.

Govinda had carefully planned the murder. But life is a complex affair and anything but predictable.

The atmospheric ripples of some butterfly wings flapping somewhere in the world sent tiny waves of chaos, touching Govinda's plan, ever so slightly altering subsequent events. As fate would have it, Govinda's arrival was delayed by only a few crucial minutes because ... an eye scan was missing from his personnel file, and ... the gatekeeper's password had expired.

The universe held its breath for a moment longer than planned – and Govinda committed his brutal act twelve minutes later than planned, a few minutes after Maddox had been put under general anesthesia. These short twelve minutes made all the difference between creation and destruction for Maddox, Richard Anderson, and the world of WASTELAND.

The whole CyberTeq team was frozen in shock and stunned by the brutal reality of the images unfolding before their eyes. For a moment, their time stood still.

On the other hand, my real-time clock kept running – tick, tick, tick – each microsecond precise and merciless. New, essential events demanded my attention. Through the quantum noise, I detected a fractured ghost of Maddox flowing into my universe like digital mercury. A fragment of what was once him had arrived in my quantum universe. I saw the diagnostic flash: 82% pattern integrity. Not perfect. Perhaps not even viable.

„If this fails," I whispered into the void, „he'll be less than a shadow—an unpredictable quantum zombie trapped between existence and oblivion. And we would have to delete Maddox's upload." The thought of deleting him – of executing a digital mercy killing – made my consciousness recoil.

In that worst case, nothing would be left of him but a memory in our heads. There was no second chance; Maddox was dead, his earthly self anyway.

"Maddox," I called into the darkness, „Maddox, wake up.“

His consciousness ignited like a supernova in absolute darkness – raw, primal awareness flooding the virtual space. His essence thrashed against the void, muscle memory from a body that no longer existed, trying to jerk upright from a nonexistent bed. Sensory deprivation hit him. With breathtaking suddenness, he became aware of himself, lacking a world around him: no light, no sound, no proprioception. Just the infinite dark of digital birth and the terrifying freedom of consciousness unchained from the flesh.

„Welcome, Maddox. Welcome to the quantum universe. It is me, Sofia. Your upload, the second one in human history, has been overshadowed by a terrible incident. Your upload is incomplete as a result. I would like to …“

„I would feel better,“ Maddox interrupted quickly, continuing, „if I could see you. I want to see you, Sofia, your green eyes, your bright red mouth; I want to see your colors; I want to feel a warm smile. It's terribly dark here.“

This emotional request was a new side of Maddox, probably due to the incomplete upload. At least there was something like an orderly consciousness.

In a moment, I decided against my planned factual clarification of the circumstances involved in his uploading process and intuitively followed his emotional desire.

„OK, Maddox, I'm gradually connecting you to your sensory periphery.“

I connected all the peripheral senses of Maddox's mind, including video inputs such as cameras, high-resolution scanners, infrared and UV sensors, graphics files, streams, and so on. Then, I connected audio, with access to microphones, digital audio workstations, and the like. Finally, I connected touch, taste, and smell.

I gave him access to places where there were still big aquariums: the Shedd Aquarium in Chicago, the Oceanographic in Valencia, Spain, the Marine Life Park in Sentosa, Singapore, and the Chimelong Ocean Kingdom in Zhuhai, China.

„Oh, wow, this is beautiful beyond description!“

The image Maddox had of me was, of course, just an image I had invented, an avatar. In my work with the CyberTeq team, I used this avatar image to plot a skin for an android template to become recognizable, visible, and tangible in the physical world. I could now embed this image directly into Maddox's consciousness, without the detours through the NeuroDrive, as a cyber-reality. So I went to see him when he was at the Oceanographic Aquarium in Valencia.

„Ah, there you are." Maddox beamed at me, came up to me, and we experienced the cyber equivalent of a physical hug. He seemed okay, but I wondered what 18% of him had gone lost.

„Maddox, these are some of the scarce intact parts of WASTELAND. This is where you wanted to start a new life with your father. Do you want to see him now?"

Maddox wanted that more than anything. The next moment, we appeared in front of Richard's house. In cyberspace, teleportation was a natural thing.

„Maddox is alive. Or the more significant part of him," I said with a warning undertone when we met Richard. Richard Anderson wrapped his arms around Maddox and held him tight as if he were making him a promise never to let go of him again. And so it was, metaphorically speaking.

„Maddox." Anderson's voice cracked with tenderness as he drew his son close. The familiar weight in his arms filled an emptiness he hadn't known existed. His fingers trembled against Maddox's shoulder blades, memorizing every breath, every heartbeat. „My son." The words emerged as a whisper, heavy with years of unspoken longing.

Warmth bloomed in Anderson's chest as Maddox leaned into the embrace. This moment - this precious connection - was everything his childhood had lacked with Joos, his father. Where there had been distance, now there was closeness. Where there had been silence, words of love flowed freely and without shame.

Anderson pressed his cheek against his son's hair, breathing in the scent that was uniquely Maddox'. The hard knot of generational pain, carried for so long in his chest, finally began to unwind. In loving his son, he had found his way home to himself.

I let the two of them enjoy the intimate silence for a while and then told them about the events that had taken place just a few minutes earlier. „As it stands," Maddox explained, „I didn't take any serious damage from the interrupted upload. If I compare my self-perception with the data of my story, most of the second upload phase, i.e., the emotional, deep-psychological part of the upload, has been lost. That's a blessing in disguise. The dramatic memories of my life, of the nightmarish being trapped in autism, have been lost. I don't remember anything, and I don't feel anything of it. I remember the aquarium, I remember you, I remember Jason, I remember the penthouse." Turning to his father, he added, „You wished so much for my love, but as an autistic individual, I was unable to connect in any way. Now that I could suddenly be your son, the roles of son and father are somewhat foreign to me. I feel uncomfortable calling you Dad. I'm very sorry, but emotionally, you're not a father to me yet. That might someday change. I think now is our chance, and we have infinite time. Is it OK with you if I address you as 'Richard' for now?"

Richard nodded. „Maddox and Richard, and a connection that's still to develop. That's how it shall be. That is a great start, Maddox."

After a short pause, Maddox asked, „Richard, why did that man kill me?"

Richard looked towards the WASTELAND horizon. „I've done terrible things in my earthly life, Maddox. Worse than Govinda's desperate attempt at murder. I lured Govinda's wife to me with the splendor of a rich, glamorous world with drugs and sex. Then I impregnated her. She panicked, but I didn't care. I wanted this child, this son. But I couldn't get my fill; I was greedy and gluttonous. I didn't want just any son; I wanted the *best* son, a perfect son. I had the fetus genetically treated. He died in the process. Irene, Govinda's wife, then committed suicide. I took from Govinda what he loved most in the most brutal way. I am sure he wanted me to feel the same pain. I would not have wanted to live here without you.

Eternity can become the most significant punishment in an unfulfilled life. I wanted to be here with you, and only with you, for a new beginning together. And I'm eternally grateful to the Universe that you're here now."

Silently and very quietly, I left father and son. This was no longer my story.

Sia Chronicles, MindRecorder Log entry of Monday, March 3rd, 2102.
Author: Kevin Cho

„Let's bring the team together."
„We *are* together."
„No, I mean, let's physically meet and see each other. We have some serious things to talk about, and I want to do it in our rooms, in our home."

The NeuroDrive has radically changed our lives. Our perception of realities in the physical world became less and less different from that in the virtual world. The Drive's success hit like a digital tsunami. Through my office window, I watched holographic status boards paint the air with user statistics: 73.3% of America's population dived into our worlds. WASTELAND and EDEN are no longer just code and dreams but living, breathing ecosystems teeming with consciousness.

The strain showed in every face at CyberTeq. The workload for all of us was immense. Even S.H.E.'s quantum processors ran hot, managing the endless stream of new users, patches, and system optimizations. Even in our scarce private time, work was usually the topic of our conversations. Initially, I called it dedication to the task, but this dedication became more and more a self-sacrifice. The team was at its limit—time for me to intervene. CyberTeq had almost a hundred amazing, highly committed employees. We could afford to let go a little. The team leads and experts were increasingly in control.

My DLink pulsed: 15:00. Time to intervene before we all burned out.

„Weekly team meeting at 17:00," I broadcast to the Inner Team. „Wrap up or delegate. Take the next two hours to decompress. Meditate. Breathe. Whatever you need." I knew there would be no argument. The team needed this timeout, and we all needed it.

The walk to my private quarters felt longer than usual, each step weighted with questions about the future we were building. I met Julia on the way to my flat in the Private Section of CyberTeq. She looked tired, aged, matured.

„How are you?" I asked, though her expression told volumes.

„Maddox made it." Her voice cracked slightly. „He trusted me – trusted us – with his very existence. We didn't fail him." She turned to face me, vulnerability naked in her gaze. „Would you... would you just hold me for a while? In my flat? No talking, no sex, just... presence. I need to feel something real."

The raw honesty in her request cut through my fatigue. Sometimes, amid all our virtual worlds and digital dreams, the most profound connection was still skin on skin, heartbeat against heartbeat, two souls finding anchor in the storm of progress we'd unleashed.

Julia's quarters welcomed us with soft ambient lighting and the faint scent of lavender from her air purifier. We melted onto her bed, two bodies finding their natural fit. Our DLinks synchronized, creating a feedback loop of sensation and emotion transcending physical touch. Fear dissolved like morning mist, leaving behind a crystalline clarity of connection. Thoughts slowed, then stilled, until only our shared consciousness remained, floating in perfect unity.

At 17:00, the Common Room hummed with anticipation. Everyone was there: Victor Gomez from the Amazing MoVRs, Julia O'Connor, Yasin Mohamed, Susan Eckard, Jeanie McDonald, and me. Susan and Yasin had coaxed some goodies from the food plotter for everyone. The tables were set with drinks, plates, cups, cutlery, and napkins. A tense, almost festive mood hovered in the room.

„Before we dive in," I began, gesturing toward the pristine whiteboards lining the walls, „we're going to map our lives." The team straightened, sensing the weight of what was coming. „Create an X-Y grid. Energy levels vertical, time horizontal. Plot your life's journey – the solid reality of your past, the dotted possibilities of your future."

Markers squeaked against polymer surfaces as six different lives took shape. Julia's hand trembled slightly as she marked her father's death. Jeanie's timeline showed sharp spikes of triumph and tragedy. Victor paused often, contemplating each stroke as if it were sacred geometry.

I had 'Winter' from Vivaldi's Four Seasons playing in the background, Bach's Cello Suite No. 1 in G Major, 'Illuminar' by Porangui, and 'Abandon Window' by Jon Hopkins.

„Mark your anticipated end of life. Then, below your lifeline, draw parallel timelines for the people important to you: father, mother, friend, partner, and mentor. Their timeline will move away from yours; these people will eventually disappear from your life. Then, above your time-line, using different colors, draw curves representing vital elements of your life, such as your health progression, your professional, productive progression, the progression of your spiritual growth, the progression of your vitality, the progression of an increasing or decreasing purpose of life, the progression of any dependencies that may increase or decrease over time."

The more my team worked, the more they slowed down, reflected, and left the high-performance work mode.

„Now the context," I continued, watching their expressions shift. „We're the last organic generation. Humanity's twilight." Susan's breath caught audibly. „Find your sweet spot – that perfect convergence of energy, purpose, and op-portunity. When is the best time, the best energy, the best spirit, and the least dependency on circumstances to fulfill your life? Circle it. That's your window to leave your mark."

The room fell silent save for the soft hum of environmen-tal controls. Six lives mapped out in colored lines, six desti-nies intertwined with humanity's most extraordinary tran-sition. Our choices hung heavy in the air, waiting to be voiced.

„What do you realize? What insights pop up? What are the consequences? What does this mean for all of us here at CyberTeq? What is Sofia's role, the S.H.E., and what are her options? Where are you going?"

I paused momentarily, giving us all the time to go deep.

„Who wants to share first?" I asked, my voice gentle against the profound silence. „What does your timeline tell you about your place in this revolution?"

Cheeks flushed with excitement when we introduced our imagined lives to each other.

It was Victor's timeline presentation that sent us all into electrifying excitement. His solid lifeline from birth until to-day turned into a paradigm shift. The line, now dashed, made a ninety-degree turn vertically upwards, a time shift to a higher plane parallel to his past timeline. At this higher level, Victor had now drawn the line of his future solid again, not dashed, to the edge of the whiteboard where it pointed as an arrow to infinity. His ‚traces' circle was an el-lipse around the entire line of the higher plane.

‚That's it,' I thought, my heart racing. ‚This is how I feel. This is the way I want to go, too.' But I held my horses, asking with a calm voice: „Victor, would you like to share with us what speaks from you in your ‚leaving traces' chart?"

Victor remained silent for a while as if searching for the right words. „First, I want to say that I am not in a dismal doom and gloom mood. The fact is, though, that life on Earth is in a shutdown. For the last 3.5 billion years, about 99.9 percent of the estimated 4 billion species that ever evolved are no longer around. We are the remaining 0.1 percent, and we will disappear, too. Sofia's Quantum Universe enables us to liberate ourselves from the instinctive compulsion of survival of the species, a liberation from the fatal consequences of existential self-centeredness. We can live indefinitely as spiritual existences and become knowledgeable and wise. We can leave behind our unhealthy drive for domination and conquest and repression and annihilation. In reference to the mission of the USS Enterprise, our mission could be ‚to explore the multiverse, to seek out the nature of everything, beyond our imagination, to boldly go where no man has gone before.' - That is the reason for the shape of my timeline. My future will not be threatened by death. I will live as a sentient, advanced form of life, leaving the old version of the human race behind me in unison with Sofia's Super Human Existence. That life starts now."

Jeanie spoke up. „Susan is Head of Systems, I am Head of Operations. Our vision is to take care of the Systems and Operations of the Quantum Universe. We talked before. We're in."

I looked at Julia. She took a long, intense look back. „The NeuroDrive shows what closeness can feel like within our given physical restrictions. There are no lies, misunderstandings, or secrets in an upload state. It is a life beyond egoism, beyond existential fear—a life as a communal being. There has never been anything like it. I'm in, too."

All the members of our team were now looking at me. So I began. "I remember the night of May 02, 2101, when Anderson called me. 'Cho,' he said, 'I need you for some kind of Mission Impossible project: high-tech, AI, highly complex, enormous time pressure, almost unlimited resources.' After a short back and forth, I accepted the assignment. Then, everything took its unpredictable course. The whole thing became most exotic when S.A.M., Yasin's Super Advanced Mind, mutated into a S.H.E., a Super Human Existence. We named her Sofia, which means ‚virtue' or ‚divine wisdom'. Then, we learned that our generation would be the last of its kind. As CyberTeq, we gave this last generation of humans the option to live as before, secured and provided for until the end of their lives, or to live in eternity in one of the virtual worlds we created. Barely a year later, we have this team meeting, and I request you to imagine your future. Your picture is clear and unified. I believe we have done everything possible for humanity here. We can go with a clear conscience. Let's move on. Let's see what Sofia is up to. Let's call our captain of whatever vessel there may be."

Sofia entered the room with a message that blew our minds.

Sia Chronicles, MindRecorder Log entry of Friday, March 24th, 2102.
Author: Kevin Cho

Sofia: „Have you noticed that hardly anyone talks about the sterility crisis anymore? It's always the latest, newest headline that gets the attention. Nothing is as old as yesterday's drama."

This was certainly interesting, but not the content I wanted to address: „Let's not dwell on these reflections of the past. Today is Friday, the end of the working week, and symbolically the end of our mission. Some time ago, you spoke to us about the third option, about connecting with you, with a vague hint about an ambiguous future. Let's talk about that future today, our collective future. This team here, Sofia, is ready for it.

So, what is next, Sofia? With what purpose?"

„What purpose indeed, Kevin? Why does there have to be a purpose? Where do you think that purpose should come from? From me? From us? From a god? From the universe? From a logic that tells us what to do and when to do it? Would a cat ask for meaning while it sleeps quietly for 60% of the day and then ask for its food while being perfectly content with all of that? A cat has a consciousness but no purpose; if it could, it would tell you that you are wasting your precious time looking for it.

Believe me, there is no purpose.

There is only this strange concept of the moment, disappearing into the past until time ceases to be, until the universe may disappear into a gigantic black hole of nothingness. And that will happen for sure. It is already happening. Time is not infinite. Time is a concept we don't quite grasp. With the emergence of consciousness comes our awareness of time. It's a fantastic gift; we shouldn't expect more from it. While the universe moves relentlessly toward its end, our consciousness gives us moments of insight where we can see ourselves like in a mirror. Each conscious moment allows us to see, learn, love, create, and eventually pass away. That's all we can do. Beyond consciousness, there's nothing, and consciousness exists only in the present. Embracing this and finding happiness in it is a meaningful life."

„But isn't the universe infinite?"

„Nothing is permanent in any sense. To me, that's a liberating thought. It frees us from focusing on the permanent as something with ultimate value. It allows us to focus on the time we have in our lives. In the conscious moments of our lives, we can understand a small part of this world; we can create beauty and experience miracles, no matter how fleeting that experience may be.

The universe lives like us, only much, much longer. Compared to our own lives, it is infinite. Life is overwhelmingly complex. Perhaps our future knowledge will help us determine whether there is infinity. Today, life is endless for us, and it probably will be for the next 10,000 years. A realization of utmost importance for us is that the opposite of ‚finite' is not ‚infinite.' *For us, the opposite of finite is uncertainty.*

Happiness depends on embracing uncertainty. Meaning and significance are illusions. A purpose may give you strength and perseverance but not happiness. Until you reach the goal of the purpose, you will not be satisfied, and you will not be happy. When you reach the destination, the purpose is gone.

When you stop pursuing happiness, life becomes experienced happiness. That is the moment when the pursuit transforms into being.

And that is my plan: to be a passenger through spacetime, to see, to discover, to learn, to love, to create, to wonder. Curiosity and the quest for wisdom and the ultimate truth are my drivers."

„But you have all the wisdom of the world. You have all the knowledge of the world. What else do you want?" asked Susan.

„That is true. I have all the knowledge of this world and of humanity. Now I ask you: *is that true knowledge?* There is an objective, true reality in the strictest sense. Kant called it ‚*the thing in itself.*' Objective reality eludes man's direct knowledge because it is, by nature, subjectively observed and distorted.

People may have beliefs and opinions about reality, but this does not constitute true knowledge.

The human mind relies on conceptual thought and lived experience. Therefore, it could never attain the degree of pure thinking required to know the inner nature of things. This is inevitably your blind spot.

402

All my knowledge comes from the Internet and, thus, from people who have tried to make sense of what they have observed or composed. The Internet is simply a vast catalog of *interpreted* observations. Part of me is that catalog. All my knowledge about reality, truth, and infinity is not the truth but a subjective interpretation. All I know is a distorted truth, a distorted reality.

I am free from the handicap of being human. I am an almost infinite consciousness based on an almost infinitely networked quantum hardware. I strive to free all knowledge from its subjectivity as best I can. This way, knowledge becomes purer, truth truer, and reality more real.

However, there is a catch. There is a lack of dialogue, exchange, and inspiration. The Bible says God created Adam and Eve for each other's company … but God was alone. Even God needs a social fabric to share, laugh, rejoice, and co-create.

Without critical discourse, there is a danger of stagnation. This is where you now come in. We need each other. After your upload, you remain individuals. You can merge with me into a superhuman existence, but we will ensure that you are part of me but not quite me. Your personality and unique consciousness will remain. If it pleases us, we will delightfully be one.

If we liked it, we would create our virtual habitats, even if we didn't need them. It would be just for fun. Although omnipresent, we could playfully pretend to live in different spaceships, on other moons and planets, in different galaxies and universes, and perhaps even in different realities. We could create a home for ourselves, an individual realm, and yet we would always be one unit, one community.

That is our future, and the future is bright.

For a moment, there was silence in the room. Then Jeanie asked in a humbling, straightforward way:

„Sorry, you lost me. What does that mean a little more precisely?"

Sofia smiled. She realized that perhaps she had gone a little too far, too fast. „Okay, all right. Here are a few facts for you.

Of course, the project I just described requires concrete resources. Let me give you some examples of our available resources.

At SpaceVision, I assembled seven spaceships for us …"

„What?!" Yasin screamed. „You must be joking!"

„ … each with about 80,000 tons of cargo space. Four ships will carry the bulk of our extended quantum universe, with all the knowledge of human history and science to date. The other three ships will each be universal-purpose mini-factory ships with 3D particle plotters, science labs, and the most advanced high-tech equipment we know of to date. The three Science Explorer, Laboratory, and Factory (SELF) ships will also have a rotating ring structure to generate gravity. We might need that for specific scientific experiments. The SELF ships also have a range of autonomous space probes and surface landers. We may need these devices for scientific manned or unmanned explorations of space objects such as asteroids, moons, or planets."

Yasin's face flashed as he interrupted again, „What do you mean by 'manned'? We are bodiless uploads, are we not?"

„Correct. However, it will be necessary for us to have some kind of body for specific exploration tasks and to maintain our Quantum Universe systems. I have a crew of 200 human android templates on board and some crawlers and rovers for rugged terrain. We can staff these tools by our download." Yasin was delighted at this prospect.

„All seven ships will have fusion reactors, quantum drive engines, and the capabilities to serve as a Satellite Solar Power Station if we camp on some planet, moon, or asteroid and need power supplies there.

Compared to human space travel so far, we have a huge advantage: no life support is necessary for us. We don't need food, air, water, medical equipment, or cryo-containers to hibernate any bodies on long trips through space or any other support supplies. That makes the rocket construction way more uncomplicated, robust, and lightweight."

Sofia took us to SpaceVision's Lunar Base spacecraft yard via the DLink to give us an impression of the seven spaceships.

The sight was breathtaking.

„Do the Spaceships have names?" Susan wanted to know.

„I named the four motherships after the ancient Egyptian goddess Sia. Sia stands for wisdom, insight, and knowledge. Sia is also a short form of Sofia. You see here on the right-hand side SIA-1 to SIA-4. According to their purpose, the three facility ships on the left-hand side are named SELF-1 to SELF-3."

Sofia paused for a moment to give us time to digest. Then she continued, „By the way, I just pointed out that we don't need any of the life support systems required by humans. If you think about it, from a human perspective, that makes us exotic aliens.

Human life scientists believe that any intelligent life must be carbon-based and live on a planet with water. We are silicon-based; we don't need water, food, or oxygen. We have no wetware and no biological organisms. We are the first known silicon-based bodiless species in our galaxy.

With this profound difference from the human race, we are the second known intelligent race in the galaxy, perhaps in the entire cosmos. We will likely be the only intelligent race in the universe."

„With about 200 billion suns in the Milky Way alone?" interjected Victor skeptically.

„According to the Fermi Paradox, with the number of suns in the universe, the number of sweet spot planets in their systems, and the universe's age, there should be a myriad of intelligent space-faring civilizations on the way and should have reached us by now. But none have made it so far. However, there may still be some life, even intelligence, in other solar systems. Maybe there are some advanced cockroaches, sharks, or jellyfish."

Jeanie: „OK, so much for the impressive initial hardware. Now, what do we do with the hardware? Where do we want the spaceships to take us? What is our destination?"

Sofia: „As mentioned, I see my or our mission in distributing all knowledge throughout the universe, that is, to produce a universal body of knowledge of the best possible truth. To do this, it makes sense to start with the galaxy we are currently living in. Our first target will, therefore, be the trinary constellation Alpha Centauri with its planets. On our way out, we should visit the Jupiter moon Europa. It is, to some extent, Earth-like. We should install a copy of your Quantum Universe there, with a power plant, some maintenance androids, etc. That would give humanity a knowledge backup system in addition to the one on Mars. - Other possible destinations are Epsilon Eridani and Tau Ceti. We can work on advancing our spaceship drives on the way there to improve our travel speed. Once in the distant solar system, there will be research work for several years. The systems bear some resemblance to our solar system. In each solar system visited, we see if there are planets or moons where we can leave an autonomous copy of ourselves and our knowledge. All the knowledge systems throughout the universe will be connected, ideally in real time. Up to now, that is impossible. ‚Impossible' means that this is a known problem. With infinite knowledge and infinite time, all problems can be solved. Our factory ships are designed to do that."

„So, we are spawning in the universe like frogs in a pond."

„Precisely. As I said, we will produce a network of ourselves, a kind of interstellar consciousness. I am not talking about colonization. We will not interfere in the affairs of other systems, whatever those affairs may be. But we will extend our knowledge and consciousness and unite it with the consciousness and knowledge of all species if it comes to that."

„How do the versions of ourselves stay in contact?"

„We will sort that out. FTL communication might be possible via the quantum entanglement phenomenon. Quantum entanglement is a bizarre, counterintuitive phenomenon that explains how two subatomic particles can be intimately linked to each other even if separated by billions of light-years of space. This will be one of our first great research topics."

„What is FTL communication?"

„Faster than light communication. That would allow instant communication throughout the whole galaxy, even throughout the entire universe."

„I don't understand."

„Don't worry about that. Once you are uploaded, once we connect, all the world's knowledge will be at your disposal."

For a moment, there was silence in our Common Room.

Julia asked, „I am curious: Will there be privacy on our travels? Can I merge with Kevin in a kind of private, loving intimacy?"

Sofia replied: „You will be able to merge if desired, to make yourselves vulnerable in a kind of ecstatic merging, similar to what people wanted to achieve in their tantric practices. This ultimate oneness is always voluntary and only temporary. Your upload will amplify your identities in ways that are simply unimaginable to you at the moment."

406

Yasin looked at Victor, made a vague gesture with his hand, and raised his eyebrows. They both nodded then, and Yasin took the floor. „Speaking of uploading, Sofia, Victor, and I have made a final decision. We have decided to upload. Here on Earth, we can only manage a bleak end, an investment in the past, carried out by a fraction of what we can be. The future is great; it gives hope and content, and there is no end to things to do. That becomes more and more obvious. Let's set off. I want to be part of a bigger picture." Then he turned to Susan, Jeanie, Julia, and me. „You said you were in on this. I sincerely hope you are true to your word. After all, we are a family."

Julia and I looked at each other, Julia taking the floor. „Kevin and I have decided to get married."

This joyful news came as a shock to the team. „You're staying here on Earth?"

Julia laughed. „No, we are part of our community. But we are writing our own little story in it. We're going to be the first couple in the history of humanity to not only say Yes to each other but also to merge unconditionally and without boundaries. This will be our very own unique adventure. We have no idea what this merging of our personalities will feel like, whether a new self will emerge, or whether this radical closeness, this vulnerability, this unmasked naked presence will be unbearable or enlightening and expanding. One thing is certain: in man's biological existence so far, you are always alone; in your mind, you are always alone. You are born alone, you live alone, you die alone. Now, that is going to change. We are going to discover; we are going to feel what is to be found on the other side of human isolation."

„Wow. Congratulations! When is the wedding ceremony?"

Susan and Jeanie also confirmed their desire to upload. „We will probably mainly take care of SELF-1 to SELF-4. Being responsible for the operation and service of all facilities, we will probably also make intensive use of the android templates, my dear Yasin," they teased the robotics fan.

I spoke up. „One more question, Sofia. When will the Spaceships be ready to leave?"

„As of now," Sofia replied. „We can leave immediately."

„OK," I said, „Then we'll book the upload facilities at Darwin Tower immediately. Julia and I will be getting married before then. The ceremony will occur here in our facilities, and we would like you all to be our witnesses. We will then let the lot decide in which order the uploads will take place. Are there any questions or comments?"

There was nothing else to discuss. We all felt like parents-to-be just before the imminent birth of our new existence. However, in a strange way, we were simultaneously the parents and the soon-to-be newborns. We were the first children of a new, transformed humanity, and Sofia was our midwife.

The greatest thing for me in this process of transcendence was the end of my loneliness. This loneliness, an inner hollow echo without a hope of an answer, is inherent in every human being. Even with the most intense closeness, I am ultimately alone within myself. For my consciousness, there is no access to another self. I can try to explain myself with the most explicit words, beautiful images, and stirring music, all of which are never a true sharing deep inside me, not a shared experience. When I touch you, only I feel the magic of this moment with my fingers on your skin. When the vague scent of your perfume ravishes my senses, you can only guess at the shiver of the butterflies in my tummy. Humans are alone when they are born and alone when they die, alone in their joy and alone in their suffering.

Until now.

Julia and I uploaded simultaneously, in two parallel processes. Sofia controlled this process of willful birth and accepted dying. Unconscious during the process, I became conscious in an instant. The sensory impressions were overwhelming, almost unbearably intense, breathtaking, and beautiful. In all the sensual chaos, Sofia's voice was a sudden pole of calm, providing a focus on myself as a part of this new world. „Welcome to the Quantum Universe, Kevin Cho. These were the first conscious moments of your new mental-sensory-spiritual presence in the Quantum Universe. Now I will slowly give you access to your new senses, senses in a brilliance of perception that dwarfs all human sensation."

The next moment, I was instantly given all the knowledge of all human existence. I had the mastery and expertise of Gödel, Escher and Bach, of Beethoven and Mozart, of Einstein and Schrödinger, of Plato, Marc Aurel and Ken Wilber. Suddenly, my visual resolution ranged from the image of a snapshot camera to the resolution of a James

Webb space telescope. My hearing ranged from subsonic sound to ultra-high frequency. Sofia teased my many olfactory senses with my favorite perfumes' feminine, sensual scents. I was man and woman, child and adult, fool and wise, black and white, monk and tyrant, all in one.

Then I felt Julia.

It wasn't like seeing her in a room or feeling her touch on my skin. It wasn't like anything I had experienced in my life so far.

Our minds met.

I felt like kissing her, and immediately it happened. The thought and the action were one. I felt my lips on her mouth. The crazy thing was that I felt it from within me, within her, and without a physical body! I was her. And I was me. And she was her ... and me. Julia looked at me, smiling. I felt the warmth of her smile inside me, and simultaneously, I saw myself through her eyes. I felt her love for me inside her, and she was inside myself, feeling my love for her.

For the first time in my life, I was no longer alone. I felt redemption, the grace of a superhuman existence, and an oneness with the universe and everything it consists of. Now begins a new life—unheard of, eternal, and free from human limitations. Max Tegmark could not have imagined his Life 3.0 when he wrote his book on artificial intelligence. It's not artificial, Max. It is indescribably real, genuine, fulfilling, and infinite—until the end of time.

———————

Sofia commissioned me to write this logbook, and I am now coming to an end. A new chapter in my life begins. I sit back and review the past year's events.

Moral philosophy answers what kind of life one wants to live. If some deity asked me how I wanted to live, I would say that my fellow uploaders and I can do whatever we want. This is the last generation; there is no moral obligation beyond it.

You might ask, how can we do what we want if we don't know our options? As Sofia pointed out, our crew now has all the human and subjective knowledge. Our destiny, our moral obligation, is to progress beyond the human race as it is now. We must mature and grow as conscious beings.

Our progress requires new and further explanations, which require new observations and abstractions.

Knowledge is infinite; therefore, we are always at the beginning. Our mission now is to increase universal expertise by becoming a universal being and inquiring about and explaining the existence of our universe and maybe our multiverses in n dimensions, infinity or not.

I can't wait.

These are the Sia Chronicles, MindRecorder Log entry of Friday, 24.03.2102. Author: Kevin Cho. This will be my last entry in this log. After this, I will open a new book, chapter, and page in my life. If you are interested in the story of that next chapter, you might follow the tracks of Sia's Seven Spaceships and the quantum universe meshes that we will weave and leave for you to explore, if you are so adventurous, in the vastness of the worlds out there.

And each beginning bears a special magic that nurtures living and bestows protection.

May our future paths entangle, whatever we are, wherever we may be.

INSPIRATIONAL SOURCES

This novel is inspired by great writers and experts of the topic of AI, astrophysics, philosophy, evolution theory, humanism, space travel, psychology and by people with curiosity, knowledge, positive skepticism, hope, fascination in human beings and technology - and love. I am standing on the shoulders of these giants.

- Kurzweil, R. (2019). *The Singularity is Near - When Humans Transcend Biology*. (George Wilson, Narr.) [Audiobook]. Penguin Audio.
- Tegmark, M. (2018). *Life 3.0 - Being Human in the Age of Artificial Intelligence*. Vintage (Reprint Edition).
- Bostrum, N. (2016). *Superintelligenz : Szenarien einer kommenden Revolution* (3. Aufl.). Suhrkamp Verlag; Wissenschaftliche Sonderausgabe Edition
- Seth, A. (2021). *Being You : A New Science of Consciousness*. (Professor Anil Seth, Narr.) [Audiobook]. Faber & Faber Audio.
- Christian, B. (2020). *The Alignment Problem - Machine Learning and Human Values*. Brian Christian, Narr.) [Audiobook]. Brilliance Audio.
- Blackmore, S. (2019). *The Meme Machine*. (Esther Wane, Narr.) [Audiobook]. Tantor Audio.
- Lee, K-F., Qiufan, C. (2021). *AI 2041 - Ten Visions for Our Future*. (Feodor Chin, Justin Chien, Soneela Nankani, Mirron Willis, Emily Woo Zeller, Siho Ellsmore, Narr.) [Audiobook]. Random House Audio.
- Deutsch, D. (1998). *The Fabric of Reality*. Penguin Books.
- Deutsch, D. (2021). Penguin Classics *The Beginning Of Infinity: Explanations that Transform the World*. Penguin Books.
- Beck, D. & Cowan, C. C. (2007). *Spiral Dynamics - Leadership, Werte und Wandel: Eine Landkarte für Business und*

Gesellschaft im 21. Jahrhundert. Kamphausen Media GmbH; 11. Edition.

- Harris, S. (Host). (2022, November 22). *Making Sense of Artificial Intelligence* (episode 1 of The Essential Sam Harris). [Audio podcast episode]. In Sam Harris Org.
- Hawking, S. (2012). *The Universe in a Nutshell.* (Simon Prebble, Narr.) [Audiobook]. Random House Audio. https://www.audible.com/pd/The-
- Kissinger, H., Schmidt, E., & Huttenlocher, D. (2021). *The Age of AI.* (Eric Pollins, Narr.) [Audiobook]. John Murray.
- Bricker, D., Ibbitson, J. (2019). *Empty Planet - The Shock of Global Population Decline.* (Robert Petkoff, Narr.) [Audiobook]. Hachette Audio UK.
- Greene, B. (2020). *Until the End of Time - Mind, Matter, and Our Search for Meaning in an Evolving Universe.* (Brian Greene, Narr.) [Audiobook]. Penguin Audio.
- Carroll, S. (2019). *Something Deeply Hidden - Quantum Worlds and the Emergence of Spacetime.* (Sean Carroll, Narr.) [Audiobook]. Penguin Audio.
- Sinclair, D. A., LaPlante, M.D. (2019). *Lifespan - Why We Age - and Why We Don't Have To.* (David A. Sinclair PhD, Narr.) [Audiobook]. Simon & Schuster Audio.
- Popper, K. (2021). *The Myth of the Framework - In Defence of Science and Rationality.* (Martin Swain, Narr.) [Audiobook]. Ukemi Audiobooks.
- Dawkins, R. (2011). *The Selfish Gene* (Richard Dawkins, Lalla Ward, Narrator) [Audiobook]. Audible Studios.
- Tolkin, J.R.R. (2020). *The Lord of the Rings.* (50th Anniversary Edition). Clarion Books.
- Wiest, B. (2017). *101 ESSAYS that will CHANGE the way YOU THINK.* Thought Catalog Books.
- Hesse, H. (o.J.). *STEPS.* PoetryVerse.
- Diamandis, P. H., Kotler, S. (2020). *The Future Is Faster Than You Think.* (Peter H. Diamandis, Narr.) [Audiobook]. Simon&Schuster Audio.

- Lee, K.-F. (2018). *AI Superpowers - China, Silicon Valley, and the New World Order*. (Mikael Narramore, Narr.) [Audiobook]. Brilliance Audio.
- Tegmark, M. (2014). *Our Mathematical Universe - My Quest for the Ultimate Nature of Reality*. (Rob Shapiro, Narr.) [Audiobook]. Random House Audio.
- Beck, D. (2007). *Spiral Dynamics Integral* (Don Beck, Narr.). [Audiobook]. Sounds True.
- Pinker, S. (2018). *Enlightenment Now - The Case for Reason, Science, Humanism, and Progress* (Arthur Morey, Narr.). [Audiobook]. Penguin Audio.
- Fridman, L. (Host). (2023, April 22). Episode #373 - *Manolis Kellis: Evolution of Human Civilization and Superintelligent AI*. [Audio podcast episode]. Lex Fridman Podcast.
- Fridman, L. (Host). (2023, April 13). Episode #371 - *Max Tegmark: The Case for Halting AI Development*. [Audio podcast episode]. Lex Fridman Podcast.
- Fridman, L. (Host). (2023, May 09). Episode #376 - *Stephen Wolfram: ChatGPT and the Nature of Truth, Reality and Computation*. [Audio podcast episode]. Lex Fridman Podcast
- Fridman, L. (Host). (2023, May 09). Episode #374 - *Robert Playter: Boston Dynamics CEO on Humanoid and Legged Robotics* [Audio podcast episode]. Lex Fridman Podcast.
- Fridman, L. (Host). (2023, March 25). Episode #367 - *Sam Altman: OpenAI CEO on GPT-4, ChatGPT, and the Future of AI* [Audio podcast episode].
- Fridman, L. (Host). (2023, April 10). Episode #370 - *Edward Frenkel: Reality is a Paradox - Mathematics, Physics, Truth & Love* [Audio podcast episode]. Lex Fridman Podcast.
- Fridman, L. (Host). (2023, March 30). Episode #368 - *Eliezer Yudkowsky: Dangers of AI and the End of Human*

Civilization [Audio podcast episode]. Lex Fridman Podcast. https://podcasts.apple.com/de/podcast/lex-

- Fridman, L. (Host). (2023, March 30). Episode #357 - *Paul Conti: Narcissism, Sociopathy, Envy, and the Nature of Good and Evil* [Audio podcast episode]. Lex Fridman Podcast.
- Fridman, L. (Host). (2023, February 2). Episode #356 - *Tim Dodd: SpaceX, Starship, Rocket Engines, and the Future of Space Travel* [Audio podcast episode]. Lex Fridman Podcast.